I0635803

VOICES FROM HADES

This Expanded Version of *Voices from Hades* includes the additional stories *Acheron, The Bone Arena, Good Will Toward Men,* and *The Half-Damned Girl*

Weird House Press Trade Paperback © 2023

No part of this publication may be reproduced, stored or transmitted in any form or by any means, electronic, mechanical, photocopying, recording, scanning, or otherwise without written permission from the publisher. It is illegal to copy this book, post it to a website, or distribute it by any other means without permission.

All stories are works of fiction. Names, characters, places, and incidents, either are the product of the author's imagination or are used fictitiously. Any resemblance to actual persons, living or dead, events, or locales, is entirely coincidental.

Publishing History:

"The Abandoned" first appeared in *The Art of Hades*, a bonus book accompanying the 26-copy limited edition of *Letters From Hades*, Bedlam Press, 2003; second appearance in the anthology *A Walk on the Darkside*, Roc, 2004. "Black Wings" first appeared in the chapbook *Unknown Pleasures*, Raw Dog Screaming Press, 2003. "Siren" first appeared in the anthology *Damned*, Necro Publications, 2004. "Sweet Oblivion" first appeared in the anthology *Dead Cat's Traveling Circus of Wonders and Miracle Medicine Show*, Bedlam Press, 2006. "The Secret Gallery" first appeared in the collection *Voices From Hades*, Dark Regions Press, 2008. "The Burning House" first appeared in the collection *Thirteen Specimens*, Delirium Books, 2006. "Piece of Mind" first appeared in the collection *Voices From Hades*, Dark Regions Press, 2008. "Acheron" first appeared in the anthology *I Am the Abyss*, Dark Regions Press, 2018. "The Bone Arena" first appeared in the anthology *The Porcupine Boy and Other Anthological Oddities*, Crossroad Press, 2019. "Good Will Toward Men" first appeared in the collection *Haunted Worlds*, Hippocampus Press, 2017. "The Half-Damned Girl" was first published as a A-Z signed and lettered hardcover edition, Weird House Press, 2023.

ISBN: 978-1-957121-55-0

Revised Text © 2023 by Jeffrey Thomas
Cover and interior art © 2023 by Frank Walls
Editor and Publisher, Joe Morey
Interior and cover design by Cyrus Wraith Walker

Weird House Press
Central Point, OR 97502
www.weirdhousepress.com

Praise for Jeffrey Thomas' Hades series

"Jeffrey Thomas' visions of Hell … are as compelling and as beautifully horrific as any ever put down on paper."

—Jeff VanderMeer, author of *Annihilation*

"Jeffrey Thomas' imagination is as twisted as it is relentless … If there is such a place as hell, the demons have a suite reserved in Jeffrey Thomas' name."

—F. Paul Wilson, author of *The Keep*

"Jeffrey Thomas offers us a unique vision of hell that's as beautiful as it is savage, as hauntingly poetic as it is heinous … I'm a hardcore fan."

—Tom Piccirilli, author of *The Cold Spot*

"Jeffrey Thomas' odyssey through hell is an imaginative and compelling journey every reader should take."

—Gerard Houarner, author of *Road to Hell*

"A very imaginative version of Hell that is as breathtaking as it is horrid. You really get an idea of what it would be like to live in hell, or at least Thomas' vision of hell, and every hidden corner of the underworld has something unique and creative that will linger in your mind for days."

—Carlton Mellick III, author of *The Haunted Vagina*

VOICES FROM HADES

JEFFREY THOMAS

WEIRD HOUSE

CONTENTS:

THE ABANDONED

Maria had been told she was lucky to have acquired work in the city of Tartarus, so soon upon her arrival in the netherworld. It wasn't much comfort. She could only take the word of her co-workers -- her fellow slaves, more precisely—that to be employed here brought a measure of protection from the Demons in place of the punishments inflicted on those beyond the city's borders. It was as reassuring as being told that she should be thankful for having one leg chainsawed off instead of two.

Seeing the Demon city of Tartarus for the first time had been the third greatest shock of her afterlife. The first shock had been that there *was* an afterlife (she had been one of the only Mexicans she'd ever known not to be devoutly religious) and the second greatest shock had been that the afterlife adjudged for her was as a citizen of Hell.

Mexico City was dwarfed by Tartarus, though to Maria's mind the population of her own former city might have been greater. Perhaps that was only an illusion because of the vast scale of this place, which rendered all (mock) life microscopic, and because of its absence of streets, of commerce. Its very expanse and scope made it seem empty, its fullness made it desolate, and most strangely, its hideousness made it terribly beautiful.

Every structure was a skyscraper, many of them vanishing into the almost solid layer of slowly churning clouds that forever obscured the sky. These skyscrapers were not so much ranked beside each other as *merged* with each other, so that often the only way one might tell them apart (if indeed they were in any sense apart) was to notice how the color of one was shaded slightly darker or lighter than another, or how a building composed of nothing but uncountable, tiny opaque windows faded into a building that appeared to be entirely constructed (within as well as without?) out of gigantic auto parts blended with a madman's plumbing system combined with computer circuit boards … some of this machinery glossy smooth, other sections corroded rust red. Though a building might be a ghostly pale hue and another so dark it seemed one existed in day while the other loomed at midnight, there was a bleak sepia tone over the whole of the city that made it weirdly homogenous. Her own former city had been notorious for its smog, but sectors of this city seemed to loom out of a more subtle mist that blurred its edges, while other areas stood out with a sharpness of line and detail that stabbed the eye. White, luminous fog wound like a living entity between the fissures and irregular gaps in the mountains of concrete and metal, and steam plumed out of apertures, some of these like grates or exhaust ports while others were more like organic orifices. Because worked into the weave of Tartarus was an unmistakable organic element, as if the city wasn't actually built from concrete and metal, plastic and stone, but had been *grown* like one titanic living body. There was thick tubing that looked both flexible but vitreous and that snaked down the faces of buildings, that ran in and out of their very bodies, like arteries. There were huge, glassy bulbs or boils or tumors of some kind which were filled with that glowing mist or else with seething black masses like gigantic worms in rows of immense egg sacs. There were portions of the city that looked formed out of translucent bone, out of some calcified matter like a coral reef, out of tons of oxidized fossil. Buildings that seemed made of polished insect chitin, structures that were not linear and hard-edged but fluid and asymmetrical and a chaos of shape and design. All of these things in unlikely conjunction were Tartarus, unified by its leeched brown color however it might shade, compressed so tightly together it was like one colossal building alone, unified by its strange silence despite the ringing and hammering heard here and there as its mechanical flanks pumped and pistoned, unified by its atmosphere of hopelessness and loneliness … like an abandoned city haunted only by ghosts. Of which Maria was one.

৩৩

Maria had been raped again. It was bad enough when a Demon raped her, but much worse when one of her co-workers did. She expected better from them, since they shared her plight. She supposed these men needed to vent their terrible, frustrated rage. Or else they simply felt that this world was a place where evil was expected, being the very substance of the walls, their masters, of their own mock flesh. Still, they expressed their humiliation by humiliating her. Spent their bottled anger by filling her up with it instead.

A Demon had come along the narrow corridor in which they lay, and had kicked the man hard in the ass. The man had scampered to his feet, his slick cock bobbing ridiculously, and scampered off down the passageway to wherever his work station was. The Demon had then strolled on, not bothering to help Maria up from the floor. As she rearranged her wrenched and ripped clothing, she watched the Demon recede. He hadn't been concerned for her, but only for the work that waited to be done.

The first man who had raped her, on her second day in Tartarus, she had afterwards struck across the back of the head with a huge two-handed wrench swung from over her shoulder. He had dropped to her feet with blood already pouring heavily out of his nose and ears. An hour later, the damage almost entirely regenerated, the rapist had sought her out with a lead pipe in his hand for his own club … but a Demon had pushed him away and told him to leave her alone. "Thanks," Maria had told the creature.

"Go back to work," it had rasped at her. And several days later, she thought it was this very same Demon who raped her against the wall of a hiss-filled boiler room … though it was hard to tell some of them apart, especially the ones like this who were less human in form.

Brushing off her bottom with both hands, Maria resumed her

interrupted journey to her current work station for the beginning of her shift. She picked up her pace, afraid of being late, and thus punished. She had been allowed a period of sleep so as to recuperate from yesterday's seemingly endless shift, and the workers were even given food to eat. These sham bodies they possessed did not really require sleep or sustenance, just as it wasn't true blood that ran in their veins or live sperm that spurted from rapists' pricks. (And nerves did not really scream at the touch of a torturer's brand or blade, however it might seem they did.)

The bodies of the Damned thought they were still alive, and so they had the urges and instincts of the living.

☙☙

Tartarus was one of those far-spaced cities of Hell in which its Demonic population was not only trained for their duties ... but made.

This was Maria's line of work. She was, for all intents and purposes, a manufacturer of the very creatures that had rustled her up for this employment.

Shifts were long. One often burned or froze their hands, depending on what sort of Demon—or what stage of that Demon's progression—they were working on. Toward the end of today's shift, a gust of hot steam had scalded Maria's left hand ... but already, on her way to this floor's showers, the pain and angry redness were fading.

Whenever she was badly burned, by steam or splashed corrosive chemical or by bumping into a red-hot metal surface, Maria was reminded of her father. His right arm had been terribly scarred as a toddler, when he had tipped a pot full of boiling water off the stove top. He had told Maria that his mother was passed out on the sofa at the time. He had told Maria that his mother was a worthless bitch and whore, and a neglectful mother who ultimately left her husband for a man who was younger but just as drunken as herself.

Maria's own mother had met her father while she was living for a time in San Antonio. He was white, she a Mexican. When she was eight years old, after an escalating series of terrifying fights, her father

4

left her mother. She had never seen him again, and her mother had moved them back to Mexico to be with family.

Maria had thought that her father loved her; that he would never leave her as his mother had ended up leaving him. Now, she couldn't even remember his face clearly. But she remembered the scars on his arm. They had never faded away, like the burn on her own hand today.

Maria nodded in mute greeting to the three men who stood watch outside the women's shower area. The Demons had not assigned them to this duty; they had volunteered, to protect the women from other men who might enter the showers to attack them. On the rare occasion, though, a Demon or even a pack might enter into the showers, and for them the men lowered their eyes and stepped aside.

Maria stripped and angled her wide pretty face toward the pelting hot streams, turned slowly around, her long hair plastering to her back. Opening her eyes, stepping back a little, she gazed upwards as she exposed her underarms to the irregular streams that fell from the machinery high overhead, the fallen water then trickling into a grated floor rough against her bare feet. This large chamber was not intended for this use, but the Demons shrugged it off, didn't bother stopping them. High above, cloudy cocoons in row after row were suspended pendulously like a crop nearly ripe for harvesting. The raining water rinsed these subtly pulsating sacs. Here and there, Maria could see a more pronounced bulge where a limb or wing pressed at the membrane that sheathed its owner.

A reverberating thud made her step entirely out of the torrents for a moment or two to listen. An explosion, perhaps. Another boiler blown? It wasn't too uncommon. A dangerous mistake on the part of a worker (though even if shredded to chum, he would reconstitute) or simply an overtaxed machine. No further detonations followed, and Maria ducked back into the downpour.

After bathing herself, she dipped her shed uniform into a mechanical recess in one wall that had collected a puddle of this falling hot water, so as to clean it as best she could—then she changed into her fresh uniform and headed out of the shower chamber, her hair still dripping wet. At the entrance, one of the guards (his name was Russ, he'd recently told her) smiled at her again and shifted in his hands the heavy mallet he carried as a weapon. "So Maria, how are ya?"

"I'm fine," she told him, smiling a little. She couldn't believe people could still ask such inane questions. Empty civility. Like robot servants after a nuclear war, making tea for mummies long dead in their armchairs. Russ was that robot and that mummy at the same time. She dropped her eyes and hurried past him without trying to look obvious about it. "You?" she called back over her shoulder obligatorily. She saw he was watching her go.

"Okay. Goin' to the mess hall?"

"Yup."

"Maybe I'll see you there in a few."

"Sure."

He was cute enough, she supposed. White. A redhead. And she could not conceive of falling in love with any man here in Hades. As numb as she was, as hollowed out inside, as automaton-like in her work and her daily routines, she was not some robot with a bolted-on grin. Her programming had been shorted out. Civility had been an illusion all along.

Affection was a sham better left to the living.

When Maria turned a corner of the cramped hallway, the rainfall hiss of the showers still in her ears, she looked up to see a Demon plant itself in front of her.

"What is your sin?" it snarled, and backhanded her across the jaw.

The Demons didn't apparently use names to distinguish one infernal race from another, but for their own convenience (since they had to manufacture them), the workers had given them designations, and this species was called a Caliban. It was like a cross between a sumo wrestler and an insect, bulgingly soft in some places and armored in others, the same sepia brown as the exteriors and interiors of Tartarus, except that its eyes glowed a bright white and its primary forearms shaded to almost black at the ends of their scorpion-like pincers. It was one of these appendages that had just sent Maria to the floor.

"What is your sin?" it demanded again, taking another threatening step toward her so that she smelled the choking incense scent burned

6

into its dimpled flesh and glossy chitin. She might have made this creature herself for all she knew.

Her mouth lubricated with blood, which drooled out over the middle of her bisected lower lip, Maria managed to get out, "I have forsaken the Father."

It was true, wasn't it?

On the night of the great and final fight, that frightening last battle like some apocalyptic war, after her father had left, Maria had found a crucifix on the floor. She recognized it as her father's, and realized her mother must have wrenched it off his chest in their shoving and slapping. Without her mother seeing, she swept it up in her fist. And buried it under her pillow that night. But the next day, the first day of her father no longer being in her life, Maria had taken the chain and little cross out into their backyard and buried it there, partly out of angry rejection, partly out of despair.

Was it that some neighbor child or even adult had seen her dig the hole, and had dug up the silver crucifix? Or was it that her vision had been so blurred with tears at the time? Whatever the case, when Maria went to exhume the crucifix out of guilt and longing a week later, it wasn't in the spot she had thought it would be. She tried another spot, and there she came upon a bundle in a green plastic trash bag. Now she remembered what she had buried in this vaguely familiar spot; their cat, which had been hit by a car a year ago. Disinterring this poor corpse was too great a punctuation mark to her pain. She reburied the cat, and didn't try to find her father's necklace again.

She had left it buried. And with it, her faith in family, in solace, maybe even in love. She had continued to attend church with her devout mother. But she had narrowed her eyes in contempt at the larger version of that symbol hanging above the altar. The man with his hands pinned where they could do no one any good.

The Caliban seemed satisfied with her answer. It shambled on down the hallway, and Maria pulled herself to her feet, blood still running off her lip. She had refused to cry, however. She prided herself on holding her tears even when she had no control over the flow of her blood. But the wound would heal, so that more wounds could take its place. Hadn't it been the same, pretty much, when she had still been alive, before she was raped and murdered?

Maria continued on her way. But not to the mess hall. She felt vaguely apologetic as far as Russ was concerned, but she had lost her appetite.

৩৩

When she reached the enormous chamber in which she had been assigned a place to sleep, Maria realized that the explosion she'd heard earlier had occurred in here.

This chamber was circular and disturbingly organic, its ceiling lost in gloom but apparently taking the form of a dome. Honeycombed into the curved walls were row upon row of elliptical openings like slots in a mausoleum waiting to be filled. Formerly, this had been a tank in which were nurtured a species of Demons since discontinued. They had been one of the more human-like breeds, and perhaps it was because of their human traits that a number of them had rebelled in the infernal city of Oblivion. Most of these Demons had been killed by now, but there were still those that had escaped the purging.

Her own little cocoon space was in the third tier, and she kept a few belongings inside, which no one had ever deemed worthy of stealing. There, she would rest between shifts, curled like a fetus, reborn—or aborted—every day in an endless cycle.

But today there had been some unknown mishap, and from the room's obscure heights, torrents of a thick, orange-colored gelatinous fluid were raining down to plop and puddle. Fortunately, the floor was subtly concave and the ooze was draining slowly toward a grille in its center. The foul-smelling matter put Maria very much in mind of the gruel they were fed in the mess hall—the only sustenance they were given—though that substance had a chemical-sharp citrus smell and taste, like slurping orange-scented dish detergent.

The irregular deluge went largely ignored by a few weary laborers who had also skipped mess hall and preceded her into the chamber, and who now climbed toward their cramped sarcophagi. Maria stared up into the leaking darkness only a few moments herself before navigating between aggregations of the viscous slime toward her section of the wall. Having arrived at it, she hoisted up one leg to begin the ascent to her own depression.

She hesitated, however, as her eyes were attracted to where some of the rotten-smelling matter had flowed down the wall and accumulated in a particularly large, glistening heap. She saw that there were several bones protruding from it; some ribs, and the bat-like struts of a wing. Not the bones of a human; humans reconstituted, their bodies were notional, they could not be killed. Demons, however: they could die. But there was more than the bones. One spot in the mound was subtly but definitely pulsing. Also, Maria could just discern a muted gurgling sound with an unsettling, familiar quality.

Holding her breath against the reek, she crouched by the edge of the pile, and from it drew a loose leg bone. She then used this to probe the slime in the area where it was undulating. There was resistance as she prodded a mass buried within it. And then, a tiny arm thrust up through the jelly, its stubby fingers wriggling.

Maria used the bone to paddle away as much of the slime as she could around the arm. Then, leaning forward carefully, she reached out and took hold of it. It was slippery, and cold, and she was repulsed by the fingers that squirmed against her wrist, but she pulled ... and in standing, she extracted a body drooling streamers of muck. She held the thing out at arm's length to examine it. Pudgy legs pedaled the air sluggishly, eyes squinted open in its sliding mask of ooze, and its wings moved as if to fan the goo from them. Free of the half-congealed amniotic fluid in which it had once been nurtured, the Demon gurgled more freely, but not loudly enough for anyone else to have noticed as yet.

Though Maria had never seen a mature version, she realized what this creature was. One of those discontinued Demons that had been nurtured in this chamber before it had been emptied and converted into barracks. It was a miracle —or, more accurately, an oversight— that it had survived this long. Overlooked in the cleansing that had eliminated all its siblings. Now, accidentally but belatedly miscarried.

Maria was afraid to bring the infant Demon close to her, but was even more afraid of being seen holding it. She glanced behind her furtively, but determined that her back had as yet shielded her find from anyone who might have looked in her direction. She then did the first thing that came impulsively to mind. Rather than drop the immature creature back into its afterbirth, rather than fetch an adult Demon to tend to this matter, she again hoisted up a leg to begin climbing to her tiny nook. In so doing, she was forced to fold the creature close to her chest.

She was afraid that at any moment, the larval Demon would snap its jaws onto her throat. But instead, it merely mewled faintly, and instinctively clung to her so as not to fall.

Working through her interminable shift, knowing what she had left hidden in her skull socket of a bed chamber, Maria was agitated and distracted and made a number of clumsy mistakes. Her function, of late, was to pour large glass jars full of maggots into molds that crawled past her on a conveyor belt. The squirming, pale brown things were not truly maggots, but close enough for the workers to refer to them as such. A co-worker, Patty, told Maria how this particular process reminded her of a carbonated soda plant she'd worked for in life, where bags of hard plastic pellets were melted down so as to be shaped into the two liter soda bottles they would become. But here, Patty and Maria were molding containers of flesh instead of those of plastic. To be filled with bile, venom and vitriol instead of corn syrup and caramel color.

Patty would hand Maria a bottle of the maggots, which she would tip into one of the molds (today, they were for Baphomets, a towering Demon with a blackened, goat-like head enshrouded in a caul of cool white flame). Maria would pass the empty jug back to Patty, who would set it aside to be washed out and reused later.

At one point Maria fumbled and dropped a bottle, which shattered below the little platform she stood on. Patty jumped back as the pool of writhing, half-alive matter spread at her feet. Fortunately, they were able to sweep it all up and dispose of it before any of the Demon supervisors could see them.

Sometimes, when there were no supervisors in sight, Maria would spit into the open molds as she filled them.

She was relieved when the shift ended at last, but also dreaded returning to her sleep chamber to find her secret discovered ... or expired. Before she could check on it, however, she first had a stop to make.

☜☞

Russ the shower guard was entering the mess hall as Maria was just leaving it. He looked like he was coming off his regular duties; his uniform was stiff with caked Demon blood, from recycling old bodies for the recasting of new. When he saw her, he grinned and said, "Hey! There's the pretty senorita. I missed you yesterday."

Maria could not speak. In her mouth she held some of the orange, gel-like gruel she had been served in a bowl by one of the human mess hall workers. She tried to smile at Russ, rubbing her belly and wagging her head as if to indicate she didn't feel well. Concern flashed into his face and he stepped aside to let her pass.

"Are you going to be sick?" When she nodded, he asked, "Can I help you?"

She shook her head, patted him on the arm as she moved forward again (hoping he didn't take the contact as having flirtatious meaning) and left her would-be beau behind.

It was not unrealistic for him to believe she might be ill. In Hell, there were microscopic Demons, or at least infernal creatures, that could infest, infect, cause grief to the Damned. Maria knew this well; from the irregular holes rotted open in the walls on the 53rd floor of this building, she had been able to look outside at a narrow building that reminded her of a spinal column, in which these viruses were manufactured by other workers like herself.

"Hope you feel better!" he called after her.

When Hell freezes over, she thought.

She had walked only a few steps when she heard Russ cry out in alarm and pain. Turning, she saw that a Caliban had loomed up behind him and seized him in its pincers. One of his wrists, pinned, was half severed and jetting blood. Another pincer had ripped his trousers down, while a third was closed around his genitals as if to masturbate or castrate. The weight of the immense body doubled him over and the creature was no doubt entering him.

"What is your sin?" the Demon wheezed.

Russ and Maria held their eye contact. Russ looked more ashamed than in pain. Maria was ashamed, too, that there was nothing she could do for him. She knew the next time they met he would be physically healed, at least … and she knew they would not discuss this.

As she left him behind, she heard the Demon grunt more demandingly, "What is your sin?"

We have forsaken our Father, Maria thought. And He has forsaken His children, the ultimate deadbeat dad.

⚭

There were more people in the sleep chamber than there had been yesterday, when she had retired without a trip to the mess hall first. Many of the orifices were already occupied, like eggs filled with termites that would hatch tomorrow to take to their labors. She climbed up the rib-like ridges that protruded between two columns of the elliptical hollows, and then ducked into her own in the third tier.

Against the back wall of her sleep space, her spare uniform lay crumpled up. And that crumpled heap was subtly moving, like the heap of gelatin had been yesterday.

Maria pulled aside her clothing to reveal the larval Demon lying on the glassy hard surface beneath it. Its eyes shifted toward her, held her gaze, blinking. Its fingers plucked and kneaded at the air. Her eyes trailed down to its puny genitalia; it was a boy.

She pinched the infant boy's nostrils shut. The creature's squirming became more pronounced, and she was afraid he would cry out. So far, he hadn't cried or made any loud sounds. In fact, even his soft burbling sounds had decreased over the hours of her rest period, which made Maria both relieved and concerned. Was he making less sounds because he was content, or because he was ailing, growing weak?

The thought of clamping her free hand over his mouth came into her mind. The Damned were immortal, so that they might suffer through eternity. The Demons could perish. The Demons were only machines, so to speak. This diabolic cherub was at her mercy. He was one of the many genera of her tormentors. And her torments might be increased in severity if she was found to have been hiding him. He was the enemy...

Last night, she had considered smuggling him out of this room and abandoning him in some little-used corridor, or in the space between two machines, and leaving him to the Fates. But there were no Fates, just Demons, and if they found him they'd kill him to further the factory recall, or genocide, of his species.

So what if they killed him? So what?

But it was *because* they'd want to kill him that she hadn't killed him. Though still a Demon, he was now something kindred to her.

Maria pinched his nose, but didn't cover his mouth. His mouth opened in a disgruntled gasp, and leaning over him, she drooled the orange, citrus-flavored gruel out of her own mouth into his, like a bird feeding her winged but flightless chick.

One could still dream in Hades. Sometimes, Maria dreamed of Los Dias de Muertos. Markets filled with flaming marigolds and family crypts in pastel shades. Seeing through the eyes of a plastic ghost or ghoul or devil mask. Rows of sugar skulls with sequin eyes. Sometimes, in her dreams, Maria imagined these skulls were the heads of Demons waiting to be attached to their bodies, and come alive. The bread called pan de muerto. Edible crucifixes, in a kind of communion...

Sometimes, Maria would dream of paging through the blood-soaked tabloid *Alarma!* and seeing photos of her own raped and murdered corpse there for the entertainment of the masses.

Tonight, she dreamed of sneaking out of her mausoleum nook ... of stealing down the curved wall of the sleep chamber ... of creeping out into the maze of hallways with a bundle tight against her breasts.

She dreamed of climbing staircase after staircase, or scrambling up ladders, or mounting inclined ramps, until at last she had reached the 53rd floor of the structure she worked and lived her undead life in. The level -- perhaps near the top, perhaps only halfway up—where great, irregular holes had rotted open in the resin-like, semi-organic walls. Holes looking out upon the immensity of the Demon city, Tartarus, where winds whistled or wailed between the tightly packed skyscrapers of bone, winds which set her long black hair flapping as she neared the lip of one such opening.

She uncovered the face of the infant in her arms, and he gazed up at her dumbly. Not crying, not cooing. She had no idea what thoughts, if any, breathed in his head. Would his interrupted progress resume? Would he mature to an adult, or remain at this stage forever? Though he would be helpless out in the world of the underworld, she found the latter possibility agreeable. That he should remain an eternal innocent.

Maria unwrapped the creature's swaddling, and as if he guessed her purpose, his wings began to flex and fan. She held him under his arms, held him up at the level of her face. For a moment, she almost kissed his bare belly, where there was a navel though it had never had an umbilicus fed into it. But she didn't kiss the white flesh, instead turned the infant in her hands to face the city sprawling beyond. She stepped closer to the rim. She held him higher aloft. Her arms slipped out into the biting wind of the air, beyond the lip of the wound. And then, she let him go.

She was afraid he might plummet, but he did not. Instinctually, his wings began to beat so quickly, like those of an insect or hummingbird, that he was buoyed up, and the currents of air howling through the canyons of skyscrapers did much of the work. Up, he rose, and up. Out over the darkness of unseen depths below. Up and into the mist between two particularly gargantuan edifices ... until he was lost from sight. Until he was free.

In a building so close to hers they were practically conjoined, she saw a figure in one of the windows. A witness to her act. But just as the figure turned away, she recognized who it was and became less afraid. She knew that her father would not betray her this time.

When she awoke and uncovered the Demon larva beside her, she found he had expired while she was asleep, his lids half closed over his already clouded eyes.

Maria did not stir for a long time. She was almost late to work because of it. But at last, she covered his head again under her spare uniform ... and this she carried with her to work as she often did, so that she might wash it in one of the basin-like recesses in the shower chamber when her shift was over.

She waited until there were no patrolling Demon guards or supervisors in view. She waited even until Patty, her co-worker, had briefly left to roll in another cart loaded with bottles of maggots. Then, swiftly, she dragged out her bundle from under the conveyor belt. Unwrapped it ... took the immobile, rubbery little body in her hands ... and dropped it into the next open mold. Then, she poured the contents of one jug of maggots over that. She watched the mold be borne away along its track.

Today they were making Calibans. Would the human-like Demon live on, in some sense, in the body of a new Demon despite its different form? Or had her act been purely one of defiance? Would the Caliban born from this mold be more human, like those rebellious Demons who were being hunted down and cleansed from existence ... or would this new Caliban one day rape his own mother?

When Patty returned with the cart she became concerned for Maria, touched her arm. She told Maria she had never seen her cry before. But Maria laughed a little, and touched her arm in turn, and they resumed their work.

THE ABANDONED

It was not Russ' turn to guard at the entrance to the women's showers today, but Maria sought him out in the mess hall, and found him, seated herself directly to his left. He turned and looked a little surprised to see her there. Her smile made his rising shame over the other day drop away again.

"Hi," she said to him.

"Hi," he said, sounding a little confused at her open tone. Maria had always been reserved with him, her smiles polite, not showing teeth. Now she smiled more warmly at him.

She stole her hand under the long table they sat at, and rested it upon his own hand.

Russ' uncertain smile grew, as well. But now it was his turn to avert his eyes shyly. He didn't withdraw his hand from hers, however; instead, curled his fingers around it.

They ate like that, side by side. Almost like a husband and wife. Almost like parents at their supper table.

Black Wings

he palace was called Urian, though amongst themselves the Demons liked to joke that it was Castle Urine. It was a great square block worked from a single stone, its luridly red-orange surface pocked and pitted as pumice, with no towers, no carven decorations, just far-spaced slits for windows and only a single door. This red cube rested at the heart of a desert of red sand, and on the rare occasion that it rained, the scarlet powder would reveal itself to be dehydrated blood, and would liquefy, become a sludgy mud flat of gore. From the desert sprouted a dense forest of bare, tree-like growths as white as coral. The surfaces of these coral trees were so rough that to rub against them was to draw blood, like the rasping skin of a shark. Their leafless, lifeless arms wove jagged thickets of bone that had never worn flesh.

There was a path through the coral reef, however, that ran to the door of the castle. From one of the narrow windows, the Demon named Xaphan peeked out at the approach of the carriage that was delivering Urian's latest guests. The carriage itself was a featureless, black iron globe between two huge wheels, pulled by a harnessed team of two dozen naked Damned children, so Xaphan could not as yet spy the guests themselves.

He started as another figure slipped beside him; he had been so intent he hadn't heard Vjeshitza's approach. She pressed her face into the crook of his neck, and bit him hard there without breaking his dark skin. While doing so, she held onto his folded wings, which like her own were feathered and black as a crow's, though the wings did not permit their species of Demon to fly. Xaphan and Vjeshitza both possessed skin of a deep chestnut hue and luster, both of them hairless, even without eyebrows. And both wore no garments. Their only embellishments were black onyx rings pierced through their nipples—and on their upper chests, raised keloids like the healed wounds of a tiger's slash, four of these tracks above each breast, where they had marked themselves with their retractable talons upon having completed their warrior's training in the city of Tartarus, where all the Demons in this region of Hell were mass produced before marching to their assigned cities, forts and outposts.

Vjeshitza lifted her face, smiling, and traced her tongue—more tender now—along the rim of Xaphan's ear. "They're newly dead," she purred, "and this is their first visit to Hades."

"Their first vacation?" Xaphan snorted. "Are they bored with their celestial pleasures so soon?"

"The man wants to hunt. His wife will be entertained here. Come away now, before you're seen loitering about. We must all be prepared to serve them."

"I hate when their kind come," he said.

"Shh," hissed Xaphan's lover, looking over her shoulder in case one of the Baphomets might be near. "You mustn't appear sullen."

"Should I appear giddy, then? I'm a Demon."

"You should appear dignified, but servile. We must assemble now. They're almost here." As she withdrew from him, she lightly raked the tips of her mostly-retracted claws across his hard belly, as if to mark him with scars again.

The Demon population of Castle Urian gathered in the high-ceilinged entry hall, the ranked warriors with their wings folded, but a few superiors, at attention near the door, with their wings opened in a majestic display. Looming over these Demon officers were the three creatures that presided over Urian, nicknamed Baphomets by the Damned laborers who manufactured them in Tartarus. The Baphomets concealed their pillar-straight forms in black robes, their bodies surmounted with the charred heads of goats, though the white flames that enveloped their skulls radiated cold rather than heat. They never spoke, but the winged Demons could read their meaning in the lapping of their flames.

A heavy, hollow rapping of the outer knocker, and a Demon lunged forward to creak open the black iron door. Into the hall walked a small procession of four white-robed Angels. The Angels were not homunculi like the Demons, but had once been mortal, had died and been resurrected in Heaven. One of them wore a white, starched head covering pointed into a cone, the other three simply with cowls that they slipped off their heads as they entered. Xaphan could see that one of these latter Angels was a woman.

They had met the one with the cone-like headdress before; his name was McDonald, a used car salesman who had died in the 1960s and found employment for himself over the past few decades as a guide leading other Angels on vacation tours through certain areas of Hades. The other three were his current tour group, who one of the Demon officers introduced to the assembly. "These are the brothers Anthony and James Colombo, and James' wife, Teresa. They will be staying with us for an indeterminate time. During that time, we are all to be at their service."

As one, the assembled Demons gave a deep bow.

The party had strolled further into the hall, slowly, as if to inspect each of the Demons in their rows. They were close enough to Xaphan now that he could hear the Angel named James Colombo snort and comment, "Haven't they heard of clothes around here? I feel like I walked into *National Geographic*." Over his shoulder, he said, "Check out their color, Tony. Big surprise, huh?"

Their guide, McDonald, put in, "Well, guys, these aren't the only sort of Demons. Some look like whites, some like orientals…"

"How politically correct."

"I think they're beautiful," said Teresa Colombo, who unlike her

19

husband had a British accent, dark and smoky. "In a scary way."

"They're okay," Anthony opined, flicking the nipple ring of one of the female Demons. Xaphan saw her jaw twitch slightly.

The woman's husband stopped, turned to her with a cocked eyebrow and said, "You do, huh? Well … they're not as bad as those things." He gestured openly at one of the towering, immobile Baphomets. Xaphan could tell by the fluctuations in its caul of cold flame that it was displeased by the comment, but he knew it wouldn't have given voice to its disapproval even if it had had a voice.

"Right," said his wife smartly, spinning to address McDonald, Mick as he insisted on being called. "Mick, can those poor children be unharnessed now from that awful contraption we rode here in, and given some food and water and maybe some rest? I never should have stepped into that thing when I saw what was pulling it."

"Uh, this is Hell, sweetheart," said James. "There's a good reason for those kids to be here, I'm sure."

"It's their parents' fault if they weren't baptized…"

Uncomfortably, McDonald chuckled and put a hand on her arm. "Don't worry, Terry—we'll take care of them. And when you leave, I promise we'll have a carriage pulled by animals."

"What kind of animals? A team of a hundred kittens with their fur on fire?"

Her brother-in-law laughed. "Whoa, that I'd like to see. Terry, you should be one of the torture designers down here."

The guests were shown off to their opulently-appointed rooms, and the ranks of Demons broke up. Xaphan found Vjeshitza and muttered, "I could devise or administer no greater torture than the smile in an Angel's voice."

☙

While Xaphan and Vjeshitza made love, a sandstorm howled outside. Xaphan hoped the two brothers and Mick were on a hunting excursion at this very moment, and had been caught out in the storm. He pictured them hunkered down in the inadequate shelter of the forest of antler-like bone, covering their faces against the stinging sands of dried blood.

That was the main reason the brothers had come to Hades—to hunt the Damned for sport. Though they had brought their own rifles, custom-made for them in Heaven, Castle Urian opened the doors of its armory to guests, and Xaphan had heard that earlier today the brothers had gone down into the tunnels below the palace to fire crossbows into targets. He didn't know if the targets were Damned prisoners from the palace's cells, but he didn't doubt it. These prisoners were released as hunting stock when the free-ranging Damned outside grew scanty in this area.

They were in Xaphan's room, which was tiny—but he counted himself as lucky, since Demons in other outposts and cities often had only communal barracks to rest in. A red silken tapestry covered one entire wall, the symbol for Castle Urian embroidered on it in metallic purple thread. The sheets of the small cot-like bed were of the same red material. Xaphan was raised over Vjeshitza on the strong columns of his arms, the muscles and cords in his neck pulled taut, his tight chest looking carved from polished ebony. Her powerful legs wrapped around his lower back, Vjeshitza had one finger hooked through both the rings pierced through his nipples, pulling on them just enough that the pleasure didn't stray too far into pain. Her feathered wings formed a black pool under her that looked like it might swallow them. His, half open, were a canopy that seemed to be casting that intimate pool of shadow.

"I helped prepare a perfumed bath for the woman today," Vjeshitza cooed, staring into her lover's eyes, which were both intensely focused but oddly detached, as if he gazed at some small object that was the only detail he could recall from a dream.

"Yes?" he grunted absent-mindedly, rocking her hips with his own, their pelvises locked like the antlers of fighting stags. "I imagine she was imperious. Insulting…"

"No. She was polite. She's bored, though. She's only here because of her husband, I'm sure. But I saw her body when she disrobed. She's a horrible thing. Fat, like a white leech gorged on blood. Like fruit that should have fallen from a branch long ago."

"She wasn't born a warrior, like us. And how old is she?"

"She was forty-two when she died, I heard. Young ... for one of them." Both Xaphan and Vjeshitza were only eleven years old. They had left the city of Tartarus, where they had been made, as adults. Had, in fact, been born as adults.

"She doesn't strike me as being terrible. For one of her kind," he said.

"Don't let her mislead you. They can't be trusted. They are all of one evil heart ... such as we Demons can only aspire to." Suddenly she darted her head like a snake and nipped him on the neck. His eyes clicked onto hers at last, and she grinned bright teeth in her lovely dark face. "Look at me." Then, more seriously, her smile becoming more subtle, she whispered, "Look at me..." She smoothed her hands over the black globe of his skull, as if to read the future in its surface.

⚬⚬⚬

Earlier in the day, Xaphan had passed Mrs. Colombo in a hallway. He had lowered his eyes and nodded his head respectfully, but when he glanced up he saw that she had given him a smile. Changed out of her Angel's customary garments, she was wearing a black long-sleeved pullover and black slacks with flared legs. Her clothing was very tight, emphasizing her overripe figure.

Xaphan felt that his lover had been uncharitable in calling her fat, a leech. Though her body was more voluptuous, more indulged than those of Urian's devils—which might be taken as a sign of grossness, decadence—he found her shape an artistic abstraction of the features associated with the feminine: her breasts plump, her hips wide (had she birthed children in life?). Also, whereas he, Vjeshitza, and the others had no hair, Teresa Colombo's flowed down past her breasts, was thick and parted in the center, as black as his own wings. It waved about her face when she moved, and she was always brushing a curtain of it aside to clear her face (with its dark eyes, heavy brows, strong nose, pink lips pressed into that little smile she gave him). Again, compared to one of his kind, her long, heavy hair might seem a sign of lush overindulgence.

But the contrast was eye-catching ... just as was the brightness of her skin compared to his own.

Later in that same day, as he was turning into a corridor, he heard her voice behind him (its British accent distinct), and turned to see that she was moving briskly to catch up with him. "Excuse me?" she called, gesturing. She smiled more broadly this time, showing large white teeth. He went to her.

"Madam?"

"Can you help me move something?"

"Of course, madam."

He went to her, and she led him back around the corner, down a hallway and to a door of one of the opulent guests suites. He realized it must be her own.

She opened the door, led him inside, and she closed the door after him.

"The desk under the window," she said, pointing. "Can you move that to the corner, and replace it with that armchair? I like to sit and read, but I prefer natural light."

"Certainly, madam." He did as she had instructed. As he lifted her desk, he noticed there were a few books strewn upon it. They were some of those written by the Damned themselves, and published by them as well in the larger cities like Oblivion. These crude booklets had found their way to Castle Urian in the possession of this and that Angel over the years, and Xaphan himself had read several of them in his idle hours (though Vjeshitza had scolded him for it, and had hissed that she didn't think it was wise for Demons to allow the Damned to express their thoughts in this way, let alone disseminate them to other Damned). He saw that she had a bookmark in one slim volume titled *Letters From Hades*, the author calling himself Dan Alighieri.

Seeing his eyes on it, Teresa lifted the book and riffled the pages. "There isn't much to do here while my husband's out hunting."

A little while ago, Xaphan had heard distant gunshots. "There is a subterranean garden, and a pool, down in the labyrinths," he offered.

"I've been to them. Yes, the pool is nice and hot, and the garden is pretty, if you like mushrooms and moss. A bit dungeon-like down there for my tastes, though." She set down the book and unexpectedly moved closer to him, reached out a finger that almost but not quite touched one of the perfect, unbroken onyx rings that passed through his black nipples. Her almost-touch made him flinch harder than an actual touch would have. "How do they get these things in you? I don't see a break in them."

"They put them in my species of Demon while we are still forming."

"Huh; I see. How strange. And these?" She indicated the slashed scars on both his breasts. He explained to her that he had inflicted the wounds upon himself, in a ritual marking the end of his training as a demonic warrior.

"Rrr," Teresa said, pretending to slash her own fingernails down the raised scars on his chest. Then she chuckled smokily. "Sorry." He didn't know whether to smile or to feel mocked, so he remained stoic.

She moved around behind him now, and though they weren't as sensitive as his skin, he could tell she was fingering the glossy black feathers along the edge of one of his folded wings. "Pretty," she said behind him.

"Thank you, madam," Xaphan muttered.

"Do you really fly?"

"No, madam."

"Hm. They're rather pointless, then, aren't they?"

He found their reflection in a mirror over a dressing table. She was obscured behind him in the silvered glass, but he felt her hand alight softly on his lower back. Slide into its hollow. Then around his side, along his hip. Now he could see her white hand on his dark skin in the mirror. He saw it glide over his hard belly, and then lower. Until it cupped his prick and his balls, and held them firmly. Her thumb stroked his demonhood, coaxing blood into its tubes.

"I'm bored," she whispered against one wing, as she slid her cheek back and forth across its silken sleekness.

"Yes, madam," he managed. She was pumping him languorously now. He grew hard quickly. Her hand barely fit around his black-veined dusky shaft. Its glans gleamed like the head of an obsidian scepter.

"My God," she husked, and she ran her tongue along the skin of his hard-muscled shoulder as if to taste its salt. Then she moved around in front of him, and sank to her knees. It made Xaphan uncomfortable that an Angel should kneel in supplication before a Demon. But when she took as much of him into her mouth as she could accommodate, he let out a small groan, and a moment later could not restrain himself from putting both hands to her head.

He had never touched a human woman's head before, except in the course of tortures he was obligated to perform. Her hair was a mass that shifted under his palms. That tangled between his fingers. His listened to the slick sounds of her mouth as her head worked forward and back. He felt her nails against the balls they cupped. Sharp, but not painful like the teasing claws of Vjeshitza.

Before he could find release inside her human head, Teresa rose before him, her dark eyes shining with something like a madness. "Undress me," she whispered.

And he did. He pulled off the form-fitting black pullover, the tight-fitting slacks, as if unpeeling a fruit. Her breasts hung heavy in her bra, and he held them in his hands, his thumbs spiraling across her nipples until they pressed at the restraining material. Then he lowered one of his hands, slipped it under the elastic waistband of her briefs, and fingered open the moist slit hidden in the coils of her secret hair. He had never touched this hair before, either, Vjeshitza as denuded there as a newborn mortal. A dark musk arose, and liquid sounds like her mouth had made at his cock.

"Fuck me," she murmured against his chest. With her tongue, she flicked the ring through one nipple, and then pulled slightly at the ring with her teeth. Then, again: "Fuck me."

He fumbled at her bra; she helped him. He skinned her panties down her legs. Seeing her entirely nude, he nearly ejaculated into the air itself. That vista of white flesh, its whiteness only heightened by the black growth below her rounded belly, and pouring down across her rounded shoulders. There were no hard ribs, points of hip bones, sharply defined arm muscles. She was like the offer of a soft bed to a monk who had been sleeping on a stone floor.

He took her body up in his arms, carried her to the bed she shared with her husband, and lay her on it. And without hesitation, he was on and in her and already plunging, pumping, making the bed dip like a boat on a storm-tossed sea, and her breasts jounced and she threw back her head and moaned deeply.

His wings opened fully above them like a black canopy.

Distantly, Xaphan heard the crack of a rifle shot echo across the desert flatness. Somewhere, a Damned had probably just died. But he or she would resurrect. Being already dead, a Damned or an Angel could not be killed a second time. In this way, the Demons were more like the mortals had once been than the mortals were themselves. Though their powers of regeneration were great, a Demon could be killed. And so the gunshot made Xaphan tense up a little. What if the husband should return and find them this way? Would he allow his wife this entertainment, see it as nothing more than a dip in the spring-fed pool? No more than his own entertainment hunting the Damned? Or...

But his mind drifted from the gunshot, as Teresa took his head in her hands and pulled it down to her breasts. He lost himself in their white softness, as if they filled all creation ... all life and afterlife. Xaphan had never seen the Creator—not even Angels had seen Him—so he could blasphemously imagine that He was a She. An embodiment of fertility, like this woman. He imagined all life pouring forth from the hole he was now stirring (like an alchemist's pestle in a mortar), and all life feeding at the orbs he himself suckled at avidly.

Yes, she was a goddess ... and he worshipped...

The bathing pool below Castle Urian, fed by hot springs that made steam curl from its surface, was enclosed by a circular wall carved out of solid rock as red as muscle. Into this curving wall, small curtained nooks had been incised so that visitors could change in and out of their clothes. The pool itself was currently empty—no Demon would dare use it while Angel visitors were staying here—but one of these small changing niches was currently occupied by the Demon Xaphan and Teresa Colombo.

She had bent over a stone bench carved into the wall, her palms spread on it, while Xaphan gripped her waist and took her from behind. When they were finished, she sank down onto her knees, her breasts and elbows resting against this rock ledge—Xaphan sinking with her, still embracing her, gently wilting inside her. On impulse, he pushed aside some of the thick black hair that was stuck to the expanse of her back with sweat, and he kissed her on her damp shoulder.

"Sweet," she whispered, in almost a little laugh, reaching up to cup his cheek for a moment. She lay her head down on one arm and sighed heavily. "Well—that was rather nice, wasn't it, my Demondingo?"

"Demondingo?"

"It's a joke. Mandingo? Demondingo? Never mind. *Mmm* ... keep doing that."

Xaphan was running his hand across her back, spreading the spilled ink of her hair, feeling the bony plates of her shoulders like unsprouted wings beneath her taut skin. "I hated you when I first saw you," he muttered, more to himself than to her.

She lifted her cheek off her forearm a little, seeming amused by his confession. "You did? Why?"

"I'm sorry..."

"No, tell me. Why?"

"Because you are valued by the Creator. And we are nothing more to Him than inanimate things. And sometimes, we don't see the difference between us. We can't understand what it is He values in you."

"Well, perhaps if you could understand that, then you *would* be the same as us." After a moment, Teresa twisted around to look up at him, no longer smiling. "Sorry, X. No ... I don't suppose there is much difference, is there? I was going to point out the horrible things your kind do to the Damned. But right now, my hubby is out in the desert hunting some teenage boys that he saw and liked in your bloody kennels down here." She snorted, lowered her head again. "I don't want to know why they aroused his interest, in particular. Aroused perhaps being the key word."

Still rubbing her skin, as if contemplating it, as if expecting to at last discern something about it that would distinguish its illusory substance from her mortal skin, wherever that lay moldering right now, he asked, "How did you and your husband die?"

"In a plane crash. Private plane. We were going skiing, in Colorado. We met on a skiing trip in Aspen, actually. I'd moved to the States a few years earlier, and..."

"Did you have children?" Xaphan interrupted.

"Two. Ten and seven. They're still alive." A few empty beats. "I don't want to talk about them, X."

He changed the subject, his voice retaining the quality of a sleepwalker. "Your flesh is so different from Vjeshitza's," he murmured.

"Whose?" A look up at him again.

Tensing up a little, Xaphan let his hand go motionless upon her.

"A mate?"

"A lover," he admitted solemnly. "We don't need to mate."

"But you fuck." A carnal smile. Was there a hint of jealousy in her dark eyes, or was it merely flirtation that pretended jealousy? He hoped she was jealous. It would cause him pain if she wasn't, he realized.

He was jealous of her husband, he realized...

"Yes," he whispered.

"I'm different from her, am I? I won't ask who you like to fuck more. It's apples and oranges, isn't it? A bright morning sky is lovely. And so is the black night sky with stars."

Xaphan grunted derisively. "Your theologian Swedenborg said, 'corporeal loves appear gross, dusky, black and misshapen, while those that are heavenly loves appear fresh, bright, fair, and beautiful.'"

"That must bother you, to have troubled to memorize it."

"It bothers me," Xaphan admitted.

She took the hand that didn't lay upon her skin, brought it to her lips and kissed it. "Don't worry—you're a beautiful midnight sky, aren't you, my love?"

"Don't say that."

"Say what?"

"Love. I'm not your love. You don't love me."

28

"Why are you…" she began to chuckle.

"Don't mock me!" he hissed.

"I'm not mocking you, X! It's an expression, isn't it? I didn't realize love was such a touchy subject for Demons. I didn't even know whether you can feel it." A moment. "Well … can you?"

"I'm not sure I understand it," he grumbled evasively.

"Well I guess we're not so different after all. I don't understand it either. I mean, I know I loved my mother, and my children … there's no ambiguity there." She veered the conversation, again, away from the children who had survived her. "I used to have a neighbor, who told me that he and his wife had once taken in a stray cat. They had it for about ten years, I suppose. My neighbor was an older man, very gruff, an old war vet. And he told me his cat was hit by a car in front of their house one day. He said to me, in his very gruff way, 'I don't know why we ever got that damn cat.'" Teresa smiled. "That was the greatest avowal of love I've ever heard…"

"Terry?" a voice called out, echoing in the circular, domed cavern beyond.

"Shit," Teresa whispered, getting to her feet as Xaphan let go of her. She grabbed up her balled robe from the stone bench, and began slipping into it. In so doing, her elbow struck the deep red velvet of the cubicle's curtain, causing it to sway.

"Terry?" The voice had turned in their direction. "You there?"

Pushing Xaphan back against the wall with one hand, Teresa parted the curtain with the other and slid out into the humid air of the bathhouse. "I was just going to take a dip, darling," she said. "Want to join me?"

Xaphan peeked out through the slit in the soft curtain. He saw James Colombo's loathsome face. Could he not smell the sex on his wife's sweat-moist body? The film of slickness spread across her inner thighs? With his superior sense of smell, Xaphan himself could clearly detect the musk of his own lifeless sperm, nestled inside her in a miniature version of this secret closet he lurked in.

"Mm." Colombo reached his hands around and cupped Teresa's full bottom, pulling her against him, kissing her on the mouth. Open mouth. Xaphan felt an animal growl rumble in his guts, fought to keep it contained. Breaking free of their embrace, Colombo groaned, "I'm beat … maybe after supper."

"How was your horrible little fox hunt?"

"I got one kid. The other got away. But the one I hit, I got with a clean shot right through the eye." He jutted a finger toward his own eye, and sniggered.

"I suppose I didn't really want the particulars," Teresa said, turning and walking back toward the row of cubbyholes. But, she was moving toward the one directly to the left of the one Xaphan was hiding in.

"They don't die, you know!" Colombo reminded her. "They regenerate…"

"Whatever. I'll join you for dinner. I still want to have my dip."

"You should," Colombo teased, turning away, "you smell sweaty."

"Thanks, James. Ever the romantic."

"Hey, you love me for my honesty," called his diminishing voice.

"Do I?" she called back. "And do you love me for *my* honesty?"

"That and your tasty ass," his voice echoed.

A moment later, Teresa ducked back into the closet with Xaphan. She curled her fingers into his nipple rings, drew him into her arms. "Mm," she moaned, as her husband had done while embracing her, running her hands around his shoulders and across the sleek feathers of his folded wings. "Thank God he's gone. I don't know why I married him, X, I really don't understand it…"

Xaphan was not moved by her statement, whether it was an honest sentiment or meant only to reassure him. He said nothing, looked over the top of her head at the dark red curtain. Its featureless smoothness soothed him a little, as her skin had done a minute or so earlier. Now that skin, bending with oppressive pleasure against his own, only confused him. What a curse, the skin. There was no escaping it, even in Hell.

As had been the case over the past several days, Vjeshitza was one of the

Demons who accompanied the visiting Angels on their hunt. Because of this, Xaphan relented when Teresa insisted he take her to his own tiny room, with its red tapestry bearing the symbol for Castle Urian and the matching red sheets on its narrow bed.

Teresa sat astride him, his hands gripping her breasts, claws extended just far enough to indent their soft flesh. Rolling her ample hips in a slow, circular rhythm, Teresa husked, "I think we're leaving tomorrow." She said it without lead-in, without segue. Its unexpectedness shocked Xaphan, although the information itself should not have shocked him.

"Your husband bores so soon?"

"I suppose so."

"And you?"

"Me? I'm not bored, X. But what am I to do?"

"What are you to *do?*" Xaphan repeated hotly. He calmed his tone, but stammered with a raw discomfort that made him bitter, "Will you return, then? Or am I never to see you again?"

"Ohh … darling," Teresa purred, cupping the side of his face. "I will come back to see you again, I promise. We're both immortal, aren't we? We have all of eternity to see each other again…"

"You're immortal. I'm not."

"You won't age. And you won't die, unless you're killed. So don't get killed, all right?" She smiled down at him. "What is it with me? I've always been drawn to either bullies or brooders."

She slid off him, left his cock suspended naked and vulnerable in the air. She rolled onto her belly and raised her rump a bit. "Here," she whispered. He got up over her, lay atop her, began to ease into her again. But she took his shaft in hand, and nuzzled its tip a little higher up. "No—here."

Lubricated with her juices and with the inner mucus of this orifice, he pressed gradually inside her. She winced, gripped the sheet in her fists, tensed up hard beneath him. A little alarmed, Xaphan said, "Do you want me to stop?"

"No," she breathed. "All the way."

"It's hurting you."

"I'm immortal, aren't I? And since when is a Demon afraid of hurting someone?"

He did as she asked, until he was in her to his hilt and rocking forward and back atop her. Teresa's eyes were clenched shut and tearing at the corners, but she gasped, "You love me, then, don't you?"

"Please don't make me say it."

"Say it. You're torturing me. Let me torture you."

"Yes," Xaphan said through gritted teeth, increasing his rhythm now with each thrust until he was slapping against her, until the bed rocked and she began to cry out a little with each stab, "I love you … I love you…"

⚬⚬

There was a commotion in Castle Urian, which Xaphan with his heightened senses detected, raising his head alertly. Teresa only became aware of it when he halted his thrusts, and she rolled over, her hair in her face, as he slipped out of her. "What is it?"

"The hunting party is back early," he hissed. "You'd better get out of the Demon quarters…"

Teresa got up, pulled her robe on. "Bloody hell. James must be more bored than I thought. Or he wants his lunch early, poor dear." On her way to the door, she gave Xaphan a quick kiss on the cheek. "I hope that wasn't our last time, love," she cooed, but he didn't think she sounded mournful, wistful. Or would no measure of emotion satisfy him, any longer?

After cracking his door and peeking out, she darted through it, and closed it after her without a look back at him. Xaphan watched the door nonetheless, as if she might reappear.

⚬⚬

James and Anthony had indeed wanted their lunch early, particularly since James was in a foul mood. He had wounded a teen age boy by blowing off one leg at the knee, and when he got up close to the boy to

32

finish him off (or to play with him, Xaphan thought, hearing the story at the banquet-like dinner table), the boy had thrown a rock at James and hit him over the eye, splitting the skin and drawing blood. There was no longer any evidence of this wound, but James was still livid.

"I want that kid tortured for the rest of eternity, Mick," he snarled to their guide.

"I've already had him taken to the tunnels, Jim," the Angel assured him. "They'll straighten him out for ya."

"Better straighten him out on a rack," Colombo grumbled, picking through a plate of edible mushrooms grown in the subterranean garden. Vjeshitza had just placed it down in front of him. Xaphan saw the Angel look up at her small, hard breasts as she straightened to remove another cart from her wheeled serving wagon.

Xaphan was one of several Demons merely standing in attendance like living statues. He had offered to take the men's guns to their rooms, since their weapons merely leaned against the wall behind their chairs, but Anthony Colombo had waved the Demon away. "Don't touch our gear, boy," he warned him absent-mindedly, while looking at freckles of drying blood that he had just noticed on the white sleeve of his robe.

Xaphan watched Vjeshitza place a glass of wine in front of Teresa Colombo, whose hair had been quickly bunched back in a ponytail to hide its disarray. She did not look up at Vjeshitza. Did she suspect that this was her lover's lover? Or didn't she even care? She had not made eye contact with Xaphan once.

But now Xaphan returned his attention to Vjeshitza, muscular and brown, candlelight fluttering on her polished skull. She had placed the glass down already, yet still hovered over Teresa's shoulder, slightly bent, as if expecting another order.

Oh Creator, Xaphan thought, realizing what was happening. When he widened his nostrils, he could smell it over the aromas of the food, too … even from across the long table he could smell it. The musk of sex on the Angel woman.

The Demon sperm, inside her. And with her superior senses, Vjeshitza would even recognize which Demon it had issued from.

From deep inside Vjeshitza's guts, from some microcosm of Hades within her, arose a growl that erupted as a bellow when it escaped her wide jaws. Even as Xaphan's wings spread open (uselessly, as if he might fly over the table), Vjeshitza seized hold of Teresa's ponytail in one fist, jerking her head back. Her other hand rose, and panther-like claws slid out of her fingertips. In a flash, she swept that hand down, and ripped open the front of the human woman's arced throat. Blood leaped like an freed animal, landing in the wine glass, toppling it, and rocking an empty soup bowl which quickly filled to its brim.

"Mother of God!" James Colombo shouted, bolting upright. Both he and his brother scrambled to grab up their guns.

"No!" Xaphan roared, leaping up onto the table.

Vjeshitza turned her feral eyes on her lover. "Traitor!" she hurled at him.

Then one gun roared like the voice of yet another Demon. Followed by several more deafening shots.

Xaphan alighted beside Vjeshitza and caught her just as she fell. Her eyes were still on his, though in those last seconds he knew she might not even be seeing him. As practiced as the hunters were, all three bullets had hit her in the chest. One of these projectiles had struck her in the nipple, punching it in, a leaving a hole streaming blood like a profusion of poisoned milk. Below her, on the stone floor, Xaphan could see a fragment of the once unbroken onyx ring that had pierced her nipple, like his own.

He lowered her slack body to the floor, then reared and spun around, wings still open wide, talons fully extended. He saw Anthony Colombo's gun swing in his direction.

One of the goat-headed Baphomets, also in attendance like a statue, drifted forward a foot or two so smoothly that it seemed to float. Apparently having seen this, the guide McDonald raised his arms and shouted, "Whoa, whoa, whoa! Let's not go crazy here, people, please! Please!"

Anthony lowered his gun warily. His brother James helped support his wife, who despite the fact that the front of her robes were soaked in gore was able to stay on her feet. Because she was an Angel, she could heal faster than one of the Damned that her husband hunted. She was in agony, Xaphan knew, but unlike a Demon, she couldn't be slain. She had an immortal soul, where the Demons had been fashioned without them, like a tin man without a heart.

"We're out of here!" James Colombo cried, incensed. "This is outrageous! Fucking outrageous!" And he began half-dragging his wife toward the doorway, with Anthony covering their retreat and McDonald still blubbering for them to calm down.

Another Demon had come forward to rest a staying hand on Xaphan's shoulder, claws extended to bite into his skin. Xaphan shook him off, and before he knelt down beside his lover's corpse, he met Teresa's eyes for a final time as she was swept backwards out of the dining chamber.

Her eyes were wide with pain. But was it merely physical anguish? The Demon had no way of telling if there were loss … regret … guilt … or only severed nerve endings that would soon weave together again, leaving no scars behind.

Though as a Demon, Xaphan was expected to be a master of pain, he realized its nuances were as mysterious to him as the emotion of love.

He took his eyes off the retreating Angel, and crouched down over Vjeshitza, picked up the halved fragment of her onyx ring. Clenched it in his fist until it bit into him. Clenched his eyes shut like fists, and wished he could take her in his arms and spread his wings and fly both of them directly up, up into the very eye of their Creator.

Not so that He might heal her.

So that they might blind Him. If He wasn't blind, already.

SIREN

Just because one had gone to Heaven didn't guarantee that one could get laid.

Heaven was a far from perfect place, in Stephen Petty's estimation. His first disappointment had come immediately upon waking up to realize he was dead, and taking in his new body, made from the stuff of his spirit. He was not disappointed that he could touch and be touched, smell, taste, and even feel pain (though his chronic indigestion and frequent back aches were no more). Being so convincingly corporeal, without fear of a second death, was something to be grateful for, relieved about. As he had neared the age of fifty, he had begun to feel the shadow of his mortality -- and with good reason, having died of a massive coronary just shy of his half-centennial.

But shouldn't this new, faux flesh he inhabited, this miraculous golem, be in the form of some celestial Adonis? Instead, he had been reincarnated, so to speak, as himself—and he had always hated his appearance, as much as it seemed women did. In grade school he had been "Tubby," in high school "Moon Face" because of its shape and pocked craters. The most he had been granted, upon being reborn, was to find that his fifty-year-old body had been reinterpreted as his twenty-five-year-old body. He supposed this was because he had been the least unhappy with his appearance at that time of his abbreviated life: his ravaging acne hadn't petered out until he was in his early twenties, and after thirty the bald spot on the back of his head had spread swiftly.

But even at twenty five he had possessed a prodigious gut. Though he doubted his new lungs were actually breathing in the sense that his mortal lungs had, he still wheezed when he exerted himself. His face was still ridden with scars as if it had been nibbled by rats and healed badly.

Despite his appearance, Petty had at last found a wife at the age of twenty-nine. But Brenda and his seventeen-year-old daughter Christina had both been killed in an automobile accident two years before his own death. Christina decapitated, Brenda's head flattened and her brains pushed out her mouth. That was what she got for letting their wild, out-of-control daughter behind the wheel. In those last few years of her life, Petty had almost come to hate the defiant, foul-mouthed (and, he suspected, promiscuous) Christina ... had only prevented himself from doing so by recalling her as the younger, sweeter child she'd once been. That child had died years before the seventeen-year-old. He had mourned them both, as if they had been two daughters instead of one.

He'd missed Brenda, too, so he had at first been delighted when he and Brenda had encountered each other by chance a short while ago. She had recognized him, though he would never have recognized her in her present form. Brenda now occupied a twelve-year-old version of herself. She explained that she had been happiest at the age of twelve. And he had to admit she was prettier at twelve than she had ever been in the years he'd known her.

But when Petty tried to goad her into sex, she rebuffed him angrily and stomped off, pigtails jiggling haughtily, and he hadn't seen her since.

So much for Heaven.

The boat bounced as it sped across the crimson waves, and Petty clung to the rail tightly, feeling his guts roil. The hood of his white robe had blown off and the monk-like circle of his thinning hair ruffled. He squinted and flinched as droplets of red spray misted across his face.

The robe itself was of a shiny, silky material, and fortunately the blood beaded and trickled on it instead of soaking through. As if the boat's speed wasn't bad enough, the stinging metallic tang of this ocean of gore was nauseating.

"Do you think we can slow down just a little?" he shouted to the pilot, Captain Eridan, who stood beside him at a control panel raised like a podium, either caked in rust or accumulated blood.

Eridan smiled without taking his eyes off the prow as it ploughed up the waters of the Red Sea ahead of them. "We want to move through this section quickly, sir. The eels are thick through here. A bit further ahead they'll be less plentiful."

"They can hurt us, too? Not just the Damned?"

"We'll taste bad to them. That doesn't mean they won't try a taste. And you'll heal faster than the Damned. That doesn't mean it won't hurt."

Captain Eridan was not an Angel like Petty. He was a Demon, who had never been a mortal man as Petty had been; the Demons were homunculi, manufactured in factory-cities like Tartarus. They came in many forms, and Eridan's breed was adapted to dwell in cities like Sheol at the bottom of this scarlet sea. Perhaps out of camouflage, or simply out of the Creator's sense of aesthetics, these aquatic Demons were fire-engine red and preferred to go nude, showing off their layers of glittering scales and the wing-like fins (or fin-like wings) that flared from their backs when they weren't folded up like fans. Petty and another tourist from Heaven, vacationing here in Hades like himself, had joked that Eridan looked like the Creature From The Red Lagoon. Eridan had looked over at them when they'd chuckled at his expense, but he was a mere Demon despite his rank, and bound to serve each visiting Angel as if he were the greatest of dignitaries.

Something slapped across Petty's chest like a whip, rebounded from him and was left in the jet boat's frothy wake. Almost dislodged from the rail, Petty let out a cry and looked back behind him. He saw something twist and writhe in the air. One of the eels that flew rather than swam, as disoriented as he was after their collision.

"Sorry!" Eridan called out cheerfully, weaving the boat between furrows of the lapping blood. "I've been trying to steer us through the thickest clouds of them." He tilted his chin to indicate a swarm of the airborne creatures, off to their left. The animals squirmed like boiling maggots, a living storm cloud above the surface of the waves.

"What attracts them to one spot like that? Fish in the sea?"

"Maybe. Or a Damned, escaping from Sheol, or from one of the Obsidian Islands. If you think they're thick here, sir, you should see the Valley of Steam. The air is a solid mass with them."

The other Angel tourist aboard the boat, who'd introduced himself to Petty as Mike Rule, was already at the harpoon gun in the boat's bow, his fists clenched around the metal handles, swiveling it this way and that. It creaked with its patina of rust-or-blood. "I hope it's a Damned," he said, pressing his eye to a scope. "Could I hit him from here if I saw him? Or would that draw the eels to us?"

"We're a bit too far to hit someone there, if there is someone," Captain Eridan said. "But don't worry, sir, you'll have your chance."

"What if I see one of your kind swimming?" Rule asked, his grin showing under the cup of the scope. "Can I shoot him? Will I get in trouble?"

Petty glanced over at Eridan's face, the entirely red eyes devoid of pupils, but the Demon remained courteous as he replied, "It is to be discouraged, sir, but of course you can do as you please."

"Thar she blows," Petty said, shielding his eyes with one hand, as he saw a flailing arm rise out of the water and submerge again. In that brief instant, eels had darted at it, and he was certain had torn chunks from it. The frenzied cloud of animals and the Damned man or woman, who could drown but be quickly resurrected to drown again, and again, were left behind them.

"I hope I see my ex-boss out here," said Rule, still swiveling the harpoon gun. "If that bastard didn't go to Hell there's no justice in the universe."

After a short while, with the shore of obsidian cliffs and glittering volcanic sand lost in the distance, Captain Eridan cut their speed to a comfortable, leisurely pace. From a cooler in the stern, Petty and Rule took bottles of beer. Rule jokingly offered a bottle to one of Eridan's crew, but the Demon shook its head and lowered its eyes, slapping away on its webbed feet to continue swabbing blood from the deck. "I'm getting hungry, Mike," Petty quipped dryly as he watched the creature. "Got any tartar sauce?"

"Can you imagine going down on one of their ladies?" Rule said. "That would really smell like fish." He looked over his shoulder at their vessel's composed captain. "But you know what they say, Captain Sinbad ... if it smells like fish, that's my dish. If it smells like cologne, leave it alone!"

On the horizon they spied a much larger craft, a battleship compared to their sleek but weathered yacht. "Hey, is that a torture ship?" Rule asked their pilot.

"An ocean liner for vacationers like yourself, anxious to see the sights beyond the pearly gates." Petty thought he detected a mocking tinge to the cliche "pearly gates." "Drink, dinner, dance, shuffleboard, harpooning the Damned. I'm sure you would enjoy it, gentlemen. Ships like that find harbor south of here, should you be interested in booking passage when you've had your fill of my humble boat."

"We'll have to talk to our tour guide about it when we get back to our lodgings," Petty said. Because he did indeed feel that he'd prefer cruising slowly on a large ship like that, instead of jouncing across the waves on this smaller craft. He had hoped a visit to Hades would shake up his jaded senses, after having found Heaven to be rather dull, rather lonely. But he hadn't wanted to be physically shaken.

"I like this boat," Rule stated, however. "Much more exciting, huh, Steve?"

"Sure," Petty muttered.

'It's good to be alive again!" Rule chirped, raising his bottle to salute the churning Red Sea and the black layer of perpetual clouds that formed the ceiling of Hades.

Petty had considered bringing his apsara with him on his vacation to Hell, but had ultimately decided against it. The apsaras were homunculi like the Demons, and made to order for those in Heaven, as servants and lovers. Because Petty had had no luck meeting a female Angel with whom to enjoy the boundless carnal pleasures he would have expected to await him in the afterlife, he had ordered one of these apsaras for himself. In life he had been a mortgage expert, so he had named his living sex doll Fannie Mae as a private joke, though she had the face and body of Demi Moore, as she had looked in her early movies like *St. Elmo's Fire* and *About Last Night* (in which she'd been deliciously nude). He had preferred her then, soft and young and small-breasted, over how she had looked in *Striptease*, with her phony-looking breast implants and her buffed body and harder face. Petty liked to think that he had a refined sense of taste, an artistic appreciation of the female form in its natural state. Not to mention that he was drawn to very young women. That they would be the last women to be interested in him made him long for them all the more.

He had enjoyed Fannie Mae on a physical level, but her uncomplaining accommodation, her dog-like complacency, and the fact that the homunculus was nearly monosyllabic had made him fairly discontented of late. Whereas Rule had come to Hades to hunt the Damned for sport, Petty had come in the vague hopes that a Damned woman would be a more willing sex partner than a fellow Angel. Or, if not willing, then an unwilling sex partner. He need not be concerned with raping a Damned woman, whereas such a thing with an Angel would be out of the question. He didn't know if an Angel like himself could be sentenced as a Damned, but he wasn't willing to risk it.

He had thought he might even persuade a female Demon to take him to her bed, but after seeing the red-scaled beings back at the Demonic seashore fortress where he and Rule had been given lodgings, he had ruled out the possibility.

He had thought this adventure would exhilarate him, like a safari. Instead, he was already finding this remarkable ocean of live red blood cells boring in its redundancy. The thought of immortality began to depress him. To escape it for a brief while, in what was dubbed the little death (or was that what they called orgasm? he couldn't recall), he decided it was best to retire to the forecastle for a nap, leaving Rule to his hunt. Though the Damned deserved to be here, because in life they had turned their backs on or denied the existence of their Creator (Petty and his wife had been church-going Catholics, Rule a Baptist), Petty wasn't sure if he could bring himself to take a turn at the harpoon gun, himself.

❧

Petty's heart, or the ectoplasmic replica of his heart, awakened him with a jolt as if defibrillators had been applied to him—again. He had been dreaming of his final living moments. Riding in the ambulance. Hearing its siren. The last sound he'd heard with his mortal ears, that banshee siren. Like a wailing cry of lamentation. It was as if the ambulance had driven him here, to the plane of the afterlife, instead of to the hospital.

He sat up on his cot, and listened to the boat's puttering. They were moving very slowly. He raised his bulk with a groan of strain, and emerged from the shaded forecastle to see what was going on up front.

"Look at this, Steve!" cried Rule over his shoulder, crouched even more avidly at the harpoon gun. "Not much sport in shooting these three, but it might make good target practice!"

"Sorry this spot was a bit out of the way, gentlemen," Captain Eridan called above the motor sounds, "but I thought you might find it of interest!"

The boat had found its way among a series of small islands, some no larger than a manhole cover, the largest as big as a parking lot. All were flattish, and Petty had the impression that these were not the peaks of underwater rock, covered in a congealing slime of blood; instead, he grew convinced they were essentially giant blood clots floating atop the calm surface of the sea in this area. These masses were gelatinous, and so dark a red they were nearly black. Toward their centers, the matter went from a glossy pudding to a hard, flaking crust. Immense scabs, Petty realized. And if the normal scent of the Red Sea wasn't bad enough—that iron reek of blood—these islets gave off a stench like rotting meat.

On the largest of these raft-like blood clots, somehow a windmill had been erected. It was a tall, metal framework with a fairly small blade at its top, which didn't even stir in this becalmed air. The whole structure was encrusted with layers of dried gore. At the foot of the windmill, three naked figures stood with their hands chained high above their heads. The legs and support struts of the windmill obscured them, but Eridan began to casually coax his boat around the rim of the island so they could get a direct view of the prisoners.

"The wind should be along any moment," he informed them cryptically.

How grateful Petty was, seeing things like this, that he wasn't one of the Damned. How foolish these poor people had been! He had gone to church like he went to the toilet; in an automatic, unthinking way—all that it had cost him for an afterlife-long membership to the celestial country club. It wasn't like one had to be a contemplative monk, teach catechism, do volunteer work. Once he and Brenda left that high-ceilinged, gilded room with the solemn lisping voice of their priest lulling them nearly to sleep, Brenda would begin to gossip about this fellow parishioner or that, and glare at them when they cut her off as they all drove out of the parking lot. That didn't matter. All that mattered was making an appearance, chanting the words the Creator wanted to hear from you, and you were safe. Was that so hard? Look what these creatures had brought upon themselves by being agnostics, atheists … running away from their Father.

They had almost reached the opposite side of the island, and as Eridan had predicted, a breeze had come up, turning sharp very quickly. He seemed to have almost cut his engine entirely, as if he didn't want to reach the far side until the wind had mounted to its full strength. But Petty still began to make out more of what lay at the foot of the windmill...

A cage of tight wire mesh covered each of the three captives. These cages, in turn, were connected by chains woven through a mechanism of gears and cogs.

And the eels. About a dozen of them wriggled through the air, circling around the cages, sinuously winding their way through the girders of the windmill's base. Once in a while one of the animals, with its phallic eyeless head and jaws overflowing with fangs, would try to nose its way through the mesh of the cages to get at the succulent meat within, but the openings were too small.

"Would anybody get mad if I shot these Damned right through the cages?" Rule whispered to their guide.

"Please be patient, sir. The wind current is approaching." He pointed a free hand up at the blades of the windmill, which had begun to spin ... lazily, then more quickly, until bursts of breeze made the metal pinwheel blur.

They were near enough now that Petty could see the three Damned souls were nude young women. He leaned against the rail, gripping it more firmly.

Suddenly, like a freight train, the wind arrived. Petty was glad he had a firm grip on the rusty rail. His hood blew off. The calm surface of the Red Sea was whipped up into a pink foam, suds of it spattering him and the deck. The intermittent blurring of the windmill blades became steady, until they were invisible. At the base of the machine, there was a screech and grinding, as gears started to turn, greasy chains to move like tendons.

The three cages began to rise, uncovering their delectable contents. The women squirmed, twisted their lithe white bodies, but their wrists were still bound above their heads. A sound rose above the gusting wind, the noises of machinery. They were wailing. Sobbing. It was an unearthly sound, like sirens calling to Ulysses and his men ... to drive them mad with lust ... to lure them to their death among the rocks.

Then, the eels darted in. One coordinated movement, like a shoal of fish abruptly changing direction. And not only that, but other eels seemed to appear out of nowhere. Out of the sea? Out of hiding places in the windmill's skeleton? Had they come up from behind the boat in a swarm? Wherever they had materialized from, the dozen had turned to a hundred … and they converged on the three screaming women in a dense flock.

"Like clockwork," Captain Eridan noted proudly, as if the torture device were of his own design.

Rule had stiffened at his gun, was obviously ready to launch a spear into one of the three newly exposed women, but the spectacle of the eels swooping in on them made him lift his head from the scope and mutter, "My God."

"*Yes,*" Eridan said, with a crescent grin.

At last, like the hand of a clock, the boat had come around to the front of the tiny island, and Eridan cut the motor so they could watch the feeding frenzy clearly.

Petty was reminded of paintings of St. Sebastian, his arms lashed above or behind him, his bare chest pierced by arrows. Except that these were females, and the arrows whipped their tails, alive, their heads buried in smooth white flesh. For whatever reason, however, whether by natural inclination or training, the beasts obviously preferred the flesh and muscle of the face. Only a few chewed at the bodies below; the rest had covered the faces of the trio, muffling and choking off their cries.

Rule spun to the side of the boat and vomited violently over the rail. That made Petty smirk a little. So much for the great white hunter.

Blood did not stream down those nude bodies from the savaged faces—the hovering eels drank it up before it could trickle far. Despite the living nightmares completely enveloping their heads—or because of the heightened contrast—their bodies still struck Petty as immensely beautiful. Like the Venus de Milo without her arms, making her torso all the lovelier. Their succulent flesh was like the white stone of that statue, a marred purity. Petty couldn't blame the eels for their passion; he almost wanted to consume the flesh himself.

He moved to the abandoned harpoon gun to press his eye to the scope, not caring what Eridan or his men or Rule might think of his blatant voyeurism.

Oh yes, that unalloyed beauty, stripped of clothes, of pretense, of society (and soon, of faces, leaving only the graceful figures without the rejecting sneer of lips, the disapproving squint of eyes). Petty was now reminded of the headless, armless, but spread-winged statue called the Nike of Samothrace. When the Romans conquered Greece, they lopped the heads off their statues. But how beautiful Nike remained, her stone gown clinging to her gentle curves, mutilated though she was...

The girl on the left was very thin, her raised arms pulling her small breasts entirely flat, her ribs showing distinctly through her parchment skin. Her ankles were also chained, he now realized, preventing her legs from kicking like those of a hanged man. But she managed to swing entirely around once, giving him a brief look at the sweep of her back, a tattoo of a butterfly in the hollow above her buttocks (one of his very favorite zones of the female form), and her small, cleft bottom. The girl on the right appeared to be the oldest of the three, her breasts heavier, her hips wide (perhaps she'd given birth?), but Petty loved sumptuous flesh. His eyes kneaded it like hands.

Like Goldilocks, however, he found the girl in the middle to be just right. She was, in a word, perfection.

Her back was forced into a tense arch, the buds of her breasts thrust out, their ends dipped in pink candy. Her skin so smooth that his eyes could feel its tautness across her sides, softer across her belly and thighs. Her pubic hair was red. He had always loved redheads, had married one in fact. Her bush was complemented by two more, under her uplifted arms. He knew most American men disliked underarm hair, but he with his refined tastes found it sexy, earthy, mirroring the hair of the crotch, and he wanted to press his nose into each of the three thatches, to draw in her intimate musk. One stray eel nursed at her skin beside the bullet hole of her navel, appearing like a new umbilical cord for her rebirth here in Hades. She was youth, she was a goddess, with her head covered in writhing bodies he thought of her as Medusa on the Half-Shell ... so hideous, and so lovely because of it.

The wind started to die down, the windmill blades to become visible again. With a metallic clatter, the cages began to descend, and conditioned to this or trained like dogs, the eels darted away from their three victims before they could become trapped inside the cages, too. Besides, their bellies were full. As the cages lowered, and the eels escaped, Petty could see what was left of the trio's faces. Bone, a few strands of hair (he could now see the center girl's remaining short red locks). Without the eels to catch it, drops of blood began to patter and trickle across the bare canvasses of their bodies, which had mercifully slumped unconscious. Was that a faint, gurgling kind of moan coming from one or more of them?

"Now they will regenerate. Heal," explained Captain Eridan. "Until the next time the wind current comes." In an odd and unwelcome gesture of familiarity, he patted Petty on the shoulder. "I thought you might find this worth the extra time."

Petty straightened from the harpoon gun's scope. He hoped the Demon didn't notice his erection, tenting the fabric of his Angelic robes.

"Yes ... it was ... fascinating," he stammered.

"Would you care to have a shot at one of them before the cages are in place, Mr. Rule?" he called. "You'd better hurry..."

Rule only groaned, still hunched over the rail, and waved them away.

Eridan turned again to Petty. "Such sights to see in Hades, eh?" he whispered conspiratorially, as if afraid the Creator might overhear. "You won't see the likes of this in Heaven."

And with that, he returned to the wheel, gunned the motor, and swung them back in the direction of the black, obsidian shore.

In his room at the Demonic fortress, overlooking the churning Red Sea, Petty lay in bed and masturbated, imaging that the red-haired girl was going down on him. The scary thought that the face clamped to his groin might be ravaged down to the bone only excited him further. He imagined his hands pressing her head to him, running across the tight skin of her humped back. With a cry, he ejaculated into the maw of his imagination.

It wasn't enough. As he lay there wheezing, the great island of his belly rising and falling, he knew it was not enough.

He went out into the fortress and asked for breakfast, sat down to it alone in a large echoing room built from blocks of volcanic glass. He asked one of the servant Demons if Rule was coming down. He was told Mr. Rule had left a short while ago, had asked to be taken south down the coast to where the ocean liners docked to pick up tourist Angels like himself.

Petty was a bit insulted, but relieved, that Rule had not invited him to join him. When the servant poured him his second coffee, he told her to send word to Captain Eridan that he wanted to ride on his boat again today; specifically, he wanted to ride out again to the series of blood clot islands.

❧

When they finally arrived, after what Petty judged to be three hours or more, the wind current had already found the islands, the windmill was already spinning, the cages already lifted. The eels already feeding.

"I wish we could have gotten here sooner," Petty groused to Eridan.

"Sir?"

"I wanted to see their faces."

"Oh ... I see ... I'm sorry, sir. Well, when the wind dies down, we can linger a while. You can nap, sir, or have a few drinks. Their faces will reconstitute. Then I can draw us in closely, sir. We can even land on the island, if you like."

Land there. Disembark. Might he be able to touch some part of the living triptych through the holes in the mesh of their cages? Might he even coax Eridan, who was required to serve him, into opening one of the cages ... even setting one of the prisoners free? That prisoner might be very grateful for her release. Grateful enough to serve him, as well...

"Yes," Petty said, trying not to betray to his guide the tremulous energies swimming through his system. "That would be fine..."

Petty fetched a beer, and watched the display again through the scope. (They couldn't land on the island until the cages had lowered and the bulk of the eels had departed, for fear of being attacked themselves.)

The wind finally roared away across the ocean of red corpuscles. The eels fled, perhaps to feed on other prisoners on other island chains. The cages descended. Now, Eridan drew them in closer as he had promised, though in a way Petty wished he had waited a while— but he supposed a half reformed face would be no less horrible than these denuded skulls. More horrible, maybe. They came close enough that he could hear the wheezing through their gaping nose cavities, the gargling blood in their throats. He saw breasts rising and falling. Drops of blood flecked their chests like rose petals on snow. So lovely.

Two of Eridan's men hopped off the boat, into knee-deep blood, and attached lines to the legs of the windmill. They drew the boat against the shining lip of the blood clot raft (and jabbed at the few remaining eels with harpoons to keep them at bay). But Petty did not climb ashore just yet. He had another beer. He watched the slow regeneration. He listened as gurgles became moans, evolved into sobs.

When they had lips again, would they curse him for being one of the blessed? An Angel, never tortured, never suffering? Well, what did they know of his suffering? In life, young beauties like these would have scorned him. It had been that way all his life. Was their Promethean torture any worse than that? Did their physical degradation really outweigh his psychological degradation?

It was unfair, was it not, that Petty was so gross and repulsive an Angel, and these Damned so perfect and lovely? Where was the justice in that? Since becoming reborn, Petty had repeatedly questioned the workings of the Creator's mind. How could it be that in Heaven he had come to feel so numb, a reanimated zombie, and yet here in the netherworld he suddenly felt vital and alive? Was it the contrast of death? Or just the lust of a younger body whose urges he had forgotten over the past few decades?

The short red hair of the center girl was sprouting anew from the scalp it had been torn from. It was like watching the minute hand of a clock, but it was happening. He noted the curly black hair of the lush-figured girl, the straight mousy brown hair of the thin girl, but the center girl had become his crucified Christ, flanked by nameless fellow sufferers, though in this case all three were resurrecting from the dead...

Yes, he wondered if this were such a good idea after all. When they had eyes again, they would hate him as much as the Demons beside him. He couldn't sneak his fingers through the mesh; they would withdraw from his touch. And even if he were able to persuade Eridan to lift the middle cage, free his little redhead, and even if she did submit to him, she would despise him. Reject him even as she gave in to him.

Maybe it was better to return to Heaven, flawed as it was. To content himself as best he could with the zombie-like Fannie Mae. She accepted him mindlessly. Wasn't that perfection, if he could get past the fact that she was essentially a robot? He mustn't be so jaded, so spoiled. Heaven, however imperfect, could do that to you...

Still, he knew he had to see this through. He had waited this long, and he wouldn't feel closure unless he could see their restored faces closely. But even as he dreaded having their eyes on him, he couldn't keep from admiring their bodies. Couldn't keep from subtly pressing his erection against the bow rail. It was a blind eel aching to feed.

He realized Eridan was directly behind his shoulder, and he flinched as the Demon purred, "Do you wish to go onto the island, sir?"

"I can see well enough from here," Petty muttered.

Muscle now layered the bone, threaded together with bright lattices of vein, elastic bands of tendon tethering this section to that. Were those raw globes in their sockets really eyes? Petty's own eyes watered to gaze upon them.

Soon, the outer rind of flesh started spreading like a fungus, a cancer, to again put a mask to the horrible beauty that lay beneath, just as it hid what lay inside the rest of their glorious bodies. The flesh asserting its mastery, even here in the spiritual world.

The rotting miasma of the island was so overpowering this close that he cupped his hand over nose and mouth. Or was that reek from the faces themselves, rematerializing in a reverse dissection, a rewound flaying?

The red hair of the center girl stopped growing at the edge of her jaw. That must have been its length when she died, and it would not grow beyond that point. Pretty red hair like copper, framing eyes that now showed blue irises, and black pupils, and which bulged and darted in mad agony.

51

Then the eyes locked on him with such a force that he almost flinched again. They remained fixed on him. The girl's struggles against the chains binding her wrists and ankles grew more frantic. Her body moved in serpentine jerks, like the eels had when they were worrying free a hunk of flesh. Her sobs rose, rose in a wail, a banshee shriek, a siren...

And there were words coming on that scream; he could sense them struggling to take form as her flesh was doing. He could feel the words riding at the top of her cry, building toward a crescendo...

"Dahhh...." the center girl screamed.

"Oh God," Petty groaned, letting go of the rail as if blown back by the cry and the stare. He thumped backwards against Eridan, who did not budge.

"Daaaahhh!"

Petty had been disappointed in Heaven, but now he knew that Hades was much worse, even for the casual visitor. Because the remade face of the central girl, this Nike of Samothrace with its head restored, was that of Petty's teenage daughter, Christina.

"Daaaad!" the cry came in full at last, like lava exploding from a volcano.

Petty whirled away and squeezed his eyes shut tightly. He clamped his hands over his ears, like Ulysses' sailors, blocking their ears with wax to keep out the call of the sirens. But then he opened his eyes and glared up at Eridan, who was watching him with a little smile, as if he possessed some secret, satisfying knowledge.

"You did this on purpose, you bastard!" Petty sobbed. "You knew she was out here!"

"I'm not the Creator," the Demon told him mildly. "Only He weaves, Mr. Petty."

"You let her go! I order you!"

"I can't, sir. She's been Damned. She should have followed her wise and pious parents to church. She should have embraced her Father."

"I'm an Angel! I'm an Angel!" Petty blubbered. "You fucks can't do this to me!"

"This is Hades," Captain Eridan said simply. "Do you wish to leave it?"

"Yes," Petty cried. He fell to his knees, palms still clamped to his ears. "Yes!"

"Daaaad! Help me!" he heard, regardless of his efforts to blot out the sounds.

Thank God that Eridan started up the motor then. The sound of it helped drown out the screams. The lines were cast off, all the crew clambered aboard, and the boat turned its nose away from the island of congealing blood.

"Your daughter is very beautiful, sir," Eridan told him casually, as he piloted them away and the voices dwindled in their wake. He looked down at Petty, still humped forward as if bowing on the deck in supplication. "Very beautiful."

Sweet Oblivion

Most breeds of Demons didn't require food as sustenance—but the Buddhas, as the Damned workers had dubbed them, were ravenous beings. They had been designed that way, in the factory city of Tartarus where most of the Demons in this region of Hades were mass produced.

The Buddhas were vast, dinosaur-like travesties of humanity, nine feet tall and wider around. Patrick thought that they made sumo wrestlers look as if they might be the Buddhas' infant offspring. Their flagrantly naked bulks were an awful canary yellow in color. These elephantine entities had heads as small as a mortal baby's, however, with eyes crushed shut and sulky pouts. Their heads reminded Patrick of human fetuses who are born with acrania—absence of that section of the skull which contains the brain.

To be born without a brain, Patrick mused. Such blissful oblivion. He had never thought he would envy such a tragic fate, until he had awoken from death to find himself sentenced to eternal damnation.

He had been twenty-two when he died. He estimated he would have been forty-four by now. He had stopped berating himself, long ago, for not having been religious in life, not bowing before the Creator. Though he had never met any of his friends or loved ones in the infinity of Hades, he doubted that any of them would pass the Creator's harsh criteria to make it through the pearly gates, the golden arches, or whatever the gateway to paradise looked like.

Patrick, Eleanor, and Wally worked close together, wading through the knee-deep (occasionally, waist-deep) bog in which they seeded, grew and harvested the food for the Buddhas. Eleanor had been in Hades the longest; she had died in 1870, when she was twenty-eight. She and Patrick had taken Wally under their wings. Although he had been much older than they, physically, when he died—sixty-seven—he had only been in Hades for a single month. He huffed and panted as he slogged through the marshy plants, cutting free the fleshy globes the Buddhas craved with his curved knife and storing them in the waterproofed leather bag he wore slung onto his back. He paused often to wheeze, to hold his chest with one blistered hand, to squint up at the blazing sky—a ceiling of churning lava. The three of them wore straw hats like Vietnamese farmers laboring in a rice paddy, to protect their flesh from being burned by that intense glow. Of course, they were immortal; their skin would have regenerated even if it had been immersed in lava. This was why Patrick often teased Wally when he saw him clutching at his heart.

"You're not going to die, Wally, don't worry."

"I should be so lucky," Wally grumbled, wiping his knife's blade clean of sap against his pants leg. "I should be so lucky to *really* die."

"Then we wouldn't have your charming company," Eleanor teased him in her good-natured British accent, flicking some water at his face. "Would we, my love?"

"*He's* your love," Wally jerked his knife toward Patrick, "not me."

"You *are* too young for me, Wally," Eleanor admitted.

All three of them turned their heads abruptly, and fearfully, when they heard the bellowing roar of one of the Buddhas roll across the swampy farmland. All three were relieved to see that one titanic yellow guard was lumbering slowly, terribly in another direction, perhaps to berate some other knot of workers, instead of coming their way. Wally wagged his head. "They invented this fruit just to give us something to do. Something hard and awful to do. And they invented *them* just to eat the fruit." By "they," he meant the Creator.

Patrick lifted another of the bright red, rubbery globes out of the water and slipped it into his own heavy sack. "Come on, Wally." He shooed a blood-drinking insect (or miniature Demon, depending on how you looked at it) that had jabbed him in the back of the neck ... then patted the older man on the shoulder. "It will drive you mad to dwell on the whys and wherefores."

They had sloshed their way to an outcropping of rock like an island jutting out of the flat landscape. They could climb up on it and rest for a few minutes, on its far side where they wouldn't be spotted, but not for too long or they'd be missed. It would give them a chance to dry off a little in the heat of the molten sky, and to pluck leeches off each other. They'd throw the leeches back into the mire instead of killing them, just in case those creatures could be considered Demons, too.

It was Patrick who climbed onto the outcropping first, gratefully slinging his sack off his shoulder as he did so. It was Patrick, then, who first spotted the cat.

The cat clearly had heard them coming; it was wary but not surprised. It was tensed, ready to hiss, ready to claw, ready to leap away. But leap away where? Into the water? Most cats hated water. How had it ever gotten to this isolated rock in the first place?

"Oh my!" Eleanor exclaimed. "Oh!"

"It's a cat," Wally observed, dragging his old, dripping bones onto the barren oasis. "An ugly one," he added. "So what?"

The cat had indeed seen better days. It looked like it might have become tangled in a tattered, filthy curtain. Or could that have been a burial shroud? Scraps of it were twined around its limbs and tail, a loop of it even obscuring one eye. And in one battered ear it wore three earrings. It had been someone's pet, obviously, at one time. Or something more important. But it looked a long way from having been anything to anyone, in its present condition.

"It's impossible," Patrick said to Wally, as tensed and unmoving as the cat.

"Why?"

Eleanor answered for him. "There are no cats in Hades. No animals can come here."

"What do you mean? These bloodsuckers ... and mosquitoes..."

"There are *infernal* animals. But no animals from the mortal world can come here upon death, Wally. According to the Creator, animals don't have souls. They don't go to Heaven or Hell. They simply cease to be."

"Sweet oblivion," Patrick muttered.

"Then this is an infernal animal, then," said Wally. "Like the leeches. Look at it. Looks infernal to me."

The cat hissed at last. Patrick smiled. "It doesn't like you, whatever it is, Wally."

"There are no cats in Hades," Eleanor insisted. "I've been here well over a century. I've covered a lot of ground in that time. I've never seen a cat, a dog, any earthly beast."

"There." Patrick pointed. "Look."

Behind the cat, and lower on the opposite face of the rock, there was a deep crack or fissure. Its edges looked black, as though charred. Wally climbed over next to Patrick carefully, trying not to startle the cat. Even in the short time he had been in Hades, he knew this rock well enough to recognize that this fissure had not been there previously.

"He came from the crack," Eleanor said. "He had to have. From some other part of Hell, do you think? Maybe animals do go to another realm, after all…"

"I had another thought," said Patrick.

"What's that?"

Wally said it before Patrick could. "Maybe it came from our world. The mortal world. You know?" He picked his way nearer to the cat, the fissure below it, less concerned about upsetting the animal now. "Maybe if he could find his way here, we could find our way out…"

The cat gave a warning yowl and hissed again, backing off just a little bit, its broken tail giving an angry flick. Seeing this, Patrick caught Wally by the arm to halt him.

"Shh, puss," Eleanor cooed, extending a delicate white hand to the creature. "Shh. Don't be afraid. We won't hurt you."

"It's probably hungry." From his sack, Patrick withdrew one of the buoy-like, bobbing red orbs they cut free of the stalks in the swampy water. He sliced into it with his tool, which always reminded him of a linoleum knife. A thick, crimson sap began to well out.

"Don't feed it blood," Eleanor admonished him.

"What else do I have to feed it? Maybe you could nurse him, eh?" She swatted his arm.

"It's seen a lot. It's been to Hell and back," Wally murmured, staring intensely at the animal as it stared back at him. "I'm telling you, it's come from someplace far away. If it can come here, we can go there."

"Think, Wally," Patrick said, while he proffered the bleeding fruit to the cat. It didn't come near it. "If where it comes from is better, then why'd it want to come here?"

"Anyway," Eleanor added, "look at the crack. It isn't wide enough even for me."

"But we could widen it!" Wally blurted, beginning to sound desperate.

In the distance, the terrible foghorn bleat of one of the Buddhas sounded. The noise rumbled across the watery fields like thunder. The three prisoners of Hell exchanged quick glances. Patrick said, "They'll notice us gone, soon."

"We have to smuggle the cat back to our barracks with us," Eleanor stated. "We can't leave it here."

"Smuggle it how?"

"In one of our sacks, of course."

"If we get caught with it, now or later..."

"Never mind the *cat!*" Wally moaned, as if trying to reason with children. "We have to start widening that hole. Every day, a little more. We have to at least explore what's beyond! Can it be any worse?"

Eleanor turned toward the old man gravely. "There are sections of Hades that make this bog look like a resort beach, Wally. Yes. It can always get worse."

"I don't care what you say!" he persisted, and began scrambling over the rock again. "I'm going to see what this hole is about..."

"Wally!" Eleanor cried, trying to snatch hold of his tunic. "Don't scare the cat!"

"To Hell with the cat!"

Patrick thought for sure the cat would start slicing at the old man's advancing hands, then. Instead, without even another hiss or yowl, the creature—oddly both bedraggled and regal—turned nimbly and scampered down the rock face toward that split in its surface. It darted into the fissure ... disappeared inside.

Wally was after it on all fours, as if by imitating it he might gain access, too. His palm slipped on a slick portion of rock and he scraped his elbow badly, but it only slowed him a moment. He reached the crack before his two companions could stop him, and thrust his arm into the crevice.

"Arr!" he cried. He was up to his shoulder in the hole. Patrick saw him lying on his belly, saw the alarm or surprise on his weathered face, and thought: Something *has* him...

A horrible dinosaur trumpet, not far away enough. Had one of the Buddha overseers heard Wally's cry ... noticed their absence, finally?

"What is it?" Patrick whispered frantically, taking hold of Wally's shoulders. Eleanor grabbed onto the back of his shirt. They began to haul at him.

"The rock is closing!" Wally groaned.

He was right; they could hear it. The rock seemed to creak, to squeal, at the stresses which reformed it. As their flesh could be regenerated after injury (after all, their bodies were no longer truly flesh), so did the stone begin to reknit itself. The only trouble was, Wally's arm was still buried in its maw.

"Ohh ... oww!" he moaned. His moan rose at the end, in the start of a wail.

Just as the rock jaws were gnashing shut, Patrick and Eleanor managed to pry their friend free. The split in the rock ground shut a moment later, making a sound like the brakes of an out of control eighteen wheeler screeching. Sparks leapt into the air.

Wally cradled a badly bleeding arm, a lot of its skin torn from it like the leaves husked from a cob of corn. The bone showed in one place through the stripped meat. He was sobbing, and Eleanor pulled him against her, wrapped her arms around his chest, rocked him.

"Well, old man," Patrick panted, "now you really have a pain you can complain about."

"Patrick!" Eleanor chided him.

"It could be worse." Patrick patted the man's bare foot, still bloodlessly white and wrinkly from hours submerged in slimy water. "You could have lost your whole arm. It's happened to me. It isn't fun. Regrowing it is worse."

"You scared my pussy away, Wally," Eleanor scolded, but she kept rocking the sobbing man.

"Wally would scare anyone's pussy away," Patrick said, peeking up over the top of the rock. "I thought they'd heard us. But they haven't noticed, thank Heavens."

"Bugger the Heavens," Eleanor said.

"So, Wally," Patrick went on. "Did you feel anything on the other side?"

Whimpering now, as his damaged nerve endings began the process of repairing themselves, Wally opened his mauled hand—which had been clenched into a fist until this moment. In it, he clutched only a strip of the dirt-caked gauze or linen which the cat had been tangled up in.

"The little thing just took a wrong turn," Patrick said. "I hope he finds the right way, now."

"I hope he sends us help," Eleanor joked.

Patrick licked at the blood sluicing from the fruit he had offered to the cat. Why not drink blood? They were the undead, weren't they? "Maybe he was a soul, after all. Maybe he was a reincarnated person."

"Shh," Eleanor mocked. "Don't talk blasphemy. There is no reincarnation, remember?"

They helped Wally sit up. Recently, he had finally relented and begun drinking the juice of the blood fruit, and allowed Patrick to feed him some now. Already, his own blood was flowing less copiously.

While Wally sat on the rock to recover some more, the other two slipped back into the water to continue harvesting fruit. They passed him orbs to tuck into his own bag, as well. One of the patrolling behemoths noticed them at last, but it must have seen that the old man was injured, merely resting until he could regenerate, and it didn't come after them. Patrick and Eleanor made a good show of it, working double fast. Patrick purposely bumped his hip against hers at one point. She gave him a flirty smile in return.

Wally looked at the place where the crack had been. Just a jagged black line there, a scar like fossilized lightning, nothing more. He reached out his healing hand and laid it flat against the stone.

"Take care, kitty," he said quietly, as if afraid to let his new friends hear the softness in his tone.

"So where do you think my puss has gone off to, my love?" Eleanor asked Patrick as they worked.

"With any luck," he told her, "sweet oblivion."

THE SECRET GALLERY

"After her death Dante realized she was more alive than ever."
    – Dante Alighieri, on his love Beatrice.

T he Demons did this from time to time.

For a good number of terrestrial years—but who could tell, when there was no true day or night by which to measure?—a print shop might be tolerated, and the bookstores that stocked its humble chapbooks and broadsheets. Restaurants that made the best of indigenous vegetation, infernal animal forms, were abundant and varied in larger Damned settlements like the sprawling cities of Oblivion and Carceri. Clothing stores that offered attire more diverse and cheery than the black uniforms they all started out with. And then, without any extra provocation, without any forewarning, the Demons would come. They would strip a shop of its wares, expel the staff or perhaps round them up for transportation to a torture factory, and burn or demolish the very building itself. There were all sizes of Damned settlements, from tiny villages to great metropolises. Sometimes the Demons would raze the whole settlement to the ground. Not often would the large cities be destroyed, because they often housed a Demonic population as well, but it had happened.

There needed to be no explanation for these raids that took place so suddenly, when these establishments had been in operation for so long. It was to be expected. They looked the other way for quite a while, let you get comfortable, let you forget just a little bit where you were. And then, one day (if such it could be called), they came to take it away to remind you where you were. Letting you have it for a while and taking it away was more cruel than not letting you have it at all, wasn't it?

The Demons that had surged into Wanda's gallery were reptilian, like bipedal lizards. Like what dinosaurs might have evolved into had they not gone extinct (and if evolution had existed), or what the Creator might have envisioned for Demons in the early days of the Earth, before He had made His plan more ambitious and designed human beings. Wanda knew it was more likely, though, that their animal-like nature had to do with the recent rebellion throughout Hades of several of the most human-like races of Demons. It had been decreed that those traitorous races would be annihilated, however long the process took, and less human—hopefully, less willful—breeds of Demon mass produced to replace them. These new kinds of Demons were often sent forth with the genocide of their brothers as their mission, but today their assignment was more modest. The demolition of Wanda's gallery.

It was only moments after she heard the commotion up front, the crashing and the cries of Rita at the counter, that Wanda saw the first of the Demons. It burst into the gallery, tearing down the black door curtain as it came and wearing it on its spiny shoulders like a cape, all naked muscle sheathed in glossy red scales, jaws brimming with teeth, eyes dead black, its head festooned with a fringed yellow crest like a tropical bird. Striking as it was, Wanda had seen more creative-looking devils in artworks like Schongauer's *The Temptation of St. Anthony* or Breughel's *Fall of the Rebellious Angels*, and so wondered numbly if perhaps the imagination of humans was more extensive than the imagination of the Creator Himself.

The Demon was more intent on the artwork than her. It barely seemed to notice her as it snatched the first framed painting off the gallery's brick wall, and tore it into two pieces with a sound (too familiar to Wanda) like flesh ripping. It was a scene, painted from memory, of

Maine's forested and rocky coast near Acadia National Park, by a man named Paul. She was glad Paul was not here to see the destruction of his work. On a more primitive level, Wanda was ashamed that she was relieved it was the painting and not her body that was receiving the Demon's violence, despite the fact that the torn flesh of the Damned would always regenerate. To be torn again, and again.

Discarding the mauled painting, the Demon raged on, swatting a clay bust of a child off its base to shatter like a skull under a mallet in one of the torture plants. It was a portrait done by a woman of her child, again by memory. She had died in 1959, when her child had been seven-years-old. That boy would be fifty-four now, but was forever a child in his mother's eyes. When she had accepted the sculpture into her gallery, Wanda had wondered just how accurate the bust could be after all these years. She had admired its detail, authentic-looking right down to the lovingly rendered intricate lines meant to represent its strands of hair, remembered as much by the mother's fingers as by her brain.

A second Demon charged in, threw Wanda a quick glare that was almost like a physical blow, making her back into another of the brick walls. But the creature moved on to pluck down a framed charcoal drawing: a chiaroscuro still life of wine bottles, a man's smoking pipe, and a stack of beautifully bound books (not like the crudely produced books available at the shops here in the city). Again, a remembered sort of scene. Like much of the art she'd gathered, maybe a little idealized, maybe a little sentimental, but real. Maybe not real here, but real from a life before this afterlife.

One of the artists had been in the gallery, visiting Wanda to discuss a special showing of her work scheduled for several days from now. The artist, Natalie, made the mistake of moving between her paintings and the first Demon. An impulsive action that she no doubt instantly regretted, as her screams pierced Wanda's ears and her blood sprayed her canvases. The second Demon rushed forward to seize hold of the woman's flailing limbs so the first could continue its shredding of the canvas of her flesh. Wanda had to look away, and her horrified numbness cracked just enough to permit tears to trickle free.

Several more Demons entered, storming from room to room. They made no sounds, no animal roars or human speech, except for the clamor of their rampage. A couple of patrons fled past Wanda the other way, one bleeding heavily from a hanging flap of scalp. The unwounded one gave her a frenzied look as if to urge her to flee along with them. She didn't. She didn't know why. Still too numb with horror, with fatalism, or was it a kind of loyalty? The captain going down with his ship?

Then, into the little museum strode an entirely different brand of Demon, as if another artist had designed him. An earlier, somewhat more anthropomorphic type (though not perhaps so human-like to be considered a threat under the new mind-set), apparently of considerable age. He was so tall that he had to duck his head through the threshold. A more classical rendering: great curling ram horns, frayed dragon wings folded against his massive back. Gray skin rough and pitted as pumice, eyes like empty holes drilled into that stony flesh, and a mouth even more overflowing with daggers than the jaws of the lizard Demons. But instead of seeking out overlooked pieces of art to rip and stomp, the Demon—likely an officer—turned to blaze his empty eye pits down at Wanda.

"You are to come with me," his booming voice rumbled in her ears, inside her very chest.

A torture factory, she thought. No, no ... not one of the torture factories again.

But that wasn't to be the case. Far from it. As far as one afterlife was from another.

Wanda's first assignment in Heaven had been as one of the workers fashioning an exact replica of Brussel's central market square, often called "The Grand Place." This magnificent complex was the home of Pastor Ed Calvin of the Eastborough Baptist Church, who had passed into Heaven a year earlier after having long served his Creator by preaching such wisdom as "When Fags Die, God Laughs." Wanda supposed there had to be some kind of limit to what souls coming into Heaven could order for their domicile, but she figured Calvin had been especially rewarded for his decades of filial service. Calvin wanted to entertain his fellow Angels by inviting them to sit in the square and listen to concerts as they were waited on by his staff of Celestial servants.

However awe inspiring her surroundings as she worked on the last of the square's ornate and opulent houses, Wanda had been glad she'd come late to the project. The sizable crew of Damned carpenters and artisans was working from precise plans, which had been drawn up in part by several of the very same architects who had rebuilt the original buildings in the 17th Century after their destruction by the order of Louis XIV of France. Thus, there was no flexibility in the proceedings, no room for personal artistic choices. It was not what Wanda was accustomed to, or preferred. She was much more gratified by the project she had now been switched to. As gratified as she could be by this labor, at least.

Wanda had only met Calvin personally once, and he had looked her body up and down as if to demonstrate that he wasn't one of his hated homosexuals. Wanda had grown afraid then, because she knew she was attractive, and she had heard rumors that Calvin and other Angels sometimes took the Damned to bed, and could be as rough with them as the Demons in Hades were. But Calvin's attention had been diverted elsewhere a moment later, to her relief, and he'd seemed to forget about her after that.

The woman whose home she was currently working on, however, struck Wanda as being much more pleasant, and she even watched her work on occasion. Presently Wanda was sketching in a figure with charcoal, making it life-size, as befitted the mural that would run the length of the entrance hallway on both walls. The woman had pretty much only specified that she wanted the vaulted ceiling to be blue with fluffy clouds and flying birds, and that lovely figures should adorn the walls, as if guests to her home would be entering a Heaven within Heaven. The homes of the Angels demonstrated that Heaven could be shaped to the vision of each blessed soul, but this woman—not being an artist—trusted Wanda's artistic ability in envisioning her vision for her.

"It's wonderful," the woman said, as Wanda roughed in one of the figure's hands, reaching out to touch the hand of a smiling child. "You don't even need to work from photographs. You have it all up here." She tapped her own temple, as if her brain and all its complex cells resided within her skull, though in reality that brain was beginning to rot in a coffin somewhere in the material world. They were both animated statues, in a way, created in the likeness of their mortal selves—the artwork of the Creator Himself.

"Thanks." Wanda smiled over her shoulder at the woman politely.

The woman, whose name was Suzanne and who had died at the age of fifty-three from cancer, shifted her admiring gaze from sketched figure to figure, in their present state a waltz of transparent ghosts. "Did you go to school for this, Wanda?"

"No, actually. Art was my hobby. I worked in Human Resources for an electronics manufacturer." Now she was part of Hades' Inhuman Resources, she thought.

"Oh my. Well, I envy you. What I wouldn't give to be able to paint, or play an instrument, or do something creative." Suzanne sighed wistfully. "Though I suppose I have all eternity to learn something like that, now. Maybe you could teach me, hm?"

Wanda smiled at her again. She knew it was said playfully. Bringing Damned laborers into Heaven to construct and adorn houses for Angels was one thing, but she sincerely doubted that the Damned would ever be employed as art instructors or the like.

Suzanne soon excused herself and drifted further into her house, to see what other progress was being made. A moment later, though, Wanda heard another voice behind her. Its quality might have made her confused as to whether or not it came from a man or woman, had she not already recognized the owner of that voice.

"You should try not to engage the Angels in conversation," it said.

Out of an apprehensive respect, Wanda turned around fully to address the speaker. "I'm sorry, but she initiated the conversation. It would have been rude of me not to respond to her." She had tried not to sound argumentative in her self-defense.

This new person let the matter drop, as it directed its eyes to the mural behind Wanda. "You work quickly. Good. It's coming along well. When do you think you can begin the actual painting?"

"It will be soon." What could she say—a few days? A week? Again, there were no real days, though the Damned did still use that term, based upon the rest periods that broke up periods of work or, if one were in a torture plant for instance, grueling suffering.

The Celestial stepped closer to the sketched mural, absorbed, as if filling in the brush strokes to come with its gaze. Wanda had learned this sort of Celestial being was dubbed a Seraph. This Seraph, whose name was Zaraiah, was one of the Overseers for the construction of Angels' dwellings, and thus in charge of this particular project. Until meeting these Overseers in the course of her work in Heaven, the only Celestials Wanda had ever been exposed to were the ones who accompanied Angel tourists into Hades to serve as their bodyguards, such as when those tourists hunted the Damned for sport. That Celestial caste of warriors was also sent into Hades to oppose uprisings of the Damned, and to do battle with factions of rebellious Demons. Therefore, with all the current turmoil in Hades, Wanda had seen quite a few of these beings. But they were mute, even struck her as automatonic. Zaraiah could have been one of them, at least in appearance. The Seraph had white-blond hair, shoulder length, and skin so white it gave off a subtle luminescence. Eyes of such an uncanny glowing blue that when the entity turned its head, brief afterimages of blue light marked the air as when a child twirls a flashlight in the dark. The toga the being wore fell loosely from a frame that was slim but athletic, and which was as androgynous as the face with its fine cheekbones and full, cupid-bow lips. So androgynous that Wanda still didn't know whether to consider Zaraiah a male or a female. She supposed that, owing to what the creature was and the fact that its kind had existed before men and women had come into being, its sex could not be an issue. Its kind were the direct creations of the Father, not of procreation. The Creator's perfect art, not human offspring like copies degraded through repetition.

The Celestials she was accustomed to never spoke a word, but she knew them to be just as harsh as the Demons whose function it was to preside over and torment the Damned. So despite the Seraph's softly modulated voice, like the voice of a feminine man or a masculine woman, she always feared saying something that might be deemed impertinent, and incurring the thing's righteous wrath.

"When I look at this," Zaraiah said, "and watch you at your craft, I see the hand of the Creator inside you … and I cannot help but wonder how a soul given such a gift could have allowed herself to become Damned."

First of all, Wanda did not like the image of the Creator's hand inside her, rammed up her ass as if she were His puppet. Second of all, she did not think she had *allowed* herself to become Damned. The game was unfair; she had not known the rules. Or had she, and just never taken them seriously? She had the letter B branded onto her forehead (the one wounding that never regenerated) to indicate her sin, her great crime: that of being a Blasphemer. She probably would have been condemned to Hades anyway, simply for not having embraced the Father in life, but she knew it was one particular act that had cinched it for her. For an art show meant to protest animal abuse, she had contributed a painting of a lab monkey crucified to a cross, the top of its head opened up and electrodes drilled into its skull like a crown of thorns, a huge syringe hanging out of its side like a spear. That was all it took. Monkey as the Son of the Father? One would have thought she was Darwin, for all the punishment she had been meted out ever since her premature death.

"Well," Wanda replied, "at least I'm doing something constructive with my gift now, right? Making pretty pictures for Angels?"

She had tried to make her sarcasm sound like sincerity, but the Seraph immediately turned its head to stare at her with bland, robot-like disapproval, leaving those blue trails in the air.

"Yes. Now you are doing good. Now that it is too late to save you."

"Here, dear, wait," Suzanne had said, scurrying to catch up with Wanda as Zaraiah and his team of silent guards, armed with sheathed swords and cradled submachine guns, escorted the slaves toward the edge of her property. She huffed as she pressed a package into Wanda's arms. "Some fruit, from the garden," she whispered conspiratorially. "Delicious. Share it with your friends if you want; there's more where that came from. It grows overnight after you pick it."

"Thanks," Wanda said uncertainly. She glanced nervously toward Zaraiah. Sure enough, the Seraph had noticed, but what could it say? It mustn't insult one of the Angels by making her withdraw her gift, right? From here, Wanda couldn't read the being's expression. Then again, even up close she found that difficult. Ectoplasmic androids, she thought.

The workers climbed into the back of a large carriage of white lacquered wood with gold trim, drawn by a team of white horses. In Hades, on their way back to their barracks for their rest period, they would ride in a black metal carriage pulled by a team of naked Damned wearing yokes fastened to their shoulders with bolts through their flesh.

The two rows of laborers rode in silence as the carriage conveyed them to the portal. When they arrived, the Celestial guards who had accompanied them watched them disembark. Zaraiah was still with them. Wanda felt the Celestial officer's eyes still following her, but she pretended she didn't notice. They began to file toward the portal, housed inside a small white structure like a pillbox. Two more Celestials guarded it, and at the approach of the Damned one of the guards turned the wheel of a metal hatch like something from the inside of a submarine. Steam hissed free as the hatch was swung open. Wanda could just make out the white-tiled walls of its interior through the bright white light that filled the little structure.

Right up until it was her turn to approach the threshold of the portal, Wanda expected Zaraiah to step forward and demand that she hand over the package of fruit. But the Seraph did not, though she still felt the weight of its cold blue eyes on her back before the white light burned her soul to ashes that would be reconstituted in Hades, which was her home.

"Did the mistress tell you what colors she wanted these figures to be wearing?" Zaraiah asked, watching Wanda as she swabbed in the green lawn of the background in rough up-and-down strokes. She would work on the fine details of grass blades later in the process.

"No; she's left all that to me. She said she wants it to have a feel like *A Sunday Afternoon on the Island of La Grande Jatte*, by Georges Seurat. Idyllic like that. But in a romantic style, not pointillism. If any of that makes sense to you."

"I'm afraid my knowledge of earthly art is limited." After a few moments, the Seraph went on, "So do you have all the colors worked out in your head, then?"

"Some of it. I'll make choices as I go along, to keep things balanced."

Zaraiah paced behind her, as if the Celestial might leave the hallway to monitor the progress of other workers in the building, but came pacing back the other way again. "You follow your instincts."

"Yes. I improvise. And I take advantage of happy accidents. I surprise myself when I push the brush a certain way and it looks just the way a wave of hair should look, or how light should fall on a fold of cloth. The trick is to not overwork it—to know when to leave it, and move on."

Wanda surprised herself that she had become so talkative with the creature, but then its inquisitiveness had prompted her, and she was less in awe of it with it behind her back where she couldn't see it.

"It's all very interesting," Zaraiah said.

Something had been on Wanda's mind for a while, and now with the Celestial engaging her in pleasant conversation she decided to seize the moment. She turned to face it, steeling herself for those beautiful and ghastly blue eyes that never seemed to blink. "In the city of Carceri I had some artist friends who contributed to the gallery I founded. They do beautiful seascapes and landscapes, sculptures and so on. I think the mistress and other Angels would love having their work in their homes. Do you think we could bring some of them into this project, too?"

"That is not for either you or I to decide."

"But could you suggest it to someone? Their talents could be put to good use ... for the benefit of the Angels."

"For their benefit? Or for the benefit of your friends? So that they too might walk in Heaven a while? Enjoy the fruits of the blessed?"

The pleasantness was slipping away, though the entity's expression and tone hadn't changed that much. Still, Wanda pressed on. "To be honest, it isn't so much that. It's that they have skills that are going to waste. Ability that could be appreciated by others."

"As I told you, it is not for me to decide or you to suggest. These matters are determined by others. They have their reasons for who they select."

"Then I guess I'm one of the lucky ones," Wanda said, with barely contained bitterness.

"You are fortunate, yes. To step within the glory of Heaven, even as a slave. And to give pleasure to the Angels is the greatest honor of your eternal existence."

"Will it buy me salvation?"

"You squandered your salvation. It will buy you respite. That will have to be enough."

Suzanne entered the hallway then, and clasped her hands together in front of her with delight. "Oh ... *oh* ... it's more beautiful by the hour, honey." She addressed Zaraiah, beaming. "Isn't she wonderful?"

The Seraph seemed to falter before getting out, "Her gift from the Creator is to be admired."

"Oh, I'm so jealous of her. Can you imagine being able to do this? And to have a face like this, on top of it all." Suzanne stepped closer and cupped Wanda's cheek, turning to Zaraiah like a proud parent. "Isn't she lovely? Some people are just so lucky. I think she's a dead ringer for the actress Scarlett Johansson."

At least Wanda had died recently enough to share the woman's frame of reference, so she smiled and said, "Thanks. Me and the Overseer here were just talking about luck."

"I have this habit of trying to compare everybody to a celebrity," Suzanne went on obliviously. "I think I look like Jane Fonda. Not *Barbarella* Jane Fonda, but maybe younger than she is now. Or am I being too kind to myself?"

"No, no, I can see it," Wanda lied.

"And what do you think about our Zaraiah here? I can almost think of someone but I'm not sure."

Wanda looked at the Seraph. A celebrity to match it? Male or female? Without thinking, she said, "I don't know … they all pretty much look the same to me."

Zaraiah met her eyes a little too quickly. The creature looked like it might become blatantly angry for the first time. In a tighter than usual voice, it said, "If you'll excuse me, I will go look in on the other workers now."

Watching the faintly glowing figure leave the hallway like a ghost headed to haunt other regions of its castle, Wanda wondered if she hadn't so much insulted the Seraph as hurt its feelings.

❧

Suzanne had handed her a package of pastries, with a wink. Again, Wanda waited for the Seraph to confiscate it from her. Again, it did not.

But when she stepped through the portal on the other side, things were different. The metal carriage awaited, and the yoked Damned, and several of the towering and ancient gray Demons. The sky of molten lava churned and glowed behind the monsters, silhouetting their great horned heads. The apparent oldest of these Demonic officers had cracks in his pumice-like skin that showed the yellow glow of magma within.

Immediately, this very Demon strode toward Wanda, trailing smoke from his empty eye sockets. Could he smell the pastries where the last time he hadn't detected the fruit, or had she been betrayed by another Damned seeking the Demon's favor? Whatever the case, he snatched the package out of her hand, tore it to fragments without even glancing at the scattered contents, and then seized Wanda by the hair at the back of her head. He lifted her off her feet until they were face-to-face. She felt the heat that blazed out of his eye holes in rippling waves.

The Demon thundered, "Enjoying our vacation in Paradise, are

74

we? Maybe you forget the true state of affairs. Maybe you need a little perspective restored … pretty little worm."

Wanda's sob was cut off by the Demon as he clamped his mouth over her own. And even the gurgle that tried to replace the sob was shoved back down her throat, into her chest, as the Demon regurgitated magma into her mouth. He dropped her to writhe, to smoke, before the horrified eyes of the other slaves. In a matter of what might be called hours she would look like the actress Scarlett Johansson again, but for now Wanda's lower face had burned away and a hole melted open in her chest, like a painted canvas set on fire.

⁂

Wanda was fashioning long folds in the robe of one of the mural's figures, having decided to give this one rose pink attire. She had resisted the impulse to make the robe blood red. Somewhere during this process a happy accident, as she called these things, occurred. Two of the folds, forming crescent loops, looked to her like a pair of skull's eyes.

She glanced over her shoulder. She heard the pounding of carpentry elsewhere in the house. She thought she heard a harpsichord playing; it couldn't be Suzanne, who professed to be devoid of any talent, so maybe a Celestial played for her, or else it was a recording. And Zaraiah—the Seraph was not to be seen.

Wanda turned back to this wall of the hallway's double mural and worked another crescent fold, smaller and lower, between the other two. Finally she added a longer drooping crescent, highlighted on its upper edge and deeply shadowed within, below the other three. A ghostly face, as if it pressed against the fabric from the other side. A dark spirit trying to tear through into the realm of Heaven.

"Do you think you could make one of the figures look like me, hon?" Suzanne asked, suddenly there behind her.

Wanda whirled, suppressing a gasp. She smiled tremulously. "Hi. Um, yeah, sure, we could do that." She looked over both walls of the mural nervously, darting her gaze from one potential figure to another.

"Would you want me to pose for that?"

"It would look more like you if you did, instead of me doing it from memory."

"Well if you don't mind doing that, then you tell me when you're ready, okay?"

"Sure. I will."

"Are you hungry now? I can bring you a sandwich. And I have some more of that fruit to send home with you tonight."

Wanda's smile turned apologetic. "I'm sorry, but they don't want me to bring home any more gifts. Against the rules, I guess."

"Oh, really? What a shame! I'm sorry to hear that."

"But thanks anyway."

"Well, you can still eat while you're here in my home—I insist. Let me go round up something for you."

"And the others? I'd feel guilty if..."

"Oh sure, sure dear, I'll see the others get some lunch, too. But you're my favorite, you know." Suzanne wiggled her fingers, and floated off into her house in the direction of the kitchen, more likely to oversee the making of lunch by her staff of Celestial servants than actually prepare it herself.

Wanda returned her attention to the morose, skull-like face she had half-concealed within the figure's robe. Subliminal advertising, she thought. She was familiar with that insidious practice and often spotted it at work in magazines. FUCK or SEX spelled out in the reflections of an ice cube in a whiskey ad. Skulls in ice cubes and cigarette smoke. Such grim images might seem opposed to the selling of a product but they still captured the subconscious eye—as did applying these techniques to ads featuring children, for instance, where a little girl might be blowing at a phallic toy saxophone while a little boy aimed the neck of a toy guitar at her from the level of his groin, wrinkles digitally airbrushed into his shorts to make it look like he had an erection in there. Yes, insidious, but it seized people's attention without their knowing why their eyes had been hooked and reeled in. The technique hijacked the mind, stole inside it, and sold products.

What did Wanda have to sell?

She tried not to hate Suzanne for her grating sweet voice, her beaming eyes like those of a drugged or insane person, her neatly cut club sandwiches and her tinkling harpsichord music. It wasn't her fault, all this, was it? Wanda felt she shouldn't begrudge Suzanne's good fortune. Instead of being petty and envious, she should be happy that this human being, at least, didn't have to suffer, too. Suzanne was kind. Human. Not one of those Angels who traveled to Hades on tours to rape women and children and hunt the Damned with bows or high-powered rifles. But for Suzanne to say she envied Wanda. To say Wanda was *lucky*. Oh, she just didn't know how it was on the other side of the portals. She just didn't have a clue. If she and others like her really cared, really empathized, wouldn't they be trying to do more than just hand out the occasional box of cream-filled pastries, like scraps of meat to a dog whose beatings they turned a blind eye to?

Wanda switched brushes. She focused her attention on the background, which she had thought was finished on this wall. She squeezed several shades of green and pink onto her smeary palette, eyeing a large rose bush that she had placed in one corner.

Camouflaged within the leaves, the flowers, she began to work the visage of the Demon who had lifted her so close to his face moments before his kiss and the molten lava he vomited down her throat. She rendered his face like that of a pagan "green man" design made of foliage, leaves for flesh, his eyes and jagged piranha mouth formed of dark shadows. No nose, as was the case, and a suggestion of his curling ram horns trailing off into the roses' twisted vines.

As she painted in deft quick strokes, not quick because she was being furtive but quick because she felt true inspiration, Wanda thought of two things. One was a line from Frida Kahlo, one of her very favorite artists: "I never paint dreams or nightmares. I paint my own reality."

This is my *reality, Suzanne.*

The other thought, as she glanced up at the hallway's arched ceiling, which she hadn't got to yet, was how easy it would be to hide things within the billowing white substance of clouds.

Wanda was on a stepladder, her forearm speckled with blue and white pigment as she pushed around the wet paint of a cloud with churning strokes, when Suzanne entered from outside with two friends in order to show off the work in progress. Suzanne introduced Wanda by name but the women only grunted, barely acknowledging her. After surveying the more completed of the two walls, one of the friends said dubiously, "Mm, it's nice. I don't know." Her gaze darted from figure to figure, from rose bush to flower bed. She was frowning vaguely.

"Hm," said the other woman, more vaguely. Without looking down at this woman, Wanda wondered if she might have spotted the word HATE in the long hair of one figure and the word PAIN in the blossomed branches of a cherry tree. She hoped she hadn't made them too obvious.

"Well, she isn't finished yet," said Suzanne, "but it's going to be marvelous, don't you think? In life Wanda worked for an electronics company, but now she's followed her true calling, haven't you, dear? You see—it's never too late to realize your dreams."

"My dreams," Wanda whispered to herself. "More like I've realized my nightmares." She thought again of the Kahlo quote.

Suzanne had ushered her friends into her home for tea, leaving Wanda smiling thinly as she continued with the challenge of hiding the fanged jaws of a lizard Demon in the ethereal softness of cloud vapor.

The work shift had nearly come to its end. When she came down from the ladder, Zaraiah drifted into the hallway, rich with its scents of paint and thinner (as reproduced by the spiritual matter of which the afterlife was composed). The being's eyes went straight to the mural in appraisal. "You go back and work again on faces and flowers and such that I thought you'd completed already."

"As the whole thing takes form, I change my mind about things."

"That, there, is our mistress Suzanne."

"Yes. She asked me to put her in the picture herself." Wanda and Zaraiah both took in the portrait. "Art's always been thought of as a kind of immortality, for both the subject and the painter. Leaving our mark on the world."

"Now you know there is a greater immortality, and that the marks you make are made on the soul."

Wanda felt emboldened by their familiarity, as such, to say, "What I've found is that immortality sucks. But at least I don't have to grow old, huh? It's ironic that I'll always be this age, young, and Suzanne is the Angel but she has to be older than me for eternity. At least I never have to worry about these things sagging." She cupped her own generous breasts through the fabric of her top. Zaraiah quickly averted its eyes. She found this amusing. Was the Seraph so modest? Or was it something more interesting than that? For the first time, Wanda wondered if it wasn't just her artwork that the Celestial being admired.

"When this piece is done, there will be another project lined up for you," Zaraiah said, staring at the painting again, this time in what Wanda felt was a conscious effort to avoid looking at her.

"And another after that? I mean, will this go on indefinitely?"

"No, it will not. It would not be allowed. You are more comfortable than most of the Damned; much more privileged, in being permitted into Heaven even in this way. You know from experience that comfort for the Damned cannot be tolerated for long. It is against the purpose of Hades, isn't it?"

"So my commission will end soon."

"We don't know when it will end. But there are other artists who will be used instead. It is beyond my control, so do not ask me to extend your commission."

"I wasn't going to." Wanda watched the creature's profile, too perfect in line and form like that of a Greek statue; too idealized to be real. Then she saw the thing's eerie blue eyes narrow. The brow became intense, perplexed. An arm rose to point.

"It looks like there is a face, there, reflected in the edge of the pool."

"A face?" Wanda turned to regard her own work. "Where?"

Zaraiah stepped close to the wall. "Here. It looks like a dark face is reflected in the water. A screaming face." Like someone drowning in the pool, unable to pull herself out as the robed figures cavorted, too oblivious to reach in for the drowning figure's hand.

Wanda's heart was thudding. "I don't see it."

Zaraiah cocked its head sideways, then looked back over its shoulder at the artist. "This seems an intentional effect, to me."

"I think it's just your own interpretation. Like people seeing figures in the constellations."

Zaraiah straightened, and the Seraph's gaze was stern. "Do not do mischief here. You have been entrusted with a special task. You are not to conduct any pranks or irreverence."

"I understand that! I appreciate this opportunity I've been given, Overseer."

Zaraiah scrutinized both walls of the mural, then the arched ceiling of blue sky, with a new look of analysis on its face. Again, the pointing arm. "That isn't a face in the clouds? A weeping child's face?"

Wanda tilted back her head. "Please, Overseer ... looking for dogs and sheep and things in the clouds is a game children play."

"It had better not be a game you are playing, my child," it said to her. "If the mistress complains to me about anything she sees within your work, you will be punished for it."

"Believe me, I respect Suzanne, Overseer. And I respect you, too."

Zaraiah met her eyes grimly. "Do you?"

"Yes. Yes, I do."

The Seraph broke their gaze first, then strode out of the hallway, throwing one disturbed look back at her. Wanda was good at psychology, from her days working with unhappy employees in the course of her former Human Resources job. But she wasn't sure she understood Zaraiah's look at all. It left her feeling uncomfortable, and doubting the wisdom of her actions. The Celestials could tear the Damned to bloody shreds with the best of the Demons.

She was surprised that the Seraph, clearly suspecting her secreted images, hadn't demanded that she do away with them. Was it going to turn a blind eye to her defiance, or would the order to destroy the subliminal images be forthcoming later? For a wild moment or two she considered going in and obliterating them on her own, but she decided against it. So what if the Celestials punished her, tortured her? Demon or Celestial, it was all the same. Either way, it was her eternal fate to endure.

೧ಬ

Just prior to the next work period, she *was* torn by a Demon into bloody shreds.

As the gray Demon with the glowing cracks in its hide twisted her arm to rip away the last rubbery strings that connected it to its socket, in her agony and panic Wanda wondered if this violence were in fact a response to her subversive acts, a punishment ordered by Zaraiah. But as she lay trembling hard and in shock, watching her vivid blood flow down the slope of rock beneath her, she thought that if Zaraiah had indeed wanted to punish her, the Seraph wouldn't have permitted her to remain on the team of artists and laborers shuttled from Hades to Heaven like children between divorced parents. And yet the same Demon who had pulled her out of line and attacked her now picked her up and flung her into the black metal carriage like a doll, to be transported with the others to the portal. He kicked away her dismembered limb, leaving it to rot, knowing that a new one would emerge from her shoulder in a matter of hours. Pain-wracked hours.

They arrived at the nearest of the portals between afterlives, and two of the other slaves helped support Wanda so she could walk. They were still supporting her when they emerged from the brightly glowing interior of the pillbox-like structure on Heaven's side. Her uniform was black but shiny with her blood, which still oozed from her shoulder though the wound had mostly closed already. Wanda lifted her head, her face a mask of glittering red spatter. She saw that Zaraiah was staring at her.

"What happened?" the Seraph asked.

When Wanda couldn't form words, one of the Damned who held her up spoke for her. "Our Demon Overseer did this to her."

"Why? Why her?"

"He didn't say." The slave shrugged timidly. "They don't need a reason. Today it's her, tomorrow it's me. They do this to us. It's Hades, Overseer."

The Seraph tore its eyes from Wanda, leaving transient brush strokes of blue in the air. "Do not let the mistress see her this way. Once we reach the estate, she will remain inside the carriage until she is healed. Make her comfortable. I will go speak to the Demon Overseer now." Zaraiah started moving toward the closed, submarine-style hatch.

"Why?" Wanda croaked.

Zaraiah stopped at the sound, faced her. "Why what?"

"Why ... speak to him?" she managed.

"This can't be permitted. You are needed to do work here, not waste time regenerating lost limbs. And we cannot have the Angels unsettled by such a sight."

But Wanda had never seen the creature's face set with such cold rage, the blue eyes dazzling like alien stars. The anger it had shown her when it realized the bitterness disguised within her painting was nothing compared to this.

"Thank you," she said.

Her words seemed to embarrass the entity, as when she had cupped her breasts, because just as then it turned away sharply and continued on to the metal hatch—to pass willingly from the beautiful dream of its home to the nightmare reality of her own.

❧

The work periods were long enough that even though it still seemed to take a good number of hours before Wanda's arm had regrown, she still had time to enter the sprawling mansion at last and resume work on her mural. Her hair and face had been washed, and her blood-soaked black clothing substituted. She wore a lavender robe that fell sensuously along the curves of her young body.

"The mistress saw your condition," Zaraiah realized, when the Overseer appeared at the hallway's inner threshold and spotted her at work.

"I'm sorry." Wanda looked nervous to be discovered this way, and her face was still white and weary from her ordeal. "The others cleaned me up a little before I came in, but she could still tell I'd been hurt. She made me take a bath and change my clothes. She's a very nice lady."

"Mm," the Celestial grunted.

Wanda made an apologetic wincing expression. "She's pretty upset. She said she was going to speak to you about it when she got back from visiting her friend's house."

"I will assure her that the matter has been seen to. The Demon who injured you has been retired from service for interfering in this important project."

"Retired?"

"Yes." Zaraiah looked away from her as if to signal an end to the subject, but Wanda wondered if the Seraph had retired the towering Demon officer with its own delicately powerful hands. Still watching the creature, she saw its eyes alight where she knew they would. How could her critic and admirer help but notice the addition right away?

"I hope you aren't offended," she said. "I changed that person to look like you. Do you think it does? Look like you?"

"Yes," Zaraiah said distantly, staring at the figure she had transmuted during the past two hours from a young woman in yellow to the androgynous Seraph in white, its perfect profile gazing off toward the horizon. "It does."

"Now you're immortalized, too. Not in the Creator's way, but in my own little way."

"Hm. Thank you." Not taking its eyes off its own portrait, after several long moments the Seraph went on, "I'm sorry to tell you that it's been determined this is to be your last assignment, after all."

"I see." Wanda nodded. She didn't doubt that this decision had been advised by Zaraiah, despite its having said that it had no input in these matters. "I understand," she told it. She was used to being fatalistic. The bad news was not unexpected.

But what she did find unexpected was, as the Seraph turned away to ostensibly go check on the headway of the other Damned laborers, Wanda caught a glistening hint of wetness in its enigmatic Celestial eyes.

THE BURNING HOUSE

1: The Angel

After Michael stepped through the doorway of blinding light, he found himself in a room lined in white ceramic tiles, floor and ceiling included. The room's only feature was a riveted metal hatch with a wheel-like valve in its center, and he saw this immediately turn with a squeal. A blast of steam entered the small white chamber ... followed by the first Demon Michael had met since his death, several months earlier.

"Greetings, sir," the thing said, unfolding to its full height. At eight feet tall, it had had to stoop to fit its body through the hatchway. "I am Iblis Al-Qadim—governor of this sector of Hades."

Michael almost said, automatically, "Nice to meet you" or "thanks for having me," so stunned into a sleepwalker's state was he by the thing's appearance. He had taken an involuntary step backwards as it had joined him in this, one of apparently countless entry points into the netherworld.

Iblis Al-Qadim's heavy black robes did not fully hide the fact that his body was an unpleasant cross between human skeleton and insect exoskeleton. His face was more human, but a human long dead, his skin a mere black parchment clinging to jutting bone, twin stars gleaming in the deep wells of his skull sockets. Even his teeth were black, in a lipless and humorless grin. He wore a black metal miter, making him all the more towering, intricate patterns of holes in this officious headpiece showing the green flames that blazed from the top of his skull ... where it had apparently been sawed open to emit them.

He carried a staff of iron with a strange swirling design at its head, either a sign of office or a weapon's blade, or both. His shoulders were bulked with a framework under the robes to make his width more commanding, as if taking a cue from football players (maybe if the ball were a human head), and on one of these shoulders perched and squirmed what Michael at first took to be some kind of familiar. It was a black octopus, its head so bloated with, perhaps, the gases it breathed that the stretched skin was almost translucent. It had small, bat-like wings growing out of the sides of its head, above its golden eyes with their horizontal pupils.

Despite that rasping whisper of a voice coming from the scarecrow-like giant's jaws, Michael had the strange intuition that—rather than being a mere familiar—it was the octopus that was in charge, and the looming skeleton creature merely its vehicle and mouthpiece. Were they both, then, Iblis Al-Qadim?

Seeing that Michael was still dazed, at a loss, the official went on, "Was it not your wife's intention to join you, sir?"

Michael recovered enough of his voice to stammer, "Yes ... well ... not today. We decided it was best, after all, if I came here first by myself to assess the situation, so I could go back and ... prepare her for it."

"I see. Very good, sir." The thing tipped its head slightly and pointed a finger twice as long as one of Michael's at the belt gathering his white, angelic robes. A holster was clipped onto this belt, and from the holster protruded the grip of a handgun. "Did you intend to do some hunting, as well, during your stay?"

"Hunting?" Michael looked down at his gun himself, and then became horrified when he grasped the entity's meaning. Horrified, and outraged. But even though he was an immortal Angel—and this creature, however seemingly important, a lowly Demon who could be killed because he had no immortal soul—Michael was too intimidated to raise his voice to the being. He kept his tone stern but even. "My son is one of the Damned now, is he not? So I should hardly think I'd want to hunt any of the Damned for sport."

"I see, sir. Many do, of course."

"I'm aware of that. And those Angels should be here in place of many of the Damned. But my Father works in ways even more mysterious than I suspected when I was alive."

The Demon paused with apparent discomfort. "That isn't for me to say, sir."

"The gun is for my protection," Michael explained tersely.

"We will see that no Damned assault you during your stay. And of course, you are not capable of being killed, or injured for very long, so…"

"I'm well aware of that."

"Of course you are, sir. In any case … allow me to take you to your quarters, now. We have insured your comfort, for the duration of your stay."

"Thank you, but I'd really rather get to where my son is, as quickly as I can."

"Yes, as I understand, sir … but you see, first we must ascertain his whereabouts, and we will assist you in every way we can, in that endeavor."

"His whereabouts?" Now Michael felt too great a heat rising in him to be cowed by the cadaverous titan. "What do you mean? Do you mean to tell me that you don't know where my son *is*?"

"We know the general vicinity, sir … we feel confident he is still in this territory that I govern, and that is why you were directed to this portal. But we have not yet been able to narrow down his exact location."

"I don't believe this!" Michael snapped. "This is unacceptable! My son is suffering here, do you understand? He's in Hell and he could be tied to a stake in the middle of a bonfire right this moment!"

"You see, sir, there is a breakdown in our former lines of communication. Gaps, and irregularities. Our methods of intelligence gathering, and monitoring of the Damned, have become eroded. I'm sure you have been informed of the conflict we are facing here—the rebellion of certain breeds of the more human-like Demons. These species are to be phased out, but they are resisting violently. There is an atmosphere of chaos, I am sorry to report, that has..."

"Look," the Angel snarled, retaking that step he had lost when the monster had entered the portal chamber with him, "I want my son located immediately, do you understand? I don't care if it takes every Demon in your jurisdiction ... I want him found! I want my boy brought to me!"

"We will do that, sir. But you understand, of course ... even when we find him, you may not bring him out of Hades with you. You cannot take him to Heaven. He will still be one of the Damned."

"I am only too aware of that, believe me. I am only too fucking aware that my son is damned for all eternity because he didn't have a little holy water dribbled on his head by some fucking child-molesting priest ... doomed the same as murderers and rapists because a few words weren't said to placate the Creator that I'd put my trust in for my entire fucking life!"

"It is a pity," the Demon stated in its emotionless, sepulchral hiss. "But as a religious man, sir—if I may presume to ask you this question—why did you not have your child baptized, since you and your wife obviously were yourselves?"

"My wife is my second wife; my son's stepmother. She was a Catholic in life, as I was. But my first wife—my son's mother—was always an atheist. She was very adamant about my son not becoming baptized or even attending church until he was old enough to make that decision for himself, as an adult."

"And you gave in to her desires."

"I gave in. Yes, I gave in." Michael was still seething. His voice trembled with his stopped fury.

"It must have been a great source of enmity between your wife and yourself—you being devout, and she denying the Creator."

"That's why she's my *ex*-wife ... isn't it?"

"And she is still in the world of the living?"

"She's alive, yes. She's there, still breathing ... still not believing. Maybe even disbelieving more than ever, in her grief. But she'll learn one day, won't she? Learn how wrong she was. When she joins her son in Hades. And then she can apologize to him. She'd fucking damn well better apologize to him!"

"Come, sir," Iblis Al-Qadim said, sweeping his arm, in a tone that almost sounded sympathetic. "Let me take you to your quarters. And I assure you—the search is already underway."

"Why did I listen to her? Why was I so *weak*?" the Angel lamented.

"Sir?" The Demon had his hand on the metal door's wheel.

Michael grunted, and in starting forward met the eyes of the mollusk-thing poised like a parrot on one of the Demon's shoulders. An uncanny intelligence glowed in them. He remembered what Iblis Al-Qadim had said—the human-like Demons being gradually phased out, because of the revolts incited by several demonic races. Was he looking at Iblis Al-Qadim's replacement-in-training?

He saw that one of its glistening tentacles had reached out and curled with insidious slowness around the handle of that great iron staff.

2: The Damned

Before they became lovers, both of them had lain with Demons.

In one region of Hades, Roger had been captured in his wanderings by a group of Apsaras, as their breed had been named by the Damned (since the Demons themselves tended not to give appellations to their many races). The blue-skinned Apsaras were beautiful and terrifying, with voluptuous perfumed bodies and long black hair that swam in the air above their heads endlessly as if they were drowned women under the sea, their dark eyes blazing and tusk-like fangs curving up from their lips. During his confinement, which may have lasted a year or more (how could he judge?), the Apsaras would seize him and arouse him against his will … rape him. Somewhere in the course of this— like a female mantis consuming the head of her mate as he copulates with her—the Demon would rip his throat open with her fangs, or dismount him as he climaxed and tear off his manhood with her powerful hands (it seemed to be a sport, with the Apsaras, to pluck the organ just as it squirted), or bite off his member as she fellated him, or slash his scrotum open with her long nails to eat the savory oysters of his testes. But there were male Demons in this territory as well, incubi known as the Asuras, and they had performed their own brand of sex acts on him, or forced him to perform acts upon them, followed by the usual mutilations. These torments became almost mundane (if no less excruciating) with time, and of course he always fully recovered later on, regenerating whole once more so that he could be rent afresh the next time around.

Davina, on the other hand, had served as one of the living spawning machines in the city of Tartarus, where many species of Demon were manufactured, so to speak, by Damned laborers. Usually the processes employed were more mechanical in nature; Demons were baked from various ingredients like cakes or injection-molded like plastic, grown in dark cellars like mushrooms or developed in bubbling solution like fetal clones—but certain types of these homunculi, these infernal golems, gestated inside human hosts. The sort of Demon that had been grown inside Davina's body were dubbed Kilcrops—ghastly cadaverous things, always laughing, that never seemed to mature beyond adolescence. She had been captured by a roving Demon squad, taken to Tartarus and put to this use. On a regular basis, she had been raped by the incubus breed called the Asuras. She had lost count of the pregnancies (maybe two hundred?), each lasting what she thought of as thirty days. There was no actual day or night, but the Damned counted days in terms of work periods. Then again, the work periods were so very long.

The farm girls, as they thought of themselves, were treated fairly well, aside from the rapes that planted the devil seed, but even those were intended more as business than punishment. Not that it made much of a difference to Davina. To her knowledge, no laborer had ever escaped a city so full of Demons as Tartarus, but after a while the farm girls and other workers were released and replaced with new souls. Her understanding of this was: rather than being a mercy, or a thanks for their service, it was to insure that they did not get too comfortable in Hades. Again, even a torture could seem commonplace and predictable with repetition. A man, say, locked in a hanging cage and pecked at by an infernal breed of crow would be liberated after a time (maybe a week, a month, a decade by human measurement), so as to wander free for a while and encounter fresh manifestations of anguish.

꙰

Hades was full of settlements, either constructed and populated entirely by the Damned, or else by the Damned and the Demons in combination. There was everything from thatch-roofed hamlets to metropolises of soaring high-rises, these skyscrapers either familiar or uncanny in their varied outlines. Many times the look of the town or city had to do with the period of human history its Damned citizens came from, though mostly these characteristics became blurred and blended with the coming of new generations.

Certain colonies of Hades alternated between freezing cold and scorching hot, as if each day contained the seasons of a year. Some were built in the shadow of glaciers, where it was eternally frigid, sleet ever stinging the skin, the rooms of the buildings heated with whatever meager measures the Damned themselves could devise.

Other cities were ever burning. Maybe not with blistering, charring earthly fire—how then could the citizenry move about freely, so as to roam to the next place of suffering?—but with a lesser blue flame that nonetheless consumed a city like Apollyon entirely, the flames lapping high into the air so that every street, every room was filled with this hot blue light, so that it filled your mouth when you spoke or slept. It needed no fuel, it never ran out, it was silent and did not crackle. After a while, you could almost forget the pain it caused in every nerve of your body. Almost.

Roger and Davina had drifted to the city of Apollyon at about the same time; it was where they met. He had been an atheist in life, a British soldier killed by a German machine gun in 1916, at the Battle of the Somme, when he was twenty-eight years old. In September of 1993, at the age of twenty-three, Davina had been killed along with eleven-thousand other Indian people in an earthquake. She assumed all eleven-thousand victims, being Hindus rather than devout Christians, must be here in Hades with her. He assumed a fair number of the million-plus casualties of the Somme offensive were here for one reason or another, as well. But Hades was infinite. Hades had room enough for all.

The first time Roger and Davina had made love, the sea of flame they were submerged in caused so much pain to their uncovered bodies that it left little room for pleasure. But they stared at each other's faces as he lay atop her. And they smiled.

Later, they had met the boy. Mark had died only recently, and Apollyon was the first city he'd encountered. He told them he had burned to death at the age of eight, and it was his opinion that he was in Hades not only because he wasn't baptized, but because he had caused the fire that had killed him ... and his parents.

Roger and Davina had pitied the child. They had taken him in as a kind of son, and it was this act as much as their love that made them kind of a husband and wife. Kind of a family.

***

At least paper did not burn in the blue flame, and the Demons of Apollyon apparently did not deem it worth their time to otherwise destroy the books that Roger and his fellow workers produced, nor the presses they printed them on. Roger was adept with machines, and had helped improve these presses and the binding equipment—all designed and built by the Damned over many years—since settling in Apollyon. Currently, he was inking up one of the presses to resume work on a slim volume called *Beautiful Hell*, a memoir written by a Damned author who had stumbled upon this city and left the manuscript in their care until he should return.

"Mark," he called, looking up but not seeing his boy. "Bring me a fresh can of black, will you?"

A clatter, a clunk (*please don't have spilled another can of ink!* thought Roger), and the child appeared from another room, bearing a metal can, looking eager to be of help. His adoptive father even paid him several coins of the netherworld's currency, every "week," for the scraps of work he performed about the shop.

Roger noticed a smear of red on the boy's beaming face, and grew concerned, straightened up. "Did you cut yourself?"

Setting the can down, Mark touched his cheek, examined his stained fingertips. He laughed. "No, Rog ... it's red ink. I was putting some cans away!"

His own hands slicked with black pigment, fashioned from native minerals and flora, Roger reached out and dabbed some ink on the boy's other cheek. "There. You can at least be stained in the same color as me."

"Hey!" The boy flashed out his own hand, and ran his reddened fingertips down Roger's forearm, leaving smudges. "Now *you're* stained the same as *me!*"

"Watch it, watch it," Roger said, drawing back in a futile attempt to avoid the swipe. In doing so, he felt an unpleasant grinding sensation in his chest, as he did from time to time depending on the nature of his movements. He often felt it while making love with Davina, and she swore she could feel the outline of the shape tucked against his ribs, though he himself could not.

"Why did you ever do that?" she would scold him in her musical accent, her heavy black brows lowered.

"You can cut it out of me if you want," he would tease.

It was not only groups, large and small, of Demons that had begun to revolt and skirmish with the Celestial infantry sent to squash them, and with their own brother races of Demons as well. No, even groups of the Damned had taken up weapons against their Demon and Celestial oppressors alike, lashing out through guerilla warfare, terrorist acts, even full-scale battle on occasion. There had even been cases where Demons and Damned had fought together in uneasy alliance. It was a turbulent time for the eternal afterlife.

Several "months" ago, a major clash had spilled over into Apollyon. The wounded remnants of a Damned rebel outfit had taken shelter in the city, pursued by a type of Demon Roger had not as yet encountered despite his many years here; a race of bipedal tick-like creatures with pale greenish chitin. He assumed it was a brand new breed, designed as a replacement for one of the humanoid species, deemed less trustworthy now. The Damned fighters had had a few guns among them. Roger figured they had stolen these weapons from some Angels who were in Hades as tourists, or to hunt the Damned for sport, or to help out in the fight against the Damned for the sheer joy of battle (being Angels, they could quickly reconstitute after even the most grievous wounds).

Roger himself had been a witness to one messy clash, in which the last of these particular rebels were overpowered and captured by those immense ticks with their awful, scythe-like praying mantis forelimbs, and other sets of arms ending in hooks, blades and pincers like surgical—or dissecting—instruments. One of the rebels had been dropped to the cobblestoned street, an arm lopped off, and had met Roger's eyes as he wailed. Roger had wanted to look away in shame for not going to the man's aid or defense. But the carnage he had experienced on Europe's battlefields, the horrors that had sent his immortal soul here, had scarred him in a way his mock cells could not repair, however miraculous their mending abilities. Or was it simply that his time in Hades had made him cowed, defeated, a dog with his growl beaten out of him? One might think that having participated in so much violence in life and endured so much violence in the afterlife would make him inured to killing, make it easy for him to resume his life as a soldier ... but Roger could not see himself ever taking part in a war again.

Even though he had not gone to the wounded man, however, the gun the fighter had been gripping went spinning out of the hand of his severed arm and ended up not far from Roger's boot. He was standing outside the print shop, and a co-worker of Roger's had hissed at him from behind, "Rog! The gun! Get it..."

Mindlessly, Roger had taken a step toward the gun, a little semiautomatic pistol of a type designed after his time on Earth; a .25 caliber, he deduced. The gun was closer than the injured man. He might furtively retrieve the weapon without entering into the battle itself, as he would if he gripped that man's remaining, outstretched hand.

He didn't know if it were because he scooped up the little pistol, or because the Demon mistook him as one of the actual insurgents, but as he rose he saw a tick scurrying at him, blood from the Damned sloshing darkly in its swollen abdomen, its arms flailing, and the next thing he knew he was on his back, his chest split wide, blood spraying up from him in a fountain. He had to close his eyes against it. The spray went into his own mouth, as if to keep the fountain recycling.

Bullets from somewhere—another of the rebels—crashed into the Demon, causing both its and its victims' blood to spatter the cobblestones, and it fell convulsing with a terrible screech. Demons could die, because they had no souls, and this one proceeded to do so.

"Rog!" his co-worker cried. This man and another dragged their friend back onto the sidewalk, then around the corner, out of sight. His co-worker took the gun from Roger's hand, examined it a moment, looked down at the wound that would have killed a mortal man. "Rog, you need to keep this. We need to hide it." He pointed the little weapon at that terrible pumping gash. "Let me put it in there, Rog. No one will find it, and you can always get it out again if you need it."

"No," the other man said, "it could be found if he's tortured and cut open some day. They'd put him in a snake pit for a fucking century, for having that…"

"Quiet! Rog…"

Did he nod or gurgle his assent? Maybe he did, in his delirium, or maybe his friend simply interpreted Roger's agony that way; he couldn't himself recall, so blanked with pain was he at the time. But the next thing he knew, his co-worker was stuffing that hard lump of metal deep inside him like a crude lover.

The co-worker had vanished from Apollyon a week later. Rumor was that the fighting had stirred him, and he himself had joined the rebel movement. And the gun … the gun still lay inside Roger's chest, healed without trace of a scar—not even the scars of the German machine gun bullets. Inside him like a black pearl. A hunk of shrapnel. Like a dead, cold organ.

"You okay, Rog?" the boy asked, noticing the wince, seeing the man's hand involuntarily touch his upper chest. "Did I hurt you?"

"*No* … I'm fine, fine." Roger smiled at him, but sadly. He hated to hear him fill so quickly with guilt, with self-blame. And he wished Mark wouldn't call him *Rog*. Or Davina, *Davina*. Maybe someday, he hoped, the boy would truly think of them as his parents.

☙☓

Roger and Davina were awakened by the sound of a child's screams.

There were two bedrooms in the little flat they rented; Mark's room was the smaller, but that was like saying the other room was the larger of two closets. Both had space enough for the bed they contained, and not much else. There were lanterns and candles for light, but even with them extinguished the air had that constant blue glow. Cold burning fire, filling each room to its ceiling. When Roger and Davina opened their eyelids, it took a blinking moment or two to readjust to the pain against their bare eyeballs. It was Davina who slipped out of bed first, her skin very brown against the white pajamas she had made for herself, and shuffled barefoot from the room. Roger trailed after, not as swiftly. He knew what the screaming was about. It was not the first time.

"What is it, my baby? What's wrong?" Davina cooed, sitting on the edge of the bed and gathering Mark up into her embrace. He wrung her in his arms, his face pressed into her chest.

"Fire," the boy spluttered through his tears. "The fire…"

"I know, my darling. I know." Davina rocked him. She glanced up at Roger, framed in the room's threshold.

As concerned as he was for the boy's anguish, he couldn't help but smile proudly, affectionately at the sight of him in his lover's arms. Her thick black hair, curly as Medusa's, wild around her face. Those huge black eyes, so solemn and concerned. Could there ever have been a more affecting portrait of a Madonna? Still meeting his eyes, she kissed the top of the boy's head and whispered comfort to him.

"It's my fault," he wept. "I killed my Mom and Dad … I killed them…"

"No, my dear. No…"

"I did! I did!"

"It was an accident, my love."

96

"It doesn't matter … it's my fault … I killed them! I killed my Mom and Dad!"

At last, Roger came to the bed and sat beside Davina, took one of the boy's hands and clasped it between both of his. "That's not why you're here, Mark."

"I'm bad! I'm *bad!*"

"No. Look at me. Look at Davina. Are we bad, too, Mark?"

The boy didn't raise his face from her warm breasts, but his muffled voice said, "No-o…"

"It's not fair, the things that happen. The fire. Us being here. Not fair, then, is it? But we don't have to accept it. We may have to live with the pain of things, but we don't have to accept them. I don't accept that I belong here. I don't accept that you belong here. That's what makes us human—that freedom they can't beat from us or bleed from us—and I've found that being human is more important than being an Angel. Or a … deity." He sighed, still holding the child's hand. "I must not be making sense to you. But, what I'm saying is, they can punish us from now until the universe burns out, but that doesn't make us evil. And you, my boy, are a beautiful, beautiful soul who would shame the most powerful, most lordly, meanest and ugliest God that anyone could ever worship."

Davina put a hand to the back of Roger's head, stroked it, and spread her lips in a smile.

3: *The Searchers*

Dawn hid her face in her hands, as if they might staunch the flow of her tears … as if, if she refused to look at her surroundings long enough they would be gone when she uncovered her eyes, and she would be in Paradise again instead of this apartment provided for her and her husband, here in Hades.

Their Demon hosts no doubt believed they provided a comfortable and even beautiful environment for their angelic guests. The glistening, metallic scarabs that covered every inch of the walls were a living (in a sense) mosaic, that shifted every so often into an entirely new pattern of color and design. And even though Michael had assured her that last night the beetles had not swarmed off the walls and across him in his bed, she still shuddered at their numbers all around her. It wasn't these creatures, though, that had brought her to such a state ... but having been met by Iblis Al-Qadim and two lesser Demons, upon her arrival into the netherworld. Even though Michael had gone back to Paradise to fetch her personally, had told her what to expect, and held her hand when that metal hatch in the white-tiled wall squealed open, she had still gasped and squeezed her eyes shut at her first sight of the three skeletal devils—the looming governor with flame lapping out of the top of his head, inside the black miter he wore, and his two attendants: comparatively smaller and without headgear, a luminous green smoke wisping out of their open skulls in place of their superior's emerald fire.

Neither of the lesser Demons had a black cephalopod perched on one shoulder, and the one on the governor's shoulder seemed to have become more affectionate, or aggressive, in the mere hours since Michael had last seen it. It now had one of its slinking arms coiled tightly around Iblis Al-Qadim's scrawny neck, like a noose.

But now Michael and Dawn were alone, and her sobs were finally diminishing ... though she still refused the ice water he offered her from a pitcher. He didn't proffer any of the brilliantly red unknown fruit, heaped for them in a silver bowl. Even he thought they looked too much like the small hearts of human children.

"And to think that Mark is in this place, huh?" Michael told her, pacing as she sat on the edge of the bed. "This is how *you* feel, even though you know you can return to Heaven anytime you want. Imagine being stuck in this place forever. And this," he waved an arm around the room, "this isn't how the Damned live, down here." He still couldn't help but think of Hades as being "down," as if beneath the Earth's rind, though he knew it was more like a parallel dimension.

"Terrible," Dawn sniffled, at last lowering her slick hands from eyes burned red. "Terrible. I don't think I ever really believed in a Hell," she admitted quietly, as if she herself might be damned by the confession. "Did you?"

"Yes," her husband muttered.

"I'm not even sure ... I hate to say it, Mike ... but I'm not even sure I really, really believed in a Heaven. I mean, I went to church every Sunday, like I was expected to ... the way my parents did. But, I don't know ... I didn't like to really think about an afterlife, even a Paradise, because ... it just didn't seem possible..."

"You see? This is what I don't understand. The Father only counts the heads that go through the doors of His churches—He doesn't look into their hearts. If He did, a lot of the people in Heaven would be here, and innocents like my son would be with us in Paradise. Instead of judging you by your acts, your purity, He's ... *petty*. He'll throw you into the pit for buttering the wrong side of the bread."

"Honey," she looked up, "shhh!"

"I don't care. I don't care anymore," he grumbled. "I never thought that all Buddhists would go to Hell, even though I was told a million times there was only one way to get to Paradise—through the Son. I never believed every Muslim, every Jew, every atheist would be punished without even a look at their souls! It's insane ... it's crueler than anything I could have imagined, even from Satan. And now, of course, I understand. There never was a Satan. Just our Dad—the big old Yin/Yang. He's the real Lucifer. The angel of light, turned ruler of Hell. Angel and demon in one. Our Creator is the Devil."

"Michael," Dawn warned him, glancing with a start at the seething, rustling walls as the insects suddenly scurried over each other to reconfigure their positions. For a moment, she had thought the bugs would pour over her husband and eat him alive for his blasphemies.

"I would hate Him less if there were a Satan to blame for this." He swept his arm around him again. "But Satan is the only Demon that was created by Man. The rest are His."

"Enough, Michael, please."

He whirled to glare at her, his goateed chin thrust forward. "I believed in Him! I worshipped Him! I was devout! And here is my son, only eight years old, in fucking *Hell*! They'd better find him, these monsters. They better bring me to him soon or they'll see some *real* wrath."

"I feel sorry for our parents," Dawn said, letting her head sag. "They don't know our souls live on. They might think we're gone forever. My poor Mom and Dad. I'm so glad they're baptized … churchgoers. My brother, too." She wagged her head. "They must be so heartbroken. Now they have to live the rest of their lives thinking about how young I was when I died. The horrible way that I died. It will haunt them, every Christmas, every time my birthday comes along." She moaned. "Why did he have to fool around with matches … *why?*"

"You blame him," Michael stated. She lifted her head. His sudden calm tone frightened her more than his furious rants. "You blame him for us being killed."

"Michael, I'm only saying…"

"He's a *child*. I played with fire, too, when I was a kid. Burning my toy soldiers, watching their faces melt. Seeing how paper burned, Styrofoam. Who left those matches out, by the way?"

"You always liked the candles I burned. Their smell," Dawn managed weakly, close to tears again. "I thought you liked them…"

"You left the matches out."

"So now it's my fault? You say I hate Mark for doing this to us, but I don't! I've gone to Paradise; I'm not the unlucky one, *he* is. But don't you think that tortures me, too? I loved him! You might not believe that, but I loved him like he was my own son. It isn't that I blame Mark … the thing is, you blame *me*! You blame me, for what happened to us. And for him being *here*."

Michael came over to her, spreading his arms open, looking appropriately angelic in his white robes. With his slicked-back, short dark hair and neat goatee, she thought he resembled a modernized Jesus. He put his arms around her and she began sobbing, again, against his chest.

"I don't blame you, baby. I don't." He rubbed her back in circles. "We didn't make this place, did we? We didn't make these rules. Look … there's nothing you can really do here. There's no sense in your staying. I'll take you back."

"But I wanted to be with you," Dawn whimpered, clutching him. "And I wanted to see Mark. Really."

"When I find him, I'll come get you again."

"But how long do you think you'll be here, honey?"

"As long as it takes."

"Well, if you find him, what then? We can't take him back with us..."

"I don't know, what then. All I know is I want to see my boy. I want to be sure he's not in pain. I can't bear it, Dawn ... I can't bear the thought of my boy *suffering*..."

◈

The Demon seated importantly behind a desk of black marble resembled Iblis Al-Qadim and his underlings in that he appeared like an unwrapped and reanimated mummy, his jointed body vaguely insectoid, but above his skull-like face his head ballooned into a huge translucent sphere, almost like a boneless fluid-filled sack that Michael was surprised the thing's neck could support. The governor and this Demon had exchanged a few guttural gurgles in an alien tongue, and now the globe-headed entity turned the fiery pinpricks of his eyes to Michael, staring at him intensely. *It's probing me telepathically*, he thought, *using me to get Mark's scent*. He could almost feel the Demon's bony digits unraveling the knotted convolutions of his brain and fingering them like the beads of a rosary.

Seated opposite the creature, Michael fidgeted in his chair, vaguely nervous, as if he were a young man applying for his first job. But it had been a long time since Michael had squirmed before a superior. He had died a career military man, an officer, a decorated veteran of the Gulf War. A man on the ground, not on a plane, not directing rockets through windows as if playing a video game. He had two confirmed kills; two faces he had looked into before he had extinguished the life behind them. And were his victims in Hell with him, even now? He had heard that in Hades, infinite as it was, the Damned were prevented somehow from encountering their relatives or spouses, even their friends from life. Would that mean that when his first wife died, she would not be permitted to join her son? It must mean exactly that. He wished he could warn her, like Marley visiting Scrooge, to change her destiny. Despite how disillusioned he had become with his faith, Michael prayed that his former wife would change her mind about religion and become baptized at last, so that she could move about freely between Heaven and Hell as he did. So she could see her son again ... if Mark truly could be located.

The globe-headed Demon broke their gaze, and Michael went a little limp in his chair. Had he merely been tensed, or had the thing's brain been holding him transfixed? The Demon looked up at Iblis Al-Qadim and gave a gravelly hiss.

"You are in luck, sir," the governor announced. "We have found him. It was helpful that he has not strayed considerably from his original point of entry. He is in a city called Apollyon—not far at all from this palace."

"Take me there," Michael said.

"As you wish, sir."

Michael rose from his seat, and nodded at the telepathic Demon in a kind of gruff thanks. But he could feel no real gratitude. The Demons did not sympathize with his plight, were merely being courteous because he was an Angel. These were the things that inflicted misery upon the Damned ... and who could tell what this being's brothers might be doing to his child even now.

4: The Skull

As Roger and Mark wound their way through the twisty, narrow streets of Apollyon, returning home from the print shop, they passed a pair of emaciated, child-like Kilcrops, but the Demons only giggled at them horribly as they turned the corner. Glancing back at the creatures, Roger couldn't help but wonder if either or both of them had been grown inside his lover's body.

"One thing I like about Hell," Mark resumed saying, now that the Demons were out of view, "is there's no school here."

"Now, now," Roger scolded. "I should school you myself, just for saying that. You're a smart boy ... you shouldn't be thinking that way."

"But why should I learn things I'll need when I grow up, if I'm never going to grow up?"

"Maybe that's another good thing about Hell," he muttered to himself. Never having to become an adult, that most awful of creatures excepting, perhaps, Demons. "It's always important to learn and learn, as much as you can, and never ever stop learning. And there *are* cities and towns that have schools, you know—I've seen them."

"I'd rather just work with you instead. Because..." he produced a few coins from his pocket " ... you don't get paid for going to school."

"Terrible. Why are you so terrible this evening?"

Mark laughed, but then stopped and said, "Wow ... Rog ... what is that thing?"

Still smiling, Roger turned his head to look at where the boy was pointing.

A moon appeared to hover above the roofs and chimneys, huge in the bluish sky of flame, but even as Roger watched the great sphere was floating closer, in their direction. The sphere was the color of bone, and skull-like sutures squiggled across its surface, and this was why the Damned had come to call the thing the Skull, though there were no other features. Roger had seen it before. Once, here in Apollyon, and in other colonies of the Damned as well. It migrated, wandered, seemingly at random. He was reminded of the Black Cathedral, on its networks of train tracks, and other such roving structures that one hoped never to see enter one's town.

"Hurry up, Mark," he said, reaching for the boy's hand. He quickened his pace.

"What is it, Rog?"

"The Skull..."

"What does it do?"

"It's a torture factory," he told him.

Roger began to look about him for a shop that might be open, into which they might duck if need be. A stranger might even let them into their house, out of sympathy. Then again, they might not want to get involved, for fear of being gathered up by the crew of the Skull themselves.

"It's getting close," Mark said, sounding worried.

"I know. Here. Under here." Roger broke into a little run, dragging Mark beneath a crumbling aqueduct. They pressed themselves against the damp bricks, and saw the great orb's shadow as it slithered across the street, darkening it in a brief eclipse as the Skull passed directly overhead, before it moved on and the street glowed blue again. At no point did they hear any sound from the titanic craft.

"It's gone," Mark whispered.

"We'll go tell Davina. We won't step outside for a few days. These things usually only stay in one place several days at a time."

"Okay," Mark said meekly.

They ventured out again, kept holding hands. As they walked, Roger explained, "They collect people sometimes because they see us making cities, communities, creating jobs for ourselves, families. They let it go on for so long. And then one day, they want to shake you, shake you badly, to remind you where you are. They allow the other because it makes you almost comfortable. You can't feel discomfort without comfort. You can't know pain without pleasure. If they skinned us alive day after day, sooner or later your mind would shut off. You would become a robot, adapt to the pain and endure it. But this way ... this way is worse, in the end."

"You *are* like my teacher," Mark teased him, trying to make a joke of it.

"Someone has to be, and keep a rascal like you in check."

Roger had taken them through a few alleys as shortcuts, and the one they currently squeezed through was barely wide enough to admit him, even having turned his body sideways. The slime on its bricks helped lubricate his passage somewhat. Mark, of course, had an easier time. He had slipped into the alley ahead of him.

A chittering sound behind Roger made him glance back nervously. He saw a silhouette flicker briefly past the mouth of the alley, where they had entered. He hadn't seen the figure clearly, but it hadn't struck him as human in outline.

He looked forward again, and saw that Mark had reached the end of the alley. "Wait for me," he hissed, his palms slapping across the sludge-coated bricks as he advanced. "Mark!"

The boy cleared the alley and entered a bright street ahead. He turned to look back into the passageway. "Come on," he whispered, extending his hand.

And then, jarringly, as if Mark had dropped through a trapdoor, he was gone. For just the briefest moment Roger thought he saw the boy's fingers rake across the bricks.

"Mark!" he called more loudly, fighting to shuffle along a little faster. He reached one arm out, clawed at the alley's entrance, caught its edge and tugged himself clear.

It was a wide street, paved in flagstones, almost a plaza. Sometimes, the Damned even held festivals here, as on the day they judged to be Christmas (though Roger himself would no longer celebrate the birth of the Creator's son). The Skull hovered there, above the street, one of its unevenly-shaped plates having opened along its sutures and lowered to the flagstones like a hatch or drawbridge. He heard screaming. He saw men and women being dragged up onto the hatch. Into the bone-colored globe.

And he saw Mark. Because he was only a child of eight, it took just one of the greenish tick Demons, scurrying on its hind legs, to restrain him and pull him along. Roger saw ribbons of blood twined around the child's arms, from where the thing's sharp pincers bit into him.

"You fucking bastards!" he roared, and began racing after the creature. He saw another one of them close to his right, and at his shout it turned and saw him, too. It whisked forward, chattering, and Roger knew it would catch up to him before he caught up to the one grasping Mark. He spun, ducked under the whooshing sickle of a praying mantis arm, came up and punched the thing in its bony face with its tiny bead-like eyes and blood-slickened mouthparts. He heard its chitin crack, or maybe that was the bones in his own hand, so hard did he strike the thing. It dropped onto its back, and he thought he could hear its feast of gore slosh in its expanded body. But from the ground, the Demon whipped its arms crazily, and Roger found himself dropping, the air going out of him.

Lying on his side, he looked down his body and saw that his right leg had been severed below the knee.

The fallen Demon scrambled to its feet, and used one of these to kick Roger in the arm and face, slashing him deeply across his jaw. It then ran to the aid of one of its fellows, who was having a difficult time hanging onto a large black man.

"Oh no, oh no, oh no," Roger was chanting, as he propped himself into a sitting position.

He saw Mark—almost at the hatch now—looking back at him as he struggled in his captor's grip. There were many people wailing and sobbing in the courtyard, but Roger knew his boy's voice. And he heard Mark call out to him, "Daaaaad!"

5: Apollyon

At first, Iblis Al-Qadim had offered Michael a ride from his palace to the city of Apollyon in a black metal carriage pulled by a team of unclad Damned, the connecting chains hooked right into their flesh, but the Angel had taken one look and refused. Now, instead they rode inside a carriage drawn by two shaggy, prehistoric-looking infernal animals of a type he had heard the Damned often killed and consumed for food.

Dotted across the landscape they traveled through, Michael saw another kind of animal, or was it an animal-like species of Demon? They reminded him of the elephants with impossibly long, thin, multi-jointed legs bearing obelisks on their backs in paintings by Salvador Dali, such as *The Temptation of Saint Anthony*, except that these would be headless elephants, and their backs were covered in squirming white objects like maggots, which Michael knew were naked human beings, apparently spiked directly to the thick hides of the slowly striding creatures. He could hear the wispy, faraway howling of hundreds of lamenting souls. Mostly the terrain here was barren, featureless, but presently the carriage rattled across a stone bridge spanning a wide river of blood. Distantly, one of the stilt-legged monstrosities waded like a stork through the sluggishly flowing gore to reach the opposite bank.

Were there children pinned to the tops of those behemoths, too?

As they rode on, Michael saw the Demon governor turn his head and gaze out his own window for a while. It gave Michael an opportunity to stare at the way the tentacles of the octopus were not only coiling around his neck, but now burrowing beneath his leathery skin. One tentacle had even snaked into a skull socket, putting out its bright little star of an eye. Michael had noted that the green flames erupting from the top of his head had diminished. He had also noticed that the black octopus Demon's head had ballooned even more, a green glow showing through the stretched membrane. The miniature bat wings sprouting above its eyes fluttered uselessly.

"Not even human," Michael heard Iblis Al-Qadim murmur. "Because I walk upright? Because I have two arms, two legs? Now I am just a human, too?"

"Pardon?" Michael spoke up.

Slowly, the terrible lipless visage cranked his way, the remaining eye seeming to have grown dim in its glow as well. The Demon appeared befuddled for a moment. And then, his voice grew strong and assured again, "Nothing, sir. We are nearly there..."

Apollyon's jagged outlines reared from the bleak landscape. Michael regarded the way a bluish glow rose from the city into the air—its atmosphere of weak fire.

"Do we know where in that big city my son would be?"

"We will need to ask about, sir."

"Ask? And how long will that take?"

The Demon didn't answer him. He found this out of character, surprisingly rude, but he didn't pursue it.

As they approached the fortress-like wall surrounding the city, Michael realized that it was studded with countless human heads, the bodies they were attached to fossilized inside the wall's concrete. There was scaffolding erected here and there, on which Demon overseers forced Damned laborers to chisel some prisoners free, and seal new prisoners up. Crows perched on a number of squalling heads, plucking at their hair to make their nests. Michael cursed under his breath. He felt strangely ashamed, should any of the heads peer into the carriage and see him there, an Angel resting in its plush interior.

Having passed through the wall's main gate, the carriage soon came to a stop outside a building with statues of winged baboon-like beasts, in something of an Art Deco style, flanking its riveted iron front doors. They disembarked, Michael and the governor and two of his lesser Demons, and mounted the front steps.

Inside, they were met by a Baphomet, as they were called, another towering breed of high-ranking Demon but with a goat-like head enveloped in a veil of white fire. Iblis Al-Qadim and this thing faced each other, but neither uttered a sound. Michael realized their communication was telepathic, unless they were deciphering meaning in the lapping of their respective flames.

At last, the governor turned to look down at the Angel. "The child is known to be new to this city, and he is known to have been taken in by a printer who lives here."

"A printer?"

"He and others produce reading materials, for the entertainment of their kind. The materials are potentially inflammatory, but they have been tolerated. For the time being."

"Take me to him," Michael said.

When Davina saw the imperial form of Iblis Al-Qadim soaring behind the white-robed Angel, she fell back with an audible gasp. They had come for her lover, she was sure of it—to punish him for smashing the face of that tick Demon...

Michael stepped through the threshold, seeing the terror on a face already wet with tears, and held up his open palms. "Wait ... hang on ... we aren't here to hurt you."

"What do you want?" she managed.

Michael looked around him. It was a tiny sort of parlor, with an even tinier kitchen separated by a half partition. And in the kitchen, tacked to one wall, he spotted drawings. They made his heart lurch, and he moved past the woman to study them closely. Davina watched him but was too stunned to move, wilting in the shadow of that hideous giant with his long staff of office in one fist and the mollusk fixed vampire-like onto his neck.

"He drew these," Michael said softly, standing in front of the drawings, rendered in rough charcoal. One showed a poorly drawn family, barely stick figures, a man and a woman and a child. But who were the man and woman? "Mark drew these…"

"Mark?" Davina said. "You know Mark?"

Michael faced her. "I'm his father."

Davina said nothing, her wide eyes staring. Then, a man appeared in the doorway behind her. He clung to its frame, sort of hopping on one leg, because the other was a stump. But at the end of the stump was a vestigial foot, where the lost one was regenerating. The deep wound on his jaw had almost sealed up, as well.

Roger took in the Demon official—hunched forward to fit his height inside the little apartment—and the two skeleton things lurking silently behind him, then addressed Michael. "Who did you say you are?" he demanded in a frayed voice, badly attempting forcefulness.

"My name is Michael Palladino. These things have led me here … they say you've taken in my son, Mark."

"You," Roger stammered, "you're…"

"Yes. His father."

Davina grasped Roger's arm. "He can get him released, Roger. He can get Mark freed."

"Freed from where?" Michael said, stepping out of the kitchen, closer to the man and woman.

"He was taken from us … today. A few hours ago. He's in the Skull, out there." Roger jerked his head toward the one window in their flat.

Michael went to it, pushed aside a scrap of curtain, looked out. He could see an ivory-hued dome, gleaming above the dark buildings surrounding it. "What am I looking at?"

"It's a torture plant. A mobile one. It flew into town today … and they kidnapped Mark. Took him inside it." Roger glared over at the trio of Demons. "Those fucking monsters."

"Torture plant?" Michael whirled to blaze his eyes at the Demons as well. To Davina, watching him, dark-haired Michael with his goatee and furious face looked as much like a Demon, if not more so. And ironically, her Roger, though damned here, was as blond and blue-eyed as an seraph.

"Yes, sir," Iblis Al-Qadim replied simply.

Michael lunged forward, to snarl, "They have my son in a fucking torture chamber?"

"This *is* Hades, sir," the thing intoned emotionlessly.

The pistol that Michael ripped out of the holster on his belt was a Beretta, of the type he had carried in the Gulf War. He thrust it forward to point up at the Demon's face. "You son of a bitch! I want you to get my son out of there, right now, do you understand me?"

The octopus's arms slithered, shifted, and the beating of the wings increased in tempo, but the host creature did not flinch. His zombie-like voice rattled, "I cannot do that, sir. It is beyond my power."

"What do you mean? You're a Demon ... a governor of Demons! You'll do it or I'll blow your fucking skull apart, and I know I can kill you ... and *you* know I can kill you."

"Be that as it may, sir, I cannot arrange it. Hades exists because it is the will of the Creator. It is the will of the Creator that those in Hades should suffer. I was able to take you to the place where he is located, but I may not interfere in this process."

"I'm an Angel, do you hear me? I'm an Angel and you have to do as I say!"

"Even Angels, sir, are bound by the laws of the Creator. The will or desire of all the Angels in Paradise combined could still not sway the Creator from His purposes."

"You mother fucker!" Michael extended the semiautomatic, which visibly shivered in the air, another inch.

"You can kill me, sir, but it will avail you nothing."

"I don't understand you. You've helped me to this point." His eyes switched to meet those of the octopus, appraising him enigmatically.

"We'll have to wait," Roger croaked, sagging onto a roughly upholstered chair. "These mobile factories ... they only stay a few days. Then they release their prisoners and move on."

Michael pivoted slowly, his eyes still feral, lowering his handgun somewhat. "Just wait? Just wait for what? My son to endure who knows what kind of agony? Even one day, one hour inside that thing is too much!"

"Do you think I don't care?" Roger snapped. "That boy is like a son to me."

"Like a son to you? Well he's *my* son, do you understand that? Mine!"

Roger dug his fingers into the armrests of the chair, and tears filmed his eyes. Through gritted teeth he hissed, "You sanctimonious bastard. Look at you ... all dressed in white like a saint. You, living in Heaven with your fountains of wine and your golden toilets while we rot and burn down here. Don't you feel this? The fire you're breathing?" He waved one hand through the pale bluish tincture of the air. "This is what we inhale, what licks at our skin, every day. Your son ... *here* ... while you tan on some beach in Paradise."

"Look—I didn't send my son to Hell. Do you think I'm happy he's here? I didn't abandon him. These aren't my fucking rules ... I don't even understand them!"

"You can't take him from us," Roger said, raising his chin defiantly. "You can't bring him back with you and you know it. So take your pompous anger back to Heaven and leave him here. He's in good hands."

"Good hands? He's in a *torture* chamber!"

"Yes. As your friend there said, this is Hades. Welcome to it. That poor dear boy is suffering. And I'm in as much torture as he is, just knowing it. But in a few days, he'll be released. He'll heal. And we'll take him back here, and care for him as best we can ... as we have been doing."

"Fuck that." Michael confronted Iblis Al-Qadim again. "I am not waiting any few days, while my son is torn apart in that thing out there. I want you to do something, you son of a bitch ... there has to be something you can do! Put me in there. Put me in his place."

"Impossible. An Angel, tortured? It could never be..."

"I'm being tortured *now!*"

The giant Demon half turned, seemed to sway. Propping himself with his halberd-like staff, he took on that distracted, unfocused aspect again, that Michael had observed in the carriage. "Things are ... very confusing at this time. An Angel ... wanting to be tortured. An Angel ... who I am ordered to deny. My flame ... drawn away from me." The creature staggered before he caught himself again. In a tone that almost sounded hurt, he said, "I am betrayed..."

Michael remembered what he had overheard the Demon mumbling inside the carriage. *"Because I walk upright? Because I have two arms, two legs? Now I am just a human, too?"* As distantly human in appearance as the governor was, could it truly be that his kind was one of those slated to be eliminated, for being too much like men? Because one particularly human-like Demon race had begun a growing rebellion, a genocide was being waged against other strains the Creator deemed a potential threat. Even this creature's barely anthropomorphic species, as well? His loyal service, up to now, no longer taken into account? *"I am betrayed,"* he had just said.

He saw Iblis Al-Qadim go more rigid, regain his composure. But Michael was aware now what was happening. That parasite, affixed to him, was wrestling back the control that had momentarily slipped away from it.

When Iblis Al-Qadim turned his imposing frame in Michael's direction again, it was to see the Berreta rising.

"Wait!" cried Roger, half starting up from his chair in alarm and disbelief, even as the room thundered with the enclosed sound of three gunshots in rapid succession.

The projectiles tore through the bulbous, sack-like head of the mollusk being, green-glowing muck splattering out of it. As it collapsed upon itself like a burst balloon, its wings stopped beating and its tentacles came slithering out of the holes they had burrowed into the host Demon's neck and head. It oozed down his shoulder, hit the floor with a splat like wet leather. Iblis Al-Qadim stood oddly naked, swayed again. Then, he tottered back, fell against the wall behind him, and slid into a broken pile of insect-like skeletal limbs.

"I am ... freed," he rasped.

"Now—free my son," Michael told the Demon.

The crumpled entity gazed up at the Angel with his remaining eye glinting inside that pit of a socket. For several moments, Michael felt hypnotized, as when the globe-headed Demon had rummaged inside his brain. And then, he and the others in the room heard a booming thud from outside, in the city. It rattled the one window in its frame and sent a vibration up their legs through their soles.

"What's happened?" Davina asked.

"I have ... contacted the Skull," Iblis Al-Qadim said. "I have brought it down for you, sir."

Michael swept to the window again, looked out. He could only see a bare crescent, the very top, of the vast bone sphere this time. It had lowered, crashed, all the way to the street.

When he looked back at the Demon, he saw that both eyes were black and empty now, and no more emerald fire flickered inside the miter atop his head.

Michael then faced the two lesser skeleton Demons, lingering by the door to the flat. He was prepared to raise his gun and aim it at them if they surged forward, but they did not move, as if they awaited instructions from a new commander.

"I need more guns," he told them.

6: Tortures

While the two creatures were off on their errand to the Demonic station where Iblis Al-Qadim had consulted with the Baphomet, Michael and Roger wrapped the dead governor's surprisingly light scarecrow of a corpse—and that of his parasite—in several blankets for the departed underlings to take away with them, later.

They returned promptly. Though Demons generally preferred swords and other such primitive weapons to firearms, they used them occasionally or stocked them for the use of vacationing Angels anxious to do a little hunting of the Damned. Thus, the two Demons came back with their bony arms laden. There was a knapsack heavy with various types of ammunition. Michael had asked for an M16 with a grenade launcher beneath the barrel, but he had to make do without the grenade launcher. Before the silent pair had left, Michael had asked Roger, "What kind of guns are you familiar with, if any?"

"Why?" Davina had spoken up.

"I can go alone," Michael said, his eyes remaining on Roger. "But I thought you might want to come with me."

"You're an Angel," Davina said. "They can't do much to you. But Roger is Damned. If they catch him, they could lock him into one horrible torture for *centuries*."

Ignoring her comment, Roger replied evenly, "I was a soldier … killed in what I'm told you people now call the first World War."

Michael smiled. It was the first time Roger had seen the expression on him. "I was in the Gulf War."

"The what war?"

Michael snorted. "I'll tell you another time. So … a simpler gun for you, huh? I recommend a shotgun; very good for close combat."

Combat, Roger's mind echoed, with a quaver.

"Roger, please, please don't." Davina held onto his arm. "They've already taken my child … I can't lose you, too!"

"He's my child," Michael spoke up. "Mark is my son—just so you know."

Davina flashed her eyes onto him, blacker than twin gun muzzles. "He's as much our son as he ever was yours."

"Listen…" Michael began.

"I would prefer a .303 Enfield," Roger broke in. "But a shotgun would do."

Michael again showed Roger that little smile, then turned to instruct the Demons.

And so, it was a 12-gauge pump-action Ithaca that the Angel took from one of the Demons and passed into Roger's hands. He was seated as he examined it, but his severed leg had already almost fully reconstituted. "I suppose I expected a break-open style shotgun."

Michael reclaimed the weapon, showed him how to work the slide, and fed a series of shells into it before he handed it back. "You just stick close to me. I'm hoping they'll be too afraid to oppose an Angel.

But … they may have the attitude of that octopus thing, and think this isn't for us to interfere in. And then they may try to stop us."

Roger rose from the chair, and looked past the Angel at Davina. "I can't bear the thought of it either, my love. Our dear boy inside that thing. In their hands…"

Her lower lip was trembling badly and she turned to face the wall, arms tightly crossed as if to hug and console herself, but said nothing more. And a moment later, she gave a little nod.

"Hey. Can you really do this?" Michael asked.

"Yes," Roger said without hesitation, sounding a bit insulted, but Michael persisted.

"It's been a long time for you."

Roger held his stare, took in a long breath. "There was a German soldier … maybe ten years younger than I. We found ourselves face-to-face. His Mauser was covered in mud; had jammed. My Lee-Endfield had run empty. But I still had my bayonet, and he did not. As he tried to clear the round, I sort of thrust the rifle at him without aiming. The bayonet went into him directly under his right eye. It forced the eye out, onto his cheek. The blade slid out and he sort of turned away, stunned … and began shrieking. My German isn't very good, but I know the word 'Mutter.' He just staggered off holding his face, crying that word again and again like a child. Which he was, really."

"And what did you do?"

"I walked after him … and I stabbed him in the back. He fell, and I stabbed him again. And the crying stopped."

"Yes," Michael said, nodding. "But—did you kill him then because you hated him, or because you pitied him?"

Roger flicked his eyes away, and to Michael that was enough to answer the question. The story, meant to illustrate his toughness, had betrayed his compassion—simply in the fact that he recalled it so vividly at all. But he muttered, "These things aren't men. They don't even have mothers." He thought of the way his Davina had been used. "Not really…"

"Yeah. But they have a Father," Michael said. "And I could care less." He hadn't taken his eyes off the other man. "So—are you ready to get our boy back?"

The British man met the American's stare again, startled by his phrasing.

"Let's go," Roger said.

๑๖

As they started off down the street, Roger and Michael glanced back to see the two skeleton beings carrying out the mummy-wrapped package of their fallen leader, to load upon the animal-drawn metal carriage. Roger felt relief that the things were not remaining with Davina, while Michael felt a funny twinge of regret. Had the Demon helped him out of sympathy, or merely out of spite for his Father? Either way, the Demon had been judged to be too human-like ... and in doing so, his Creator had only proved Himself right, by pushing the creature into a human-like act of vengeance.

It wouldn't have been unusual for an Angel to be seen walking along the streets of a city in Hell carrying an assault rifle in his hands, but to see a Damned man striding beside him (with a faint limp) openly carrying a pump-action shotgun would be quite the shock—had there been anyone on the street to witness it. The citizens were still keeping themselves out of sight, though the Skull's crew seemed to have taken aboard all the prisoners they intended to. But Roger glimpsed a figure ducking behind the edge of a second floor window, and realized he was at least being peeked at around makeshift window shades, and through cracked doors, by his bewildered neighbors—perhaps alarmed by his actions, perhaps stirred.

"That brand on your forehead," Michael said. "It stands for your sin..."

"Atheist," Roger stated.

"And your wife ... uh, girlfriend. H?"

"H is for Hinduism."

"Does Mark have one on his head?"

"Yes. A U—unbaptized."

Michael made a hissing sound. "His mother—my first wife—wouldn't allow it. I could shoot myself for listening to her. Not that it would kill me, now. It's my fault ... my fault, for giving in."

"As you said, we don't make the bloody laws. You mustn't blame her. Or yourself. It isn't his father's fault ... it's his Father's fault." Roger nodded his head upward, as if at something hovering unseen above them. "Anyway ... if it's anyone's fault that Mark is inside that place now, it's mine. I didn't protect him well enough. I shouldn't have let him go into that alley ahead of me. I should have said we'd stay in the alley for an hour or so, until the Skull's crew had finished rounding up their prey."

Michael looked over at him as they strode side-by-side. "Now it's you who's talking shit ... because it seems to me, you and your lady back there have been doing a very good job of looking after him. Thank you."

"Guilt," Roger mused aloud. "Yours. Mine. His. He torments himself, you know, over what happened to you and your second wife. The fire he caused."

"He torments himself," Michael repeated, making a wincing expression. "I've got to reassure him. I have to show him that Dawn and I still love him—could never blame him for that." After several more steps he said, "When we first got to Heaven, I guess my wife and I were ... humbled. We tried to accept our fates, our Father's judgment ... to trust in the system. We settled in a town called Nepenthe. I chose it because it has features that reminded me of places Mark loved. A park, with trees. A mall. Huh. Heaven's full of shopping malls. Anyway ... it wasn't any solace. It only made my loss sharper, until I couldn't take it any longer. How can they call it a Paradise, when I'm grieving every day because my only child is trapped in Hell? How can I call that place my home for eternity, without him?"

They turned a street corner, and found themselves at the end of that long, wide avenue as open as a plaza. At its other end, the huge bone orb rested in a little crater of shattered flagstones. In dropping, it had even caved in the front of a brick building facing onto the plaza. Not only had Iblis Al-Qadim prompted it to land, somehow, but that hinged skull-plate had lowered open, a hatchway. Steam was billowing out from inside. How long before those aboard the craft were able to override the mental command the governor had given, or repair

117

whatever damage he might have caused? Might the craft be borne aloft again at any minute?

Michael tossed Roger a glance again, and the British soldier looked blanched, the shotgun drooping heavily in his hands. But the man's wounded stride didn't waver, and Michael felt an odd affection suffuse him. Who was he to question his resolve, or abilities? He had obviously killed more men than himself in battle, in a war more earth-shaking than his own, which Michael was a bit crestfallen to know Roger wasn't even familiar with. The affection Michael experienced was like that he had felt for other warriors, walking beside him many years ago. Like the affection he might have felt for a brother.

Together, they reached the lip of the hatchway ... together, walked up through the steam's obscuring clouds.

7: Unholy War

Just inside the shell of the Skull, the two humans encountered three Kilcrops bent over a series of valves, one of which was leaking steam around its edges and another dripping a greenish fluid. At the sight of the men with guns, they froze with their hands on the great valves' wheels. One of them held a large wrench, but didn't raise it as a weapon. Despite their surprise and paralysis, the naked creatures—bony and sunken-faced as starving children—suppressed cackles and giggled behind their fixed grins.

The men moved past them carefully, and left them behind in the steam. Michael said, "Maybe I should've killed them so they wouldn't raise an alarm. But the gunshots would've done the same..."

Their path branched off into different directions immediately. Narrow corridors, some with walls of metal but one with walls apparently carved or grown from the same bone substance as the craft's exterior. A metal ramp rose toward a higher level over there, but over here was a flight of metal steps, and then they saw a metal spiral staircase in the distance, in the light from a caged gas jet in the wall. Roger was about to ask which way they should choose, when they both heard an echoing, haunting cry. It was a woman screaming, apparently off down that bone corridor. They headed that way.

They moved through a mist not so much of steam, now, as incense. Whereas in the more mechanical sections of the Skull bluish gas jets burned along the walls, in the long bone corridor there were organic-looking sockets or hollows in the wall in which burned candles or the incense they smelled. As they proceeded, they heard more reverberating banshee shrieks, from both men and women. So far, none of the cries sounded like the voices of children.

Toward the end of the bone corridor there were two rounded doorways on either side, facing each other. Michael and Roger exchanged looks, then Michael swung into the threshold on the right while Roger did the same on the left.

Michael saw three white Xs floating in the murk of a smallish room. They were the spread-eagled nude bodies of three women, their wrists and ankles shackled to a trio of metal hoops hanging on chains, the ends of which were lost in the darkness of a surprisingly high shaft. When they saw the Angel, they whimpered and sobbed, no doubt thinking he was here to enjoy their torments along with their Demon captors. Their weeping alerted a grotesque tick-like creature, the likes of which Michael hadn't seen before, bent over a table spread with gleaming metal instruments that it didn't even seem to require, since its various pairs of arms looked sufficient for any torture it might devise. The entity whipped around, and just from the way it raised its bladed forearms—and from the way its nearly translucent belly was a bottle filled with blood, and the way the three women dribbled blood from various puncture wounds on their bellies and thighs—Michael decided to pull his trigger, and the M16 was set to fully automatic, and the stream of lead caused hunks of chitin to spring into the air like shattered pottery. He drove the tick against its counter of tools, which spilled over it as it fell dead ... blood gushing from the broken bottle.

Understanding now that the Angel was not here to partake of their punishments, the women began babbling at him, pleading to be unshackled. "Just shoot through my wrists and ankles," one woman begged, wild-eyed, "I'll heal ... it's okay ... shoot me down, please!"

Her request stunned him, until he was shaken by the sound of a shotgun blast, and he spun toward the doorway. "I'm sorry—forgive me," he mumbled too softly for the women to hear.

In the opposite room, Roger had found an elderly man lashed down onto an iron bedframe. The man's decapitated head had been placed on a shelf several feet away, but rubber hoses and segmented metal cables had been inserted into the stump of its neck, connecting the head to the trunk. The head's eyes streamed tears as the old man watched two ticks that had bent over him, one with a tubular proboscis plunged into his thigh and the other snipping off his fingers with one of its pincer limbs.

Despite the horrors he had been witness to—and himself suffered—over the decades, Roger was dazed by what he saw. It was Michael's gunfire that shook him out of his stupor, and even as the two ticks jerked upright at the sound, Roger fired at the one on the right with his shotgun. The weapon jolted in his arms, but the tick jolted even more—exploded across the wall behind it like a water balloon full of gore. The one on the left flew at him, arms spinning, so fast that he barely had time to swing the gun in its direction. He stabbed the thing with the barrel as if there were a bayonet at its end. The blow was only enough to make the Demon stagger back a little, but it gave Roger time to pull the trigger again, and the point-blank eruption of fire and OO buckshot obliterated the top half of the monster.

Roger whirled with the shotgun leveled as he heard a third presence behind him, but he was able to restrain himself from shooting when he saw that it was Michael. "Come on," Michael, the seemingly older of the two men, directed him, and they stepped back into the corridor and emerged from its end. Roger heard the old man's severed head calling after him.

The next hallway was wider, running transverse to the one they had just exited, and they entered at its midpoint. From its high ceiling, metal cocoons hung in two rows of a half dozen. They were like iron maidens, and both men wondered if there might even be spikes inside them, or if these were merely holding vessels until their human contents could be properly tortured later on. The cocoons dangled and swayed like a strange crop of fruit, emitting a chorus of sobs and pleas. The two men passed under them, toward another doorway at the right hand end of the hallway.

The left hand end of the hall was nothing but a mass of twisting steam, and the men pivoted around when they heard a clatter of armored feet and the chitter of inhuman voices within its depths. Then, they were bursting out of it: three smaller ticks, not yet gorged and slowed with feasted blood, so swift that even though both men fired upon them simultaneously, the sound of their combined thunder deafening, they only just barely cut the things down before they reached them. The last of the creatures skidded to a stop at Roger's feet, causing an array of spent 5.56mm and shotgun shells to scatter. Now the air was misted with gun smoke in addition to the steam and incense.

"Who are you?" a voice called from one of the cocoons above. "Are you rebels?"

"We're looking for a boy!" Roger shouted, not sure which of the containers the man's voice issued from. "Eight years old…"

"Not that way!" the voice yelled down, meaning the right hand path they had chosen. "The other way—into the steam. There were children in these things just like twenty minutes ago, but the bugs switched our places."

"Why?"

The unseen speaker seemed to hesitate. "It's their turn."

Michael snatched Roger by the arm. "Thanks!" he called.

"Just kill these fuckers!" the disembodied voice replied.

They plunged into the hot steam, apparently originating from a ruptured pipe above them, and could see nothing for several moments except for three evenly-spaced, orange-glowing smudges along their right side. When Michael got close to them, he discerned three tanks set into the wall, containing a luminous orange fluid in which three human faces—flayed from their skulls—were suspended on wires. Though the staring eyes did not follow him and the slack mouths had no muscles to move them, he knew there was a living consciousness in each of the masks. The bodies they had been sliced from had been incinerated, so when these scraps of flesh were eventually freed they would regenerate into their complete human forms again.

Regarding the faces as they regarded him, Michael was momentarily transfixed with horror, and not for the first time felt a vague kind of shame for being an Angel. But mostly, he was just grateful that he didn't recognize any of the faces; none was that of a child. Tearing himself away, he left the apparitions behind him.

Roger was the first to emerge from the steam, and as he did so heard a *whoosh*, a curved sword missing his neck by two inches as it cleaved the air. It was a blue-skinned Apsara, her eyes and tusks gleaming. She reminded him uncomfortably of his Davina: the sensual curves of her nearly naked body, her general facial features, the large eyes and heavy brows and thick black hair, the Demon's swimming in the air as if each strand had its own independent life. He hesitated for only an instant, but that was too long for Michael, who let loose with his M16. With just a grunt, as if punched in the stomach, the female Demon was slammed backwards into a wall. She left smears of red on it as she sank, her animated hair falling in lifeless curtains to obscure her face.

Michael spotted another Apsara hovering in a doorway, a spear in her fists, but either his gun or the fact that he was an Angel caused her to duck back out of sight before he could swing the rifle her way. Roger approached the open threshold and peeked in, wary of the succubus, but he obviously didn't see anything encouraging, since he waved for Michael to continue onwards.

The hallway dead-ended in a high curved wall. The two men realized they had reached the opposite side of the Skull, but a spiral staircase with steps that clanged under their boots took them up to a metal catwalk. They crossed this, back into the fog of escaping steam, feeling their way along by holding onto the catwalk's railing.

Behind them, they heard more feet clanging on the steps of the spiral staircase. These new feet struck the metal with a lighter but sharper sound. In only seconds, there were many of these ringing footfalls … accompanied by the rustling sound of multiple bodies scraping against each other, and a chorus of whispering, chittering voices…

Michael and Roger began to run, guessing what sort of creature was swarming behind them … but as they cleared the churning cloud of steam, they saw more of the tick Demons ahead of them, a small horde, razored arms spread into waiting embraces.

Michael skidded to a halt and spun around, opened fire at their pursuers as the first of them sprang out of the wall of steam. "Get through them!" he roared at Roger. "Clear our way!"

Back-to-back, the two men fired their weapons repeatedly, Roger bucking with the explosions from the shotgun, Michael emptying a magazine of his clattering assault rifle and deftly slapping in another.

Two of the ticks went down under one of Roger's blasts, the OO buckshot having dispersed into a spray of heavy slugs. Another discharge sent one of the arachnid beings up over the railing, but a barb on its foot caught in the mesh of the handrail and it swung from the catwalk lifelessly, blood raining like candy from a burst pinata. Three last ticks leapt over the bodies of their fallen brothers. Roger fired, hit one of them, and then the other two were only a few feet away. A whipping claw struck the end of his barrel just as Roger jerked the trigger again, causing the shot to go wild. He followed through with the momentum of the Demon's blow, however, and with all his force swung the wooden stock of the weapon into the thing's plated little face. The cracking impact sent it reeling, its back striking the handrail.

Roger jumped back as the remaining tick took a swipe at him. He blocked a second blow with his shotgun. But the entity had multiple pairs of arms, and Roger felt one of them get under the shotgun, stab into his body and rip upwards. He grunted, fell onto his back on the hard catwalk surface.

Looking down at himself, he saw blood welling out of him … saw that he had been rent deeply.

He tried to angle the shotgun to point up at the thing, but it kicked the gun and its clawed foot not only sent the weapon out of his hands but nearly severed one of his fingers. It hovered above him, its arms spinning and clacking as if in a mad sign language, wordlessly speaking in tongues. The sight of his pumping gore seemed to tantalize the creature. It sank down over him, appeared to stare into his eyes a moment, and dropped its head as if to fellate him. Roger felt another deep stab, as the tick shot its proboscis into his inner thigh … heard a terrible gurgling sound as his blood was sucked up into the vampire.

Wheezing in pain but steeling himself, Roger slipped his injured hand into his shirt. And deeper than that. It burrowed under the lip of his wound.

Either Roger's motions or another metallic rattle from the Angel's M16 broke its lustful spell, but the arachnid jumped to its feet, the bloody proboscis withdrawing. It saw Roger rummaging inside his soaked shirt and descended upon him, lashing out with a mantis arm. Roger rolled to one side and the claw banged against the catwalk. The creature lifted its head and chattered, its mouthparts twitching like bloodied fingers. Roger had rolled onto his back again, and he was tearing something out of his chest. It looked like an organ, red and drooling strings of blood. He had known just where to find it. The hunk of metal had been a nagging weight inside him, an irritation and a burden—a pain now extracted, liberated, and returned to those who had inflicted it upon him.

Screaming in a mix of agony and war cry, Roger tugged back the little .25's slide, aimed it up at the tick and squeezed off round after round. The semi-automatic's immersion in his body had not dampened its gunpowder. The bullets were small, but they drove the tick back, shrieking. He emptied the pistol. The very last slug sent his attacker flipping backwards over the railing. He heard it crash far below.

Michael had emptied his fresh magazine and popped in yet another, mostly firing blindly into the steam. But soon, he saw only a heap of demolished bodies at the edge of the mist, one or two badly wounded Demons screeching, the ingested blood of their victims streaming through the holes in the catwalk's floor.

He turned back toward Roger to see that he had gone down. A last tick was moving in on him, its cracked face oozing its own greenish ichor. He saw that Roger was without the shotgun, gripped only a toy-sized pistol that had apparently run dry. Michael sprayed the wounded Demon before it could get to him, white fire flashing from the M16's muzzle, the impact launching the vampire off its feet. He then rushed forward to Roger's side. When he took his arm to help him up, the

British soldier let out a terrible groan, and that was when Michael saw how the front of his shirt was saturated with blood.

"Can you make it?" he asked numbly.

"Listen!" Roger hissed, clinging to the man's arm so as to hold himself up, staining the Angel's robes.

From beyond the end of the catwalk, they both heard crying voices. Watery with echoes, distant and ghostly ... but distinctly, the cries of children.

"Come on," Michael said, slinging his M16 over his own shoulder and retrieving the shotgun from the floor. He put one arm around the Damned soul. Roger kept his left hand pressed to his chest as if to hold his split body together. Every step made him wince, every other step a stagger that almost toppled both of them. They made it through the bodies of the Demons Roger had killed, loped like a wounded four-legged animal until they could make out a polished door of bone set almost seamlessly into a wall of bone, at the end of the bridge-like catwalk.

8: Avenging Angel

The wall, when they reached it, was made up of plates separated by rippled sutures, like the outside of the Skull itself. Roger leaned against it while Michael took hold of the door's latch. It was not hinged, but slid along grooved track into the wall.

In the room beyond, Michael saw three Kilcrops hunkering near the foot of a row of coffin-like containers—metal, rusted and riveted— bolted horizontally into the floor. There was a hatch in each one, the hatches currently hanging open, where the faces of those inside the sarcophagi would be. It was from these open hatches that the wailing voices came. One child was sobbing hysterically, another crying for her mother, but Michael couldn't tell if any of the cries belonged to his son.

There was a hose with a nozzle at its end hanging from the ceiling, over the coffins, and its base end was connected to a huge glass orb in the center of the room. This orb was filled with a yellowish solution, and inside the miniature yellow sea writhed a colony of white worm-like eels or eel-like worms. Their threaded bodies almost formed one immense living ball inside the globe. Following the line of the suspended black rubber hose again, Michael could guess its use: for delivering the contents of the orb into the dozen metal coffins. They were water-tight, then. And he had no doubt the worms were ravenous.

Though the snickering Kilcrops didn't try to attack or flee, having heard the approaching gunfire and thus waiting to see what the two men intended, Michael treated one of them to the contents of a 12-gauge shell. When the gaunt body had stopped flopping and rolling across the floor, the other two began to giggle more wildly in nervousness, one clutching at the arms of the other. Michael jerked his gun barrel at their grinning faces. "If you don't want to end up like your friend, open those things up *now*."

One Kilcrop dashed to the far end of the row, the other to the nearer. They reached to a clasp system on each, and the lids of the sarcophagi began to swing open. An adolescent black girl crawled out of one like a spider, fell to the floor. Roger managed to help her up while still pressing his chest. She started to flee from the room in a panic, her eyes crazed, but Roger held her at the elbow and croaked, "Stay with us, dear ... we'll all go out together."

Michael almost wanted to push past the emerging children to get a better look as the pair of Kilcrops converged at the center to unlock the last two chrysalises.

From one of these, Mark rose into view. His eyes flicked from the robed Angel quickly to Roger. Michael saw recognition dawn on Mark's face then, and it was a piercing realization—that his son had recognized his surrogate parent, but not him. The boy hadn't expected to see his father come to this place to rescue him. When Mark spotted Roger, a grin opened in his tear-crusted face. "Dad!" he cried, clambering down from his cocoon. He darted to the man but came short of hugging him, seeing how badly he was injured. Roger smiled, and released the traumatized girl to slip one arm around Mark's shoulders.

Tears flooded Roger's eyes. Tears of love, and relief ... and pain. Twice now, the boy had called him "Dad." But he felt that when Mark finally turned around and saw who it was that had accompanied him here, the child he thought of as his son would never call him by that name again.

Only when his arms were slipped around Roger did Mark glance at Michael a second time—Michael, who stood momentarily wordless, helpless as if paralyzed. At last, the boy understood who he was seeing. "Dad?" he said. There was a leeriness in his tone, mixed with disbelief and delight. This obvious confusion of feeling pierced Michael again. He could tell the boy was a little frightened of him. The gun in his hands, the blood splashed across his robes. He was still afraid his father was angry at him for causing his and Dawn's deaths.

"Mark," Michael said, his own eyes wet and agleam. "I came for you."

"Daddy," his son whimpered, face crumpling, regressing into an even younger child.

"Go to him," Roger whispered, and kissed the top of the boy's head before releasing him.

Mark took a timid step forward, and Michael closed the distance—swept him into the curve of his free arm, clenched him against his body.

"I thought you hated me," Mark sobbed.

"I love you," Michael told his son. "I love you, forever…"

Blinking at his tears, Roger glanced around at the faces of the eleven other children, ranging in age and race but all of them ragged, all of them waiting for the adults to give them some sort of guidance. "Children," he told them, "you stay with us."

"Come on—we're out of here," Michael said, moving back toward the doorway, his arm still around his son's shoulders. "Roger … can you walk?"

"We'll help him," said another boy, and he and the shivering black girl took Roger under both his arms.

Out through the bone wall, across the catwalk littered with cracked and draining tick bodies, one or two with a limb still twitching. Down the spiral staircase. Michael had the shotgun in his hand, at the ready should one of the bodies spring up alive, but none did. He had passed his Beretta to Roger, easier to manage in his condition. Through the steam-filled corridor into which the three flayed faces stared, the children held hands in a chain. Michael saw a Kilcrops dart across the end of the corridor, but didn't fire at it.

Under the dozen hanging cocoons. "Is that you?" the familiar voice called down. "Did you find him? Hello? How about us, huh? Please? Hello? *Hey!*"

"Can't save them all. Not every soul in Hell," Roger whispered into the ear of the tall black girl. "Can we, my love?"

Down the bone corridor. Suddenly, candles and burning incense sticks spilled out of several of the organic-looking sockets in the walls and two ticks emerged, dropped into the hallway, charged with flailing jagged limbs ... but before they could pick up speed Michael had let go of Mark and leveled the shotgun, and Roger had pushed the black girl behind him and pointed the Beretta. The children flinched and covered their ears, but it only took a few short bursts from both men to bring the ticks down, and a few moments later the party was advancing again.

The entrance to the Skull was near. Here was where corridors, ramps, doorways branched into numerous directions. And as the party moved toward the main entrance, scores of ticks flowed out of these hallways and thresholds as if coordinated by a silent command, scampered down the clanging metal ramp, descended a ladder fixed to the wall. In just seconds, the humans' path was blocked by what looked like a hundred of the greenish creatures. They gave off an insidiously low chittering, but it quickly rose into a metallic buzz-saw sound. Again, the children clamped their hands over their ears. "Dad!" Mark cried.

Michael looked back the way they had come. He saw the light going out in the bone corridor as more and more candles were knocked out of their hollows by ticks emerging through the walls. Soon, the corridor would go completely black, masking the advancing rear army.

"Here," Michael said, passing Roger the shotgun. He saw Roger stand as straight and steady as he could so as to accept the weapon. In turn, Roger handed the Beretta to the black girl, the oldest child.

Her eyes were still wide and half-frenzied, but she accepted the pistol. Michael took his M16 off his shoulder and leveled it grimly. "Roger ... will they dare to stop me?"

"These things? I think they will. They may not hurt you, but they'll disarm you. Incapacitate you, until they recapture the rest of us. Until they can repair this machine. Then they'll let you go ... and they'll fly this thing so far away you might never find it again."

"I'm not going to let that happen. They'll *have* to hurt me." Michael took a step forward. He saw the ticks at the fore of the group shift back ever-so-slightly, either the gun in his hands or the look in his eyes filling even their robotic minds with fear. He took a second step.

From the left, then the right, two Apsaras appeared. A third, and a fourth. One held a curved sword, and the others carried metal spears. Their movements as eerily graceful as stylized dance steps, their forms beautiful in a nightmarish way, they positioned themselves at the front of the mass of ticks. At first Michael expected them to lead the battalion forward ... but they extended their spears at waist-level and turned their nearly nude bodies slowly, using the weapons to urge back the teeming arachnid warriors. The creatures seemed reluctant, but complied. Michael realized what the human-like Apsaras were doing: parting the ticks, opening a path for him—the Angel.

He glanced back over his shoulder. There was just enough guttering candle glow left in the bone corridor for him to see another of the blue-fleshed succubi standing with her arms spread, a sword in each fist, her hair lapping the air. Ticks fidgeted restlessly behind her, but none tried to push around the fearsome Demon.

Facing forwards again, Michael slowly advanced. The children followed meekly, Mark holding onto his father's robe. His chest wound healing even as he staggered along, Roger kept the shotgun ready ... but none of the divided assembly of ticks surged around the Apsaras and the weapons they had used as if to create invisible barriers. Michael entered this living corridor first, expecting it to close around him at any second. It didn't. He glared defiantly into the ranked, expressionless faces as he passed them.

He turned and guarded the entrance to the Skull as the children cleared the gauntlet, ducked out the doorway and sprinted down the ramp into the city of Apollyon. Its burning blue air had never seemed inviting to them until this moment. He saw them scatter in all directions. The black girl had his Beretta still in her fist but he didn't call her back. A rebel in the making, maybe. She could not grow up, but she could mature, harden ... like a stone sharpened into a spear head.

At last, only Michael, Roger and Mark stood in the doorway, looking back into the Skull—meeting the gaze of all those glittering black eyes, and the more human eyes of the Apsaras.

"I'm immortal," Michael said to the Demons, like troops gathered for his inspection. "You're not. If you ever touch my boy again ... if you ever go near him, or try to take revenge on this man," he nodded toward Roger, "I'll spend eternity killing every last one of you mother fuckers."

And with that, the two bloody men and the boy between them stepped wearily out of the Skull.

9: The Family

The child slept on the little sofa they had purchased from a shop in the city, where the Damned manufactured crude furniture, and he was covered under a quilt Davina herself had sewn together from scraps of cloth she'd collected. She sat on the very edge of the sofa, lightly caressing his forehead, her brown fingers trailing over the raised U branded there ... a wound his body hadn't been allowed to regenerate. She had told him it stood for "Unbelievably Cute."

Roger sat in a chair opposite, shirtless. The groove in his chest was raw pink with puckered edges, but no longer an entrance to his interior. He watched his lover's face, the way her uncanny huge eyes glistened. Still weak, he used the chair's arms to push himself to his feet, crossed to her, took her head against his chest and stroked her thick hair. He heard her sniffle, felt her kiss his healing scar.

"He won't really stay, will he? He says that now ... but don't you think he'll change his mind?"

Roger knew the man better than she. "No, my love. I think he means it."

"But he won't be allowed to, will he? Aren't they told how much time they can spend here? Isn't there a limit?"

"I don't believe there is. I think he can stay here as long as he wants. Forever, if he likes."

"But his wife won't want to, I'm sure."

"Yes, that's the only thing. She isn't the boy's natural mother." He regretted the words the moment he said them. Davina's head lifted, as he knew it would.

"Neither am I, his natural mother. But she may love him enough to remain here, too ... do you think?"

"I don't know her, my dear. We haven't met her. We can't say."

"I hope she doesn't love him as I do." Davina looked down at the boy again.

"That isn't a good thing to wish, Davina."

"But do you want to let him go? After all you went through to get him back?"

"I went through that to take him from the hands of Demons, who meant to torture him. But these are the hands of his father ... who loves him enough to leave behind the Paradise most of us down here will yearn for, forever."

"I don't begrudge him," Davina moaned. "How can I hate the man my son loves? And I thank him, for what he did. But I only wish ... I only wish he would go home. Just come back to visit from time to time."

"I know, love." His hand slid down and inside her veil of hair to stroke her wet cheek. "I feel the same way. We just have to wait, and see..."

∂♌

After his experience inside the Skull, Michael and Dawn would not enter into the administrative building of the Demons, with its Art Deco winged baboons flanking the front steps, until a carriage arrived in Apollyon bearing an Angel accompanied by two Celestials—an androgynous heavenly race, almost ghost-like in their silence and with their empty stares, but wearing all-too-solid swords in scabbards.

The Angel had been a priest in life, so in the afterlife had been given a position of some authority. When he and his guardians stepped down from the carriage and the couple moved forward to meet him, he pushed back the hood of his white robe and beamed a smile, extending his hand. Michael felt a kind of disgust for him already. Weren't the Demons better, in a way? They didn't hide their hatred for the Damned behind bright grins. Well, except for the Kilcrops...

"So nice to meet you," the man said, next pressing Dawn's hand between his two. "I'm Reverend Worthy." In life he had been called Father Worthy, but in Heaven there could only be the one great Father. "Shall we go inside to talk?"

Finally, Michael consented to enter the building that he hadn't been in since Iblis Al-Qadim had taken him here to consult the goat-headed Baphomet. He saw that entity watching them from across the foyer as Worthy led them to a doorway. A corridor beyond, but no Demons waiting to ambush him, no ticks springing from holes in the walls to slash at him. They entered a small office, where Worthy seated himself behind a black marble desk. The Palladinos sat in front of it.

"So..." began Reverend Worthy.

"So," cut in Michael, "my son ... Mark. I'd like to take him back to Heaven with me."

The former priest's smile rippled at the corners. "Ohhh, Mr. Palladino ... I'm so sorry, but that is utterly out of the question. It's impossible—just not allowed."

"Maybe because no one has persisted before. Maybe the Creator could make an exception."

"You must know ... *many* people have persisted before. But the Creator can make no exceptions; it would be against the very reason that Hades, and more importantly Heaven, exist. But I am truly so sorry." He spread his hands, which Michael had found too soft and puffy.

He saw Dawn look over at him, as he lowered his head and nodded.

"I understand. I didn't expect you to say yes ... but I had to ask, anyway." He didn't add that he had promised his wife he would try. That it had been her idea to ask. But he was actually relieved, in a way, by the Angel's words. How could he think to take his son into Paradise, away from the two people in Hades who adored him? Could all the replica Disney theme parks and replica McDonald's burger stops and glittering shopping malls in Heaven replace those two Damned souls?

"Well," Reverend Worthy said, "I'm told you were considering remaining in Hades, then."

"Yes." Michael raised his head, but was afraid to meet the eyes of the woman seated beside him. "It's my choice to do so."

"It's ... something you are *allowed* to do. But do you know how very awful it is in this place?"

"I believe that's been well illustrated for me," Michael said ominously.

"Yes ... of course. Well, as I say, it is permissible. An uncommon request, but not without precedent. And you ... Mrs. Palladino?"

At last, Michael summoned the strength to look over at her, but now it was she who lowered her head and murmured, "I won't be staying."

The former priest nodded slowly, looking suitably pained by their dilemma. "I see. But you know you can visit your husband here any time you wish ... and he can visit you, without his son, as often as he likes."

"Yes," she said quietly.

"Will you be returning with me, then, to the palace?" It was the palace where the governor Iblis Al-Qadim had resided, also housing the portal through which these Angels had entered into Hades.

"Yes, Reverend. I just ... I just need to talk to my husband alone, first."

"Of course, of course." Worthy floated to his feet, out from behind the desk. Michael hated the perfumed proximity of him. "I will leave you two alone to talk for as long as you wish. In the meantime I will be speaking with the Baphomet, Mr. Palladino ... to instruct him that you are not to be interfered with."

"And my son. And those two Damned."

"I cannot guarantee that any Damned soul will not be punished … all I can guarantee is that you will not be opposed, if you step in to protect them."

"However you want to phrase it," Michael said darkly.

"A devoted parent, to be sure. You are to be admired."

"If only the Father of all children were as devoted … eh, Reverend?"

"Michael," Dawn whispered.

The former priest's smile faltered more than before. "I know your pain makes you … unaware of what you say, Mr. Palladino."

"I am only too aware of what I say. And maybe now you think Hades is the place I should have been sent to all along."

"I would not think that. The Father, in His great love for you, judged that you should be in Paradise."

"I'm sorry to disappoint Him, in not wanting to be there any longer. Then again … He's been a disappointment to me, too."

For several moments Reverend Worthy looked horrified, as if afraid to be consumed along with Michael should a lightning bolt crash through the ceiling just then. But there was no sign at all that the Creator was even in attendance, and now it was Michael who reached to shake hands, squeezing the other man's filmy silk handkerchief of a hand in his own firm grip.

"Goodbye, Reverend."

❧

There was a knock on their door, and Roger went to it with his shotgun ready. He let it droop when Michael crossed the threshold.

"You won't need that anymore," he said, gesturing at the weapon.

"I'll still feel better to keep it." Roger tilted his head toward the sofa behind him. "He's sleeping."

Michael stepped close to the sofa to gaze down at Mark's gentle profile, his mouth open against a pillow. The room's stinging blue light made it appear as though the boy had fallen asleep in the glow from a TV, as when he had been alive. "Let him sleep," he whispered, then he looked up at Davina—who had risen to her bare feet. "Thank you, for taking care of my boy."

She nodded, but crossed her arms tightly.

"Back at the Demon outpost, there, I acquired a lot of the money you people use here, when I told them I'd be staying in Hades."

"I don't want your money," Davina told him.

"I didn't mean it the way you think, Davina. What I was going to say is, I paid your next door neighbors, over here, to move to another apartment ... so I can have that one." He turned to study one of the room's walls, rubbing his goateed chin. "We could put a door right there, don't you think? So Mark can go through it, any time he wants?" He shifted his eyes to meet Roger's. "So that one house is no more his house than the other?"

Roger's eyes began to fill. "Thank you," he managed.

"Well, I'm not as unselfish as all that," the Angel replied. "It's for this guy." He smiled down at his child, but a half-stifled sob made him look up at Davina. She came to him, put her arms around him. He laughed uncomfortably, patted her back, "Hey, you can share my son, but you can't share me ... sorry." He flicked his chin at Roger. "This guy is pretty bad-ass ... I wouldn't want to mess with him."

"What about your wife?" Davina asked huskily.

He slid out of her embrace, his smile strained. "No," was all he could answer.

🙙🙚

Another knocking at the door, and this time Michael rose to answer it. Despite what he'd told Roger earlier, he brought his M16 with him. Mark was awake now, and watched his father with concern.

Michael unlocked and opened the door to see Dawn standing in the hallway beyond, escorted by the two eerie Celestials.

"Honey..." Michael said.

He saw that her eyes were red, but she smiled and told him, "I'm staying, too."

Michael pulled her through the door, into his arms. The ethereal

Celestials looked on without feeling. After they had held each other for a good minute, Dawn peered over her husband's shoulder and said, "Hi, baby…"

Mark approached them uneasily, but Dawn gathered him into their embrace.

"I'm sorry, Dawn," he mumbled.

"Shhh. I love you, baby," she said, her lips moving against the top of his head.

Roger slipped his arm around Davina, should she become troubled by the sight of the reunited family, but she was content and whispered to him, "What about Mark's real mother, when she dies? She was an atheist; she'll be here. But we Damned can't see our loved ones from when we were alive—we're kept impossible distances apart. So do you think Michael can make them bring Mark's mother here, too?"

"I don't know if that's possible," he told her. "But this man is … rather determined. And there's always the apartment of our neighbors, on the other side." He indicated the opposite wall.

"Hm." She pressed her smile into his neck. "I'm so very proud of you … my husband."

"And I, you … my love."

Piece of Mind

– For Minh Nguyen

1: The Underworld Wide Web

Out of the sea of fog rose black metal towers like stove pipes or chimneys, a forest of them. Recesses gaped in the towers at various heights, and suspended in each black socket was a glass globe containing a luminous orange fluid. Floating in the fluid of every globe was a human brain. And attached to each and every brain by threads of nerve/muscle/blood vessel were two eyes that could not blink, that could do nothing but stare. Watch. Observe. Witness, like the unblinking lens of a television camera.

From underneath each brain sprouted a long structure like an immense spinal column. It emerged through a watertight rubber collar at the base of the sphere and extended into the distance like a tightrope, like a telephone line.

And so this was all that remained of Leon Brown besides his brain and eyes. All that was left had been stretched and extruded, broken and torn and then woven together again into one long rope. All his muscle tissue. All his veins and arteries. His bones, pulled apart into thin white fibers. And his nervous system, of course—most importantly. All of his body drawn out like taffy, like a bundle of cables, reaching far across the misty void until the other end was secured to a metal ring in another tower. Just as the cord of a person confined in that tower was secured to a ring somewhere above his globe. He could not lift his eyes to see it. But he could see the great web spread directly in front of him, of which his body was just one of countless crisscrossing strands.

He watched with dread, wanting to weep tears but lacking the mechanism, as a spider-like form picked its way across the neighboring strands. Slowly crept toward his own.

The orange fluid in which his consciousness floated did not preserve his brain tissues, per se. Instead, it prevented them from regenerating, as they normally would. In Hades, no matter what injury was inflicted upon the human body, it would always reconstitute itself. Burned flesh would go smooth again. Bullet and sword wounds would close up. Severed limbs would grow back like the arms of a starfish. It was a miraculous form of healing ... but only so that more tortures could be inflicted afresh. All this was possible—the miraculous healing of flesh, the spinning of flesh into a far-reaching cord of yarn—because it was not real flesh, of course. It was flesh as hallucinated in the mind of the Creator.

The spider-like thing was drawing nearer, so that Leon could see it more clearly. Not that it was the only creature of its kind. They were all over the web, diligently setting new globes into the hollows in the metal totems, or taking old globes away to release the brains at last, so that they could finally regenerate after having been part of the web for months, perhaps, or even years of terrestrial time. But mostly, these creatures seemed to be nibbling at the strands. Plucking and sawing at them, as if to set off a vibration only they could hear. A kind of music; an orchestra of suffering.

Yes, Leon could imagine those multiple pincers and claws and scalpels of the insect-thing when it finally climbed onto his cord. His cord with its raw, exposed nerves, which it would scrape and abrade, slice and gnaw.

The approaching Demon—for such it was—lifted its head to look his way, and orange light from the many glowing spheres flashed back at Leon's naked eyes, flashed back from the mirror that was the Demon's face.

2: Hell on Earth

In a way, Leon Brown was probably better prepared than most of the people who found themselves committed to Hades. In life, he had been a television news journalist.

In Sierra Leone in 1995, he had seen numerous people who had had their hands cut off with machetes by rebels. One woman whom he interviewed said that after a rebel had lopped off her left hand she had begun sobbing prayers to God. The rebel had told her if she pointed to heaven with her remaining hand, God might spare her—then he proceeded to hack at her right hand. But after three failed attempts he had to leave it dangling partially attached. This woman told Leon that she felt her appeal to God had prevented the machete from cutting all the way through her wrist. Leon did not have the heart to tell her that if God had felt like dispensing miracles that day, He should have had the rebel trip and fall on his own machete. Or struck his machete with lightning when he uplifted it. Or prevented men from looking for hands to chop off at all.

Twenty-thousand people—children included—had lost limbs in this way. And as if that hadn't been enough of a demonstration of inhumanity, instead of inspiring compassion the amputees were shunned by their neighbors as "half people." Because they frightened their neighbors. They were a reminder of the dangers that could come so easily amongst them. They were a reminder that all was not right in the world.

Who were really the "half people"? Leon wondered.

He had been to Somalia, where tens of thousands of people had died of starvation. Americans had been sent to capture Mohammed Farah Aideed, who was considered to be the obstacle in the way of aid distribution. Ultimately, some of these Marines had their bodies dragged through the streets of Mogadishu, beefy American carcasses flaunted by jubilant thin-limbed Somalians.

Brown had wondered what their parents felt. When they saw those pictures, did they remember the milky smell of their babies' heads when they kissed them, their first Halloween costumes, crying a sweeter brand of tears as they sent them off for their first day of school?

He had been to Rwanda, seen heaps of machete-hacked bodies (always, always, the machetes). Hundreds of thousands had been exterminated by the *interahamwe* —"those who attack together." Even tall Hutus, mistaken for Tutsis, were slaughtered. When the murderers became too exhausted in their work, they would slash the Achilles tendons of their victims to prevent them from fleeing until they could be "processed" the next day. In addition, thousands of women had been raped, and even those who survived the machetes or sexual mutilation often found themselves HIV-positive later on.

He had covered the issue of violence against women in Senegal, where two out of five women suffered physical abuse, often from husbands who believed the Koran gave them the authority to beat their wives.

Brown had been in Liberia, where thousands upon thousands of people had been killed in their civil war. Practitioners of juju had committed ritual murder and rites of cannibalism. Children had been forced to rape their mothers. He had personally witnessed the killing of a man by a group of Krahn militiamen. One of the killers had been a nine-year-old boy, who had stabbed the fallen man in the back with a kitchen knife. Later, he had seen this boy and others playing soccer with a human skull still dressed in rags of skin and hair.

Leon knew why he had been sent to these places in particular. He had been told on a few occasions that it was good to have the perspective of an African-American at these African locations, but he knew it was not that so much. It was because he was a "good" black man. While reporting these horrors, his civilized demeanor and articulate delivery on camera would reassure American TV viewers that they need not fear or hate their black countrymen. He was like the "good Mexican," perhaps a cook or sidekick or pretty senorita, included in a western movie to offset the "bad Mexican" villains.

Whatever had caused him to be in these places, Leon had always come back horrified, disgusted, sickened in his very soul. If he were indeed to consider these "his" people, it was frustrating to him that they should be killing their own kind. But he was sure the Hutus had not thought of the Tutsis as "their" people, any more than the Crips of Los Angeles County thought of the Bloods as "their" people.

Leon would wonder if the hard lives human beings endured excused them somewhat for their evil acts. Was empathetic behavior a luxury that only affluent and civilized societies could afford? Did achieving a better way of life result in compassion and mercy, or did compassion and mercy lead to that better way of life?

Leon had sometimes forgotten in which country he had seen this or that specific murder scene or howling orphaned child. He and his crew had repeatedly been stopped in their van and threatened by militia with AK-47s and mobs with machetes. But somehow he had lived through it all himself. Somehow he had come back without a scar.

No—it was in the United States, in his apartment in New York City, that Leon Brown had died, at the age of forty-eight. Of a heart attack, of all things. He had been murdered by one of "his" people: himself. As if all of the suffering he had ingested—the smell of blood that stung his nostrils, the taste of rot that got into his very mouth, but mostly it was his eyes, his eyes taking it all in—had accumulated in that one small organ in his chest. A malicious genie's bottle too small and frail to contain it. But he knew of course that his heart had not been the true repository.

It had been his brain, of course, entrusted with that solemn responsibility. His brain was the videotape. The glossy news magazine. The archive, the history book. It was his complex and miraculous brain that proved he was the masterwork of all creation. But it was also his brain and all it had soaked up that told him "his" people—that is, the human race—never should have come into existence at all.

As he lay on his kitchen floor dying, wishing he could phone his married son ... his remarried ex-wife ... he had felt a physical panic, of course. That much was a primitive instinct. But he had also felt a kind of desperate yearning. A yearning for his physical pain to end ... a yearning for all the pains of his life to end. Because his one life seemed to contain the lives of all the people he had seen killed, crowded into one skin. He yearned to escape from those countless ghosts into his own private nothingness. The videotape wiped clean.

The history book burned. In dying, he wanted to forget it all. Forget even himself.

3: *The Ritual*

"Hey, it's Leroy Brown," said Dan, turning just his head because the rest of him was bolted into the wall. "Baddest man in the whole Damned town."

Men, women and even children were affixed to the metal walls of this fluidly twisting and turning labyrinth of corridors, crucified like frogs for dissection. Leon and other Damned souls, dressed in their ragged black uniforms, marched through the high-walled corridors slowly, each carrying a burning stick of incense. The incense filled the maze like steam.

He knew he would be released from this sector of Hades soon; set free to explore its infinite reaches again. Of course, only to be captured by new Demons, with new methods of torture. But maybe the next sector wouldn't be as harsh as this one. There were even communities of the Damned. Cities. He would try to reach one, maybe find work there for a while. He had started out here as a mere set of brain and eyes, forced to watch the taut thread of his essence as it was worried at by the Demons. Then, he had been one of the crucified ones, like Dan. And now, after an unknown passage of time, he was one of the harvesters—those forced to look after the Demons' needs. But once every "day" (if eternity could be broken into such units), he and the other harvesters were required to march with their incense through the maze of the crucified. And torture their own kind.

In neighboring passages, Leon heard people cry out and curse. A child screamed from around the bend of a nearby branch. Leon had hoped never again to have to hear such a sound.

He had come to a stop in front of Dan. He smiled painfully. "I'm sorry, Dan," he said. "That time again."

"Hey," said the man, spread-eagled naked against the black metal, "better you than someone else. And better me than you have to do this to a kid, huh? Aren't we the lucky ones?"

Dan was the soul that Leon, in the mysterious logic of Hades, had been assigned to torture daily. But for the moment, he stood motionless with wisps unfurling from the orange glow at the incense stick's wavering tip. "You'll be free like me soon," Leon assured him.

"Free? Is that what you are, man?" Dan licked cracked lips and grinned again. A movement above them drew his glance upward. The top of the maze was covered over with only a metal mesh, and they saw one of the Demons crawling up there, its claws making a clinking sound. It paused to swivel its flat, circular mirror face down at them. Leon saw himself and Dan reflected in it, like images on a TV screen. Dan hissed, "Hurry up and do me, man, before they get after you."

But the strange being continued along toward some infernal errand or duty. The Demons were black, looked like insects, looked like skeletons, but Leon was of the opinion that they were actually machines. Automatons.

Rumors found their way even among the Damned, and rumor had it that a rebellion had started up in Hades. It had two faces. On the one hand, it was the Damned who were arming themselves with the weapons of Demons and those people who, having gone to Heaven and become Angels, liked to venture into Hades on occasion to hunt the Damned for sport. These Damned rebels were emboldened by the fact that they could not be killed a second time. Recaptured and tortured in yet more horrific ways, with no period of respite, yes, but these brave souls were willing to risk it.

The other face of the rebellion was this: that some of the more human-like species of Demon themselves were going against the infernal order. They were battling other strains of their own kind, sometimes even joining forces with the Damned, as unthinkable as that was. As a result, it was said that all of the most humanoid races of Demons had been condemned to eradication. From now on, only nonhuman Demons would be created to restock those who were killed in the war (and Demons could indeed perish, since they were not immortal souls as the Damned were). And so this was why Leon felt the mirror-faced, metallic-looking insect Demons were actually robots, instead of imitation flesh and blood like the human-type Demons, and

143

like the Damned. As safely removed from humanity as the Creator could devise.

Thinking of these things now, Leon again tried to reassure his friend. "The rebels will find their way here, Dan. And when they do, they'll free us. And we'll *join* them."

"That's the spirit," said Dan, but it sounded like he was just humoring Leon. Leon didn't take it personally. Mockery was Dan's way of coping.

Leon let his eyes return to the cruel orange embers floating between them. "But I won't spill a drop of blood myself. I've seen way, way too much blood. I'm not going to do that. I'm not that way."

"So what will you do when this big revolution reaches us? Do a news report on it?" Dan deepened his tone of voice. "This is Leroy Brown, reporting live from Hell. Back to you, Stacey."

Leon chuckled. But they both heard the nearing claws of another Demon, crawling on all fours somewhere overhead. He said to Dan, with smile fading, "Where do you want it today?"

"On the end of my dick. Just kidding! Do it on my face, man. My cheek. That way I can press it against my shoulder afterwards, you know, for just a little comfort until it heals."

"I'll do the shoulder instead," Leon said, stepping closer. "You can do the same thing. Press it against your cheek."

"Whatever. Go for it, brother." Dan closed his eyes and tensed up as Leon touched the end of the incense stick to his bare shoulder. A sizzle, and the smell of blackening flesh.

Leon winced as much as Dan did. "I'm sorry," he kept whispering over and over. "I'm sorry, Dan..."

"I don't hate you, Leon ... don't worry," Dan said through gritted teeth, still squeezing his eyes shut as they both waited for the prescribed amount of time to pass before the ember left his seared flesh. "I don't hate you. They can't make me hate you!"

4: Harvesting and Sowing

Demonic life came in all sizes and forms, and Leon smashed a blood-sucking insect against his own brow. As he wiped its juices away, his fingers ran across the raised B branded upon his forehead. It marked him for his sin: Blasphemer. The sin of blasphemy, as judged, was not merely taking the Creator's name in vain, but feeling a real hatred for Him in the process. When he had first arrived in Hades, and been told the crimes that had sent him here, Leon had protested that there was a mistake. All of this was insane and unfair. He came from a religious family, had been baptized—and while he had stopped going to church decades earlier, he had never renounced God.

"We know your soul better than you do!" the skeleton-faced Demon official in his metal miter had hissed at him. "You have cursed your Creator. You have despised your Creator. Many times."

"People!" Leon had cried as he was dragged away. "It was people, not God!"

But was that true, really? Wasn't it really both?

He stood knee-deep in marshy water from which sprouted a forest of bamboo-like stalks, mist rising off the water making them appear as ghostly silhouettes as they receded into the distance. And here and there, vastly larger silhouettes reared up from the marsh, their tops lost in the fog of the sky, though orange points of light glowed dully like a constellation of dying suns. These were the metal towers that supported the great web, and the orange suns were the globes containing the brains of imprisoned Damned.

Leon heard the whack of curved, sickle-type instruments like the one he clutched in his own hand, as other Damned laborers cut down the tall stalks and further chopped them into segments small enough to fit into the woven baskets they carried on their backs. Later, Leon and the other harvesters would insert a stick of this sweet, sugarcane-like infernal plant into a circular opening in the midsection of each Demon. Food, said those who felt this race of Demons was organic (so to speak), but Leon thought it was fuel for mere machines.

Either way, it was yet another humiliating punishment. Being forced to nurture the very entities responsible for their enslavement.

He had hacked a thumb-sized segment of the sugarcane for himself and now withdrew it from his pocket to bite into, sucking out its sweet fluid and then tearing off some of its tough fibers to chew on, before returning to his sweaty labors. It gave him a defiant satisfaction stealing this pleasant sensation, though his mock body did not actually need it for nourishment.

In the distance, beyond the whacking of blades into stalks, Leon heard another sound. He had heard it often enough in life to recognize it.

The crackle of automatic gunfire.

He paused again and listened for more, but none came. Just some Demons, he thought. Their many races seemed to prefer swords, if they adopted any specific weapon at all, but it was not unknown for them to use guns. More likely, though, was that he had heard a hunting party of Angels, drinking beer and shooting at pretty women and fleet-footed children.

But ... what if it had been something else?

If there were Demon rebels out there, should he fear them? Should he fear them, even if they were Damned rebels? He had seen the handiwork of many a rebel in his time on Earth. Then again, he owed the creation of his country to rebels. One man's rebel was another man's murderer. One man's freedom fighter was another man's terrorist. One man's God was another man's Satan.

Leon detected movement sloshing his way, and flinched—expecting a Demon to materialize from the fog and punish him for growing lax in his duties. But it was a human figure that came toward him, silhouetted, and resolved itself into a woman. She wore her thick, curly red hair tied back behind her head, her face pale but freckled, short of stature in her black uniform. Like him, she carried a wicker basket on her back.

She smiled at Leon as she approached him. She was attractive; he thought he should recognize her, since she was obviously at the same level of decreasing punishment as himself ... but he didn't. "Hello," he said to her in a cautious whisper.

"Hey." She nodded. "Taking a little break?"

Her question made him suspicious, but why? Did he expect her facade of skin to tear open like a cocoon, a mirror-faced Demon emerging from inside her? He realized he trusted no one anymore. Not even his fellow Damned. His life as a live man had showed him that fellowship often merely consisted of hacking people up alongside your fellow sadists. Causes were excuses for hatred. And hatred was the way people expressed their unhappiness for existing at all.

"Just catching my breath," he told her. "Did you hear that? The gun?"

Stopping near him, the red-haired woman grunted, "Mm. Maybe someone tried to escape?"

"The Demons around here don't use guns," he said. And shouldn't she know that?

She shrugged again. She was playing with the weight of the sickle in her hand. "You're right; they don't. They aren't really much better armed than we, are they?" She gave a lazy swipe through the air between them. Leon tried not to look concerned that the blade might touch him.

More sloshing, behind him. Leon felt oddly reluctant to take his eyes off the woman, and not because she was attractive, but he half-turned to see another figure moving toward them through the swampy water. A tall black man, his skin a darker shade than Leon's. He wore the standard black uniform and basket on his back. Carried the standard sickle in his hand.

"Hello," the man said. That one word, spoken in a deep rich voice, gave away an accent. An African, though he would need to speak more at length before Leon might hope to identify the accent specifically.

"How's it going?" Leon asked, wary. He didn't recognize this fellow worker either.

The man joined them, nodding to the woman in familiarity. Well, at least the two of them recognized each other.

"I'm Leon," he said, switching his tool to his left hand so that he might extend his right. "I don't recall meeting either of you before." He was going for a casual tone.

The black man switched his sickle, too. His grip was strong: solid meat. Not a hollow flesh sleeve hiding a bony Demon arm. "I'm Salim."

"Salim." Leon still couldn't place the accent. "Where are you from?"

"Darfur. I was killed there, in the genocide." The man seemed to be watching Leon's face for a reaction, watching him as if he might even recognize him from TV.

Darfur. Leon knew about *that* genocide; hadn't the death toll already been 400,000, at the time he died in his safe little apartment in New York? Children with their heads bashed in by rifle butts, men castrated and then shot, women raped—by the Arab Janjaweed militias brought in by the Sudanese government to do their dirty work. He had wanted no part of that story, had even turned down the assignment offered him, no matter what his superiors thought of him for doing so. He had drawn the line at Darfur.

Was it a coincidence that he should run into a victim of that genocide here? Not with 400,000 dead, at least, Leon thought. In fact, he was surprised he had never before encountered one of the victims of the holocausts he had covered in his career. But Hades was big. So big.

"I'm Megan." The woman shook his hand, too. Though she didn't have an Irish accent, with her name and her red hair he cynically wanted to ask her if she had died in some old IRA bombing, but he didn't.

Despite the introductions, Leon still didn't trust them. He knew there were those Damned who worked closely with the Demons, as spies and snitches and betrayers, in order to minimize their own punishment. But these two seemed suspicious of him, too. Did they fear the same thing?

Leon returned his attention to Salim, and saw that the man had caught a flying insect that had been feeding on his blood. He pulled off one of its wings, and then the other. The Demonic creature's legs writhed. He flicked it away, then wiped the thing's blood on his trousers. Involuntarily, Leon touched the smear of blood on his own forehead. He had told his friend Dan that he would never spill a drop of blood here in Hades. But he had, hadn't he? When he'd crushed that tiny primitive Demon against his head just minutes ago. Yes, some of it had been his own ingested blood. But not all of it.

The tall African craned his neck, gazing off into the swaying forest of tall shoots. "We should move on ... before the Demons catch us talking."

Megan nodded, and then looked at Leon again. "See you around."

"You two stick together?" he asked.

"You don't approve of interracial relationships?"

"No, no ... that wasn't what I was thinking."

She smiled. "We aren't a couple, anyway. We just like working together."

Looking back as he started away, Salim said to Leon, "Maybe you can work with us, too, sometime."

Leon stood watching the strangers as they vanished again, like ghosts, into the fog.

He found himself listening for more distant gunfire. Waiting, and listening.

5: Feeding and Digesting

As he pushed a segment of stalk into the orifice of the Demon before him, Leon surreptitiously kept an eye out for Salim and Megan. Shouldn't they be feeding the harvest to the Demons, now, too? But he saw neither of them. It confused him, and inflamed his suspicions, as unformed as they were.

Leon tried not to feel disdain, specifically, for the man who'd called himself Salim. It made Leon feel a kind of shame, but it was hard to avoid. He had seen so many men who looked just like Salim with blood on their hands, bloodlust in their eyes. It was hard for him to think of any of them as victims, now. Then again ... he had seen men who resembled himself on his assignments, as well.

A scream, and he jerked his eyes to the right to see that a woman had been struck down by the Demon she had been in the process of feeding. What had she done to enrage it? Turned her head to look away, too obviously? Pushed the stalk in too roughly? Or was there any reason at all, beyond that she was here in Hades? Diminished level of punishment or not, their masters didn't want the Damned to become too comfortable in their station.

The woman's body gave ghastly jolts, some of her brain matter bulging out of her riven skull. But she would regenerate, without any loss of memory. Too bad, maybe, for that.

Leon made sure he kept his eyes forward now—as the next Demon in the queue stepped up for its meal, rising on its hind legs—but his mind wandered back to Rwanda.

It was an anecdote that his network had not allowed him to relate. Leon had interviewed a father who had found the murdered body of his son, his head hacked open by a machete. A chunk of the boy's brain lay apart from the body, and there were ants feeding on it. The father said he felt strangely angry at the mindless ants for the way they desecrated his boy, more angry at that moment than at the men responsible for the crime. The father had picked up the fragment of brain to deny the ants their meal, had brushed them off it. And he had saved that piece of his child in a bottle, where it had shriveled like a holy relic, the remnant of a saint. It was a strange thing to keep in order to remember one's child, but Leon wondered if maybe the father felt his son's memories of him resided in that scrap of his mind.

Leon lifted his eyes from the stalk, as he fed it like a pencil into a pencil sharpener, to the mirror that was all the Demon had for a face. His own face framed there, serving as the Demon's. Why? So he would hate himself? A symbol, to show him that he was responsible for his own damnation?

Later, during the rest period that those in this level of lessened punishment were allowed, Leon was told why that woman had had her skull split. She had explained the reason herself to her fellow Damned, now that she was mostly mended already.

The reason the Demon had struck her was that she had seen her face in the mirror, and out of a strange compulsion—a defiance she had not planned—she had stuck her tongue out at herself.

6: *Trojan Horse*

Gunfire awoke Leon Brown, and he thought he was in Sierra Leone in Liberia in Rwanda in Somalia in New York City. He opened his eyes, sat up on his bunk in the barracks of the Damned. The man who had the bunk above his jumped down, and Leon asked him, "What's going on?"

"The rebellion!" another man cried, delirious with excitement, as if mere bullets could blast them a hole in the wall of Hades itself. "They're here!"

They? Who were they? Demons? Damned? Both?

More and more gunfire, from everywhere at once.

A man burst into the barracks, with a submachine-gun in each hand and a revolver tucked in his waistband. "Here! Hurry!" He passed one submachine-gun to the man nearest him, and the pistol to a woman. Another man lunged into the structure after him, with two sawed-off pump shotguns and two semiautomatic pistols.

"Where did all this come from?" Leon shouted.

"A bunch of rebels infiltrated the area yesterday!" one of the men dispensing weapons said. "They pretended to be harvesters, but they had guns in their baskets!"

Salim, Leon thought. Megan. And others he hadn't met.

But why hadn't they told him, when they had talked with him? Maybe they hadn't been ready to reveal themselves yet? Or was there a vibe about him that had made them feel he was untrustworthy? Or at least, ineffectual? The latter was even more insulting.

A shotgun was offered to one older man, but he backed off with his hands in the air. "Don't involve me! We're almost phased out of this sector, anyway."

The man offering the gun looked incredulous. "What are you, crazy? We can overthrow these bastards, make them pay!"

"Yeah? Are you going to overthrow the Creator, too?"

"He's probably a spy," a woman snarled, glaring at the older man. "Is that it, Marty? You one of their spies?"

"What, you wanna shoot me? You want to shoot me, too?" The man named Marty spread his arms wide. "I'm not a spy, but I'm not a fool, either. You can't do anything except make them angry!"

"Maybe you aren't a spy," said the man with the shotguns, as he pushed past Marty to approach Leon. "But you're definitely a coward." Now he offered the sawed-off twelve gauge to Leon instead. "Here, man, come on."

But Leon only stared at the weapon, too.

"What is this?" the woman exclaimed.

"Their spirits are broken," the man offering the gun said in disgust.

The woman snatched the shotgun herself, with a withering look at Leon.

"I just hate violence, okay?" Leon said. "I don't want to be like they are."

"Are you saying we're like they are?"

"I'll come with you. I'll help free the others. But I'm not killing anything."

"They're just Demons! They don't have souls! Anyway ... I think these Demons are just machines."

So, Leon wasn't the only one of that opinion. Still, he wouldn't take one of the weapons.

But when those who had armed themselves with guns—or with the bamboo legs of tables and bunks—poured out of the barracks, Leon went with them to do what he could. Even so, he felt a bit removed from the action. Like a reporter, just tagging along.

Ineffectual.

7: *The Rescued*

The streaming prisoners branched off in several directions. Leon veered toward the maze where Dan was crucified to the wall. After all, Dan had been assigned to him. It was Dan he would free.

But just outside the maze, a man plunged out of the mist straight at him, moving swiftly despite his hobbled gait, a sickle in one fist and a wild grin on his face. At first Leon didn't recognize Dan, because he had only ever seen him bolted to that wall. Blood still streamed from the stigmata of his wrists and ankles.

"Leroy Brown!" he blurted, stopping before him. He held the sickle out to him. "You better take this, brother. My wrists are still killing me; there's nothing I can do with it until I heal a little bit."

Leon looked down at the tool. Maybe because he had used its like before, he accepted it.

Dan said, "You were right, man. I didn't believe you, but you were right."

"Right?" Leon said numbly.

"The rebels! They're here! We can fight these monsters!" He pointed beyond Leon. "Come on. Let's go to the towers."

Leon glanced behind him. Distantly, he saw the ghostly outline of the nearest metal tower looming into the ceiling of fog. "The towers?"

"Yeah! We have to free them, too, right?"

They ran side-by-side. They joined several others racing toward the tower, which became as wide as the base of a lighthouse. Rungs that the Demons used to mount it were welded to its black iron flank. Dan waited for the others to crawl up the side like ants, and then waved for Leon to follow them. "I'd better go last, with these hands."

Leon obeyed his instructions, too dazed to think for himself. He began climbing, keeping the sickle in hand. He glanced down and saw that Dan was making his way up, albeit slowly. And he still had that rapturous, mad grin on his face.

Much of the gunfire—automatic bursts, blasts from shotguns—came from above him, and when Leon was high enough for the "living" web to be visible through the haze, he was shocked at what he saw. Damned with guns, at the very tops of the towers or clinging to their sides, were not just shooting at the spider-like Demons crawling along the webs. They were shooting out the spheres of luminous orange fluid. The brains within, with their eyes like the horns of snails, were either blown into gobbets, or slithered whole out of the shattered globes to plummet far below.

But after the initial shock, Leon realized this was their way of freeing the brains from the containers that would not allow them to regenerate. Now, the prisoners would be able to reconstitute from their mutilated state, as Leon himself had done after his stint in one of the iron towers.

He continued climbing, until he came level with the lowest strands of the vast web. One of the spider-things was scurrying nimbly toward him along its tightrope. Below Leon, Dan cried, "Cut it! Cut the cord!" But Leon could not raise the sickle. Could not slice the strand, because it was the attenuated body of a Damned, with nerves that felt pain. He knew that only too well…

Thunder from someone's twelve gauge. Sprayed with buckshot, the Demon was knocked off the web and vanished into the clouds of fog below.

Leon climbed on. He did not know why ... what he could do. The Damned were being freed with bullets, the Demons killed with bullets. But he had been swept up in the furor. Maybe he was just here to witness. There must always be witnesses. It was a sacred responsibility—was it not?

That's what he told himself, as he reached the top without having shattered a globe with his blade, without having severed a cord along which a Demon moved.

The obelisk tapered toward its summit but still provided a flat surface, and up here a man was firing bursts from his submachine-gun at another spire in the distance. He was so absorbed in this, and Leon absorbed in watching him, that they didn't see the Demon pull itself up onto the platform until it had lashed out with its multi-bladed limbs. With a shriek, the machine-gunner toppled over the side and plunged out of sight. The Demon then turned its mirror face Leon's way—and surged at him, arms slashing.

Leon raised his left arm. A chop from the Demon sliced his forearm to the bone. He fell onto his back, struck the rear of his skull on the floor in so doing. The Demon jumped over him. It pinned his head down with one pincered claw that gripped his hair. The other foreleg cocked itself back and he saw a corkscrew-like digit click into place. He saw his own face hovering above him.

Not his face ... not his face ... he couldn't be grinning like that! Blood splattered on his skin, and his tongue wolfishly lashing over his lips, like that...

An explosion, like a bomb going off. Deliriously, Leon thought a plane had flown right into the side of the metal tower. The Demon suddenly flew off him, as if it had jumped away. A man stooped over Leon in its place, a shotgun in one hand. With the other, he helped Leon to his feet. He recognized the black man. Salim.

"You must be the good Mexican," Leon mumbled.

Salim frowned. "Mexican? Are you daft? I told you ... I'm from Darfur."

Dan was there, too, taking his other arm. Together they supported him, while he recovered his senses.

The three of them surveyed the scene before them. They couldn't see any more orange suns through the mist. No more Demons scrambling along those strands of the web that had not been hacked away.

"Can you make it back down to the ground?" Salim asked Leon.

"Yeah ... yeah," he said, but he was still a little disoriented as he stooped to retrieve the sickle he had dropped.

8: *Bloodlust*

As they reached ground level, a line of the Damned was marching past them. The group was bloody and torn, but there was a triumphant gleam in their eyes. Toward the end of the miniature parade, Leon recognized the woman who had glared at him back in the barracks. She was carrying a bamboo rod against her shoulder, and bound to its end by its hair like a hobo's sack was a severed human head. Leon recognized this person, too: the old man named Marty. His eyes rolled frantically and his mouth moved like that of a fish, opening and closing without a sound. There were some other living heads being carried, too. Displayed as traitors.

The woman spotted Leon, and her eyes hardened. She looked like she was about to point him out to the others. But then she apparently noticed the sickle in Leon's hand, and she nodded at him, as if in approval. She tramped away with the rest.

Leon realized he was wagging his head. Numbly wagging his head.

A thudding sound of bodies colliding and an inarticulate cry close behind him made Leon spin around, to see that one of the Demons had descended the tower, head-downwards like a fly, and launched itself onto Salim. It had him on his back, striking madly at him, perhaps recognizing him as one of those who had smuggled the rebellion into the heart of this particular Demonic enclave.

"Shit, shit, *no!* You *bastard!*" Dan was shouting, crouched as if he might jump upon the Demon's back, but knowing he would have no chance against its strength.

Leon pushed Dan out of the way, drew back his arm, and swung his sickle down squarely into the Demon's jagged spine.

Red blood squirted out of the wound he left. It was a shock to Leon. Yes, he had seen red blood on the Demons during this battle, but he had seen red blood on them so many times before. He had thought it was the blood of the Damned, as it always was. But now he realized that they had red blood of their own. That they were not machines, mere robots, after all. Alive, in their way. Just as he was alive, in his way.

The thing made no sound, but jerked its mirror face around at him in a fury that needed no voice, no face of its own. Anonymous and distant and hidden, like the Creator of all this. Leon swung the sickle again, into that mirror. Shattering it.

The Demon fell off Salim, and Leon kept hacking at it, again and again, ignoring the pain in his own slashed left arm. Dan helped drag the badly lacerated Salim to his feet, and Leon went on smashing the creature with the tool's heavy curved blade.

He crouched over it, panting. It lay quivering on its back. It was dying. Blood ran from a dozen deep gashes. It had regurgitated a greenish ooze of partially digested sugarcane from the orifice in its midsection. It was pathetic, vulnerable, lying there. Spread-eagled like a beaten woman waiting to be raped. So with one final, extra-powerful swing, Leon buried his sickle's blade into the center of its bony black chest.

He grinned, gasping, felt the thing's splattered blood trickling down his face. It dribbled onto his upper lip, and unconsciously he licked the drops away with his tongue.

And then, even though the thing's mirror face was broken, he saw his own face reflected. In his mind. The mad, lustful leer glowing through the war paint of gore. The wolfish tongue...

"You bastards," he croaked. It was the Demons' final humiliation. Final punishment. Once, they had forced him to feed them, care for them. And now, they had forced him to kill them. To break his vow. To spill blood.

Tears welled up in his eyes, at what they had made him do. As if this creature had planned it; yet another psychological torture. He wanted to strike it again, he was so filled with trembling rage, but he only tugged his sickle out of the dead thing's heart. It would not regenerate, as he would. It was dead forever. And that made him hate it all the more. Because it made him envy it.

"Damn you," he sobbed at the creature. "*Damn you...*"

9: The Rebel

Leon, Salim and Dan eventually caught up with the group they had seen marching past—this time with Leon and Dan supporting Salim between them, since he was the most badly wounded, with one hand almost severed and one eye gone from a gouge to his face. They had waited a little bit, until he was able to walk, until he was not moaning terribly with the pain. By now, Dan's stigmata was nearly gone and the wound in Leon's arm had become shallow.

They found that the group had congregated at the area where once they had fed the queues of Demons, and even more Damned had joined them. There were tables upon which they used to pile the freshly cut segments of those sweet-tasting, bamboo-like stalks. But now, on one of these tables a row of glass containers had been set. They were spares of the globes that had formerly been mounted in the hollows of those black iron minarets, in which brains like Leon's own had been stuffed and an orange fluid added to prevent the brains from regenerating until they were released again.

These globes had been inverted, with their black rubber seals at the top instead of the bottom. But the entire rubber collar on each globe had been pried off to make the opening wider. This had been done to accommodate the larger objects that had been forced into them. Not just brains, but an entire row of human heads. More than a dozen of them.

Marty was one of them, and all of the heads possessed mouths that worked as if trying to breathe or speak, eyes that blinked and followed the movements of their captors.

Leon turned to see that someone had stepped up to Salim, and put a hand on his shoulder. The red-haired woman, Megan, concern on her face. He smiled at her bravely through his agony.

Megan switched her gaze from Salim to Dan. She motioned with her head toward the row of glass spheres. "Are these the people you felt were working with the Demons?"

Dan looked over her shoulder. "I guess," he said reluctantly.

Leon was still staring at them. He was reminded of tales of the French Revolution, and the guillotine. How it was claimed that every so many heads lifted from the wicker basket had eyes and mouth still moving. A few horrid seconds before the life went out of them. But here, the life would not go out of these heads. Not ever. For all Leon knew, one of these Damned might even have died during the French Revolution, only to find himself here in Hell. This place where all mortal suffering was rewarded with more, and more, and more. Eternal, no real death, no oblivion, no forgetting, a suffering always alive and eating the brain from inside as the Demons ate at the outside. There were two Hells. This infinite macrocosm. And the microcosm within one's skull. Both could not be escaped from...

He stepped forward uncertainly, unconsciously, like a sleepwalker.

He stepped forward with the sickle in his fist, its scimitar blade painted in Demon's blood. Dan started to say something to him. And the woman who had glared at him in the barracks looked up, recognizing him as he approached the table.

Leon reversed the sickle in his hand. And when he struck the first glass sphere, it was the back edge of the harvesting tool and not its blade that shattered it. The luminous orange fluid spilled out like a pregnant woman's water bursting, and from the fanged glass womb rolled Marty's head. It dropped off the edge of the table and lay on its side, gasping soundlessly for air. The eyes turning up toward Leon. But Leon had moved on to smash the second glass globe.

"Hey! Hey!" the glaring woman shouted. She and others surged toward Leon.

"Stop!" a man's voice shouted.

Everyone turned. Salim stood tall despite his severe wounds. And Megan left his side, to cross toward the table. She moved between Leon and the crowd. They still had guns and lengths of bamboo and sickles of their own in hand.

"Leave him be," Megan told them. "He's one of *you*."

Leon watched the stalemate for a moment. Would the next war begin so soon? The war between Damned and Damned? It was inevitable, wasn't it? It was the way of things.

But the crowd recognized the woman as one of those who had come amongst them to sow the rebellion, and free them, so they did not move on Leon. They watched him, as he resumed breaking the containers and liberating each head so that it could fully regenerate again, into a whole person.

And with each person he freed, it was like he freed another part of himself, bottled up and trapped inside him. Something demoralized into numbness, something beaten into submission, something terrified into helplessness. With each bottle he shattered, with tears in his eyes, he felt his own wounds healing. For the first time in what seemed all eternity, he felt like a whole person, himself.

ACHERON

-1-

Tattersall knew there was more to the Demon Surgat when he and another Damned man named Cutler were standing at the ship's starboard rail looking down into the sea of blood, and Cutler pointed at something floating near the hull, saying, "What's that?" Surgat stepped up to the rail between them, startling the two men, who hadn't known he was behind them despite his imposing bulk. He surprised them even more when he looked where Cutler had pointed, and offered an answer.

"It is runoff from that fabrication plant," he rumbled. His was a voice a granite boulder would make if it could.

Surgat, captain of the *Acheron*, was a foot taller than the Damned men and as wide as both of them combined. He was built on the scale of a classical Hercules, meaty and thick, not some terrestrial weightlifter defined by steroids. His head, shaggy with a long gray mane, reminded Tattersall of masks of Indonesian demons, with its huge flared ears, great canines curving down over the chin, and greater tusks that swept up from the lower jaw and framed the wide-spaced, bulbous eyes, with their enormous black pupils outlined by red sclera. He was of a very old make of Demon.

He was naked, his albino skin densely tattooed in black ink: ornate vine-like designs that branched off into spirals, interspersed with odd geometric patterns and sigils. Strangely, the Demon's tattoos always reminded Tattersall of his father, the barbed wire tattoo that had encircled his left bicep. Surgat had no genitals, smooth as a doll between the legs. Some Demons did possess them, but this was either so that they might abuse the Damned, or be equipped to sexually service the people—called Angels—who had been granted passage into Heaven, should those blessed former mortals ever grow bored and jaded enough to desire a vacation in Hades, tourists in the most convincing of theme parks. But none of the seemingly infinite varieties of Demons reproduced—that was why the fabrication plants existed.

The object bobbing like a crude raft on the sloshing blood was a mass of translucent matter, its predominately yellowish coloring and gelatinous appearance suggesting a monstrous blob of fat. As it drifted a bit closer alongside the ship, a smell came up off it, cutting even through the strong iron tang of the waves of blood that buoyed the glob. It was the road kill reek of decay, and Tattersall flinched back a little from the rail as he took in a good lungful of it.

He looked up toward the fabrication plant that Captain Surgat had indicated with a jerk of his spiral-tattooed chin. Perched on a rocky prominence that broke the Red Sea's surface was a looming fortress-like compound with high walls of black metal, like iron that somehow resisted corrosion, limned in red against the ceiling of churning black clouds that forever obscured the sky. Every structure contained within this wall—at least, those that rose high enough to show above it—was constructed of the same metal. Windows were few, but chimneys numerous, trailing sooty gases that looked like immense, writhing black caterpillars. Even from this distance they could smell the plant's pollution, which made one's eyes water when the wind across the sea gusted it directly toward the ship. Furthermore, from the plant came the muffled clamor of gargantuan machines. One might imagine that within those walls beat the very heart of Hades, a black infernal mechanism. Except that this was just one of many such factories distributed across the infinity of the netherworld.

In such plants, new Demons were produced from raw materials. In the same establishments, it was sometimes also the case that Demons that had failed or disappointed in their duties were reduced to their fundamental matter to be recycled. Tattersall had heard there were similar plants in Heaven in which were manufactured the various Celestial races that served the Angels in any number of ways. He wondered how laboring in one of these Demon factories compared to serving aboard a ferry vessel like the *Acheron*.

This was the closest Tattersall had been to one of these plants in the time that he had been in Hades. And how long was that? How could time be measured in the dominion of infinity, where there was no day or night, no ending to anything but for one manner of suffering giving way to another, no second chance to die? But it hadn't been long, compared to some of the others who served with him on the ship. He and Cutler had gravitated to each other because they had come through the same soul gate at the same time, and had both been immediately assigned to this vessel.

The *Acheron*—over 1,500 feet long and itself formed entirely of black metal impervious to rust—curved in its course around the steep protrusion of rock, and now Tattersall could begin to see a row of huge circular openings at the base of the enclosing wall. As he watched, one of these tunnel mouths disgorged a rush of soupy material, yellowish streaked with red. This vomited process waste spread out upon the heavy, slow-rolling waves of blood, to ultimately dilute and break up. Already he could see a few sizable chunks of matter like the one Cutler had pointed out, drifting away to decompose in time.

No doubt because the normally stern, silent ship's captain had deigned to answer his blurted question, Cutler asked the Demon in a timid and respectful tone, "If they make the Demonic races out of... um, out of stuff like *that* in there...where do those materials come from?"

"Grown," Surgat grunted, staring off toward the island of rock. Tattersall wondered which plant he had found his own origin in, most likely hundreds of years earlier. "In tanks of solution. Some are harvested from large pools. Other materials are seeded in soil, or poured into molds and cured in ovens."

"So, all this stuff is like bioengineered cells, then." Cutler's voice had gained a touch of anxiousness. In life, he had worked in the fermentation department of a biopharmaceutical company, which manufactured proteins and antibodies from mammalian cell cultures. Tattersall wondered if Cutler was going to volunteer his expertise, to escape his current slavery … if he pictured himself drinking coffee in a spiffy cafeteria with Demonic department managers.

Surgat turned slowly to stare down at the Damned crewman, his lidless eyes seeming to actually glow red around their black pupils. "It is the stuff of the *Creator*. As is the illusory body that represents your soul. As is the illusory metal of this ship." He brought his palm down on the rail. It rang with the vibration. "All that you believe you see and believe you feel, all that exists in any guise, is composed of His essence. In Hades, as in Heaven. On Earth as in the afterworlds. The spiraling universe is but His thumbprint." He raised one finger in front of his fearsome visage. "And there is no Satan, no fallen Lucifer, no counterpart of the Creator. There is *only* the Creator."

Cutler went on babbling, encouraged by Surgat's willingness to talk and educate them. He reminded Tattersall of a meek schoolchild trying to get on an older bully's good side—or himself as a boy, trying to impress his taciturn father. "So we're all a part of the Creator, then … like brothers, right? You Demons, us Damned, the Angels, the Celestials."

Surgat snorted, and looked out to sea again. "You and I are not brothers."

"Oh, I didn't mean…I'm not implying we're, like, equals or anything," Cutler said, his words tripping over each other.

Surgat ignored him, and continued, "The Angels and the Damned are brothers, because you are immortal spirits. The Celestials and my kind—we are not souls." After a moment he added in a quieter voice, "We are only machines."

"You're not immortal? You mean…are you saying Demons and Celestials can die? Die forever?"

Surgat faced Cutler again, sharply. "And why do you ask me that?"

"Sorry, sir, I just –"

"Do you now think to wait for me to drop my guard? So that you might try caving in the skull of this old machine with a wrench?" The

164

fangs overflowing his mouth marred his rising voice, making it sound animal-like, a warning snarl.

"No—of course not!" Cutler held up his hands and backed away a step, his retreat stopped by the rail. "I'm sorry!"

Looming over Cutler, the *Acheron*'s captain went silent for a moment, in which he seemed to regain his composure. His voice, though gruff, resumed its usual calm. "Mind your tongue when we reach our destination. Captain Beleth is not as lax and senile as I have become. Do not speak in his proximity at all, unless you would rather stay with him on his island. You would miss this old tub as if it were Heaven itself."

"Of course, sir, of course," Cutler squeaked, still looking horrified. "Thanks for the warning."

Tattersall himself said nothing.

"Return to your stations. Do not be idle outside your rest periods." Surgat started away across the deck, but after several strides twisted half around to say, "Captain Beleth gives his Damned workers no rest periods. Remember that. Be thankful for your fate. Even in hell, there is greater hell. Suffering is relative." He made an ugly contortion of his mouth that Tattersall realized was an attempt at a bitter smile. "In Heaven, I hear, the Angels are vexed if their steak is not cooked to their liking."

Their steak ... made of the stuff of the Creator, Tattersall thought. *Take, eat; this is my body.*

Surgat lumbered away, turned the corner of one of the numerous, varied structures mounted on the ship's deck like buildings crowding a city street that had been set adrift. He disappeared from view.

"Suffering is relative," Tattersall repeated. "It might be worse on that island he's talking about, but then again we might find another place that would be better than this ship."

"What are you saying?" Cutler whispered.

"That we should try to get off this thing ... go ashore. Live in the wilderness, and keep away from Demons and their tortures and the work they force us to do."

"Jesus, man, how could we do that? In case you hadn't noticed, there are no lifeboats to steal. You want us to jump over the side and swim for it? There are *things* living in the blood … they'd get us."

"All I know is, I'm not going to spend the rest of my life … well, you know what I mean. If I see an opportunity, any chance to make things better for myself, I'm going for it." Tattersall sighed, looking out to sea. "Anyway, let's go below." He turned back to Cutler, and found the other man quaking with soundless sobs. At first he thought Cutler was feeling defeated by his own lack of courage in contemplating the escape that he'd suggested.

"Surgat talked to us like men," Cutler said.

Tattersall tried to joke. "And what do I talk to you like—a woman, sweet cheeks?"

"I mean, he talked to us like we're men and not just animals."

More to himself, Tattersall murmured, "He talked to us like *he's* a man."

His gaze trailed away, then up and up the shaft of a monolithic smokestack in whose shadow they stood. From it poured an endless chain of black fists of smoke, like the chimneys of the plant perched on the island they skirted. The smoke was a product of the fuel used to generate steam for this vessel's engines.

That fuel was the Damned.

Only adult men and women were forced into the furnace to be burned. When children were part of the ferry's cargo they were kept in the vast hold, were not fed to the flames and were not even witness to the procedure. All this time Tattersall had thought it was simply some infernal law that children should not be punished in the same manner as adults, who were more culpable for their sins. But somehow after their surprising little exchange with the *Acheron*'s commander— particularly in regard to the different approach of Captain Beleth, whose island they were headed for—he wondered if it was Surgat's own directive that children being borne on the great ferryboat were not to be subjected to that particular torture.

-2-

Zelma was inside the house, curled on the sofa where she'd fallen asleep watching something on HBO Latino. He'd been watching a horror movie on Netflix in the basement. It was like that now on Friday nights. They might as well have been long married, but they weren't married and it hadn't been that long. Not even a year yet since she had moved in. That was the way it was with people, he had found. Spouses and lovers, friends too, even family; at least his family. They liked the *concept* of being deeply involved with other people, the lofty illusions propagated in movie and song, but achieving or at least maintaining a deep connection in reality was something else. Too often, he thought, the reality was not a convergence and blending of two malleable entities, but a grating of implacable objects that only threatened to grind away chunks of each other, if not sink each other entirely, like two ships meeting in the dark.

Or so it seemed to Tattersall, as he sat out on his deck with a third glass of Maker's Mark resting cool on a knee bared by his khaki shorts. He hadn't refreshed the ice, it was dwindling in the heat of a Texas night, and he'd compensated for the loss with a more generous portion of whisky.

When she'd first come into his life, Zelma had been the intoxicant to replenish his glass. He'd met her one Saturday when he'd driven out to Airport Park, on the northern shore of Lake Waco.

He'd been feeling nostalgic that day, remembering the occasions when his father had taken him out on the lake in his motorboat, fishing for crappies. His father had been in the Navy in Vietnam, serving on a river patrol boat, and despite whatever unpleasantness he had no doubt experienced during the war—experiences he had never shared with his son—being on the water seemed to soothe him. He was huge and gruff, and Tattersall had been in awe of him, even afraid of him, but he had admired him ... had always yearned for his approval, for some blatant expression of affection that had never quite come. Even alone together for a whole day they would speak little, and in his father's final years their relationship still hadn't changed. Tattersall wished one of them had told the other that he loved him. Why had he waited for his father to be the one?

He met Zelma in a Mexican restaurant not far from Airport Park, where she worked as a waitress. Petite to the point of being childlike, hair black as crow's feathers and pulled back in a ponytail, her cuteness had given him the courage to pull off at least a little flirtation that first time. He ventured to the restaurant two more times that week, ostensibly because he was no good at cooking at home. By the third trip, he'd asked her out to a movie.

Even after she'd accepted his offer of a date, though ... even after they'd ended up in bed ... even after she'd moved into his little house...he'd felt a kind of dread tick-tocking in the background like a pendulum blade. The end of the affair was as inevitable as death itself; it was only a matter of where it would pencil itself in on the calendar. There was no such thing as the eternal.

He'd once had faith in love. He'd lost it with his marriage. Yes, he had been married once, if not to Zelma, who never had; she was twenty-four to his thirty-six. Just as he'd lost his faith in God at some much more ill-defined point in his life.

Not knowing, back then, that loss of faith was enough of a crime to sentence one to everlasting punishment.

Zelma had always been quiet, but her quiet had a different quality these days. He felt her shyness had become sulkiness. He tried to tell himself he was only projecting his insecurities. Tried to warn himself that he had better be careful lest his fears become a self-fulfilling prophesy. He had never been much of a drinker, but over the past few months his drinking had increased. Of course she disapproved, but she didn't voice it much, only gave him looks with her heavy-lidded dark eyes that were even worse for their silence. Oh, but he read loads in her looks. Judgment. Like a judgment on his whole existence. So of course the answer to that was to drink more. *Insulation. Isolation. Alienation.* He ticked off the words in his head as he sipped his drink again. *Disorientation*, he thought. Yeah ... soon.

Dissolution.

Two uncomfortable days awaited him in lieu of a weekend. She'd probably spend one of them visiting her family. Once he would have felt jealous about that. Now he hoped it would be so. Then Monday, work again. And work the next day and the next, and then after some as yet unknown number of further days he would die and it would all be over, and his entire flicker of existence would not have mattered a whit to the universe.

He glanced down at the bottle near his foot to gauge whether a fourth glass's worth remained in there. Golden nepenthe. His faith in that, at least, was unshakeable.

The bottle, or the whisky already in his head, caused his thoughts to circle back to his family. He had one brother, Nicolas, a few years older than him, with whom he had also never felt sufficiently close. Nicolas had been too involved with his friends, and was wild as a teenager: trouble with the law, and drugs, and drinking. As a man Nicolas had never held onto employment for long. Nicolas hadn't been able to hold onto his wife, either. The night she had thrown him out, Nicolas had come to Tattersall—then married himself—and asked if he could stay for a while. Fearing that "a while" would turn into a long while, and disgusted at his brother's directionless, drug and booze saturated life, Tattersall had turned him away. Nicolas had stepped back into the darkness, out of the light of Tattersall's front door, and sobbed drunkenly, "Well fuck you, traitor!" And then he had gone.

Now, Tattersall didn't know where his brother was in this wide world, but he doubted he had changed, and he was probably even worse off. Living on the streets, for all Tattersall knew. Sometimes, like the surprise thrust of an assassin's knife in the center of his chest, he felt a pang of guilt over not opening the door for his brother, giving him the shelter that might help him find balance—that might *save* him. That knife was all the sharper now that Tattersall had taken to drinking himself. Maybe, he thought bitterly, the person he had been so disgusted with wasn't Nicolas but his own future self, that he had glimpsed embodied in his older brother. And now, was he shutting the door, so to speak, on Zelma too? What was it about himself, he wondered, that would not allow him to step up and engage people in a way that might make a difference to them? That might protect and nurture them, make the way better for them? Wasn't he only excusing himself when he accused all humanity of this selfish disconnectedness?

A distant animal cry, shrill and ululating, roused him from this reverie, caused him to look up and face the night again. The tranquility of this blandly attractive condo village was mostly still intact, but that funny trilling howl continued.

He realized it was not animal in origin. Someone was screaming. A woman.

He stood up, set his glass down on the deck rail, was already slipping a hand into a pocket of his shorts for his cell phone. A domestic situation was more likely in this neighborhood than a rape or robbery, but then he spotted a fuzzy yellow glow against the darkness toward the end of the long straight lane his condo faced onto. Maybe he had been smelling the smoke these past few minutes and had subconsciously dismissed it as someone's outdoor fireplace.

Tattersall worked an eight hour shift as a low rung inventory manager at a data storage company, but he was also a volunteer firefighter for McLennan County. A few years ago, he had been one of those who responded to the site of an ammonium nitrate explosion that has taken fifteen lives at a fertilizer company in the city of West.

He almost lost his balance going down the wooden steps, as if he were making his way along the deck of a sailing ship tossed on the waves of a storm. He thrust out a hand to grab the rail, spiked a long splinter into his palm for his trouble. Cursing, he lurched out onto the sidewalk and punched 911 on his phone. He started running as he blurted to the dispatcher.

He wavered to the sides as he ran, the straightness of the lane mocking him, every footfall sending a jolt up through his belly. He thought he might have to stop and vomit, but he fought to keep the urge tamped down. He continued shouting into the cell phone between panting.

Was this a machination of Fate? An act of divine providence? Had he become a firefighter, or chosen this specific lane to live on, just so that he might be present here on this one night to respond to this one fire, right down at the end of this straight path? Was this the hand of God, showing him that He did exist after all? That Tattersall, however seemingly humble a creation, was a valuable part of His design? Someone who *could* impact the lives of other beings in a meaningful way?

Despite the nausea sloshing in his belly, something else whooshed up inside and suffused him. Something beyond the excitement of adrenaline. Something like exhilaration. Like hope.

-3-

When he had been assigned to the *Acheron*, shortly after having been delivered into Hades through one of its manifold gates, Tattersall was shown how fuel was driven into the boiler's furnace, to heat the water that yielded steam to power the ship's engines. Just one time, as part of his orientation, since he worked at the other end of the process. So he had only witnessed the Inferus at work on that single occasion. He hoped never to witness it again.

The Inferus was a proto-Demon, one of the precursors of the Demons that the Creator would later design to oversee the punishment of human beings. These early draft creatures predated humans, some of them predating even the earliest forms of terrestrial life. As such, they often had no telluric analogue, since He had evolved humans and Demons along a parallel course, each informing the design of the other to some extent.

The Inferus was a mountainous cone of translucent yellow flesh, almost amorphous, its base a layered skirt of rubbery membranes. Radiating from its middle were a circle of boneless limbs, long and whip-like and studded along their lengths with curved ivory barbs. It was blind and voiceless and all but mindless, despite having two blank heads, their faceless fronts connected by a segmented trunk or tube, as if they breathed the same foul air back and forth between them, and had been doing so for millions if not billions of earthly years.

It was the Inferus that drove the Damned from the stoking chamber, which accommodated up to fifty of them at a time, through the wide opening of the furnace before it was fired up. Tattersall had watched this through a thick circular window in the stoking chamber's riveted metal door. The Damned men and women, of varying age and ethnicity but all wearing the standard black uniform of shirt and trousers they'd been issued upon their arrival, had crowded into each other when the shutter was cranked up to reveal the Inferus...crowded into an even tighter mass, shrieking and calling out for mercy, as the towering creature glided out on a glistening trail of mucus, its bobbing twin heads almost grazing the high ceiling.

Two Damned shipmen were always made to aid in this procedure, positioned to either side of the precursor Demon to help herd the Damned into the furnace chamber, prodding with long spears those who tried to dart past the Inferus or duck its whipping limbs. Cutler was one of the pair who had been given this task. On his first occasion he had dropped the spear to the floor, fallen to his knees and wept, unable to proceed. The Inferus had swept him up into its coiling tendrils and with its hooks in him had torn him into two pieces. Then, with his lower half flung into the furnace and his upper half tossed into a corner to slowly and agonizingly regenerate, he had *truly* wept. Thereafter, he had performed his role as expected, though in the early days sobbing all the while, begging those who screamed and cursed at him to forgive him.

It was understood that it was not only to aid the Inferus in its function—both practical and punitive—that Damned workers were made to do this. It was a form of punishment for Cutler and his partner, as well, to have to assist in the infliction of misery on their fellows. No soul, however cooperative, was exempt from suffering in Hades.

The other man assigned to this duty was unpopular among the Damned crewmen. He never interacted with any of them because of this, but also because his language was not English, though Tattersall sensed there was yet another reason why the man never spoke to anyone. They knew two things about him, even if Tattersall didn't understand how the knowledge had come amongst them: that his name was Samoshkina, and that he was one of the terrorists who in 2004 had captured a school in the Russian town of Beslan. Word was, when Russian forces moved in to liberate the hostages, a little girl who had had nothing to drink but her own urine for several days went rushing to drink water from a fountain, and was shot in the back by Samoshkina. And she had been only one of his victims.

The other Damned called him Baby Killer, even to his face. He never objected to this, or their harsh comments.

One time when the two of them had been alone, Tattersall had asked Cutler, "So, did he escape the siege and only die recently, or has he been serving on the *Acheron* for over a decade? Earth time, that is."

"Couldn't tell you."

Tattersall said, "The man seems traumatized to me. Shell shocked."

"Probably just disillusioned that he didn't get his seventy-two virgins," Cutler said. "A guy like Baby Killer, he belongs here. I'm all for that. But me? Okay, man—I was a druggie, I admit it. A frigging meth addict. Yeah, surprising, I know. Me, the biopharma guy, helping develop drugs to benefit people, doing this hateful shit on the side. It got so bad, I'm healthier now dead than I was alive." As his words grew more impassioned, Cutler's eyes dampened. "I was a pitiful loser, I destroyed myself, yeah...but I didn't hurt anybody else but *me*. Is that why I'm here, though? *No*. It's just because I was an atheist, man. What can I say? God didn't tap me on the head and let me know He was there!"

"Shh," Tattersall warned, looking behind him.

"But it's not fair!" Cutler hissed, only growing more animated and teary eyed. "People here for being Buddhists, Jews. Children here because they weren't baptized. Is that right? Is that a loving God? It's not really about sins we committed...it's about not kissing the feet of a petty tyrant."

"It's beyond our understanding, I guess," Tattersall whispered. "They'd probably tell us He did tap us on the head, every day, but we didn't listen."

"Bullshit, man," Cutler said, gulping agitated breaths into his sham lungs. "See...and you're here just for being a frigging agnostic." He gestured toward the raised symbol branded on Tattersall's forehead. These forehead brands designating their offenses were the only wounds inflicted on the Damned that left a permanent mark. An eternal scar.

At the time of this conversation Tattersall hadn't replied aloud, but he had said to himself internally, *What I'm here for, and what I should be here for, are two different things.*

"Aw, fuck it," Cutler had gone on, breaking into outright sobs. "Maybe I do deserve it. I'm still a loser, an absolute waste, and I'll face that till the end of time."

Tattersall had then put his arms around Cutler to quiet and comfort him. With this spontaneous gesture, which wasn't like him, he had surprised himself. "Okay, brother, come on now," he had soothed the other man. "You were right the first time: you don't deserve this, and you aren't a loser. You hear me? You aren't a waste."

Cutler had wept a little in his arms before finally pulling away and composing himself, but Tattersall had felt strangely reluctant to let him go. When he had held the man and couldn't see his face, he could have sworn that it was his brother Nicolas he was embracing, instead, and his own eyes had dampened. He should have held Nicolas this way on his doorstep that night.

"Thanks," Cutler had said afterwards in a small, calmed voice. Tattersall wished it was Nicolas's voice.

Since then Cutler hadn't discussed his former addiction again, perhaps out of embarrassment for having broken down, and Tattersall had never brought up the brother he had rejected—though at the time he had felt an impulse, or need, to do so.

The number of Damned the *Acheron* picked up along the coast of the apparently infinite Red Sea varied, as it traveled from one to another of the locations where existed the portals through which the Damned passed from the earthly plane into Hades. The ship would then transport its cargo to whatever region this group of Damned had, for whatever reason, been consigned. Tattersall supposed the migration of souls was handled differently further inland, but thus far he himself had been aground only briefly. He couldn't begin to understand the system that directed these Damned to be sent here, others to be sent there, though he knew part of it had to do with making sure no Damned soul ever encountered a person he or she had known in life— lest the reunited Damned provide each other comfort. But the soul gates themselves seemed to function as filters to disperse new arrivals far and wide throughout Hades.

However many Damned the immense ferry craft picked up to transport, a good percentage of them—as many as half—would be kept aboard to be used as its fuel. Only after these individuals had been rendered down to ash, then reconstituted, would they be let out at the ship's various ports of call. An individual might need to be cycled through the burning process twice or even more times, depending on how long it would be before new fuel was acquired. Fortunately, in spite of its massive bulk, it didn't seem to take a great deal of steam to keep the *Acheron* endlessly roving. Considering that an earthly aircraft carrier of similar size would be nuclear-powered, the *Acheron*'s engines were a wonder of infernal design. Cutler had suggested to Tattersall that if the Demons had wanted they could have powered the ship without steam at all, but the whole operation was as much a floating torture chamber as it was a means of propulsion...because, as Cutler put it, "In the end it's all about the torture, here, isn't it?"

Even the matter of who was burned and who was not appeared to be predetermined, though Tattersall didn't know how much Captain Surgat and his unnamed advisor—a silent Demon of a type the crewmen had dubbed Bubbleheads—had to do with the planning of all this, themselves.

Today (and Tattersall still couldn't help but think of work periods in terms of days), the latest fifty Damned had already been chased into the furnace, with the Inferus only having had to fling three of them into the chamber—in various pieces. The fire had come up, and from inside the sealed furnace the muffled screams had intensified, as terror turned to agony.

If the Inferus was positioned at the mouth of the furnace, Tattersall's station was at its anus. On his side he could hear all those comingled screams within, before the flames were sucked into throats and lungs and the voices were drowned to silence.

"*Mami*," the voices always seemed to cry, at least to his ears, and though they were the voices of adults they were so shrill and terrified they sounded like those of children. "*Mami!*"

He no longer sobbed when he heard those familiar screams, but he was always grateful when they ceased. The screams would frequently return in his dreams, though, and he almost resented the rest periods that all his fellow crewmen anxiously anticipated.

He was partnered with another Damned laborer, a Ghanaian

named Mac-Jones, who despite having served aboard the *Acheron* for a considerable time still quietly wept and muttered to himself whenever he went about his work inside the furnace. Tattersall suspected he was broken, as he believed Samoshkina was broken. And was that because they had been in Hades longer than he? Instead of one gradually becoming numb and inured to the suffering of others and oneself, did the internal torment only increase? Would he become broken, too?

When the jetting flames had been extinguished and the furnace had cooled down sufficiently, together Tattersall and Mac-Jones turned a metal wheel set into the wall that would draw aside a panel in the floor of the incineration chamber, revealing a pit below. This done, they turned a second squealing wheel, this one centered in the hatch on their side. They hauled it open, then stepped into the furnace with their tools.

A fine mist of ash hung in the air like fog. For as long as he could, Tattersall held his breath against it, and against inhaling the heat. It was still almost intolerably hot inside. In no time his mock pores leaked mock sweat that saturated his mock uniform.

They moved as lightly as they could across the carpet of bone shards, the gravelly smaller fragments and gritty underlying sand crunching and grating under their shoes. Using implements like metal hoes and push brooms, Tattersall and Mac-Jones scraped and swept toward the central floor opening the heaps of cremated remains.

By the time they were finished their black uniforms, their hair and faces and hands, were powdered gray with ash. Stepping back outside, they resealed the hatch, turned the wheel on the wall to close up the hole in the incinerator's floor.

Now they would wait a while, before venturing down to the pit into which they had swept the cremains. It would take some time for the reconstitution process to really get underway.

Both men sank down to sit on the floor, propped against opposite walls of the room. Tattersall folded his arms atop his knees and lowered his forehead onto them. With his body still and his eyes closed, he believed he could sense the subtle rocking of the *Acheron* on the waves of blood.

-4-

The screaming woman stood in front of the burning house, barefoot on the lawn, wearing a faded nightgown and holding a girl of maybe eighteen months on her hip. A few other neighbors stood around her, with more moving in from various directions. Several had their phones out to call for assistance, themselves. The woman spotted Tattersall loping toward her, huffing, and the determination she must have seen in him caused her to turn toward him in particular, her eyes wild, the child's eyes huge and uncomprehending. She was Mexican, like Zelma—he didn't know her name, but knew her well enough to greet her whenever he saw her. She cried in English, "My children are inside! Please help me, my children are still inside!"

Tattersall knew she had three boys, though he wasn't sure of their ages. He recalled the youngest boy had an unfortunate port-wine stain—called a firemark—covering half his face.

"Where's your husband?" he panted.

"He's at work...he works nights!"

"Stay clear," he told her, waving her back. "I'm a fireman—I've already called it in." Then he was turning away from her, toward the blaze.

Immediately, though, he staggered back. The front of the little house, almost identical to his own, was a jack-o'-lantern—yellow fire flush against the window panes and filling the threshold of the open doorway through which the woman had apparently narrowly escaped with her daughter. He assumed the fire had begun in that room while the family slept.

The alcohol in his head made the fire glow more softly, phantasmal, around the outlines of the door and windows.

Starting forward again, he veered around the side of the house instead, headed for the back door, which like his own would be accessible via a raised deck.

He grabbed the rail to the deck's steps, flung himself up them. He tripped on the penultimate step, stumbled forward and almost dove onto his face, but his hold on the rail prevented him. He lunged for the back door and took hold of the handle to slide it open.

It wouldn't budge. Locked for the night to protect those inside.

To one side he spotted a garden statue type of decoration, a cherub in cast stone, wings open across its back. Might a key be hidden under it? He lifted the cherub, found no key there. Still cradling it in his arms, however, he spun toward the sliding door and hurled the statue with all his strength. The glass shattered, dropped both inside and outside the house. Tattersall thrust his arm inside, clawed for the inner latch, found it. Now the door slid open.

Heat and smoke rolled out across him, and so did the shrill, comingled cries of young children somewhere within. A wailing, terrified chorus.

"*Mami! Mami!*"

He plunged into the house, already darkened for the night and darker still with the smoke. He was in a kitchen, he knew from his own condo, but he couldn't see any towels that he might clamp over his face so he used his left hand instead. With his right he groped ahead of him. Fluttering yellow light from the blazing living room overflowed into a hallway ahead.

"Boys!" he shouted from behind his cupped hand. "Kids! Where are you?"

Starting for the hallway, he began to call out to the screaming children again, but as he drew in a breath he sucked smoke deep into his lungs. Instantly he doubled over, coughed hard to eject it. As a result, he ejected more than just the smoke. The whisky he'd been drinking came up, too, unbidden. He dropped to his hands and knees and vomited on the floor.

The screaming intensified, becoming less coherent. Was it going from terror to pain? *Where were they?* He couldn't even recall the floor plan of his own house at this moment. There would be a basement, but no second floor. Bedrooms…they would be off the hallway. He hoped the children were all huddled together in one spot, not scattered in different rooms.

As he began unsteadily hauling himself back to his feet, he looked up to see the fire had spilled into the hallway itself, feeding on the carpet, racing up the walls in lascivious orange tongues. He was prepared to continue forward, however, and try the first open door, when he finally realized the screams were not coming from any of the three black doorways he could now distinguish in the glare of the flames. The cries were coming from behind him, back toward the kitchen.

No...from the basement. The door to the basement would be in the kitchen, as in his own place.

He whirled around to retrace his steps, the heat rippling across his back as if to seize hold of him, yank him backwards into the fiery maw. By the advancing glow he could make out the outline of the closed basement door ahead of him, just where it would be oriented in his own house.

For God's sake, why would they have fled down there? No...no... maybe they slept down there. Four kids in one small house. Or maybe there was a TV in the basement, as in his, and they'd been up late playing a videogame while their mother slept with the baby.

The fire chased him to the door. To avoid swallowing more ember-tinged smoke, to avoid ejecting more vomit, he held his breath and pressed his left hand tight across his lower face as his right hand threw the basement door open. The screams, released like scattering birds, spiked his ears. Smoke surged out at him. The insidious smoke had already found its way down there, somehow. It was pitch black below. The stairs might as well have been endless.

Tattersall slapped around for the railing, found it, and began to descend blindly. Like a man who had found his faith again, though he hadn't, he thought *dear God, please don't let me fall.*

With his eyes stinging, struggling not to gag, lightheaded and shaking violently—and with the fire close behind—he kept descending.

-5-

Tattersall's eyelids snapped open. For a sliver of a second he was transported back to that moment when he had first opened his eyes to the understanding, already ingrained into his very essence, that he had been claimed by Hades.

But he stifled the scream that had half risen, because he was greeted by the familiar sight of Mac-Jones sitting against the opposite wall, awake and staring at him as if he had been doing so all the time Tattersall had been dozing. The man's face was ghostly with its coating of ash, making the whites of his eyes look yellowish.

"Do you think it's time?" Tattersall groaned, slowly and achingly sliding up the wall to his feet, to stretch his muscles.

"Yes," Mac-Jones said, rising too.

Taking their tools with them, they went out through another of the room's doors, this one delivering them onto the landing of a stairwell. They descended two flights of metal steps, reached a corridor lower in the bowels of the ship. In front of them now was the door to the reconstitution chamber. To either side of it was stationed a Demonic guard.

At maximum capacity, the *Acheron* might carry five thousand people. Four thousand of those would be newly Damned souls, with as much as two thousand of these passengers reserved for fuel. (Of course, the cargo was often half that number or even much less.) Of the remaining thousand people, roughly five hundred would be Damned crewmen serving any number of functions, with the other five hundred being Demons under Captain Surgat's command. As most of the labor on the ship was given to the Damned, these Demons primarily just served to guard and mistreat the prisoners...for every Damned was a prisoner, and mistreatment was a Demon's job.

These two, guarding the hatch to the reconstitution chamber, were similar in make to Surgat, though on a smaller, more man-sized scale, except that one's skin was bright yellow and the other's cobalt blue. The yellow Demon was covered in tattoos very like his commander's but less ornate, inked in black against the yellow, while the tattoos of the blue Demon were in white ink. They were naked except for leather belts, from which hung a short sword in a scabbard. Tattersall opened the hatch, respectfully keeping his eyes downcast all the while, but behind him he heard one of the Demon guards lean close to Mac-Jones and snarl threateningly. Not for the first time, Tattersall fantasized about turning his metal hoe around like a spear and putting its end through a Demon's eye, then grabbing its sword to engage its partner.

They can die, he reminded himself, *and I can't die again.* But the time wasn't right to fight back … to escape.

Once they were inside the chamber, Tattersall closed the hatch and turned to face the familiar sight he dreaded even more than a Demon's random animosity.

This was the chamber into which Tattersall and Mac-Jones had swept all the cremains, through that hatch up there in the ceiling. Most of those cremains still lay scattered all over the floor in this spacious, featureless room. Only one chunk of every Damned who had been utilized as fuel—the largest and hence most viable shard of bone, be it from a skull or pelvis or what have you—would regenerate back into that person. The rest of the debris would rot away like mortal remains, and so it was up to Tattersall and Mac-Jones to clean up that useless matter.

Scattered upon this bed of bone fragments and gritty ash, though, were the fifty regenerating souls. They were well on their way, but the process was excruciating and none of them could yet get to their feet. They lay mewling and hissing, twisting and writhing weakly on the floor, reaching at the air with skeletal arms, eyes rolling feverishly in veiny translucent heads.

Other Damned workers were here to see to the reconstituted Damned, also. Some of them were gently dragging the half-formed bodies across the floor by their arms or legs to clear the way for Tattersall and Mac-Jones to commence raking and sweeping again. Other workers waited beside carts full of new black uniforms, neatly folded, to replace those that had burned away in the furnace directly above. These uniforms were produced in a little factory right here aboard the *Acheron*, by Damned laborers, from rolls of material picked up occasionally at various ports. The Demons made sure the Damned were always clothed, lest in their nakedness they stimulate each other—pleasure of any kind being something the Damned could only experience furtively, if at all.

Yet Tattersall couldn't help but witness the nakedness of these fifty bodies reforming in his presence, as he raked up bone chips between them. He and Mac-Jones gradually maneuvered the piles they made toward another opening that had been uncovered in the floor. Only this time, the unviable cremains would ultimately find their way out into the ocean of blood, trailing in the *Acheron*'s wake as discarded waste.

Tattersall stole glances around him and began to recognize the faces of several of the reforming Damned. Then, with his heart suddenly pinned like a struggling butterfly, he recognized a person he had known in life among them. A small, dark-haired woman.

"*Zelma*," he said under his breath.

He was horrified that his girlfriend had somehow met her end prematurely, too, and been condemned to Hades—Zelma, who had been a devout Catholic. At the same time, though, he felt a leaping elation to discover her here. How had he not noticed before that she was aboard the ship? He wanted to scoop her up into his arms, hold her against him. Whisper comfort in her ear, as he had done with Cutler. He would never let them drift from each other again.

But Zelma had possessed darker skin than this woman he'd focused on amid the tangles of bodies. Zelma had been a little more chunky and compact. How could his eyes have tricked him so? Perhaps it was that his eyes themselves were the stuff of illusion.

This small woman he had noticed was not Mexican, but Asian... in her early to mid-twenties at the time of her demise, he reckoned. At least in that regard she was like Zelma. And now that his vision had sharpened he remembered her. This was not only because he had glimpsed her elsewhere on the *Acheron*, but because this was the second time he had watched her reconstitute in this room. Already tiny and slight in build, in her unfinished state she appeared fragile enough to shatter with a touch. She looked to him like a strange giant insect, ghastly but beautiful at the same time. Stepping around her a little to get a better view of her face, he saw it was sheened with sweat, her eyes like thin black slits in paper, her lips full and slack. Even as she experienced a rebirth worse than dying, he found her striking.

Through damp plastered hair he recognized a symbol branded on her forehead, knew it meant she had been committed to Hades for having had an abortion at some point in her life.

As he stared at the woman, he realized her own eyes, glittering black through strands of hair, had locked on his.

"I'm sorry," he said to her quietly. He wasn't sure why he apologized. Was it guilt for being part of this procedure, or guilt he felt toward the dissipated illusion of Zelma?

She croaked something back at him. Tattersall knelt down closer to her. "What'd you say?" he asked her.

She rasped the words again. "Fuck…you…*traitor.*"

Tattersall straightened up, averting his gaze. "I'm sorry," he repeated, ashamed to have been admiring her pain-racked form, and he resumed sweeping.

-6-

The Red Sea had gone so calm, at least in this locality, that the surface had begun to blacken and congeal to a thick, gummy state. The mammoth vessel plowed on through it, though, without inconvenience. Tattersall found the smell worse than the regular wet penny tang of blood, more decayed or infected, but he felt this tranquility was better than when great waves tossed the ship, and winds blew mists of blood across one's face if one had to venture onto the deck. Worst of all was the hammering rain of storms at sea…those torrential downpours of blood.

He had sneaked out here onto the elevated platform of one of the ship's superstructures—avoiding any Demons who might turn him away—and now stood leaning against its rail for a few moments of solitude, if not serenity.

He thought again of going out on Lake Waco with his father. The silence between them that was part discomfort, part harmony. On one such excursion, his father had related the only story of his time in the Navy that he'd ever shared with his son. One day, he'd looked off the stern of his PBR to see a gigantic Burmese python, over a dozen feet long, swimming after the river boat. That wondrous and nightmarish image had imprinted itself in the boy's mind, and it came back to him vividly now.

Despite what might dwell in this sea of blood—things worse than giant snakes—*could* he dive over the side? Tread water, make his way eventually to shore? Find shelter in some infernal forest, or stay on the move to avoid recapture? Such fantasizes filled his idle time ... kept him from giving himself over to insanity.

Through the haze of distance he could make out a hilly landmass, though he didn't know if it was the coastline or only a substantial island. Could it be the island of this Captain Beleth, of whom Surgat had spoken? Still, it seemed the ship was pointed along a course parallel to the landmass, rather than headed toward it.

"Hey," a voice said behind him, only loudly enough to be heard.

Tattersall turned to face the speaker, surprised though not alarmed. The voice of a female human, not a Demon.

A small figure hung back in the shadow of the threshold through which he had stepped out onto the platform. Hair black as crow's feathers, dark eyes that caught glimmers of light. He almost said under his breath again, "*Zelma.*"

His surprise at being addressed was greater when the figure took a step forward out of the shadows and he saw that once again he had been mistaken about this person. It was the Asian woman he had spoken to in the reconstitution chamber. She had, of course, completely regenerated by now, her hair dry and falling a little past her shoulders, wearing a new black uniform. Her face—pallid, not brown—glowed against the ship's black metal.

Tattersall stepped toward her in turn. "Hello," he said warily.

The surprises came in threes: she smiled at him, looking shy. "I'm sorry for what I said. I wasn't exactly feeling my best."

Relieved that she hadn't sought him out to further chastise him, he smiled too. "Understandable."

"I didn't mean to call you a traitor. You're only doing what you have to do. I'd do the same; anybody would." He liked her voice, small and a little squeaky. In life he might have pegged her as geeky, and he often found those types cute. She went on, "It's not like they're giving you special treatment. It must suck, having to do the things they tell you."

"It does," he admitted. "It's a punishment all its own, having to help them do stuff to other people. My buddy has it worse; he's one of the guys who have to force folks into the oven. I'm just the guy who shovels up the mess."

She spread her arms. "And here I am—the mess."

"You're looking better than when I swept you down the hole."

She laughed a little. It wasn't a sound one customarily heard in Hades. "Thanks."

In fact, though, he wondered if in part it *was* special treatment that he had been made a crewman of the *Acheron*. His lot did seem somewhat better than it might be—it was certainly better than being fuel—and he pondered whether that was because he had died at least attempting to save the lives of three children. Three children he could only hope had been baptized by their parents according to the Creator's unforgiving mandates, so that they wouldn't have been sent *here*.

Then again, he didn't really know much about how the Damned lived inland. He'd heard rumors that inland there were communities ranging from small villages to full-blown cities, where the Damned lived under relatively minimal Demonic supervision. If that were true, then he envied them. Would his service aboard the *Acheron* end at some point, or had this mode of afterlife been selected for him because in essence it mirrored the way he had lived? In life he had moved from job to job, unfulfilled by all of them. The same could be said of his relationships. In his adult life, his general feeling was of being detached from anything meaningful. Unmoored...adrift...ultimately, of being without a true direction.

Of the work he had done, only volunteering as a firefighter had given him a real sense of pride. He wanted to laugh. Look how that had turned out. Look what he had allowed to happen to himself.

And to those children.

The sad thing, the hilarious thing, was that his failure to rescue them wasn't even the reason he was here.

"I'm Jin," she said, bringing his focus back to her. She held out her hand.

He stared at her small hand for a moment, then took it into his own. It was soft, warm; its fingers squeezed his. It was as though he had never held a human hand before. His eyes began to fill up. He let go of her hand and looked to the side a little, hoping she didn't see his eyes shimmering. To distract her from that, he told her his own name.

Jin didn't seem to notice that he was close to tears, or was too polite or embarrassed to call attention to it. She regarded the expanse of sea, and said, "I wonder what waits for me after we pick up the next batch of people at this island. Man...if it's far to the place where we're supposed to drop them off, who knows how many more times I'll have to go into the fire. That was my second time."

"I know," he murmured.

"The first time they burned me, I tried to tell myself the fire is only an illusion. My body is only an illusion." She snorted. "That didn't work for shit."

"When we bring the next group to their destination they'll release you, too. People from that group will become the fuel."

"I wonder if things will be more bearable out there, on land." She gestured toward the misty hills they saw like a mirage on the horizon.

He told her then of the stories he had heard from other Damned, of villages and even cities in which the Damned dwelt alongside their Demonic masters. "I hear people have apartments. Jobs. Shitty jobs, but hey, the jobs I had in life were mostly shitty anyway. I hope you end up in some city like that."

"Thanks. Me, too. What about you? I don't suppose you can elect to go, too, if you wanted?"

He shook his head. "People can't elect a whole lot, here."

"Well ... you can't give up hope that things can still get better for you than they are now, to some degree."

"*Hope?* Talk about illusions, Jin. I'd put hope right up there with justice...fairness...goodness. How can those things exist if even the Creator doesn't understand them?"

"Then I hope one day He'll learn."

He sighed, wagged his head. "Were you a motivational speaker in life?" he teased.

"No, it's my new job," she kidded him back. "Inspirational speaker. How am I doing so far?"

"Great. I feel inspired already."

"Good. Remember—you have to grab the afterlife by the horns."

"You can stop now."

She laughed. Again, that human sound, as human as her soft hand. It was an intoxicant.

"You're right, though," she said. "Hope is a passive thing. You might need to take matters into your own hands, somehow."

"From inspirational speaker to mind reader," he said. "I've been thinking the same."

She nodded gravely. "Then do that."

"I'm looking for a way. Waiting for the time."

"Well, I know we have all the time in the underworld, here, but there's no time like the present."

A loud, flat *whump* that resonated in their chests caused Tattersall and Jin to look back to sea. For a panicky moment, Tattersall feared the Creator had overheard them speaking disrespectfully, and was enraged. Then, he saw a black pillar of smoke rising from behind the remote line of hazed hills, like a fast-sprouting giant tree.

"What's that?" Jin asked, putting a hand on his arm. "Is that a volcano?"

Below them on the deck, off to their left, Tattersall noticed Samoshkina, the Baby Killer, stepping out of the shadows and up to the rail, to look toward the smoke himself. As a former soldier, a former terrorist, were the booming thud and billowing smoke familiar to him?

From Samoshkina's reaction, Tattersall said, "I think it was an explosion."

Jin's face twisted. "Like a bomb?"

Then, two more figures appeared from directly beneath the platform Tattersall and Jin stood on, and they too approached the edge of the deck, to gaze off toward the black column. At the sight of them, Samoshkina spun away from the rail and hurried away in the opposite direction.

The two imposing figures were Captain Surgat and his advisor, whose name, if it had one, the Damned sailors didn't know. This towering entity, its thin body hidden under a cloak made from a single sheet of black leather, had the fleshless grinning face of a skeleton, with white points of light blazing in its skull sockets, but its head was a semitransparent balloon squiggled with black veins like that of a hydrocephalic infant. The Damned had nicknamed this sort of Demon Bubbleheads. Teams of them scrutinized each and every one of the Damned shortly after they had been delivered into Hades through a gate—briefly, with those fiery eyes—as if to weigh or judge their soul, or determine where that soul should be sent in the vastness of the netherworld.

"What's out there?" Surgat asked in his growling voice.

His advisor didn't respond audibly, but were the Bubbleheads telepathic? This was Tattersall's impression, because when Surgat next spoke, it was as if he were repeating a word that had just been conveyed to him.

He said, "Oblivion."

Jin shrieked then. Tattersall began to shush her, though he knew it was too late—surely the Demons below had heard her, would know they were loitering outside up here—but when he looked to her he saw that a small flying animal of some kind had alighted on the side of her neck. Infernal animals of boundless varieties populated Hades, nearly all of them meant to harass the Damned.

Tattersall couldn't grasp, at first glance, what this creature was. A bony white ring, with a vagina-like interior, and two thin membranes that served as wings, waving languidly. Only when he realized that it had glued its base to the skin of Jin's neck, and her frenzied clawing hands couldn't dislodge it, did he understand it was a kind of airborne barnacle.

Before Tattersall could try to pry the creature loose himself, a high-pitched whistle speared his ears. He glanced over the rail again and saw that Surgat and his advisor were staring up at the pair. Surgat had made the whistling sound through his front teeth.

At the sound of the whistle, the barnacle somehow broke its hold and fluttered up into the air, darting away like a hummingbird.

Still looking up at Tattersall and Jin, Surgat said, "One of Beleth's pets. We are almost there."

Another shriek pierced the air, but this time it wasn't Jin; someone further down the length of the ship. Had that same barnacle creature affixed itself to another of the Damned? This cry was in a man's voice.

Tattersall saw Surgat and his advisor turn sharply toward the sound. He and Jin looked that way, too.

That was when they saw that the sea of blood had come alive.

-7-

Sometimes in their travels the *Acheron*'s crew saw giant swells, like inflating balloons or bubbles with semisolid skins, rise up from the blood's surface, then subside like whales that had briefly breached and submerged again. This was because the blood was made of phantom cells, phantom organic matter, and except for plant life (and not always then), most every mock organic entity in Hades however primitive was programmed to be hostile toward the Damned. Sometimes, even the ocean of blood could attain something like idiot consciousness. This was why storms at sea were like deliberate, malicious attacks.

But Tattersall had never witnessed a manifestation like this before.

Something like a bluntly tapered spire of blood had arisen right alongside the ship, but the scabrous outer skin was black and crusted as if burnt, reeking of decomposition. In its size and general shape, Tattersall was again reminded of a whale—a whale that had flung almost its entire body out of the sea, hanging poised on the end of its tail. This blind, elongated mass had somehow extended two long, thick appendages like tentacles where its pectoral fins might have been. One of these limbs was wrapped around the waist of Samoshkina. He was still shrieking in mad panic, as the tentacle sought to pull him off the deck, but he had wrapped his arms and one leg around the ship's railing.

Surgat whipped around to point up at Tattersall. "You!" he bellowed. "Get down here and lend me a hand." Then, the *Acheron*'s captain charged toward the effigy of blood, as it somehow kept pace beside the moving ship, merely rising and falling slightly with the languid roll of waves, and wavering a little at its top like a tree blown in the wind.

189

Tattersall swung himself over the rail of the platform he stood on, let himself drop to the deck. Immediately, he set off after Surgat. The obelisk of blood all but blanked his mind with fear, and yet he was even more afraid of disobeying the Demon captain's command.

Tattersall passed the Bubblehead, which only revolved as if levitating to watch him without joining in their advance. Ahead of him, a little short of where Samoshkina clung desperately to the rail, Surgat stopped at the rail himself, and took hold of it. This gave Tattersall the opportunity to almost catch up with him, though he wasn't clear on what the Demon expected him to do to help the Baby Killer—if help the insignificant Damned man was, for some reason, Surgat's intention.

Tattersall saw the thick muscles in Surgat's arms and chest tighten and bunch as he gripped the rail, and he couldn't comprehend the Demon's actions until suddenly a length of the metal pipe that made up the railing tore free with a metallic screech. Its ends were jagged twists.

"Grab him!" Surgat shouted at Tattersall.

As if it had understood, the blood monolith wrenched more violently at Samoshkina, and his leg became unhooked from the lower rail. His screaming mounted to a level of pure frenzy. Another tug from that tentacle limb and his arms slipped from around the top rail, but somehow he managed to seize it in both fists, his body pulled out horizontally toward the main mass of the ocean's manifestation, as if it meant to suck him into itself—drag him down below, where he might drown, be resurrected, drown and be resurrected again, on and on for who could say how many terrestrial years, or centuries, or millennia.

Tattersall covered the last few steps in a leap, and grabbed hold of Samoshkina's straining left forearm in both hands, planting his feet on the deck as best he could. From the corner of his eye, he saw Surgat rushing toward them. The Demon held the long piece of railing pipe cocked over one shoulder like a bat.

Surgat brought the pipe down against the serpentine, blood-formed limb. There was a loud thump, and the limb's tense skin might have quivered a little, but it didn't uncoil from Samoshkina or even loosen its hold. It kept tugging. Surgat wound up again, swung a second mighty blow against it. Again, the pipe merely rebounded.

In a flashing movement, Jin was on Tattersall's left, grabbing hold of Samoshkina's right wrist in both her hands. It had taken her longer to get down from the platform and run across the deck. He stole a quick glance at her, saw the hardened look on her face, and liked her all the more.

A third blow from Surgat's club bounced off the appendage. Oddly, as if he were looking back in time at himself from outside his body, Tattersall saw himself desperately hurling a cherub statue through a sliding glass door. He wanted to cry out to his mortal self, cry out to Surgat, to hurry before it was too late.

Samoshkina's grip began to give way, his thumbs coming off the rail.

With a roar of frustration and fury, Surgat took a step back and cocked the pipe over his shoulder again, but this time holding it in one hand as if it were a javelin. With a surge of his whole powerful body forward, he launched the pipe like a spear at the main body of the blood creature.

The spear lanced the thing's outer skin, broke the tension that held it together. It burst all at once, and a waterfall of blood cascaded down from the sky, crashing back up from the sea in plumes. A spray of blood washed over Tattersall and Jin as if thrown from a bucket, and they shut their eyes against it, but neither of them let go of Samoshkina. Still, when his body fell vertical again, he began to slip down out of their slickened grasp, his fingers at last coming off the rail.

Then Surgat was beside them, his body knocking Tattersall aside, and he snatched hold of the Baby Killer by the hair. He lifted the Damned man up over the rail easily and let him fall to the deck. The terrorist lay there whimpering and gasping, a fish out of water, staring up at them with eyes wide and bright in a mask of blood. If his sanity hadn't already been shattered, as Tattersall had speculated, it looked that way now—or was he only confused as to why this Demon, and any of his fellow Damned who so despised him, would have struggled to rescue him?

Surgat straightened and looked out to the ocean, which had returned to its sluggish, becalmed state. He spoke directly to it. "You cannot have my men," he said in the defiant voice of one whose every moment was bent toward mastering the sea. "They have work to do."

Then he nodded toward that turret of black smoke that had bloomed on the horizon. "Whatever is happening there," he said, only vaguely explaining what had just occurred, "has caused a disturbance."

Without another look at them, he turned away and left the three blood-soaked Damned there at the rail, heading back toward his waiting advisor.

They did hear him grouse to himself, though, as he passed the section of railing where he had dislodged that length of pipe, "Now this needs to be repaired."

Samoshkina gathered his senses sufficiently to scramble to his feet and dash away in the direction he had been headed earlier, before the blood creature had risen to seize hold of him. Watching him flee, Tattersall said, "You're welcome."

"Hey, look!" Jin said, pointing. Tattersall wondered, with dread, *what now?* Bombs? Barnacles? Blood?

Indeed, it was more infernal animals, a school of them, that had surfaced and were swimming parallel to the ship like a pod of dolphins, sinuously threading their way in and out of the lazy swells and the troughs between them. Double sail-like fins on their backs, red like the rest of their sparkling bodies, cleaved the surface.

Then Tattersall recognized these twin fins or wings and understood the graceful red creatures were not animals, but a type of aquatic, humanoid Demon he had encountered in person before, during one of the *Acheron*'s stops. He'd heard many of them populated a city called Sheol at the bottom of the Red Sea, and there were supposedly other such cities occupied by their race. He explained all this to Jin.

"I wonder if whatever's going on with that smoke has disturbed them, too," she mused, as she wiped blood from her face with her hands. "Anyway, they're beautiful, huh?"

Beautiful? Tattersall looked at the swimming figures again.

Yes...though they were Demons, he supposed they were beautiful, as least as seen from here. Actually, they were undeniably beautiful.

Seeing the Demons anew through Jin's eyes, the notion struck him: that beauty could exist in Hades. Beauty in the very entities, creatures, and locations that had been designed to cause Damned souls terror and despair. It was all in one's perception.

If beauty could be found here, if one *chose* to perceive it, what other positives might one extract from Hades through perception, and perhaps more than that? Perhaps through force of will? In fact, wasn't electing to distinguish beauty where it wasn't intended a small act of rebellion?

-8-

The island of the Demonic commander Captain Beleth was not of great size, mostly only providing enough area to support a utilitarian walled palace that appeared to be entirely formed of coarse white coral, as if carved from a single prodigious piece. The island itself was not composed of rock, but of heaped up layers of melted-looking yellow matter that put Tattersall in mind of both the factory runoff they had seen afloat, and the blob-like proto-Demon called an Inferus. Did this seemingly organic matter extend down to the sea's floor, or was the artificial island only floating on the surface, and anchored here—just as the *Acheron* had dropped anchor at its edge?

As Tattersall and the other Damned crewmen assembled in neat rows on the deck, herded by their Demon guards, he observed that the only other feature outside the wall of Beleth's palace was an immeasurable number of those flying barnacles, piled up on each other in high mounds, at rest with their flying membranes only lazily pulsing. These thick assemblages of barnacles seemed to completely surround the palace, massed against the outer wall and covering much of what little remaining ground area the island offered.

Soon virtually all the crewmen were ranked on the upper deck, facing toward the palace, in which Tattersall guessed resided one of the multitudinous gates through which souls were funneled into the netherworld. The only Damned sailors not yet called to attention were those who were extending a metal ramp from the *Acheron*, and spiking its end securely into the rubbery edge of the island.

To the right of the Damned, Captain Surgat and his Bubblehead companion stood at the head of rows of fearsome looking Demons of every stripe, though the majority of them resembled their Captain at least superficially. Surgat had fixed a leather belt around his waist, from which hung a long ceremonial sword that reminded Tattersall of a Scottish claymore, except that the captain could probably wield it one-handed.

The Baby Killer, Samoshkina—once more his quiet self—stood stiffly at attention like a soldier on Tattersall's left, and Cutler was on his right. Tattersall had begun to turn his head toward Cutler slightly, and mutter a comment from the side of his mouth, when a sudden blast of sound cut him off and caused him to flinch. It was a deep, reverberating bleat like the forlorn trumpet of a mastodon sinking in a tar pit, coming from the direction of the blank coral palace. It rolled off across the Red Sea's surface like thunder. Quickly on its heels came a second blast. Then, with a clattering sound, a gate of crisscrossed black iron bands was raised at the fore of the surrounding wall, and through its threshold started a procession of more Demons, though quite different from the *Acheron*'s contingent.

These Demons were like man-sized, bipedal praying mantises, metallic black in hue, moving in strange sudden jerks as if frames had been erratically snipped out of a strip of motion picture film. Their deep eye sockets were as empty as those of a skull, and from the front of their heads a long spike or beak was thrust, putting Tattersall in mind of a plague doctor's mask. Their weirdly bent forelimbs, though, ended in human-like black skeletal hands. The first two Demons in the column carried poles from which banners emblazoned with a mysterious glyph snapped in the ocean breeze, but those creatures that followed carried something else in their hands.

Cutler hissed to Tattersall, "Are those *machineguns?*"

The weapons borne in the Demons' jointed arms did appear to be assault rifles of some type, perhaps even patterned after a terrestrial model; Tattersall was not enough of a weapons enthusiast to know. As obsidian black as the beings that carried them.

How were these emerging Demons supposed to pick their way over the tall heaps of barnacles? No sooner had Tattersall asked himself this, though, when one of the two flag-bearing Demons at the front tilted back its head and made a shrill, ear-piercing whistle from within its beak.

All at once, every one of the formerly torpid barnacles shot up into the air, wing-like flaps in a blur. Their shells clinked and clacked against each other, like thousands of dice, and the chorus of their rapidly fluttering wing membranes was an uncanny susurration. Yet the flying arthropods quickly scattered in every direction, darting away as if in terror, blowing above the ocean in clouds like swarms of locusts.

Now Tattersall saw what had been buried, imprisoned, under those mounds of barnacles all this time.

They were the Damned. Those whom the *Acheron* was here to pick up, and either transport to their next destination or retain as crew replacements or fuel. Men, women, children, all wearing the standard black uniform, and heaped up as if they'd been tossed into a charnel pit. They began to untangle themselves from each other with aching slowness, none quite ready yet to attempt standing. A formerly muted chorus of moans, sobbing, cries of despair had risen into the air along with the barnacles the moment the animals had released them. They had not been unconscious in their prison, however. Only too conscious, while they waited for the ferry ship to arrive.

Beside Tattersall, he heard Cutler whisper, "Bastards."

Children screaming—as if they were burning alive. Nausea yawed in Tattersall's guts at the sound.

The parade of Demons proceeded down a ramp, now cleared of those masses of barnacles, and the Damned who had been entombed by them pitifully crawled out of the procession's path as quickly as their cramped and crushed bodies permitted. The ramp slanted down toward the edge of the island, where the end of the *Acheron*'s own ramp was nailed.

At the center of this column that flowed centipede-like from within the palace wall, Captain Beleth loomed distinct above his entourage. He was even less anthropomorphic than they. Beleth's body was nothing but layers of wet-looking black sheets, like long leather cloaks draped one upon the other upon the other, this mass seemingly hovering above the ground but actually carried along by myriad hair-thin legs or cilia that somehow upheld him. He possessed no upper limbs, and no real head surmounted the leathery pillar. Just a blank, bony black knob resided there, like the spherical post cap on a staircase banister.

The marching insect-like entities continued from the end of the palace's ramp to the start of the *Acheron*'s gangplank, and ascended this...began to pour onto her expansive deck. There, Beleth's creatures formed rows just as the *Acheron*'s own Demons and Damned had done.

As Captain Beleth came aboard the *Acheron*, proving himself even more tall than he had appeared at a distance, Tattersall realized that not all the wails of children came from the Damned who had been trapped under the barnacles. Around the base of the bony orb that topped his form, Beleth wore a necklace. A string of severed heads, the heads of human infants, the stumps of their necks sealed with metal caps to prevent their bodies from regenerating. Tears wetted their cheeks, their faces twisting in grimaces of anguish.

Stunned and overwhelmed by this vision, almost growing faint, Tattersall then seemed to see these strung heads through a gauzy and distorting veil, like smoke. The faces were now not those of a dozen infants, but three brown-skinned boys of varying age, the youngest of them with a purple firemark covering half his face, staring back at him imploringly. Their wailing of "*Mami...Mami*" mounted in intensity inside Tattersall's head, like the siren of a fire engine enclosed within his skull space.

But no, no, they were infants, and they couldn't be making any sound without vocal cords. The screams only seemed to be coming from their soundlessly working mouths. Their screams were only in Tattersall's head.

Despite those deafening cries in his mind, to his left he heard Samoshkina mumble something to himself. He appeared fixated on the necklace, too.

The procession had come to a halt. The three dense congregations—Beleth's island force, Surgat's Demonic crew, and the ship's Damned sailors—faced in toward each other, with the two Demon captains a short distance apart. They couldn't have looked more different had they come from different planets.

About halfway down the front of Beleth's figure, the layers that made up his body parted in a vertical elliptical shape, like the folds of a woman's sex, and uncovered at the opening's center were a human-like pair of glistening black lips, also vertical. They seemed to smile, revealing black teeth, and a very human-sounding voice issued from them.

"Surgat!" the overseer of this island's gateway exclaimed. "Your travels too seldom bring you to this humble outpost. It's good to see you again."

See? Tattersall thought. Could this monstrosity see? And for that matter, his soldiers with their hollow eye sockets?

"Captain Beleth," Surgat replied simply, in a formal tone.

The tower of black flesh pivoted slightly toward Surgat's Demons with their tattoos and sheathed swords. "And your hardy crew. A little ragtag, but as one would expect from a seafaring lot, eh?"

As Surgat's Bubblehead counselor stood beside him, so did Beleth's counterpart crouch like a favorite dog at his side, but Tattersall hadn't seen it from a distance because it was lower to the ground than his soldiers. It was roughly in the form of a giant black spider, with its head swollen into a translucent gray sphere above its eight eyes. Its complex mouthparts were in constant twitching motion, as the thing seemed to nervously apprise Surgat.

Beleth shifted a little again, and Tattersall felt, with a shudder, the Demon's gaze sweep over him with something like a mild electric shock through his nerves. "But where are the children among your workforce, Surgat?"

"I like strong workers, to get the job done quickly," Surgat replied tersely.

"Ha…I see. And why didn't you assemble your fuel up here for me to inspect, as well? I might have found a new bauble or two to add to my necklace. Do you like it, Surgat? It's new. I noticed you admiring it. Ah, but I suppose you still choose not to utilize children as fuel.

ACHERON

Wait…let me guess…you like adult bodies because they burn longer."
A chuckle came through the grinning vertical lips. "Am I right, Surgat?
You have a soft spot for the little ones?"

Tattersall's suspicions had been confirmed. It was the decision of
the *Acheron*'s captain not to use as fuel the children who were conveyed
aboard his ferry ship.

After an uncomfortable hesitation, in which the air around him
seemed to seethe invisibly, Surgat grumbled, "The Son said, 'Suffer
little children to come unto me.' Would you mock the Son as being
soft, Captain Beleth?"

"He meant *blessed* children, you old fool," Beleth laughed.
"Damned children need only *suffer*."

"They suffer," Surgat said.

"As well they should. As the Creator demands."

Surgat changed the subject. "Are the souls you gathered ready to
be directed aboard?" He gestured past Beleth at the Damned who
surrounded his palace's walls, most of them now having shakily got to
their feet, though their chorus went on only somewhat subdued.

"Presently, Surgat. Why be in such a hurry? I want to invite you
to come have dinner with me tonight. You can set sail with your cargo
refreshed in the morning."

Tattersall cringed inside to imagine what dinner would consist of
on such a barren island. Probably not animals from the ocean of blood;
more likely the flesh of the Damned, maybe individuals penned for
that purpose, harvested for new meat each time they had regrown it.
Not that Demons *needed* to eat to survive.

Beleth said, "But listen to me…*tonight*…*morning*. Here I am a
youngster designed to be as little like a human as possible, and I let
myself be polluted with earthly conceptions. In any case, you must of
course accept my invitation!"

"Thank you." Surgat sounded less than grateful, but Tattersall
believed the Demon held rigidly to a code of respect, either ancient or
solely his own.

"Excellent. I'll have quite the banquet laid out, I assure you."

Surgat began to grunt further thanks, but a sound interrupted him.

It was another of those deeply felt booms from far out across the waves, where a black pall of smoke hung over that distant landmass.

Tattersall noticed that the fidgety spider Demon's mouthparts had become even more agitated, its pedipalps in spasms. What was this oracle sensing?

Surgat looked off toward the smoke. "Do you know what that is, Beleth?" he asked.

"Ah yes," the other Demonic officer said. "Trouble in the city of Oblivion, we hear. A little rebellion has been brewing."

Surgat turned back to him. "Rebellion?"

"An uprising of some of the Damned who live there. Can you imagine the negligent Demons of Oblivion allowing things to get to such a point? But the problem is worse than neglect. What my friend here –" and he meant the spider "– has heard is that there are even Demons who have taken side with the Damned rebels, against their brother Demons."

"But...why would they do that?" Surgat glanced off again in the direction of the city of Oblivion.

"Sympathy from the Devil," Beleth joked. "I know—I too had never heard of such an unthinkable collaboration before, but for some time now the older races of Demons have been growing too sentimental and weak. Too...*soft*. The Creator has anticipated this, though. This is why recently we have seen a move away from anthropomorphic races of Demons, like yourself, who are more likely to identify with humans— and vice versa—in favor of new breeds like, say, my own. I'm sure He'll step up that process in light of this Oblivion situation. As more new Demon types are produced, the older types will be eliminated... recycled for their materials at best." Beleth chuckled again. "I'm afraid it's only a matter of time before you and your motley crew are replaced, too, Surgat."

Surgat once more faced Beleth. "Is that what your friend has heard, Beleth?"

"Oh, there is no question. You haven't foreseen this, yourself? Poor old Surgat; you spend too much time adrift! You're disconnected from what's going on. Or maybe you've been left out of such discussions intentionally. In any case, who are we to question the Creator's decisions? He never stops perfecting His craft. Think of it as... evolution. You'll obediently go to meet your end when the time comes, I know you will—respectfully and honorably. Your service has been commendable, Surgat; you are a monument to older times. But even monuments crumble. Yet, the stone can be reused. In that way, at least, you will live on." That vertical mouth leered, black teeth glinting.

"Your body might be inhuman," Surgat said darkly, "but you talk in the manner of a human."

"Oh? How so?" When Surgat didn't elaborate, Beleth went on, "I myself have never listened much to what humans have to say. I'm only interested in their screams. Now, will you and *your* friend please accompany me back to my citadel? I'm eager to share my hospitality with you."

"Lead on," Surgat said.

When Surgat, the Bubblehead, and a group of about a dozen of the *Acheron*'s Demons had joined Beleth's retreating party, the Damned and the remaining Demons assembled on the ship's deck broke up to return to their regular duties.

Tattersall and Cutler lingered, staring off toward where the Demon officers had indicated the city of Oblivion lay.

"Can you imagine?" Cutler whispered excitedly.

"Did you see that fucker's necklace?" Tattersall asked.

"Kind of hard to miss it."

"That's too much, man. Of all that I've seen here ... that's too much for me."

A pair of tattooed Demons came toward them, drawing their swords in readiness to poke them and get them moving, so the two Damned men hastened away before they could.

-9-

It had taken a fair amount of time for Tattersall to sneak unseen through the craft, up to the deck, and from there to a position close to the lowered gangplank. He crouched down behind a vent hood for what he gauged would have been over an hour, until his legs ached from muscle tension. He listened to the diminished sobs and the soft drone of conversation from the Damned who still surrounded the palace's wall, hunkered down and waiting to be transported when the *Acheron* lifted anchor. At last, over their sounds and the lapping of blood against the ship's hull, Tattersall heard noises from the island that indicated Surgat and his entourage were returning from Beleth's questionable feast.

When Surgat and the Bubblehead beside him had mounted to the deck, preceded and followed by soldiers, the latter Demon stopped suddenly in its tracks and let out a kind of rasping hiss, like an alerting cry. It was the first sound Tattersall had ever heard the advisor make. Had it sensed him hiding? If he had doubted whether he could go through with this, it was too late to retreat now. Tattersall rose and stepped out from behind the vent hood. "Captain Surgat!" he called.

Immediately, the six Demons who had led the way up the gangplank rushed him. Despite his impulse to do so, he didn't spin away and flee. Even if he had, they'd have caught him, and the outcome would have been worse. He allowed two of the Demons to seize him in powerful hands, twisting his arms behind him in a way that might have left a mortal man with lifetime injuries. Even so, Tattersall cried out sharply in pain. One of the Demons gripped him by the hair, another laid its sword blade across his throat.

"I know him," Surgat said, coming forward. "One of the furnace crew."

"Tattersall," he groaned.

"Let him up," Surgat ordered. When Tattersall had straightened, though the Demons still held his arms, Surgat asked, "What do you mean jumping out at me?"

"Sir," Tattersall managed through his discomfort, "I wanted to speak with you."

"So speak."

"Can we speak in private?"

The Demon holding a sword to his throat snarled, "Who do you think you are?"

Ignoring his man, Surgat asked, "About what?"

201

"About Captain Beleth."

Surgat was silent for a moment. Then, in a more subdued voice, he said to the Demons who had hold of Tattersall, "Bring him to my cabin."

Tattersall was hustled below, to a portion of the ship he had never been exposed to before: the level whereon the Demons had their quarters.

Surgat's cabin was humble: small and Spartan. His head almost brushed its ceiling. Against one wall, a long narrow bed was bolted to the floor. There was a desk built of the same riveted black metal as the walls, piled with some huge ledgers and a number of books apparently bound in human skin—including several with a living, moving eyeball set in the front cover. Damned souls prevented from reconstituting. Seeing this made Tattersall again fear that he was wasting his time approaching this Demon.

Surgat dismissed his men, who had lingered uneasily in the corridor, and closed the heavy hatch that was his door. He unbuckled his belt, lifted his great sword to rest it in brackets mounted on one wall. Watching him do so, seeing the tattoos entwined around the Demon's bulky arms, he again thought of the barbed wire tattoo around his father's left arm. Again thought of the mix of admiration and trepidation he experienced when alone with his father. The connection that, despite their hours together on the water, had never seemed to reach some elusive point of acknowledgment or expression.

As he set his sword in its brackets, Surgat still kept his eyes on the Damned man. Tattersall remembered when Surgat had admitted to him and Cutler that Demons could be killed, whereas the Damned could not. Was this monster actually feeling trepidation, or at least wariness, about him, too? The thought made Tattersall feel a little more confident.

"Talk," Surgat demanded.

"Sir," Tattersall said, wincing as he flexed his own arms, "I'm not leaving Beleth's island without that necklace of his."

"*What?*"

"Beleth's necklace...those baby heads."

"I know what his necklace is made of."

"I want it. I want those babies set free, to grow their bodies back."

Surgat took a step closer to Tattersall, who correspondingly backed up a step, almost into a wall. "What tone is this? Are you making some kind of demand, here?"

"Sir, it's not within my power to demand anything of you. I'm asking you."

"Asking me to…"

"To help me get the necklace somehow, to take with us."

"And release those infants to what? Grow full bodies that will experience the suffering of Hades, instead of merely their heads, their minds, suffering? What good do you think that will do them?"

"You told me yourself. *Even in hell, there is greater hell.*"

"Why does it mean so much to you?"

"They … it speaks to me. In a personal way."

"And you would like my help in what way? You want me to trade something for that necklace? Ask for it as a gift? He knows it has no appeal for me. He was taunting me with it."

"Yes. He taunted you quite a bit, sir."

"My dealings with him are not for you to contemplate or discuss."

"Sir…with all respect, and I'm sure I respect you more than Beleth does…I will not leave without that necklace."

"Really?" Surgat thundered. "Then maybe I will leave you behind when the *Acheron* sets sail. Is that what you want?"

"What I want is for you to help me. To steal that necklace if we must. Or…take it by force if we must."

"By force. Do you mean I should oppose Beleth with *violence?*"

Tattersall held the much taller being's laser red gaze. "Yes."

Surgat cocked his arm as if to give Tattersall a backhanded blow. Such a blow would have left Tattersall in need of much regenerating, and he flinched in anticipation. But the *Acheron*'s captain stayed his hand in that position. Through gritted teeth he growled, "For me to oppose another Demonic leader in the way you suggest is the same as asking me to go against the Creator's design. To go against the Creator Himself!" Surgat began to visibly quiver with the effort of controlling his fury. Did his eyes glow even redder? "You have lost your mind—now I understand. It happens here."

Tattersall wanted to say it was the Creator who was mad—for what sane or loving being could sentence infants to eternal damnation because their parents were atheists or Muslim or Hindu?—but he didn't dare. "I haven't gone crazy. I'm getting clearheaded. I thought maybe you could, too."

"So you believe me muddled. Insolent human, do you presume to teach *me* something?"

"Beleth's the one who presumes to teach you something. He wants you to believe you're of no more worth. No value. He thinks you're a joke. He called you an *old fool*."

"*Enough!*" Surgat roared. The metal walls rang, or was that just the inside of Tattersall's skull? The Demon spun away, glaring at a wall as if to bore twin holes through it. Not looking back at Tattersall, he said, "Rescue a dozen Damned souls from another Demonic leader. Do you have any idea of the punishment I would face, if it were deemed I had acted against the Creator's will?"

"Yeah…I do. But you'd only be facing that punishment once, then you'd die. I face those punishments for *eternity*. So do those children. You're going to die one way or the other, Captain…you heard him. It's only a matter of time. After all these, whatever, hundreds of years you've served the Creator loyally, are you just going to walk into one of those factories like a pig to slaughter and let them melt you down? Recycle you, to make more like *Beleth?*"

Surgat turned toward Tattersall with ominous slowness, but his fiery eyes looked more contemplative than enraged. "I have seen this. Sometimes you Damned, understanding you cannot really be destroyed, lose your fear—no matter what tortures you are threatened with."

"You can lose your fear, too."

"I am afraid of *nothing*."

"You're afraid not to be obedient."

"You *are* insane. Talking to me in this way."

Tattersall nodded at the sword on the wall. "That's mostly just a symbol, isn't it? A decoration. You've probably only used it for discipline, not in any kind of battle. You're a proud warrior, Captain. A proud warrior who's never dared fight a war."

"You insult me more than Beleth."

"So prove me wrong."

Surgat had his fist wrapped in the front of Tattersall's shirt in such a blur of movement he hadn't even seen the arm coming toward him. The Demon lifted him clear off his feet, until his own head nearly struck the ceiling. Tattersall realized with horror he had misjudged Surgat, that he had been naïve and foolish, that the Demon would find some new means of making him remember fear and obedience. That Surgat would see his spirit broken again.

Surgat drew Tattersall's face close to his own. The smell of meat on the monster's breath indicated he had indeed partaken of Beleth's feast. The heat of it was like that from a furnace. From a burning house.

The Demon said, "I need prove *nothing* to you, human! Nor to Beleth!"

Though his voice was choked by the material of his shirt bunched at his throat, and choked by the return of trepidation, Tattersall was still able to get out the words, "How about to yourself, then?"

-10-

The last of the Damned who had most recently arrived on Beleth's island via the soul gate at the heart of his palace had been driven aboard the *Acheron* by Beleth's Demons, and from there herded by Surgat's Demons into the cargo hold. Now only one bit of business remained before the *Acheron* once more set to sea.

Standing straight and staring ahead just as he had done when Beleth first boarded the *Acheron*, but this time positioned along with his coworker Mac-Jones to the left of the stoking chamber's door, Tattersall heard Captain Surgat's guttural voice carrying ahead of him from around a bend in the corridor.

"I thought it best to begin with a look at the *Acheron*'s method of propulsion," Surgat was saying.

"The object of my greatest interest," Captain Beleth's smoother voice replied. "I've heard it's an extraordinary technology, and of course a wonderful means of dispensing torment, besides. This is very considerate of you, Surgat. How many times have your ship and others come to my island, without any of you captains once inviting me aboard for a tour?" "Forgive me if I have been remiss in the past. I felt it only fair to return the courtesies you have extended to me."

Cutler and his coworker, Samoshkina the Baby Killer, stood to the right of the stoking chamber door. Like Tattersall and Mac-Jones— who were usually stationed at the far end of this process—they had the aspect of imperial guards, each of the four men holding erect in one fist a long metal spear used to help drive Damned prisoners into the furnace.

Beleth continued, "For all your flaws, Surgat, I'll tell you…I prefer you to old Vassago, captain of the *Phlegethon*. He's all but a human in Demonic guise. Have you heard that he takes to bed some of the Damned females he transports, and favors them…protects them? They say he even fell in love with one of them, and tried to keep her as a fixture aboard the *Phlegethon*, but when word of it reached higher ears he was obligated to deliver her to her intended destination. Such ridiculous and unacceptable behavior! This is precisely what I've been talking about…the sort of insanity that has to end."

By now, the touring party had turned into this section of corridor, preceded by two of Beleth's beak-faced underlings, both carrying those jet black assault rifles. After them, so much taller, came Beleth and Surgat, the latter looking majestic with the sword he wore like a sign of office. Following them were their respective counselors: Surgat's Bubblehead, and Beleth's arachnid-thing. Next, two more of Beleth's soldiers, and bringing up the rear a pair of Surgat's Demons wearing their own sheathed swords.

Around the base of the bony protuberance atop Beleth's nonhuman figure, like his own sign of office: that necklace of silently bawling Damned infants.

Tattersall's heart blubbered as the party came to a stop a short distance opposite him, Beleth's unknown means of perception again momentarily falling upon him with that same electric buzz along his every nerve. He found himself unable to draw in enough breath, tried to remind himself he didn't need to breathe because he wasn't alive.

"This is the stoking chamber, where it all begins" Surgat explained. "The fuel is brought here, and directed inside. These men are workers assigned to the feeding and cleaning of the furnace." He nodded to Cutler. "Open it."

Tattersall turned his head ever-so-slightly to watch as Cutler leaned his spear against the wall so he could take hold of the wheel in the center of the large hatch. He noticed that Samoshkina's eyes were darting between the assembled Demons wildly, his face filmed in sweat. No one had said anything to him about this visit. No one ever spoke to the former terrorist but to abuse him.

As he turned the wheel Cutler shot a look at Tattersall, wearing the faintest of smiles on his lips. The smile seemed to say—and in his mind Tattersall could almost hear the words, but spoken in the voice of his brother Nicolas, sober and strong at last—"*I'm not a loser. Not a waste.*"

As the door was hauled open, Beleth asked, "Is it these workers or your Demons who force the fuel into the furnace, once they're in the stoking chamber?"

"I have an Inferus," Surgat explained.

"Ah!" Beleth cried in delight. "I saw one once! Where is it now?"

"Locked up. Better that way. They are difficult to control. It only really listens to me."

"Yes, savage old things." Beleth lowered his voice confidentially. "You know, the Creator had the right idea from the start, with those early races not being anthropomorphic. Of course, not that there were humans around to influence His design back then, but you know what I mean. In any case, I'm happy He's getting back to that."

Tattersall and Cutler stepped into the stoking chamber first, to lead the way. The group of Demons then followed the two workers inside. Surgat had to bow his head as he passed through the threshold, and Beleth likewise folded forward about a third of the way down from the top of his form. Tattersall saw Mac-Jones gesture to the bug-eyed Samoshkina, and these two men entered the stoking chamber last, to flank its inner doorway.

Cutler turned another wheel, this one set into the wall near the door through which they'd come. A large panel at the far end of the room began to gratingly inch open: the entrance to the furnace itself, currently as cold and silent as a cavern. Alongside the wheel Cutler turned were gauges, a few small valves, and two large levers. Surgat indicated the control panel. "The furnace can either be operated remotely, from the engine room's central controls, or manually here."

Surgat himself led Beleth to the furnace's opening once the thick metal panel had risen high enough. "We can accommodate fifty Damned in here at a time," he said, leaning his upper body inside, his voice reverberating hollowly. Beleth drew closer, appearing to hover on his whispery cilia, for a look.

"Ah, can you sense it, Surgat?" the visiting Demon purred. "Echoes. Echoes of screams, soaked into these walls. *Delicious.*"

The two advisors hung back. Surgat's Bubblehead was as still as a statue, but the spider-creature was unsettled, its pedipalps vibrating in a blur as it shifted restlessly on its jointed legs. Its behavior caused Tattersall's heartbeat to gallop all the more riotously.

The spider Demon seemed to sense that Tattersall was surreptitiously watching it, for it suddenly scurried around to face him directly with its eight onyx eyes.

And then it let out a terrible screech.

Having bent forward a little beside Surgat to take in the interior of the furnace, Beleth abruptly straightened and wheeled toward the cry of warning.

Mac-Jones leapt out through the threshold of the stoking chamber and slammed the door shut after him, a moment before one of Beleth's mantis Demons whirled around and fired a burst from its assault rifle. The bullets sparked off the closing hatch. On the other side, the wheel squeaked as Mac-Jones sealed the stoking chamber tight.

Tattersall lost all but a vestige of his hearing, then, from the enclosed gunfire, and it only got worse from there.

"*Surgat!*" Beleth bellowed, his shout just as deafening.

The captain of the *Acheron* drew his huge sword from its scabbard and swung it toward the other Demonic officer all in one whooshing arc.

Tattersall lowered the point of the spear he'd been carrying and lunged forward, driving the leaf-shaped tip into the front of the spider Demon's globe of a head, just above those glittering eyes. It shrieked again and tried to scramble backwards, but he ran forward with it, holding onto the shaft, shoving it in deeper. There was an eruption of gray fluid, like dirty water released from a burst balloon, and the spider folded down onto its many legs.

Surgat's blade had cleaved straight through the tapered upper section of Beleth's body, this severed portion toppling to the floor. The black orb clanged against the metal floor like a dropped cannon ball. Along with it went the necklace of living heads, thumping to the floor a few inches away.

A black tongue as long as a python, studded down its length on both sides with black serrated teeth like those of a great white shark, whipped out of Beleth's mouth and lashed crazily at Surgat, opening a deep gash in his upper chest. He stumbled back, but Beleth bore down on him.

At the control panel, Cutler cranked several valves, then threw one of the two levers forward. Inside the furnace, countless jets of flame burst to life from rows of tiny holes in the ceiling, walls, and floor, forming a single maw of fire—its yellow light and a wave of intense heat flooding into the stoking chamber.

Seeing this, the mantis Demon who had fired at Mac-Jones let loose another spray of bullets. They punched across Cutler's back, dropping him. A split-second later, however, the blade at the end of a metal spear went through this insect-being's head. As the Demon crumpled, the Damned man who had killed it let go of his spear and swept up the fallen assault rifle instead.

Two other of the mantises fired on the pair of Surgat's soldiers who had formed the party's rear. Both of them were cut down, stitched by automatic fire, but with his dying momentum one of Surgat's men managed to swing his sword and split the head of a mantis Demon down the center.

Groaning miserably, bullets drilled right through him, Cutler still managed to claw his way back up the wall far enough to reach the control panel's second lever. He pushed it forward, then collapsed in a heap.

A shutter that took up almost an entire side wall of the stoking chamber began to grind upward.

Surgat's sword had chopped off the end of Beleth's lashing tongue, but even truncated it still kept whipping at him. One slash across the top of his hand caused Surgat to drop his sword, and a second swipe across his face ripped through one of his blazing red eyes. Surgat's back crashed up against a wall.

The shutter kept rising.

Tattersall tried to pull his spear free from the dead spider, but he had jammed it in too well. He looked around in time to see Surgat's Bubblehead killed, felled by gunfire from one of the two remaining mantis Demons. The other mantis, spotting Tattersall, turned its weapon his way and fired. Tattersall threw himself to the floor. Bullets flew over his head, but these bullets were crossing paths from two directions.

From the floor he saw Samoshkina with an assault rifle in his fists, the gun he had taken from the Demon he had speared. With the skill of one who had used such weapons before, Samoshkina fired a prolonged burst at one mantis, then switched to the other and unloaded the rest of his magazine. The exoskeletons of both Demons were broken apart, shards of chitin jumping and scattering.

Tattersall had just sprung back to his feet when his attention was called to his left, as a mountain of rubbery yellow flesh surged into the chamber.

Beleth had been coming at Surgat again with mouth appendage flailing, but he halted and swiveled around to see the Inferus bearing down on him. "How can you?" Beleth cried, his formerly mellifluous voice distorted by the monstrous tongue he had extended. "*Why?*"

The Inferus, even greater in height and bulk than both Demon captains, glided across the floor at startling speed and crashed its full weight into Beleth. The thud of their bodies meeting was a sound as of worlds colliding, if worlds were made of flesh. Beleth's tongue hacked at the primeval Demon once, ineffectually, as his body was knocked back through the mouth of the furnace. Falling into the inferno, he roared in outrage and agony only briefly before fire filled whatever he had for a throat.

Still, Tattersall saw the Demonic leader's body thrashing in the flames, and was afraid he'd fling himself out again. He bolted to the control panel, stepped over Cutler's slowly regenerating body and slammed down the lever to lower the furnace's door.

Surgat slid down the wall, black blood like ink flowing from his lacerations and from his punctured eye, as if to alter the patterns tattooed on his naked skin. From his place at the control panel, Tattersall saw the ship's captain glance dazedly around the room at the carnage, and settle on the bullet-riddled carcass of his loyal advisor.

The Inferus shifted around to stand over Surgat obediently, protectively. Tattersall had the impression Surgat had prepared the Inferus for this encounter beforehand, that it hadn't acted only spontaneously. Before all this, the captain had only instructed the others to be ready to unleash it.

Tattersall considered that they should also burn the bodies of Beleth's men, and Surgat's dead Demons besides, to destroy any evidence of what had transpired here, but would that even matter? The lesser Demons still abounding on Beleth's island would sooner or later let others know that their leader and his advisor had never returned from their tour of the ferry ship *Acheron*.

The furnace door had lowered halfway.

Tattersall saw Samoshkina drop his empty gun, and break into a run toward the furnace. The former terrorist appeared to be after the severed chunk of Beleth lying on the floor. Did he mean to throw the orb into the flames, too, irrationally afraid that the Demon might regrow from it just as the Damned regenerated? But no, Tattersall realized; it was the strung circle of babies' heads, next to the fragment, that the man wanted. Coming up on the necklace, still not stopping, Samoshkina reached down and swept it up in his hand. But even then he didn't stop hurtling forward. He gathered the heads against his chest in both arms.

Tattersall wanted to cry out in protest as Samoshkina ducked under the furnace door and plunged into the heart of the flames, but he stopped himself. Anyway, it was too late.

He lost sight of the man, and the subsiding body of the dying Demon, as the furnace door came down the rest of the way and met the floor with a resonating clang.

Tattersall slumped back wearily against the wall where the control panel was set, and said, "See you on the other side."

-11-

As Cutler and another Damned crewmen pulled up the spikes that had secured the end of the ship's gangplank, a group of mantis Demons emerged through the gate in the wall surrounding Beleth's palace to mutely watch. Cutler looked up at them, waved, and shouted cheerfully, "We're just taking Captain Beleth for a few laps around his island, to show him how the ship operates. We'll be back soon!"

The other crewman called, "Bye!"

The immense ferry ship *Acheron* reversed away from the island of flesh, and once clear began to move forward at an unhurried rate, a ponderous leviathan, its bow parting the rocking surface of blood that upheld it. A few flying barnacles would skitter along the blood now and then, like stones skipped across water, but none approached the ship to harass the many Damned who were freely milling on the deck to watch Beleth's island recede.

Jin stood in the open air cradling one of the babies, an Asian boy, against her chest. It had finished reconstituting, looking plump and healthy and wrapped in a black uniform shirt. In being burned down to ash, it had been freed of the metal cap that had formerly prevented its body from growing from the stump of its neck. The baby was asleep, its face at peace for the first time since Tattersall had seen Beleth's necklace.

He came beside Jin and put his arm around her shoulders. She didn't protest. Tears flowed down her cheeks, but she was smiling. "Isn't he the most beautiful thing you've ever seen?" she asked him.

"Besides you, maybe," he told her.

She flashed a bright grin at him before returning her focus to the sleeping child. She grew reflective. "They'll never get any older," she said. "They'll never grow into adults."

"Maybe they're luckier for that."

"We'll have to always protect them."

"So we will."

Tattersall looked up and saw Samoshkina standing further down the deck, holding another of the babies in his arms and gazing at it solemnly. It was a baby girl. No one approached him to take the child away. From that point on, behind his back and even when they spoke to his face, the other Damned would call him the Demon Killer.

Captain Surgat stood at the edge of the deck, holding the rail and staring out across the Red Sea with his one remaining eye, the other socket caked thickly in drying black blood. Tattersall slid his arm from around Jin's slight shoulders and moved to stand beside the Demon. He saw other scabbed wounds on the captain's body, wounds that had split and interrupted the network of tattoos that had covered him for centuries, heretofore a rigid map. Surgat glanced down at the human before returning his attention to the sea.

"You should wear an eye patch now," Tattersall said. "Become a pirate."

"You are in high spirits. But I have lost three of my people."

"Yes," Tattersall said. "But they didn't die walking into a recycling plant."

Surgat grunted.

"You're not...you're not going to take all the Damned aboard to the destination you were supposed to let them out at, are you?"

"There is no going back to the way things were, now. Not for any of us."

Tattersall nodded, relieved. He looked Surgat up and down again. "How do you feel?" he asked, not only in regard to the Demon's injuries.

There was a long pause, as if Surgat were reluctant to admit to his personal feelings. As if he were reluctant to *have* personal feelings. But when the words did come, they were firm. He said, "I feel *good*."

"How do you intend to keep the *Acheron* moving? Please tell me it can be done without burning the Damned."

"For now, Beleth's stinking carcass will keep us steaming. We do not have far to travel, in any case."

"No? So where are we heading?"

Surgat lifted his arm, and pointed toward the horizon. Tattersall followed the gesture.

In the distance he spied that hazy line of land, a black veil of smoke still hanging over it, fed by ongoing battle.

"Oblivion," Surgat said.

Tattersall digested this, and smiled.

He felt, then, that he now possessed something he had never truly known in his mortal life.

A direction.

THE BONE ARENA

The Demon named Naberius wore only a loincloth of gold material, his beautiful onyx muscles on display for all the crowd, delineated with his glaze of sweat. A diadem of black metal was bolted into his skull, this decorated with three canine heads with rubies for eyes. He was a striking figure, but he had lost one of his great raven-like wings to a powerful blow from his opponent, and it lay in the sand behind him. He had also taken several deep lacerations, one across his left pectoral and a worse one across the top of his right thigh, a gaping crevice that sent a constant flow of red blood pulsing down his leg. Naberius tracked his own gore around as he bobbed and weaved, swung at the other combatant with his long, straight-bladed sword, also of black metal.

The other Demon, named Furcas, was of a different Demonic race. Though he was taller and bulkier than Naberius, he had the appearance of an old man, with flowing white hair and beard, but hollow pink skull sockets in place of eyes. He was granted vision by a single orb, twice the size of a human eye, that hovered just above his head. He carried a long weapon that sported a trident at one end, an axe-like halberd blade at the other. It gave him a greater reach, and this plus his superior strength had put Naberius at a disadvantage.

"Fight!" Furcas bellowed at his adversary, spittle flying. "You look like you're about to faint, you fool! Fight as if you mean to kill me!"

"I do mean to kill you!" Naberius panted, dancing black and

forth, looking for an opening as Furcas slowly spun his double-headed weapon in front of him. As much a flourish for the audience as a means of keeping Naberius uncertain which end would come for him.

"That's the spirit!" Furcas snarled. Then he lunged.

Naberius swung his sword, but Furcas trapped the blade between two tines of his pitchfork and turned it aside. He followed through by spinning his body around—allowing the redirected blade to slide out from between the barbed prongs—and swinging the axe blade toward his foe.

Up until fifteen minutes ago (if an earthly reckoning of time could be utilized in the netherworld), Naberius would have been able to jump back or duck under the halberd, maybe drop his sword and catch the staff in both hands. He was weak from blood loss, however. Though stronger than human beings, with greater healing abilities, Demons could be wounded ... injured ... and mortally so, because they had no souls, and were thus not immortal like the humans who in death had gone on to Hades as the Damned, or to Paradise as Angels. Unlike these former mortals, Demons could truly die. They were the real mortals.

And so, the halberd chopped sideways through the front of Naberius' face, at the level of his eyes, slicing through both orbits. With that one stroke, the beautiful Naberius was made a crude copy of the older Demon. He cried out, stumbled back, fell onto his remaining wing at a bad angle. Furcas heard the crack of bone. Blood poured from the upturned vessels that had a second ago housed Naberius' eyes.

"I'm sorry, brother," Furcas grunted, and he stepped forward, twirling his weapon around, cocking it back in both hands to plunge the tines into the fallen Demon's chest in a merciful coup de grâce— which in these games was known as Charon's blow.

A klaxon's bleat, like the deep-chested roar of some gigantic animal, filled the arena ... almost causing its walls to shiver. A single, circular wall, actually—a titanic, seamless cup of bone. In this way the amphitheater itself was like a skull socket. This ivory-tinted, glossy material was the same illusory bone that made up the skeletons of the Demons, and the Damned, and the Angels, and the Celestials—who were the equivalent of the Demons, but servitors to the Angels rather than tormentors of the Damned. Every form of matter even in the mortal world was simply another type of illusion than this. The Creator was an artist Who worked in multiple media.

At this blast of sound, which rumbled in his chest, Furcas turned his body and swiveled his floating eye to face toward the box centered in the lowermost tier of seats, wherein sat the highest ranking Angels in this considerable group, that had journeyed here to Hades to enjoy these games.

Behind him, Furcas heard Naberius moan, "Will you kill me, Furcas? *Kill me!*" Yet Furcas remained focused on the occupants of that box, it too seamlessly a part of this bone coliseum.

The box held a handful of Angelic high officials, and their retinue, which included of course a squad of armed Celestial guards. From here Furcas saw a number of women and children in the party, draped in white robes, as were the officials and every other Angel seated in this arena. From his gold miter, Furcas could tell one of these visiting officials had been a Roman Catholic bishop in his mortal life. He'd overheard that another of them had been a prominent Southern Baptist minister and a spiritual advisor to a string of American presidents. Furcas knew nothing about the others; he understood he was only an ant contemplating the world of dinosaurs.

Then again, not an apt comparison. Though he had never visited the mortal plane, he knew that dinosaurs had long ago gone extinct, while ants still thrived. And he and his kind—Demonic races that had been patterned along anthropomorphic lines—were scheduled for extinction themselves. It was the very reason he stood here, waiting for the orders of his masters.

And they were soon forthcoming. An amplified voice, following the deafening bleat, solemnly boomed, "Stay your hand and hold your place, Damnatus Furcas. Charon's blow will be delivered by the guest of an eminent visitor from Paradise."

At this announcement a tsunami wave of wild applause reared up all around Furcas, filling the arena's bowl. It almost drowned out Naberius' desperate groaning words just behind him. "*No!* I don't want

217

to die by some pampered Angel's hand, Furcas! Kill me! Are you afraid of them? You're soon to die in this arena yourself ... it can't be much longer."

Furcas didn't respond, instead scanned the faces stacked above him in the arena's sweeping curve, feeling their collective gaze weighing on him, crushing him immobile. The arena could accommodate 50,000 spectators, but for this current set of games there were only about 30,000 Angels in attendance—bussed in from Paradise, figuratively speaking—all seated in the stadium's lowest three tiers. Many wore white conical hats, though many others wore only attached cowls instead, and most of these let their cowls hang behind them. The majority, no doubt, under their robes wore "street clothes" of the type they had favored in life and wore in their native realm of Paradise.

In the fourth and top tier of seats, with the most distant view of the games, sat local Demonic officials, their immediate entourage, and a few thousand of their troops. These newer breeds of Demons had been designed not to look so much like human beings, such as the earlier forms of Demons that had presided over the torments of the Damned for so many centuries. From down here, in their ranks Furcas discerned large numbers of insect-like beings. Bird-beaked figures. Tentacled creatures. Entities for which there was no terrestrial counterpart. The Demonic officers, of course, were themselves nonanthropomorphic: regal, oversized, wildly and excessively nonhuman monstrosities. The *former* officials of this region of Hades had been the first to go— executed with much ceremony, in tribute to their former service. Despite this bloated show of respect, several of them had resisted—as if to prove the very need for the elimination of the old guard—and these embarrassing ingrates had been among the first to die in these gladiatorial games.

Above the uppermost tier, the sky seemed to cap the top of the bone area with a ceiling of restless but unbroken black clouds, hiding the inverted sea of molten rock behind it. The heavy cloud cover and his inability to see anything beyond the high surrounding wall of the amphitheater caused Furcas to feel fatalistic. There was indeed nothing more than this space, this bloody dance. His existence, his service of hundreds of years, was near its end. His former duties as an overseer and torturer of the Damned had been replaced with his current role as entertainer for those Demons that had come from the infernal factories to replace him. And, more importantly, entertainer for visiting Angels—eating mock hotdogs and drinking illusory beer in the stands.

A door opened in the base of the wall just under the box in which the Angelic officials were seated, and out into the arena stepped two Celestials, with platinum blond hair and unblinking blue eyes, maybe male or maybe female or maybe no sex at all, wearing togas and carrying assault rifles. Furcas didn't understand enough about such things to know if these guns were identical to any particular model on the mortal plane. On the sandaled heels of the Celestial guards emerged an adult Angel, garbed in white robe and conical hat. He represented the pinnacle of the Creator's handiwork: white, pot-bellied, bespectacled, with a thick graying mustache. Beside him walked a boy of about ten, the hood of his robe hanging loose behind him. Short sandy hair, face rounded with a vestige of baby fat. Two more Celestials followed, then the door closed. The little party walked straight toward Furcas, and the applause gradually died down, replaced with murmurs of anticipation, as the group reached the two blood-slathered Damnati.

The official in the conical hat nodded at Furcas, in a minor gesture of respect for his performance, but made a little brushing gesture with his hand for the triumphant Demon to step aside. Furcas complied without a word. Then, the Angel turned to one of the Celestials and motioned toward the short sword carried in a scabbard on its belt. The Celestial transferred its rifle to one hand so as to draw the sword and carefully pass it to the esteemed visitor.

In turn, this man handed over the sword to the boy. In what Furcas had come to know as a southern accent, over centuries of handling the Damned—and in a rehearsed lofty tone besides—the Angel said, "'Smite with thine hand,' William. You will never become a man in body, for your body is no more, but your soul will become the soul of a man. With Demons such as these—Demons of human guise—in recent times sympathizing with those Damned that rise up in rebellion

219

against the Creator's order, you may in the future be called upon to take up arms against them in earnest, to help destroy the last of them."

Furcas wanted to protest. Though indeed great numbers of the Damned had finally begun fighting back against their Demonic overlords, and troops of Angels and Celestials had come to Hades in an effort to help contain the uprising, he himself had never sided with the Damned as a good number of his Demonic brethren had done. It was said that these Demons sympathized with the former mortals because they shared a similar form, but he felt this was an unfair generalization. He believed he knew the other Demons held in the outer buildings of the arena, awaiting their own gladiatorial service, well enough to say that the majority of them still maintained their loyalty to the Creator's plan. Furcas felt this damning of every anthropomorphic race of Demon, after thousands of years of loyalty, was a monstrous injustice. And on top of that, this final indignation: so many of them now being imprisoned and forced to execute one another in an arena in which, in the past, only the Damned had fought as Damnati.

The Angel went on, condensing biblical text to suit his purpose, "'The evil abominations shall fall by the sword.'"

"Where should I stab him, John?" the boy asked.

"*No!*" Naberius sobbed loudly, wagging his blind head, spattering blood onto the sand. He had heard the boy's voice. "Don't let me be killed by a child, Furcas! *Damn you*, Furcas! Kill me before they have a child kill me as a *game!*" He began propping himself up on his elbows, but two of the Celestials stepped forward quickly and hammered him back down with blows from their rifle butts. One blow opened a gash on his left eyebrow and he fell onto his back again, moaning.

"Silence, Devil!" the Angel snarled at Naberius as he was being subdued. "Die with dignity, for the love of the Creator." He then looked down at the boy and said, "You won't stab him, William." He rested a hand on the boy's back, ran it up and down in what was almost a romantic caress, and Furcas finally registered that the boy hadn't called the Angel "father." He wondered at the full nature of their relationship. The Angel went on, "You will strike him across the throat."

220

"Ohhh…" Naberius moaned. "Furcas…"

A Celestial handed its gun over to one of its comrades, knelt in the sand and grasped Naberius' head in both hands to hold it still. At the other end of him, another Celestial knelt to hold down his legs.

The Angel helped position the boy, like a baseball coach teaching a child how to cock back his bat. The boy looked up at the man with eyes and twitching smile agleam, and then he looked down at the wounded Demon and swung the short sword.

Furcas flinched, as if the blade had bit into his own illusory flesh. He wanted to close his eyes, but then he only had the one floating eye, and it had no lids—and besides, he wouldn't really have hid his face from the death of his fellow Demon in any case. It would be another kind of disrespect.

The first blow gouged the sand as much as it did Naberius' neck. The Angel urged the boy to strike again, and this chop struck Naberius on the chin instead, cracking bone.

"Bastard!" Naberius gurgled. "Cowardly pet!" At this, he spat out a mouthful of blood. The boy tried to lurch back but the hem of his white robe was splattered.

Die with dignity, Naberius, Furcas thought, echoing the Angel's words. *Die like a good warrior…*

But then, Furcas thought—as he watched the boy chop again … and again … and again, until Naberius finally writhed and moaned no more, his neck and lower face a pulped mess—he *had* died as a warrior, hadn't he? Defiant until his defiance had been smashed beyond recognition.

The various barracks the demonic Damnati dwelt in between games, outside the arena, were heavily guarded not only by newer breeds of Demons, but by a contingent of Celestials—owing to the proximity of Angels visiting Hades for the games, housed in much finer accommodations not too distant. A minute ago one of these Celestials had unbolted this particular structure's metal door and stepped into the threshold, eyeing the Demons who sat on the edges of their bunks in low conversation. At first, Furcas thought the being—though wordless, as all Celestials were apparently—would gesture for them to be silent and get into their bunks for their rest period, but its flat blue eyes only took them in for a moment before it stepped outside again, and they heard the heavy bolt squeal back into place.

"They're just mindless machines, their lot," a Demon named Pithius whispered, as if the beautiful, blank-faced entity might be lurking beyond the door eavesdropping. "But we were given minds, and one might argue hearts, if not eternal souls. Why would the Creator have wanted us to be this way, if we would only end up being condemned for it?"

"Mortals have minds, and hearts," another Demon seated nearby, named Sabnock, argued. He had a noble hooked nose, and a pair of long corkscrewed horns like those of an antelope. "And they're punished when they err. Why do you make it sound like we alone are being persecuted?"

Pithius had pearly white flesh, bat-like wings collapsed tightly at his back. Hunched forward on his cot, he wagged his head and murmured, "They call those of us who are fighting alongside the Damned traitors. Maybe so. But to me, they are also traitors."

"Who is 'they'?" asked Sabnock. "Our new demonic leaders? The Angels? The Creator? Is the Creator a traitor, Pithius? You're skirting blasphemy."

"Who really knows the mind of the Creator? I'm leaving Him out of this. But do you not feel betrayed?"

"It's regrettable what is taking place, but I must retain my honor."

"You said 'err.' But how have I erred? I haven't aided a single Damned, in any way whatsoever, in regard to their rebellion. Though now, I swear, I wish I had."

"Fool," Sabnock said. "Even saying that, you prove our overlords correct in their actions."

"So be it!" Pithius snarled through gritted teeth. "So be it, my self-hating friend! My defeated friend!"

"Defeated? I will die with head held high, Pithius. It will be my *honor* to give my life for the greater good, as it is for any soldier."

"Your life was never yours to give, Sabnock. But it could be yours to *take*."

"Bah!" the long-horned Demon laughed, looking around to see who else felt as he did. Some of the Demons housed in this room grinned or chuckled. Others only watched him stonily.

Furcas didn't insert himself into their conversation; not then, in any case. Later, however, when Sabnock had stretched out on his cot and Pithius had wandered into a hallway between barracks rooms, to stand peering out through a narrow barred window, Furcas came beside him and said in a lowered voice, "I too feel betrayed, Pithius."

"I have seen that in your face, Furcas," Pithius said. He turned to face the taller, bulkier, more ancient Demon. "I'm not sure of our exact number in these barracks, but there are many of us. At the start of the next series of games, they'll parade all of us into the arena, as they always do—all the Demons and Damned that will fight in that program. Can you imagine, Furcas, if all of us agreed beforehand to fight back as one? Demons and Damned together? Of course, we couldn't communicate our plan to the Damned beforehand—they being in their own barracks—but when they saw what was happening I have no doubt all of them would be inspired to join in. Why wouldn't they? They have less to lose than we—they can't die a second time!"

"What would we do?" Furcas said in a hush.

"Spring up into the box where the Angel officials sit," Pithius said, his grin a harsh slice in his face, revealing his elongated canines. "Climb up there on each other's bodies if we have to, to reach them. Then we'll drag them down into the arena and tear them to shreds. Shrieking in agony. Screaming for mercy. We'll give that audience a show they never counted on."

"They'll just regenerate later," Furcas said, though the image blazed in his imagination.

"Of course they will."

"And the Celestials and the new Demons will mow us down with their guns."

"Of course they will! But we're going to die *anyway*, Furcas!"

"We would die in disgrace."

"In disgrace in the eyes of the new Demons. In the eyes of the Angels. Yes, and even the Creator." He took a step closer to Furcas and hissed, "But not in disgrace for *us*."

In the room behind them, they heard that metal door open again—slam open this time. A commotion of movement; the two Demons standing at the window turned toward the sound, and a second later two demonic guards stepped into the short hallway. One had a sleek-feathered head with a long, thin beak like a hummingbird's, and four thin red limbs like the legs of a stork. The other Demon had the appearance of a giant, greenish tick, standing on one pair of limbs and cradling an assault rifle in its uppermost limbs, as did its comrade. Both Demons immediately opened fire. In the enclosed space, the sound of their fully automatic weapons was punishing.

Furcas flinched back involuntarily, but it was Pithius who was hammered by both weapons. He flew back against the wall, his white flesh pitted by bullets. He then slumped to the floor, one wing half unfolding, its membranes punctured, holes chiseled in the wall where rounds had drilled straight through him.

Then the two Demons swiveled their guns at Furcas, and he threw up his hands, waited to be spiked through with holes himself. But the guns only smoked, and in a strange high-pitched voice the bird-like Demon said, "We heard your stupid friend, talking by the window. You don't hold his delusional views, do you, old one? You were only listening ... you were not swayed ... *were* you?"

How much had the guards outside overheard? Had they heard him say, at the start of the conversation, that he too felt betrayed?

"'Yes ... I was only listening to him," Furcas said, ashamed at his own words. At the shakiness of his words. He was soon to die ... so why was he afraid to die sooner than that? "I was only curious ... about what he was thinking."

"Would you have reported him for his treason?"

Furcas hesitated. So far he hadn't really lied. He didn't want to lie...

The bird-faced Demon laughed, a horrible twittering sound, and thankfully spared him from answering, by saying, "Let this be a lesson to you, old one." It turned to address the Demons who had gathered at the doorway through which the pair of guards had come, cautiously peering into the hallway to see what had happened. "Let this be a lesson to *all* of you. Don't die like this. Die with a sword in your hand."

They slung their weapons, by their straps, over their shoulders. No one moved forward to overpower the guards, though they were greatly outnumbered, and seize their weapons. The human-like Demons only watched, and parted to make way, as the two guards took hold of Pithius' corpse and dragged him from the room. Furcas stared at the swath of blood left on the floor in Pithius' wake. He heard the heavy door clang shut, the bolt driven home. He shifted his gaze to the chiseled wall, and reached to touch the bloody smear where Pithius' body had slid down. He looked at the blood on his fingertips, as if he meant to write something with it, some defiant slogan on the wall, but then he only let his hand drop to his side.

All the present Damnati—Demon and Damned alike—had paraded through the arena, under the eyes of the Angels and the next generation Demons. Obediently, cowed, they had all remained in formation. Not a one of them had broken rank to lunge toward the stands. The cyclops Furcas, in marching, had only stared ahead with his single hovering eyeball.

Then, the next program of games had commenced. From where he waited in the suffocating bone labyrinth beneath the tiers of seats, Furcas couldn't see the duels that preceded his own, but he heard the clash of metal weapons, the abrupt cries of pain, the vast cheers of the crowd.

At length, he and another Demon were called forth, pushed by their handlers out into the light. Their appearance was greeted by hoots and whistles of hungry eagerness. Furcas saw he had been paired against a Demon he had long known, and worked alongside: Gamigin, who was built on a heroic scale rather like himself. Like Furcas, Gamigin was without wings. His face was long and almost equine, his ears pointed, a Mohawk cresting his head and running halfway down his bare back. He carried a bow, a quiver of arrows slung behind him. Furcas himself had been handed an oblong shield and a gladius with a two-foot blade.

As they walked toward the center of the arena, Gamigin looked to Furcas and said, "Give me all you have, old friend."

"That and more ... count on it," Furcas told him.

Gamigin smiled. "I would expect no less from you. I promise, though, to kill you as painlessly as possible."

"Ha," Furcas said. "My friend Gamigin, always the dreamer."

"If I were a dreamer," Gamigin said, "I would dream that right now you and I were lying in the grass beside a gentle stream of blood, drinking flasks of wine."

"Those times are gone forever, aren't they?" Furcas said.

They had reached the heart of the arena. A klaxon sounded, vibrating their bones. Without another word, without hesitation and no longer smiling, the two Demons sprang at each other.

Furcas had expected Gamigin to backpedal to put distance between them, so he could notch his first arrow. No doubt aware that Furcas would expect this, Gamigin had instead turned his bow in both hands and thrust one end of it at Furcas' levitating eye. Furcas jerked his head to one side, saving his eye from being crushed or punctured, but the tip of the bow still grazed the orb's side. Furcas shouted a curse at the pain, angry for having taken a hit immediately, and he was the one who backed off—swinging his sword wildly to cover his retreat.

Now that Gamigin had put some space between them, though not in the way Furcas had anticipated, he swiftly drew an arrow from his quiver, notched it, pulled back on his bowstring and launched it. Furcas raised his shield just in time: the arrow lodged into it. Furcas knew he had to close up that space again, before more arrows flew. He dove forward, but too late: a second arrow twanged through the air. Its tip struck him under the left cheekbone, raked across the row of his teeth. The arrowhead emerged at the back of his jaw, below his ear, the arrow's shaft having skewered through his face, but it had only injured flesh, and mock flesh at that.

Not squandering even a second to yank free the arrow projecting from his face, Furcas leapt and swung his gladius in one movement. He hacked Gamigin just below the nose, splitting his upper lip and his lower jaw, straight through the chin. With no time to notch his third arrow, instead Gamigin grasped it by its shaft and thrust it up under the ribs on Furcas' left side. It went deep.

They had collided into a kind of embrace. Panting. Bleeding. Both hurting badly.

His words distorted by his bifurcated jaw and mouthful of blood, Gamigin said close to Furcas' ear, "We're too good at this, old friend. We can't prolong things for them for long."

"Good," Furcas said. "It's time this all ended. At least for us."

"I love you, my brother."

Furcas cocked his head, cocked his blurred and smarting eye, and chuckled mirthlessly. "*Love*, brother?"

"Why not?" Gamigin said. "We have nothing more to lose. We can love."

Furcas shoved Gamigin back, and snarled, "Then, I love you!" And he drove the point of his gladius up behind Gamigin's breastbone.

The ancient Demon Gamigin staggered backwards, glancing down at his pouring wound, then grinned bloodily up at Furcas and said, "Thanks, you bastard, for making me look so incompetent."

"I'm sorry, my brother," Furcas said, "but why extend our humiliation?" He drew back his arm to chop at the side of his friend's neck. It was time to put an end to this sad farce.

The klaxon again. It seemed to ring through the length of Furcas' blade, making it a tuning fork. The sound froze his arm, fixing him in place like a dramatically posed statue.

An amplified voice, following the deafening bleat, solemnly boomed, "Stay your hand and hold your place, Damnatus Furcas. Charon's blow will be delivered by the guest of an eminent visitor from Paradise."

"Oh Creator, no," Gamigin muttered. He sank to his knees. Furcas reached forward to take his arm, to help ease him into a kneeling position. Gamigin looked up at him, his halved mouth managing a grin, and said, "Allow me to take a moment to say fuck you, old friend."

A door opened in the base of the wall just under the box in which the Angelic officials were seated, and out into the arena stepped two Celestials, with platinum blond hair and unblinking blue eyes, maybe male or maybe female or maybe no sex at all, wearing togas and carrying assault rifles. On the sandaled heels of the Celestial guards emerged an adult Angel, garbed in white robe and a tall gold miter: that former Roman Catholic bishop. Beside him walked a boy of about twelve, the hood of his robe hanging loose behind him. Thick dirty-blond hair, too-pale skin and too-pink lips, his far-spaced blue eyes almost as dead as those of the two additional Celestials who brought up the rear. The door closed behind them, and the little party walked straight toward Furcas. The applause of the audience gradually died down, replaced with murmurs of anticipation, as the group reached the two blood-slathered Damnati.

"Well done, Demon," the bishop said to Furcas. He then motioned for one of the Celestials to pass him a sword.

Furcas found himself grateful that the Angel had not asked for his own blood-slicked gladius.

The bishop in turn passed the Celestial's sword to the child beside him. He rested one hand on the boy's back, and Furcas intuited it was not the first time the Angel had touched the boy so tenderly. The bishop said in a loud, grand tone, paraphrasing the Bible, "Duke, our swords are appointed for slaughter at all the gates of the rebellious Demons, so that their hearts may melt and stumble. Yes! Your sword is ready to flash like lightning; it is drawn for slaughter. Dispatch this traitor, and become a warrior! Become a *man!*"

The boy, whom the bishop had called Duke, accepted the sword with a smile just as bright and cold as its blade. He turned to face Gamigin. Gamigin stared back at him, blood from his bisected jaw streaming down the front of his bare, scar-crossed chest. *A mighty Demon,* Furcas, thought, *brought low. Too low.*

"What are you waiting for, little *boy?*" Gamigin said. "Kill me."

"Shut up, freak," the eternal child said, winding his arm back. Furcas figured he was already an expert at killing Demons—from having done so in video games, in life, many times before.

Before the child's blow could descend—in that moment when he hesitated, drawing out the suspense for the crowd, drawing out his triumph—Furcas took only a single step forward, swung his own sword, and chopped it through the exact center of the boy's head.

The crowd of 30,000 roared as one. It was not the sound any of them had expected they'd make.

"Uh!" Duke said, blinking dumbfoundedly, shocked with pain, as Furcas jerked his blade free. The child collapsed to the sand in front of Gamigin, who still rested on his knees.

"Kill me," Furcas saw Gamigin's lips mouth, though he couldn't hear him over the furor.

Furcas swooshed his arm sideways, cleaving Gamigin across the throat. He followed through with his blow, not taking the time to watch his friend pitch forward onto his face. Furcas slashed the bishop in two great blows, marking a terrible X. One diagonal blow not only sliced the old man's face into halves, the lower half sliding away from the upper, but badly dented his gold miter and sent it tumbling away.

The four Celestials came for him, suddenly and from all sides.

Oh, the boy would regenerate. His icy beauty would be restored. It would outlast the dying of every star in the universe. But so would his memory of the pain he had felt, at having a Demon's blade buried in his skull. So would his humiliation.

Furcas hacked this way and that, meeting this Celestial and then another, spinning, grinning, even laughing, with Gamigin's two arrows still poking from his body. He, who had never truly lived in the corporeal sense, felt *alive* perhaps for the very first time.

He flat-out killed two of the Celestials, who because they too possessed no mortal soul could also be killed in the realest way. He critically wounded the other two.

Finally, it was bullets from assault rifles—he didn't see who was shooting them, couldn't tell if it were Celestials or Demons—that dropped the Demon Furcas to the sand beside the body of his friend

Gamigin, and the body of the Angel child named Duke, who was already beginning to heal.

But the healing process was agonizing, and the child wailed for his mother, and it was the sweetest music the Demon Furcas could have hoped to die to.

GOOD WILL TOWARD MEN

1: The Five Stages of Drowning

e didn't know for how long he'd been drowning.

The liquid he was suspended in wasn't water, being of a more viscous nature and of a smoky gray tint throughout. Still, it was fluid enough that it had filled his lungs when he'd been thrown from the edge of the crater in which the liquid formed a wide, deep pool.

Though his body was in truth only an illusion, a spiritual representation of the physical vessel his soul had occupied in life, when the Demons that he and the other Damned called the Torus had cast him into the gray pool he had experienced much of what was called the five stages of drowning.

First Stage: Panic, as he thrashed his arms in a futile attempt to keep his head above the surface. However, in life he had never learned to swim. Even as he splashed frantically he recalled his older brother, an experienced swimmer, teasing him and calling him a baby for not even allowing their parents to support his body in the shallow end of his Aunt Marge's swimming pool. He'd cried, all but hysterical, when his father had tried to carry him in. This panic stage lasted about forty-five seconds, if eternity could be said to be portioned out in the terrestrial sense.

Second Stage: As his head sank below the surface, he held his breath in an attempt to prevent himself from ingesting fluid. Here was where a difference occurred between drowning in Hades and drowning in the earthly world. In life, he would have likely lost consciousness now due to lack of oxygen. However, in the afterlife his sham body only pantomimed the functions of a material body: he experienced hunger and thirst but didn't require food or drink; his heart beat but his body didn't actually utilize the mock blood it drove through him; he seemed to breathe, but didn't need air to survive because he was immortal. And so, he was only too horribly conscious of the stages that followed.

Third Stage: Despite his mind being aware, after about a minute and a half of trying to hold his breath his body persisted in its emulation of mechanical processes and went into respiratory arrest. His mouth gasped open and his lungs filled like sacks of sand. He sank lower in the gelatinous fluid until it grew darker around him. He finally hung in a shadowy oblivion between what lay above and what lay below. Below was ominous blackness. Above, if he tilted back his head, he saw the silhouetted curve of the crater's rim, and the ambient golden glow of the air, though the ceiling of the sky itself—an inverted sea of molten lava—was covered by a blanket of dense black clouds. Also silhouetted against the fiery air were several of the gigantic Torus beings, looming there like statues and seemingly gazing down into the pool, though they had no eyes, their heads darkly outlined as great zeroes.

Fourth Stage: His spiritual body went through the motions of hypoxic convulsion, going rigid and jolting with spasms as if he were being electrocuted. A thick white foam rose up from between his lips, and he didn't even have the breath to dislodge it by blowing it away. Unlike a drowning mortal, he did not suffer sodium deficit or potassium excess or fallen calcium levels, because he was no longer comprised of chemicals, but he could feel his imitation heart stutter to a halt and go still like a rock in his chest.

Fifth Stage: Death. But he was already dead, so he dreamed.

2: The Sea of Memory

Though he never truly slept, sometimes in a sense there were nightmares.

Unbidden, bad memories would push their way to the forefront of his mind, like scarred black whales breaking a calm surface to spout geysers of blood. However, if he relaxed his mind sufficiently that he achieved something like meditation, something like a self-imposed coma—internalizing his consciousness completely, forbidding it a peek at any window— he could distance himself from his surroundings and situation, so that for all intents and purposes he was *away*. (Dare he even say...*free?*)

Because damnation was eternal and the passage of time so difficult to gauge—there was no day or night—he would never know for how long he had been in one of his *away* periods before being disturbed from it. For there were disturbances. The Damned did not share this pool of perpetual drowning with each other only. Every now and then he would be roused from his dreaming state by a vicious tug on his foot or hand, nose or ear. His eyes would snap open to see a large eel-like creature had clamped onto him. Only one of an endless variety of infernal lifeforms, this creature had a long, segmented body like a human spine of black bone, its black head with its four white-glowing eyes composed of two matching halves resembling the heads of human infants, twins conjoined at the mouth, so that the lower jaw of each was the upper part of the other. Their shared mouth was full of needle teeth, and the eel would tear away a hunk of flesh or maybe even a few toes or fingers before it swished away again into the depths below, or to feast on another of the Damned.

He could only be grateful that apparently just one of these animals haunted the pool, and not a whole school of them in an unending feeding frenzy. He could only be grateful that, given time, his mock flesh would regenerate, the perception of physical agony would recede. He had taught himself to be thankful for such things, as a coping mechanism.

He was always grateful when he could return to his dreams.

He dreamed of, or rather remembered, his childhood. The Sunday drives his father would take him and his mother and brother on, after church, with no destination in mind, stopping for ice cream or to play in some little park they'd never been aware of before. He remembered

Christmas mornings, bleary from too little sleep but high on adrenalin, sitting cross-legged on the floor near a live (or rather, undead) tree almost lost under the cheap mortal magic of tinfoil icicles reflecting multicolored fairy lights, he and his brother admiring (sometimes jealously) each other's presents as they tore the shimmering skins from them.

He remembered his adulthood. He could clearly see his future wife's breasts the first time she'd let him expose them, in his car in a parking lot outside a steak house where they'd just eaten; could almost feel their softness again, smell their warmth, taste their dark nipples, hear her little sigh.

He vividly recalled being drunk at his wedding dinner, blissfully disoriented as he stared into the pink-lighted miniature fountain tinkling under their elevated wedding cake, thinking, "I'm a *husband* now."

… And vividly recalled thinking, "I'm a *father* now" as he watched his blood-slick son emerge from inside his mother, bluish as if born dead (and from his first breath, already on the lifelong path of death like all mortals)…the doctor rushing him to a table to suck out the meconium he had aspirated. Seeing his airborne son's penis, he had told his wife, "It's a boy!" The doctor had paused, swung around with his son aloft and said, "Oh yeah, it's a boy," and then had continued to the table.

… And dueling with his seven-year-old son with toy light sabers in a department store, falling to the floor mortally wounded and looking up to see a pair of parents watching his performance from the end of the aisle.

… And walking into his son's room (*no, not this again!*) and seeing the fifteen-year-old hanging from his neck (*oh no no no!*) with his toes just lightly touching the floor, as if he had been frozen in a graceful leap upward, a leap *away*, an arrow caught in flight, never finding its mark. A document left open on his computer, a confession of his shame. An account of his seduction at the edge of twelve and three subsequent years of abuse by their family's priest, Father Gordon MacArthur, who was already on administrative leave as his Diocese investigated him in regard to several other allegations. The rope choked off his son's voice, his bulging tongue gagged him, but his document poured forth a gush of words. In the document that cast its blue light upon his hovering body, making of him a ghost bearing witness to its own testimony, the boy apologized to his parents. He couldn't face them when they found out, couldn't face his classmates should his name be released or leaked, couldn't face this mortal realm of betrayal and grief any longer.

... And walking up behind the man on the sidewalk, barking his name (*Father MacArthur!*) because he wanted the priest to see him, to *know* him, and when the man turned shooting him with a .357 Python in the belly. Standing over him while the priest curled himself around the bullet like a fist. Listening to him whine and whimper and groooan before finally ... *finally* ... pointing the revolver again, this time at his head.

... And then (*this again ... always this again*) lifting the gun's muzzle to his own temple, while he heard people screaming across the street, while he sobbed out loud an apology to his wife, who was back at their home unaware, his son's mother, whom he had failed because he hadn't protected their child from a predator, because he (*Damn him! God damn him!*) had insisted his family attend church every Sunday just as he had as a child, insisted they believe in its words, and in the messengers of its words, and the promises of eternal love and justice and reward and he had pulled the trigger, and like a bullet through a skull, a bullet through some mysterious veil, he had fired his soul *here*.

3: The Dubious Rescue

A stern finger poked his shoulder to arouse him from his dreams.

His mother? Was it already time to go to school again, the weekend gone so soon? He groaned inside.

The finger poked him again, hard, in the side of his neck. *"Mom!"* he wanted to protest. How could she hurt him this way? It wasn't like her. He opened his eyes, and at the same time the finger curled and hooked him with a pointed nail under the edge of his jaw, puncturing his skin. It ripped upward, tore free, leaving a deep gouge along his cheek.

With his eyes open, he saw in front of him the void of grayness and remembered where he was with something so much more than a groan inside him. It was more like the howl of a man plummeting down a bottomless pit, forever and ever and ever.

He also saw the shadowy form of another Damned man not too distant from him, like himself suspended in the thick solution. This man was thrashing his limbs as if drowning; had he only just been tossed into the pool by the Torus? But no…he was being towed upward on a taut black cable, as if being rescued. So why was he resisting? Then, he realized that wasn't a cable. It was a long, rigid pole of iron. He realized this even as a similar pole caught him in the left eye socket with its hooked end—which in his dream he had taken for a finger, that had failed before to snag his jaw—popping the jelly orb therein and taking hold of bone.

Then he himself was being hoisted up toward the surface. He himself flapping his limbs like ineffectual wings. He would have sucked fluid into his lungs, in his attempt to scream at the pain, had they not already been filled to capacity.

The shock had jolted his heart into beating again.

As he was reeled in like a fish the outer air brightened above him… and as the fluid around him correspondingly appeared lighter, with his remaining eye he saw a half dozen other Damned—men, women, a girl of maybe twelve—being pulled up by hooks caught in their flesh or bone, too. He imagined other Damned behind him were also being drawn upward. A ring of the giant Torus were arranged around the circumference of the pool, effortlessly working their long metal pikes.

Then he was breaking the surface, sputtering, trying to sob. Hand over huge, gnarled hand the Demon that had snared him pulled him toward shore. Identical to all the others, the Torus was twice the height of a human, its body hidden under layers of black leather robes imprinted with glowing white insignias that emitted wisps of vapor, its eyeless head a great circle of amber-colored flesh with the vague shadow of its O-shaped skull visible within.

He was dragged away from the rim of the crater, and with a deft flick of its wrists the Torus unhooked its pike from him. He was left floundering, blood running from his eye socket and the gouge in his cheek. He rolled onto his side and began vomiting up the gray fluid that had filled his lungs for however long it had been. Beside him and all around the perimeter of the pool, other Damned were doing the same.

The pain and the violent effort of his body to empty itself caused him to lose consciousness in a way he had never done while floating, as if in outer space, in the drowning pool—but just before he did he saw there were other, smaller beings standing in a cluster off behind the ring of towering Demons. These beings were not dressed in black, but in robes of white.

4: The Visitation

He awoke as if from a night's sleep in his mortal life—on his back, atop a narrow bed (*was this his childhood bed?*), dressed in dry clothing. He saw, though, that this was not his childhood bedroom. It was a tiny barren cell, three blank walls with the fourth wall, facing a corridor beyond, comprised of iron bars covered in three-inch spikes. A series of grooved tracks running along both the ceiling and floor accommodated each of the bars, so that the wall of bars could be cranked closer and closer to the cell's occupant—this advance done either swiftly, or with excruciating anticipation over slow daily increments—inevitably pinning and crushing the prisoner against the pocked and bloodstained back wall. He knew this because he had been a prisoner of one such cell in the past, before being dragged to the pool of perpetual drowning.

So had the Torus realized at last that he had learned to overcome his panic and physical discomfort in their deep well, and even achieve periods of tranquility? He had heard that the Demons liked to vary the torments in Hades, lest the Damned become too accustomed to any one of them. He experienced a more acute sense of despair than he had known for some time. Was his new punishment to take place in this crushing chamber, or was it only a temporary holding cell until he could be moved to another of Hades' infinite regions, presided over by another of Hades' infinite races of Demons?

It wasn't that his clothing had dried out, but that he had been dressed while unconscious in a brand new uniform of long-sleeved black top, loose black trousers, thin-soled black shoes like Kung Fu slippers. Gone was his old waterlogged uniform, threadbare and torn by bullets and blades, his old shoes with holes in the imitation matter that composed their soles. (Which didn't heal up on their own, as did the holes in the imitation matter of his soul.) He was at least thankful for these…gifts.

He sat up on his cot, felt at his cheek where the groping pike had lacerated it. Smooth once more. He realized he was seeing with two eyes again. The only scar remaining, that always remained, was the conflated symbol branded on his forehead that announced his doubly damning sins: the sin of Murder, and the sin of Sacrilege for having killed a servant of the Creator.

As he was feeling around his regenerated eye with his fingertips, he became aware that he was hearing a distant murmur of voices from somewhere out in the corridor. Curious but apprehensive, he got to his feet and crept closer to the thorny bars.

The voices were somewhat louder, echoy with the corridor's acoustics, but from this angle he couldn't see anyone…just a few other cells like this one, facing his. They were untenanted, however, with their doors standing open. Leaning closer to his cell's door in the hopes of making out the unknown speakers' words, he curled his hands around two of its bars between their spikes…and the door shifted forward, swinging out a little. He had been left in an unlocked cell.

What kind of trick was this? Some diabolical game? Were those apparently human voices meant to lure him into a trap?

He eased the door outward some more, grateful that its hinges didn't squeal, and dared to poke his head into the corridor. His reactivated heart was pounding at maximum power.

To the right, the corridor went on a good ways, showing only more abandoned cells, but the sounds had come from the left and in this direction he was met with an unexpected sight. In an open intersection of corridors, about twenty Damned—all in fresh black outfits—stood facing a group of six human beings in snowy robes with the hoods drooping behind them like crumpled wings. These were undoubtedly blessed souls—people who had died under the good graces of the Creator. *Angels*. The only time he'd ever seen Angels before, they were tourists venturing into Hades on safaris to hunt the Damned. Evidently Paradise grew boring.

Standing to either side of the Angels, no doubt to protect them from the Damned, were two taller figures wearing cone-like red hoods, through the eyeholes of which a white light glowed, their bodies also cloaked in red. They carried assault rifles. These were obviously Celestials, the equivalent of the Demons: entities that saw to the needs of the Angels just as Demons saw to the punishment of the Damned. They were said to be more terrible than Demons, but like Demons they could be destroyed—*killed*—because they had no immortal souls. And what Damned didn't dream of killing Demons and Celestials?

One of the Angels, a corpulent elderly man, bald but for a semicircle of white hair tucked behind his ears, looked over and spotted him and motioned to the others. Even the hooded Celestials turned his way. He felt the irrational urge to dive back into his cell…as if that would protect him if those crimson-robed warriors came striding down the corridor.

Another of the Angels, a tall woman perhaps in her early sixties, with silver-white hair flowing to her shoulders, smiled and raised a hand to gesture to him. "Come here, sir…don't be afraid. We bring you season's greetings!"

5: The Most Wonderful Time of the Year

He hesitated. The tall woman, who must have been model-beautiful in her younger days and was still striking—poised and sapphire-eyed— gestured again but maintained a patient and gentle tone. "Come on, don't be shy now. What is your name, sir?"

He was reassured that at least the Angels didn't have guns. Obediently, he started down the corridor toward the unlikely party. When he was close enough for his nervous voice to be heard he said, "Andrew Nabors."

"Andrew! Did your parents name you after Andrew the fisherman, brother of Peter, son of Jonas?"

"I don't know."

"Any relation to Jim Nabors?" the corpulent man asked in a wheezy voice, grinning.

"Not that I know of," Andrew said.

"Andrew, my name is Eva," said the woman, apparently the leader of this group. Andrew resisted the urge to ask if her parents had named her after the first woman. "This is my son, Patrick." She indicated the corpulent man, who had obviously died many years after his younger-looking mother. Eva went on to introduce the other members of her party...aside from the nameless Celestial escorts.

Andrew nodded to each Angel in turn, and at the end muttered, "Nice to meet you." He noted that the other Damned were watching him expectantly, as if he might tell them what was going on, their faces no less uneasy than his own. Several of them were children. One of the Damned women held a boy of maybe five in her arms, straddling her hip. Surely not her own child, because—as was clearly not the case in Heaven—one of the punishments of Hades was to never allow family members or spouses to be reunited in death. Hades was vast enough that they could be distributed impossible distances from each other, that even an eternity of traveling might not be traversed. The boy made Andrew think of his son at that age, and the thought of the boy's fear compressed his heart in a vise.

"Well, Andrew," said Eva, "you were the last we were waiting for. Now that we've all been properly introduced, why don't we go on to the main hall to talk about the reason why our little expedition came here today."

The Damned followed the Angels through a series of corridors until they entered a large chamber with a high arched ceiling that Andrew hadn't seen when he'd been briefly held in this facility before. The room was undecorated, windowless, but a long table made of black wood from infernal trees, with benches pulled up to both sides of it, dominated the floor. A miniature cloud, glowing white, billowed and knotted in upon itself in the air above the table, giving the room its illumination. Were banquets held here for visiting Angels? Meetings for Demonic officials? In each of the room's four corners, unmoving as titan suits of armor, stood a Torus Demon with a spear. The vapors curling from the sigils on their robes were like an audience of ghosts lurking furtively at the fringes.

Eva turned to face them all, passing her smile from one to the next, and announced, "Today, my friends, is Christmas Eve."

Another of the perks of Heaven? Andrew wondered. The passage of time was charted, known?

No one reacted, except for the dark-skinned boy on the woman's hip, who twisted around alertly in her arms. In life he might not have celebrated that holiday, but he obviously knew of its festivities. Seeing the child's instinctively eager reaction out of the corner of his eye squeezed from Andrew another dollop of pain.

When no one said anything, Eva went on, "A group of us in Paradise have undertaken to forego our own Christmas celebrations this year to bring them, instead, to unfortunate souls like yourselves. We call ourselves the Carolers, because in life some of us—myself included—went door-to-door singing carols outside people's homes on Christmas Eve." Her smile grew more beatific at the memory. "There are presently almost two hundred of us. Because Hades is so immense, we can't possibly reach out to all of you, but we hope for more volunteers to join the cause in years to come. Nevertheless, we Carolers have spread ourselves out as best we can, and our particular group has chosen this place—chosen *you*—for our visit."

Some of the Damned exchanged wary looks. When was the trick going to be revealed, the trap sprung? Andrew, however, felt Eva and her group were sincere. He had grown up with religion. He recognized the missionary, the evangelist, the midwife to those who would be born again. But it was too late for any of them to be born again, wasn't it, when in Hades they had been consigned to eternally die again... and again.

Eva looked a bit embarrassed or disappointed that no spontaneous exclamations of gratitude, nor even a single smile, had greeted her announcement, but she soldiered on. "Tomorrow morning is

Christmas, and we'll have some festivities for you…some special surprises. But for now, we want you to enjoy the anticipation that makes the night before Christmas so magical. We invite you to openly interact with each other, to talk freely and move about this facility as you care to. There will be no punishments, no torments, nothing to fear tonight. This respite is our gift to you. Tonight you can reflect on your lives…on Christmases past. We encourage you to sing songs together, play games! And we most certainly invite you to talk with us, as well. I'm sure most of you have regrets about decisions you made in your lives. We will listen to those regrets with open hearts, and you may find a degree of comfort in the telling. Confession is good for the soul, and it's unlikely that in life or thereafter you've ever taken the opportunity to truly confess. To confront your sins in a manner that is contemplative; that doesn't simply involve the punishing consequences of sin." She spread her arms, palms upturned, saint-like. "We welcome you to talk of this, or any other thing you may care to express."

"Ooh," her son Patrick wheezed, looking toward a doorway at the far end of the great room. "Here come some treats!"

Into the chamber came a procession of a dozen Demons of a smaller size than the Torus, better adapted to this structure's maze of narrow, low-ceilinged corridors. They were very much like old but still powerful chimpanzees, shaved completely hairless, their pale and stubbly bodies and even their faces luridly and colorfully tattooed with scenes of Holocaust, and child molestation, and the tortures of Inquisition. Overlarge penises swung between their legs as they loped along. They often ravished female and male Damned alike, even the children, and the Damned had nicknamed their species Rapes. But now, incongruously, they bore platters of illusory food for illusory bellies. Breads and crackers and cheeses, ruby-red grapes and other infernal fruits that didn't quite correspond to earthly varieties. Earthen jugs of wine, water, and milk derived from infernal animals. Pastries and candies and nuts. The platters were laid out along both sides of the banquet table. Then, with a few flashed snarls at the Damned and a couple of barking cries, the Rapes turned and waddled out of the room again, their great arms swinging at their sides.

"Please," Eva said, waving her arm like a woman revealing a car behind a curtain on a game show, "enjoy yourselves!"

6: The Breaking of Bread

Though some of them no doubt suspected poison, or razor blades or broken glass secreted in the food, not one of the Damned refused partaking of it, so strong was the hunger they constantly suffered. The young woman who had taken it upon herself to care for the little boy sat him beside her on the bench and plucked grapes for him.

Partly what reassured the Damned was that Patrick and a couple of the other Angels were digging into the feast, themselves. "Mm," he mumbled, chewing, "this is a helluva good cheese!"

"Patrick," his mother warned, casting him a chastising glance. She continued speaking with one of the Damned who had approached her, a timid-looking man who had died in his seventies. He had revealed that he was a newcomer to Hades, the drowning pool having been the first of the punishments meted out to him. In a quavering voice he had confessed his sin: in life he'd been an atheist.

"Is it true," he asked her, "there's no Satan...never was? Only the Creator?"

"Yes, Richard," Eva replied. "A truly loving and strong father knows when to spank just as he knows when to caress." She laid her hand on his shoulder. "One cannot blame Him for their fate; one can only blame himself. Those who sin bring about their own punishment. They wield the sword against themselves."

"I'm sorry I didn't believe, Eva, I'm sorry!" Richard sobbed, breaking down. "Now I know better! Why do I have to suffer for all eternity just because I made a mistake...a stupid, blind mistake?"

Listening in on their conversation, chewing a cheese sandwich he'd put together, Andrew cut in before Eva could reply. "In life, supposedly, we can be forgiven for our sins if we confess to them and repent. Why can't we be absolved after our deaths, if we feel contrite?"

"Oh Andrew," Eva said, facing him, "by then it's too late; judgment has been cast. The opportunity to die in a state of grace has passed, but the opportunity was there. May I ask you—and of course you needn't answer if you'd rather not—what sin brought you here?"

Andrew put down his plate, and his voice gained strength, defiance. "I shot a man. A priest, who'd been abusing my son and who knows how many other boys, for years."

"I'm sorry to hear about your son. Did you kill this priest while he was attacking your child, to defend him?"

"No. I hunted him down after the fact. I shot him in the street. And for that, for killing that monster, I'm here. I was a devoutly religious person in life, but here I am. And I strongly suspect that Father Gordon MacArthur is at this very moment enjoying Christmas Eve in Heaven, attended by a flock of golden-haired Celestial slave boys. Is that true, Eva? Did he make it into Paradise?"

"Andrew," Eva sighed, "I don't know of this man. But if he felt honest regret in his heart for his actions, if he made confession and paid his penance in life...*in life*, before you killed him...then yes, Andrew, he would have."

"I see. Sure. Make some bullshit insincere confession, go through the motions, and why not? So tell me this...how about my son? Where is he now? Because I forgot to tell you this part, Eva: my son was so distraught over what that scumbag did to him that he hung himself. He killed himself, only fifteen years old." His voice choked on the last few words.

"Oh, dear," Eva said, wagging her head sadly, her tone that of a compassionate doctor relating that a loved one's prognosis was dire. "If he committed suicide, then I'm sorry to say he'd be denied entrance to Paradise."

"Of course!" Andrew blurted, though this news was not unsuspected. "Of course he would!"

One of the two Celestials, who had been lingering nearby, shifted forward and raised its assault rifle a little, but Eva waved it back.

Andrew lowered his voice to a hiss, pointing toward the child eating grapes, who was oblivious to their conversation. "What about him? What could he have done at his age to deserve being here?"

"He told me his name is Ravinder," Eva whispered, leaning toward

Andrew. "I'd say he was born of Hindu parents. I'm sorry, Andrew, I know how this sounds, but I don't make the rules. The rules are not kept secret, though. In any part of the world where people live, people of any color or creed, who is not aware of the Son's words, whether they choose to follow them or not? 'No one comes to the Father except through me.'"

"And that poor kid has to be tortured for eternity because he didn't defy his Hindu parents and say, hey, fuck that, this Jesus guy is for me?"

Eva recoiled slightly, her expression gone chilly at his profanity. "You talked about contrition, Andrew, and forgiveness. May I ask you another question? Even if you could be forgiven for murdering that priest, and ascend from Hades to Heaven, can you tell me you are truly sorry for having killed him?"

Andrew didn't even have to think about it. "No," he said flatly. "I'm not sorry."

"Well there you go."

7: The Eternal Night

None of them sang songs or played games that night, after the Angels had all left through that doorway at the far end of the banquet hall, presumably to retire to more comfortable quarters than the Damned had access to. They did, though, break off into pairs or little groups to talk in subdued tones while continuing to pick at the feast. Only a couple of them sat alone, perhaps reflecting too much on Christmases they had known in their mortal existence, one old woman weeping quietly and continuously.

Within Andrew's earshot, a man approached the young woman tending to the small boy and asked haltingly, "Would you want to share a bunk with me tonight?"

"I'm caring for him," she said, nodding at the child.

"Well...couldn't someone else watch him? How about just for an hour?"

"Sorry."

"I'm just looking for a little comfort," he said, his voice catching. "I'm comforting *him*."

The man drifted away, mumbling. Andrew thought he might next ask one of the older Damned women, or the men, or even the twelve-year-old girl, but he didn't.

Eventually people began leaving the hall, seeking cells in which to indulge in the luxury of undisturbed sleep. Andrew heaped a dish with more food, though he was full almost to discomfort, and took it with him. He didn't think he'd find the same cell he'd woken up in but imagined it didn't matter. He settled on a cell that was unoccupied, with an unoccupied cell to either side but other people close enough at hand along the corridor that he experienced a faint measure of reassurance at their presence. He closed his cell's door most of the way, but not entirely. It felt good to know it didn't have to be closed all the way.

He set the plate down, removed his shoes, stretched out on his back with his fingers laced behind his head, and gazed at the ceiling with its striped rows of grooves for the bars to pass through when the wall of spiked bars was cranked forward. But not tonight. No such tortures this one night. Tomorrow was the birthday of Christ. But... hadn't Christ died for their sins?

So why did they have to die infinite deaths to pay for their own sins? How did that work?

He realized he had never understood religion at all. That it was unfathomable except, perhaps, to the alien mind of the Creator. If He even understood Himself.

Andrew had almost dozed off when a stealthy shuffling from the corridor caused him to angle his face that way. It wasn't Santa Claus with his sack. It was one of the Rapes, the front of its body tattooed with a scene of lingchi, the Chinese torture of Death by a Thousand Cuts. The simian-like Demon, its eyes entirely black, curled back its upper lip in a snarl-like leer and pointed one finger at him. Its member was erect, the head protruding between the bars. It might as well have said to him, though it said nothing, "*Soon...soon enough.*" Satisfied that Andrew had seen it, the Rape turned away, loped off down the corridor presumably to look in on the next prisoner.

Andrew thought, *So much for Eva's promise of one night of peace.*

He got out of bed, and though it wouldn't lock he closed the barred door all the way.

Then he returned to his bunk, finally fell into a doze.

He dreamed of Eva, in fact. She was crouched down compassionately beside several African children with cadaverous faces, emaciated limbs, bloated bellies, flies crawling in and out of their nostrils. They stared back at her benevolently smiling face with glazed yellow eyes.

She was handing each one of them a Bible.

8: *The Holiday*

"Wake up, my friends!" Eva's cheerful voice, her hands clapping, like the nicest drill sergeant in the history of humankind. "Rise and shine!"

She appeared beyond the spiked bars of Andrew's cell. "Time to get up, Andrew! Merry Christmas to you!"

He sat up on his bunk with a groan, and was thankful Eva and her companions continued on toward the next occupied cell so he wouldn't have to return her greeting. He put on his shoes, stepped out into the corridor. Others were doing the same.

"Everyone on to the hall!" Eva called back to those behind her.

They trailed after her like a train of obedient, groggy children. They followed her into the great hall, where she swept around to beam at them and watch their reaction.

The hall had been transformed as had Ebenezer Scrooge's home upon the visitation of the Ghost of Christmas Present. A feast had been spread upon the massive table of ebony wood that put to shame the party snacks of the night before. Heaps of steaming vegetables, golden roasted birds, more bread, more fruit, more jugs of beverage, The centerpiece was a whole roasted boar with rows of fantastical tusks curling out of its jaw, rows of horns curling out of its skull.

And in the middle of the table stood a Christmas tree, its trunk fitted into a heavy iron candle base. It was a coniferous tree, like an evergreen, but its needles were obsidian black. The infernal tree had been decorated with pinecones painted gold and silver. Throughout the black branches flashed tiny red lights. These, Andrew recognized, were an infernal insect, a bioluminescent beetle like the earthly lightning bug. Except that these beetles, which inflicted a nasty bite, drank the blood of the Damned. Somehow they had been directed to lie passively upon the branches of this beautiful, this terrible, Christmas tree.

The miniature cloud that provided the hall's light had condensed greatly until it was a mere disk, hovering just above the top of the tree like a crowning star, or a halo. So concentrated, so radiant, it was hard to look at directly.

"Merry Christmas, everyone!" Eva and the rest of the Carolers cried out as one.

The tree—and the Angels—went barely acknowledged as the Damned dug into their repast. Andrew found himself standing beside a portly white-haired man who was piling his plate with several types of mashed vegetables. This man said to Andrew, "I'm a Jew. Do you know what I used to do every Christmas day? I'd volunteer to serve meals to homeless people. Not to insult, but how many Christians do you think ever spent one day feeding homeless people? So do you know why I'm here in Hell?"

"Because you're a Jew," Andrew said.

The man chuckled humorlessly. "Mm hm." He pointed his fork at the boar carcass. "And I'm not touching that thing. Not kosher."

While the Damned feasted, true to their name, the Carolers serenaded them with Christmas songs. They were able to goad only the twelve-year-old into singing along with them, robotically, her expression shell-shocked. Mercifully, she had probably lost her mind many years ago. Andrew had heard her tell Eva in her ghostly, empty voice that she'd died from a scarlet fever outbreak in 1874.

"O Christmas Tree! O Christmas Tree! Thy leaves are so unchanging!"

Andrew heard one Damned mutter to another, "I hate them worse than the Demons."

"What?" said the other person.

"The Demons don't talk to us. They aren't full of shit. They don't lie to themselves that they care about us."

"Thou bidst us true and faithful be, and trust in God unchangingly."

After the Damned had eaten much—the boar a torn, partly skeletal ruin—and after a good number of Christmas carols, Eva went to the door at the far end of the hall and motioned for several Rapes to enter. Between them they pushed an odd contraption on wheels. Within an elaborate brass setting that was also the framework for the mobile cart rested an apparently glass orb the size of a basketball, cloudy gray marbled with milky and inky swirls, like the globe of an alien world.

"Friends," Eva explained, "this is another gift we've arranged for you. It's a device normally reserved only for use by Demonic administrators. This is a scrying ball, which can be used to view scenes greatly removed from the viewer…in Hades, or Heaven, or even in the mortal world. For our use today, those who lent this fantastic device to us have adjusted it in such a way that any soul who gazes into it will be able to view a loved one, alive or dead, to whose soul they're connected. The scrying ball can detect and trace that connection." She let this sink in, watching her audience's faces. "We've arranged for each one of you, if you choose, to be able to view one loved one…whether they be alive on Earth, or whether they've passed on to one of the afterlifes."

The Damned still stared mutely. Still absorbing, chewing their food dumbly.

"Who'd like to go first?" Patrick asked, sweeping his arm toward the globe like a stage magician asking for a volunteer for the box of piercing swords.

Finally, one of the Damned raised her hand and stepped forward. She approached the device meekly, Eva taking her by the arm to help position her. Leaning forward hesitantly as if she expected to see some rotting corpse's face swim up in the glass, she asked, "Do I have to tell you who it is I want to see?"

"The scrying ball will know," Eva told her.

They all watched her as the woman watched the sphere. They couldn't see what she was seeing—from where he stood, the globe looked unchanged to Andrew—but within seconds the woman clapped her hand over her mouth and behind it said, "Oh! *Ohh!*" Tears flowed down her cheeks. After a few seconds more, one of the Angels helped her walk to the table and sit down. The woman cast a longing look over her shoulder, back at the globe.

"Who's next?" Patrick asked, looking quite satisfied, like the proud inventor of some remarkable new invention, or a car dealer who had just made a sale.

Another of the Damned stepped forward.

Andrew came up alongside Eva and said, "You can't let Ravinder look into it. That would be cruel, Eva, not a kindness. What's he going to see? The mother he'll never be reunited with?"

"I understand that he couldn't put something like that into perspective, Andrew," she replied. "That's why he was given the toys instead, for his gift." Indeed, earlier Patrick had handed the little boy several giftwrapped packages to open, containing miniature cars and jointed little figures, toys such as children in Paradise no doubt played with. Contentedly, he sat on the floor playing with them even now.

"How thoughtful of you," Andrew said. "How concerned. And tomorrow, when our special holiday is over, do you know what will happen to Ravinder? A Rape will grab those toys away and smash them on the floor in front of him...right before it sodomizes him."

"Stop it!" Eva said.

"Do you think I'm lying? I'm just telling you how it is here. Why wouldn't they do that? And what could you do to stop it? Order the Rapes, order all the Demons in Hades, not to touch the boy's toys? Not to ever harm him again? You don't have that kind of power, any more than you have the power to take that one boy back with you to Heaven."

"I've done what I can for him, Andrew!" Eva snapped, tears warping the surfaces of her brilliant blue eyes. "I've done what little I can to relieve your suffering for a day or two at least!"

"A day or two of *eternity?* And will we at least have this respite to look forward to again next year? No...you already told us you Carolers are spread too thin. Next year it'll be another spot of Hades you'll visit. Right?" She didn't dispute this, only looked at him in helplessness, tears streaming. "You should have just left us in the pool. We were better off in there, without your *mercy*. Why do you think they let you come here? They knew it was only a new kind of torture. Whether you wanted it this way or not, you're just Demons with halos."

"Oh, Andrew," Eva sobbed, wagging her head.

He brushed past her, toward Patrick and the scrying ball. "Okay, let me have my turn. Let's get this punishment over with. The sooner this farce is finished, the better."

Patrick glanced at his mother dubiously, but she nodded at him. The Angel shifted aside so Andrew could stand over the orb and look down at its glossy, clouded surface.

But it didn't remain clouded for long.

9: The Gift

The sphere became clear, became a lens, revealed to him a distant scene. It was obviously a landscape in Hades: an arid lakebed of dried mud split into tiles, as if the party of people he saw moving across this hellscape were walking upon the vast scaly body of the Creator/Satan Himself. There were three men and two women in this little group of Damned in their dusty and torn black uniforms. One of them carried an assault rifle, identical to those of the Celestial guards in this room. Another carried a compact submachinegun. Several of them wore swords in scabbards...swords such as many races of Demons carried. Swords that had to have been stolen, like the guns, either from Demons or Celestials. Demons or Celestials who had been *killed*.

One of the members of the party, with a pump action shotgun in his arms, was his eternally fifteen-year-old son. His tongue no longer bulged from his mouth, his toes no longer touched the earth ever-so-lightly. He tramped solidly, determinedly, across the desert floor, his eyes squinted and hard. He looked to be in search of something.

More Damned to join their little band. More Demons to kill.

His son wouldn't be aware that his father had killed himself after his own suicide. Wouldn't be able to reach his father even if he did know, no matter how long he and his friends marched. But he was fighting back. Defying the keepers of Hades. Defying the order of the Creator. He was young. Defying was what the young did.

Gray clouds spiraled in to cloak the orb once more. Andrew staggered back from the scrying device, turned toward Eva with tears on his own face to mirror hers, but he was also grinning. "Thank you, Eva" he said. "That was a wonderful gift you gave me, after all."

She pivoted to watch him, uncomprehending—only he had seen the vision in the orb—as he crossed the great hall to seek out his cell, and wait for the end of their holiday.

10: The Gray

One more gift awaited the group of twenty Damned, come the next morning.

Eva and the other Carolers had departed. They'd tried to round everyone up to say goodbye first, but Andrew had avoided them. He heard from the young woman who had been a temporary surrogate mother to Ravinder that Eva had gently taken his toys back, promising to return them next time she saw him. A lie, but Andrew appreciated that she had done this, rather than have Ravinder lose them in the way he had described.

The Rapes led them all from the building, outside again, and from there the looming Torus took over, conducting them along a trail back to the crater. Back to the drowning pool. Andrew had never been so grateful…that is, aside from his glimpse the day before into the scrying ball.

When one of the Torus picked him up and hurled him into the pool, he didn't resist. As his lungs filled and he sank, his body fought against it but his mind did not.

He welcomed the gray void. Welcomed the dreams.

The Half-Damned Girl

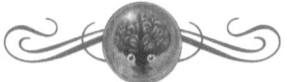

-1-

"**S**he's the last!" Laura heard the monster call out to the other monsters, its voice guttural and deep, like that of an animal mimicking a human voice. It was at least seven feet tall, upright like a man and with a man-like face, but this face was framed with the thick and matted white fur that covered the rest of its body but for the palms of its hands and presumably the soles of its feet. It wore tall boots, but no clothing other than a cyan blue poncho-like garment that flapped in the howling icy wind. From the top of its head sprouted long black horns, spiraled like those of a blackbuck antelope, but it had three of these. A little white jet of fire hovered above the central horn, like a candle flame. The monsters this one commanded had only two horns, or a single horn centered atop their skull. All of them, regardless of visible rank, had entirely black eyeballs with gleaming dots like drops of mercury for pupils.

One of the monsters with two horns had reached down into the room Laura had returned to consciousness in, only minutes ago by her sense of time, and caught her by her long hair. (How many times at school had other girls gushed over her thick, black hair?) Twining its hand into this, while she screamed and screamed, the monster had pulled her up through a circular opening in the ceiling of the cell-like space, with its walls and floor of gleaming white tiles.

She had no idea how she had come to be in that cell. She had awakened naked upon its floor, curled like something waiting to be born. She had roused, groggy, disoriented, and then noticed that she lay in a circle of blood like a red halo around her body, that was flowing into a drain set into the floor near her belly. She had sat up then to find the half of her body that had been in contact with the floor was smeared with this blood. Long strands of her hair were plastered to her bare skin with gore. She had looked down at herself at that point, and seen the three neat black holes punched into her: one in the sternum, one to the right of her belly button as if to mimic it, and one in her right upper thigh. Blood pulsed slowly out of these wounds, as if it were growing more viscous. She couldn't see them, but later she would be aware that the exit wounds on the other side of her body had not been as neat. By then, though, they would already have begun rapidly filling in as they healed.

Upon discovering these wounds, a memory had come to Laura and she had scrambled to her feet, looking about wildly, shouting, "Hello? Hello?" Panicking, because what she had remembered was being the first to leave her Spanish class, emerging into a locker-lined hallway of her high school, and seeing a man striding toward her, youngish but at least a decade too old to be a student, wearing a greasy baseball cap and a thick blondish beard and black body armor, and carrying an AR-15 assault rifle.

All these clinical white tiles. She must be in a hospital—*and oh, the agony, pain without a vocabulary sufficient to express it, that she suddenly became conscious of...as if it too had only just revived after a period of dormancy*—but why were her wounds uncovered, why wasn't she in a bed, why...

...and then, a wheel in a bright metal hatch in the ceiling had begun to turn and turn, and the trapdoor itself had been lifted open, thick like a submarine hatch. The awakened pain had doubled Laura over—she'd almost dropped to her knees, the air snatched out of her so that she couldn't even cry for help again—but she had managed to straighten a little to look up toward that opening trapdoor. And that was when she'd seen the first of them, the monsters, leaning into that circle above her, with a wintery sky behind its head, full of snow spitting sideways. That obsidian-eyed face bordered with fur. Its shaggy arm, thickly muscled like that of a gorilla, reaching in for her. Before she could dodge it, it had grabbed hold of her hair, and then she was kicking her legs like a hanged person and she could see herself reflected in the pool of blood below as she rose and rose.

When it had hefted her all the way out, the monster had cast her to one side like some inanimate item unpacked from a box. She had plunged into snow, several feet deep…had become fully immersed in it. She was blinded, it went up her nostrils, filled her mouth, she couldn't breathe, her agony robbed her of the strength to stand and gasp for air, but other arms drove into the snow and found her, hands curled around her own arms, and she was pulled into a standing position by two people, one to either side of her.

These two, one a woman maybe in her thirties and a man perhaps in his fifties, were bundled in warm clothing, wore thick coats with hoods trimmed in white fur (*fur-framed faces!*), but she saw they were humans like herself, not monsters. The woman got close to her ear to be heard over the wind, over Laura's strangled sobs, and said, "Shh… it's going to be all right. We have you. It's going to be all right."

That was when the monster with three horns roared, "She's the last!"

It stood upon a long walkway or platform of black metal, elevated above the snow on numerous metal legs. The open hatch was at the very end of the platform. But, beneath that trapdoor, beneath the platform, was snow. So where was the room she had just been removed from? Buried in the snow, with an empty space between it and the hatch? But, the snow looked pristine in that spot.

Resting near the platform was a great metal sled, with twenty human beings harnessed to the front of it like reindeer. They were heavily bundled, too, but didn't look comfortable for all that. The sled bore an upright framework that helped support a crane, from which was suspended a heavy crucible pot filled with molten metal. Upon hearing the words of their commander, several lesser creatures with only a single horn directed the crane so that the cauldron was positioned over the open trapdoor, and the pot's hinged lid was pulled open via a cable. Then, the steaming pot was tilted, and the orange-glowing molten metal began pouring into the hatch's opening as if to fill a mold.

Weirdly, the poured metal vanished into the hatch but could not be seen below the level of the platform, as if that tiled cell existed in some alternate plane…some in-between place.

Laura watched in a kind of delirium, too numbed by the cold to feel it, but fortunately the cold seemed to numb a lot of her pain as well. Her mind, though…the agonies of her mind were a whole other matter. Paralyzed or frozen outside, a maelstrom inside. But she kept watching, as the pot was tipped empty and the crane then swung away. The monster with two horns that had pulled her from the small cell lowered the hatch back in place, worked its wheel several turns to reseal it. Straightening, it said to its commander, "No more Damned will be coming through this portal. We should go."

"We will go," said the monster with three horns. It turned toward the twenty human men and women hitched to the front of the sled, their legs buried in the powdery snow. Laura realized this team had been watching the filling and sealing of the tiled cell avidly. The monster commanded its crew, "Release them."

Several monsters with two horns, also wearing boots and blue ponchos, leapt down from the black metal platform into the snow to help the single-horned monsters remove the harnesses from the sled team.

"Should we hitch the girl up to her load?" asked a monster with two horns who had remained on the ramp beside the commander. This underling pointed to a smaller sled off to one side. There was a harness for only a single human being at its front, but it hung empty. Upon this sled rested something that looked to Laura like a rough-textured block of cement, with a tarp lashed over its top. It was rectangular, about the size of a refrigerator.

The commander swung his black stare to meet Laura's eyes, his pupils glittering like distant stars. He boomed, "No…don't bother. Why would we? We don't need to follow those routines anymore. We're abandoning our stations, aren't we?"

"Thank you, master," said the woman who helped hold Laura upright, apparently thanking the monster on Laura's behalf.

"You're free," the commander said to her. "All of you, here. As free as you can be."

The man in his fifties said, "But master...can't we come with you, wherever you're going?"

"Come *with* us?" the lead monster repeated. It seemed incredulous at the suggestion. Then it puffed up with pride, on the verge of anger. "You've no doubt heard, as we have heard, that some legacy Demons have joined forces with the Damned to oppose the new wave of Demons, and thereby defy the modifications of the Creator's design. We are not those Demons...we are not your friends. We are not your compatriots. We leave here with heavy hearts at defying the Creator even this much, but we leave here only to survive...to prevent the New Ones from eliminating us...not to join a battle. We hope to disappear somewhere in the vastness of Hades, to escape the purges, to escape their notice. The only thing you Damned here and we, your former captors, have in common is that we are now free, too." Again it added the words, "As free as we can be."

"But will they come here? The New Ones? Should we stay at the Mall or should we flee, too?"

"Who can say if they're coming? But we feel they will, sooner or later. We can't risk staying. Demons have no souls; these forms can be destroyed." The commander thumped its own chest. "You Damned souls are eternal; you can suffer mightily, but never be destroyed. So, you have less to lose if you remain. If you care to risk it, that is for you to decide. But do not follow us. Do *not*. Or we will bury you so far beneath the ice it will take you a century to dig yourselves out again. Be grateful for the gift we give you, to choose your own direction."

"We are grateful, master," said the woman beside Laura. She shot a warning look to the man in his fifties. "We are."

Laura stood nude—glazed almost white from the cold, and the blood on her body mostly cleansed away from her having been immersed in the snow—and stared as if drugged as the monsters tramped off into the distance, to meet up with another, much larger group of monsters

257

who waited for them like a long fringe of snow-covered trees. The commander was in the lead, the flame hovering above his middle horn a pale beacon. As they had departed, the monsters had torn off their cyan ponchos and let them flutter away in the wind. This made them harder to spot from far away, to any who might think to follow or to hunt them, and soon their caravan merged into the blizzard's mists and was gone. In their wake, some of the humans recovered a few of the discarded ponchos and donned them over their own garments. The woman at Laura's side motioned for one of the ponchos and it was handed to her, and she slipped this over Laura's head.

Before the poncho covered her body, Laura looked down and saw that the bullet hole in her sternum was now only a kind of deep dimple, from which no more blood oozed. The lower two, also.

The man in his fifties gave some commands, and Laura was lifted out of the snow and placed onto the sled in front of that cement-like block, so that her back was propped up against it.

"We should push that thing off into the snow," one of the men who had lifted Laura said, gesturing at the tarp-covered block. "You heard them; why follow the old routines now? We already have plenty of gray cake in storage as it is."

"We need it for food," the man in his fifties said.

"Uh, actually we don't," the other man said. "We *don't* need food."

"Well, tell that to your growling belly the next time it tells you it's empty."

The people who had been harnessed to the mobile foundry balked at wearing a harness again, so finally it was the man in his fifties and the woman in her thirties who each slipped an arm through a loop to pull the smaller sled. They strained and grunted as they got it started moving, ploughing up snow ahead of its curled front end.

"Aw, shit," one of the members of the former foundry team—a young black man—grumbled, coming around to push the sled from behind. As he passed Laura he said, "You're lucky, girl. I had to pull my block all the way to the Mall myself. We *all* did."

Two more men came forward to help push the sled. One of them sighed, "Let's just get the poor kid home."

"Train!" someone exclaimed, pointing off toward the horizon, in the direction opposite from that into which the caravan of monsters had disappeared.

The entire party paused, as if holding its combined breath, and looked. Only a black plume of smoke showed in the distance, leaning away from the direction in which it traveled. They all listened to a faraway rocking sound, of the locomotive's wheels along a track.

"New Ones coming?" someone whispered, as if someone on that train might hear them even at this remove.

"Maybe a shipment of more blocks for us?" someone else suggested.

"No...no," the woman in her thirties said. "Look...it's going to keep going. It's not stopping here."

"Thank G—" the man in his fifties began, but he caught himself and said, "Good."

The trailing plume of smoke and the rumble of the train faded away and were gone, and the party resumed its journey, though Laura was in no state to grasp their destination.

One of the travelers said, "Now where are the Damned going to come through to get here?" He gestured behind them at the newly sealed hatch, steam rising off its shiny metal surface.

"Are you kidding?" another of the men pushing the sled snorted. His breath misted the air, though Laura would learn eventually that none of the Damned truly breathed; their mock bodies only pretended to, only went through the motions of being alive, like clever machines. "They've got an infinity number of doorways, all across Hades. I guess our boys just didn't feel right about abandoning their post if the portal they were responsible for was still open and unattended. See? The Creator's good little robots, even when they think they're not."

-2-

They had finally reached a complex of buildings the party of humans had referred to as the Mall. Dominating it was a blocky, mostly featureless building that covered a lot of ground but was only a couple of stories high. Surrounding this were smaller buildings of different sizes and configurations; Laura had been told they were mostly warehouses and factories of various kinds. Columns of steam unraveled from the chimneys of the latter, seeming to join eventually with the dense ceiling of storm clouds overhead. The humans had taken shelter in the first building they came to, which was a kind of hangar-sized garage containing more sleds and sleighs, and toward the back stacks of boxed supplies on pallets. It was warm in here, at least compared to the outside, and they sat on some of the boxes to thaw out.

"How old were you, honey?" asked the woman in her thirties, who'd said her name was Lynn, as she held and rubbed Laura's hands in her own.

"I'm fourteen," Laura said, in a small voice. "I'm going to be fifteen in October."

"There ain't no October here, girl," said the youngish black man, whose name was Emmanuel. "You're going to be fourteen forever."

"Better than being fifty-seven forever," said the man in his fifties, whose name was Brad.

"How did you die, Laura?" Lynn asked her gently.

"This guy came into our school. I don't know why...he wasn't a student. I think he shot more people than just me. When he shot me and I fell down—I was in a hallway, I'd just come out of my Spanish class—when I fell down, before I blacked out, I heard a lot more shots...and screaming. I think he chased some kids back into the room...and he went in after them."

She began to cry, and Lynn put an arm around her shoulders. They had by now layered her in a few more of those blue ponchos. Lynn said, "If he wasn't just plain crazy, I'm sure he had some crazy reason. Conspiracy nut...domestic terrorist..."

"But why kids?" Emmanuel asked.

"Because it's crueler," said Brad.

"But the Demons set us free," said Emmanuel. "Ain't that funny? They could've locked us all up in cages or torture machines or whatever before they left, but they set us free."

"So what's your point?" Brad asked. "That people are more evil than Demons?"

"Can be."

"I wouldn't disagree," said Lynn.

Against Lynn's shoulder, Laura sobbed, "Why am I in Hell? What did *I* do?"

"Are you Christian?" asked Emmanuel.

"No…my family isn't religious. My parents are atheists."

"Well, then there you go, that's all it might take. You see this?" He pointed to a raised symbol branded like a keloid upon his forehead. Laura hadn't noticed that all these people had brands on their foreheads until they'd arrived at the garage, and some of them had shucked off their furred hoods. "M…for Muslim."

Brad tapped his own brand. "A…for Agnostic. The Demons gave us these brands when we first came through. They're the only scars we can't heal from. You're lucky—they didn't stick around to follow protocols with you."

Emmanuel went on, "That asshole who shot you? If he's Christian, he'll go straight to Paradise. If he shot himself after he shot up your school, that's where he is right now. We've seen his kind come around before, down here."

"*Down?*" Brad chuckled. "Like Hades is at the Earth's core?"

"You know what I mean! Anyway, we've seen his type. When they die, they go to Paradise. They become what they call Angels. And the Angels get bored up there, even with theme parks and mansions, casinos and fountains of wine, and all those beautiful Celestials to see to their needs. The Celestials are a race like the Demons: they're *made*, except they aren't made to torture the Angels, they're made to service them in every way…I think you get what I mean."

"She's fourteen," Lynn reminded him. "Keep it clean."

"Keep it *clean?* There ain't no clean down here!"

"There he goes with *down* again," said Brad.

Emmanuel continued, exasperated, "Anyway, what I'm trying to say is, they get bored, the Angels, so sometimes they come down…they come here to rape and pillage and kill us. They hunt the Damned and they kill us for sport. Yeah, I know, not all the Angels are like that, but we never see the ones who ain't."

"It isn't fair," Laura whined. "It isn't *fair!*"

"Well you're damned right it isn't."

"The Creator is an asshole, Laura," Brad said.

Lynn bulged her eyes and hissed, "Brad!"

"Oh, what's He going to do, damn me to Hades?"

"There's always worse here, you know that. There's always worse."

Brad sighed, and asked, "How's the pain, Laura?"

Laura moved the hems of the layered ponchos away from her upper thigh, where she'd been pierced by one of the bullets. Her ghostly white flesh had been partly restored to its natural olive tone that, like her long black hair, friends at school had praised as if to console her for not being particularly pretty. There was now the barest pockmark in her smooth, otherwise unblemished skin. She felt the back of her thigh; more of a divot there, but smooth-edged and not bleeding.

She replied, "It still hurts inside, but not like before. It's like... maybe like heartburn now."

"I got my head chopped off once," Emmanuel said matter-of-factly. "Not here—it was at another place, this big-ass amazing city called Oblivion. I don't know how many Damned live there, and –"

"*Live?*" Brad said.

"Will you shut up, man? You know what I mean. I don't know how many Damned there are in Oblivion, and Demons too, but a *lot*. I liked it...at least compared to the other places I've been to here. Anyway, I got involved with a female Demon. She treated me good, looked after me, but we got found out by the New Ones. The new kinds of Demons, that are being made to replace all the old races of Demons...the *human*-type Demons, I guess because the Creator thinks the old Demons sympathize with us too much. I don't know what they did to poor Naamah—that was my girl's name, Naamah—but me, they chopped my head off, burned my body, and tossed my head into a train car. Train brought me out here. By the time they unloaded us heads, we'd all grown back our bodies again. Well, not full-sized—more like kid-sized bodies—but those got bigger soon enough. I tell you what, that process was no fun."

"Oh God," Laura wept.

"Too late to appeal to Him now," Brad muttered.

"So what about this?" someone said. The others looked. A middle-aged woman, with sweaty brown hair and a haggard face, had unlatched the tarp from the top of the block they had carted here and folded it back.

Lynn said, "We'll drag it to the warehouse when we've caught our breath."

"No, I mean, *this*." The haggard woman, whose name was Marjorie, tapped her fingers at the center of the block's upper surface. There, inserted flush in its very center, was a block-within-the-block, only about the size of a deck of cards but the color of rust, or dried blood. "If we aren't following protocols, are we going to give this to the kid to eat?"

"No!" Emmanuel snapped. "Why would we? Are we Demons? No...we ain't! Why infect her with that shit?"

"We all had to do it," someone grumbled. "You too."

"Fuck yeah, I had to. Which is why I don't want this poor kid to do it. Things are different now, don't you get that?"

"I didn't say I *wanted* her to," the grumbler retorted.

"What is it?" Laura asked meekly.

"Haven't you noticed we're all sick here, Laura?" Brad said. "With this or that? I have a fever...I'm woozy as hell. Though I should be used to it at this point, because it never goes away."

Laura had in fact noticed that during their trek to the Mall complex, Lynn had been constantly wiping snot on the sleeves of her overcoat. She looked to Emmanuel, remembering that she'd heard him sneeze several times, and saw his eyes were reddened, watering, as if he were crying though he wasn't.

Another man opened the collar of his coat and pulled it down to reveal a ring of overlapping purplish boils or buboes encircling his neck, crowding up against his jawline. "You see this, cutie? You don't want this, believe me. You don't want to eat that crap."

Brad explained, "When we all came through that portal back there, before we came to the Mall and got branded, we each got assigned one block to drag here. This whole place and everything in it, even the food we eat, is made from those blocks. And inside everyone's block is a red cake—that's what we call them. The Demons would make us eat our one red cake. And once we started eating it, we'd *want* to, see? Because you never tasted anything better in your mortal life. There's nothing I can compare it to. But that stuff...oh yeah, that evil stuff..."

Lynn said, "In Hades, hon, there are what they call infernal animals. Out there –" and she pointed beyond the open garage door, into the stark whiteness and curtains of driven snow "– are animals that will prey on you if you try to walk far enough. These giant crabs, covered in white fur, big as cars. These gigantic, I don't know, furry snakes or worms maybe, that burrow under the snow. They'll grab you, feed on you, and you'll regenerate...and if you're still in that area recovering, they might do it to you all over again. I'm sorry to scare you, but you have to know everything sooner or later. But those aren't the only infernal animals. In hotter areas of Hades there are blood-drinking ants, poisonous flying spiders. And even smaller animals. Small as bacteria and viruses...do you understand? That's what the red cakes are made of. Little organisms, kind of like how coral is made from colonies of...of..."

"Polyps," someone said.

"Right. Anyway, but the red cakes...they made us eat them as a punishment for every one of us here at the Mall, because this is Hades, right? Punishments vary here, like the Demons vary, and the environments vary. But this is what *we've* had to deal with specifically, here at the Mall. You, though...you're the last one to come here, unless some stragglers find their way across the wasteland in the future, or get delivered by the train like some of us did. With the Demons gone, there's no need for you to have to go through some of the things we have, and –"

"Hey!" Brad shouted. "Marjorie, what are you doing?" Yelling sent him into a coughing fit and he doubled over, extra feverish and drained from their journey here.

The others snapped around to see that while they'd been conversing, Marjorie had dug her nails into the crease around the red cake inserted into the center of the cement-like block, and pried it out of its hollow. She had hunched over, with the red cake cupped in both hands, and bitten into its hard porous surface. She crunched a mouthful, and the grating sound made it seem she was chewing gravel and broken glass, but part of that sound might have been her teeth shattering. Still, she chomped another bite. After all, her teeth would regenerate.

"But it's so good," she said in a muffled voice, while chewing. "She doesn't need it, right? She doesn't *need* it!"

Lynn rushed at the other woman, reaching out. "You'll only get sicker! You want that? You want to be sicker?"

Marjorie spun her back toward Lynn, and protested, "But it's so *good*, Lynn!"

Emmanuel lunged and seized hold of the half-eaten red cake, snatched it roughly out of the woman's hands. "You crazy? You got enough of this shit inside you as it is!"

But another man, just behind Emmanuel, reached around and grabbed the object out of his hand. Instead of eating it on the spot, however, as Marjorie had done, this man ran out into the snowstorm.

"You goddamn idiot, Eric!" Brad called after the man, between lung-searing coughs.

"Let him go," Emmanuel said. "Let them be stupid."

Marjorie sank to the garage floor, sobbing, blood flowing over her lower lip, trying to lick traces of the red cake off her fingers. "But it's so good," she wept. "It's so *good*."

Laura was sobbing again, too, from having witnessed this latest horror. Noticing this, Lynn said to the others, "She's seen enough! Let's get her into the Mall, right now."

-3-

Laura found that "the Mall" was not merely an easy nickname, but a literal description.

Before giving her the tour, Lynn had first taken the girl to a public restroom, which in the back also featured a long row of shower stalls. Thankfully, the water was even lukewarm instead of icy as she might have expected. When she emerged, Lynn had returned from somewhere with a rough-textured towel, a pair of what appeared to be laceless canvas sneakers, and a somewhat faded black pajama-like outfit of long-sleeved top and pants. Lynn explained, "When you first come to Hades, these are the unforms the Demons usually give you. I still had mine; it's yours now. We'll get you more clothes soon enough. You can shop for them, in fact."

Then—with Laura's hair hanging in wet tangles, and with her body no longer bearing the slightest trace of bullet wounds or accompanying pain—the two of them went out to explore the Mall, which Laura had only glimpsed, and marveled at, briefly.

The interior of the structure reminded Laura closely of older, smallish malls she had been to, those that her parents had fondly recounted they'd visited when Laura was just a baby tucked in a stroller, before more sprawling megamalls with more elaborate layouts had arisen in their area. There was a straight main concourse, with a high ceiling, ringed by the balcony of a second floor. Shorter hallways branched off on either side, spread out along the main hallway's length. There were even two sets of escalators, positioned near either end of the concourse, though Laura asked why none of them were working. Surely the power hadn't been shut off when the Demons abandoned the place, because there were still lights overhead, and colorfully lit shopfronts.

"See that little door?" Lynn said, pointing to a closed panel in the base of one of the escalators. "There's a kind of treadmill in there. Some of us had the job of going in there every day—what we call 'day' here, anyway—and they'd take turns walking on it for hours to keep the escalators moving." She snorted a bitter laugh. "Remind you of the technology in *The Flinstones*, but with people instead of animals?"

"But who would want to do that all day?" Laura asked, gaping at her guide.

"No one would…that's why they're not moving since the Demons left. That's minor; I wonder what else might break down now, without them to oversee us. The Demons were harsh, no question about it, but they were…well, I can't call it fair, but there was a system here, set rules, and you knew what to expect if you broke them. They were cruel to us because that was *their* job. If *I'm* going to be fair, I'd say that in their own way, they were prisoners here, too."

One of the shorter sub-hallways contained a miniature playground, in which a number of children were frolicking on equipment fashioned from painted wood, rope, lengths of pipe. A burly man sat on a bench watching them intensely, a makeshift metal spear across his knees.

"What's up with him?" Laura whispered, concerned. He looked too dangerous to be near those children.

"That's Mitch. Like I say, with the Demons gone things could get really unpredictable. Not all the people here are in Hades just because of their religious affiliation, or lack thereof. A bunch of people truly belong here. You have to watch your back, Laura, you even more than these kids. Before, the predators here would have been too afraid to victimize other Damned. Now…they could definitely be emboldened. And that's why Mitch and others are keeping an eye on the children."

"Do they live with their parents?" Laura asked, watching the children of various ages and races run and swing and climb, seemingly happy in their innocence and adaptability.

"No, though people volunteer to take on that role. Their parents might still be on the Earth, alive, but even if they're not…one of the greatest punishments of Hades is that, somehow, we never meet our loved ones from life. Hades is so immense—limitless, for real—and the Damned so spread out, that you simply won't ever find them."

"Oh!" Laura said, staring at her new friend with eyes growing wet. She had comforted herself, to some degree, with the thought that her parents would one day join her here. Not that she wished them to be condemned to the netherworld, but if it was to be their unreasonable fate anyway as atheists…

"I'm sorry, Laura," Lynn said gently, obviously knowing what was going through her mind.

Onward. The next off-branching hallway was dimly lit and featured nothing but an imposing double door at its end, the panels composed of riveted metal. Lynn paused to indicate the doors, and said, "Those used to go down into a basement level. That was where the Demons ran their operation. There were cells for people who got on their bad side…and torture machines, too."

"Oh no! Did they ever…like, do that to you?"

"No, thank goodness. But when I first came here, like every other Damned who came through the portal you did, they took me down there through another doorway, on the outside. There was this one different type of Demon that always stayed down there...we called it the Brainiac. It looked kind of like a giant black preying mantis, but with this huge round head –" she framed her own head with her hands "– like an exposed brain. Because it wasn't human-looking, it must have been one of the New Ones. We new arrivals would be brought before it, and the Brainiac would just stare at us for a while, like it was looking directly at your soul, and then it would make this chittering sound that must have been instructions to the shaggy Demons, which we called Yetis, and then the Yetis would brand us with the symbol for whatever our greatest sin was, in their eyes."

"Where's the Brainiac now? I didn't see it with those other guys... the Yetis."

"I noticed that, too. I suspect they killed it before they left. Like I said...one of the New Ones."

"Oh wow."

"Anyway, those doors to the basement are sealed now. The door on the outside of the building, too." Lynn turned to her pupil. "You aren't branded, catalogued, or infected, Laura. It's like you're not officially Damned. I wonder how much that allows you to fly under their radar." She smiled grimly.

"The Demons' radar? Or, you mean...you know...His?"

"Come on," Lynn said, on the move again.

They passed others of the Damned going in the same or in the opposite direction, past all the open shopfronts, and a number of them said a word in greeting to Lynn, because they knew her, or gawked at Laura with curiosity, because they didn't. Though the ailments they all suffered weren't always immediately apparent, Laura saw a woman whose cheeks and nose were mottled with a severe red rash, followed by a man who on his forehead bore several huge, black-red blisters that looked ready to explode, as if he suffered gas gangrene.

"I thought the only scars we keep in Hades are the brands," Laura said, after the man had passed. "Can't these people get better, like I did from my bullet wounds?"

"The red cake is a different story, hon. Like I told you, they're microscopic infernal animals. They stay in you as long as they want, doing their work."

"These people aren't, like, contagious, are they?"

Lynn smiled. "What's the matter? Afraid you'll catch the flu from being with me?"

"I was thinking of that guy who just passed."

"No, we can't infect each other, it doesn't work that way. You get your cake when you come here...well, you used to...and the Demons would make you eat it, and whatever was randomly—I guess randomly—inside your cake was yours and yours alone."

"Our bodies are just illusions here, though, right? If we know that, why can't we program ourselves to take control of the illusion? You know, *will* ourselves to get better...to be younger, if we came here with an old body...or to look different or even be another sex if we want to?"

"Hon, the illusion of our physical bodies isn't *our* illusion. It's the Creator's." Lynn put a hand on her arm. "I like your spirit, though. Ah, to be young again."

"How long have you been here, Lynn?"

"Hard to say, without asking newcomers like you what year it was when they died. There's no real passing of time in Hades itself...no real day or night, except according to how we choose to perceive it. You know? Anyway, I've been here longer than some, less time than others."

"Do you...are you like the leader here, or one of them?"

"Me? Oh no, and I wouldn't want the responsibility. I'm not tough enough for that. We don't have a leader...the Demons were our leaders. Now, though...will we elect someone, or a board? Or will someone strong or just power hungry step up and proclaim that they're the new leader? I guess 'time' will tell."

Having covered the Mall's ground floor, in both directions, they ascended one of the immobile escalators to the second floor. More small shops lined it on either side, separated by open space. A good number of shops displayed roughly made but not necessarily unattractive clothing, folded on tables or hung on racks. Other shops offered furniture formed from plastic or some other substance, unidentifiable to Laura. There were shops that sold pots and pans, plates and cups and utensils, apparently made from this same substance, usually gray but sometimes dyed in various colors. Shops that sold handmade toys, shops that offered merely decorative items like vases and small sculptures (of that ubiquitous material again?). A surprising array of articles, given that this was Hades. Lynn addressed this fact.

"There are much worse places in Hades—much, much worse. I've only been here, but others like Emmanuel have seen some of them. All things considered, we're lucky to be here."

"Was it the Damned's idea to make this place into a shopping mall, or the Demons'?"

"The Demons, as I understand it. See, the fact that it's comfortable and familiar here seems like a gift, but it's also a curse. Sometimes the worst punishments are the things that remind you of the way things used to be, and should be. The things that remind you of *home*. And that, I'm sure of it, was their intention."

"Where does all this, like, merchandise get made?"

"Here. Some of it gets made right in people's quarters, but most of it is made in these little factories, that you might have noticed outside the Mall. Pretty much everyone has a job. Some of us work the factories, some of us work the shops, look after the generators, repair the water pipes if they burst from the cold…and some of us work crazier things, like escalators, or play music over the intercom in place of Muzak. We don't earn money, though, so we trade the things we make. Or food. Or…our bodies. Sorry, but you have to know."

"Well, that's not the job I want." Laura hugged herself as if to suppress a shudder. "Okay, but, so where does the, um, material come from for everything?"

"Once in a while a big shipment will arrive on the train, out there, and the Demons would send us with sleds to pick it up. Fabric, wood, glass, things that are harder to get around here. We'd put all that material into storage for the factories. But the main building blocks here are the blocks like the one you were supposed to drag here by yourself. That coral stuff. We call it gray cake. The walls here…well, the whole building: built from those types of blocks. You can process gray cake in all kinds of ways in the factories. Melt it into something like plastic. Tease it out into strands to weave it into clothing. We even break it down and process it in different ways and flavor it so we can eat it. Our minds know we don't have to eat…but these imaginary bodies of ours think they do. If we don't eat, we suffer. But we get sustenance other ways, too. We melt ice and snow for water. There are hunting expeditions that go out there for meat. I sure wouldn't want *that* job, but I'm grateful for the crab meat they bring back, not to mention that crab fur is pretty soft once you wash it and all. But yeah, those blocks…so much of what's around you comes from them. But of course, more were needed to build the Mall than what the Damned dragged here. I think the Demons organized special work crews to build it before any of us got here, and the train has dropped off a lot of blocks in the past, too. Will it keep making deliveries, now with the Yetis gone? Who knows? I hope so…but I hope the train crews don't realize we're on our own now. They're mostly Damned, but of course overseen by Demons."

"Old-time Demons, or…the new types?"

"At this point, who can say?"

Just then, music came over speakers distributed throughout the Mall, performed somewhere within the complex by several somewhat talented musicians. In this big open space, the music had an echoey, distant quality that Laura found melancholy. Lynn tilted up her head to listen, and said, "Well, seems like things haven't fallen into chaos here just yet. The question is, are they playing because they're just so used to their role, or because they actually enjoy playing?" Then she smiled in recognition. "Oh, I remember this song…yeah. It's just as well that it's an instrumental, and no one's trying to imitate Leon Russell."

"Who? What is it?"

"The song's called *Lady Blue*."

"That's me," Laura joked, affecting a weak smile. "Lady Blue."

-4-

From the second floor balcony, with the open front of a shoe store directly behind her, Laura looked down at an argument in progress. Two men, the younger of them with several friends standing behind him trying to look intimidating. Laura felt they were successful at that. The older man had only one friend behind him, but Laura recognized this friend as Mitch, who remained silent but held his metal spear with its butt resting on the floor.

The younger of the two men was pot-bellied, wore a baseball hat, and spoke too loudly and gestured too forcefully. "It would take twenty people to go out there and bring that sled back here. Are you going to want to do that, Gabe, 'cause I know I don't…and I don't know who will."

"We're going to need that crucible back in our foundry, Sam. The longer we wait, the more snowed in it's going to get. Who knows how long it'll be before we see a little thawing around here again."

"Well, don't ask me and my boys to do it; I'm not your fucking sled dog. We might have to abandon this place soon anyway—who knows?"

The older man, Gabe, replied, "We aren't likely to find another place as comfortable as this anytime soon."

"Tell it to the New Ones when they come here and decide to change things up. Because you know those things are gonna happen; it's just a matter of when."

"So we just give up, Sam, and let things fall into disorder around here?"

"So it begins," said a voice behind Laura.

She whipped around, startled, and found an unfamiliar man looming close, large-bodied and smiling. She should have heard his hiccups approaching; he seemed afflicted with a chronic case of them. Was that his personal infirmity?

"What begins?" she asked timidly.

"People making gangs…fighting for control. Eh, who needs it?" Hitches between his words. The smile turned to a grin. "Hey, new girl—my name is Billy. I've seen you around. How you doing so far? Look, you need a place to stay?"

"I'm staying with Lynn," Laura said, edging back a step, her hand sliding along the balcony rail. She pointed to the shoe store behind him. "She makes shoes."

"I know her—she's okay. You comfortable living with her? I think she likes girl, myself. Not sure, but something to keep in mind." He wagged a finger, like a father lecturing his daughter. "I have a room above Warehouse B; that's where I work. It's cozy, but big enough for two."

"I'm all set, thanks. I should get back inside...Lynn's talking with the owner." She gestured at the shoe store again, but when she shifted as if to walk toward it, this man Billy shifted as well to remain in front of her.

"In the Warehouse B breakroom we built ourselves a pool table. You should see it—it's awesome. I can go right downstairs and play pool anytime I want."

"I don't really play."

She realized the arguing men below her had moved on; she didn't hear their voices anymore. There were other voices in the Mall, but they all sounded too far away, like ghosts haunting the place.

"Hey," Billy said in a lowered, more conspiratorial tone, edging even closer to her and reaching into a pants pocket. He withdrew something pinched between finger and thumb, showed it to her down low: a reddish pebble that reminded her of the kibbles she had used to feed her family's cat. "You like this stuff? Like I said, I work in the warehouse. Can I trust you with something? One time by mistake—I guess it was a mistake—the train delivered a load of blocks and one entire block was made out of red cake. We never saw anything like that before. Anyway, we still have a good chunk of it left. I'd be happy to share it with you, if you want."

"Aren't you afraid to get more sick?" Laura said, recoiling hard against the balcony railing.

Billy hiccupped, then said, "You just take a little tiny bit at a time! You do it like that, and it's like there's barely any problems. Come on, you know how great this stuff tastes."

"No, I don't. I didn't eat mine."

273

"You *didn't?* Oh man, you don't know what you're missing." He returned the pebble to his pocket.

Laura saw another man coming toward them quietly, behind Billy, this man somewhat shorter than Billy but somewhat wider.

Billy went on, "Well, how about you come and check out that pool table I was telling you about, um…what'd you say your name was again?"

"I need to get back to Lynn."

Billy reached out and took hold of her arm. He put no force behind it, and he was still smiling (and hiccupping), but when Laura tried to pull away his fingers closed just a bit more firmly.

"Come on, tell me your name."

"Lady Blue."

Laura watched with some relief, even satisfaction, as the tip of a metal spear delicately poked into the hole of Billy's ear.

Billy flinched back and spun around, cupping his ear where it had been nicked inside. Mitch still held his heavy metal spear angled up toward him.

In a calm voice Mitch said, "Move along, Billy."

"I was just telling her –"

"Don't make me put this thing through your head again. I don't want you talking to this girl."

"Okay, okay, I was just trying to be friendly." Looking humiliated, Billy shambled along.

Laura eased her back from the balcony railing. This near to Mitch, she saw how his bald head—wider than it was long—was scarred and pitted from a rough mortal existence. "Thanks," she said to him. "He was creepy. Are you, like, the police around here or something?"

The man held his spear like a walking staff again, and began to turn away. All he said was, "I'm Mitch."

❧

Lynn's apartment was more like a wall cavity between one flank of the Mall and the rear of a structure called Warehouse C. Lynn had hung up a white sheet to partition off a little corner for Laura to use. "I guess I'm subletting," Lynn had joked.

This space was narrow but fairly long, and Lynn had set up some work tables at which she and a few other workers under her made shoes like the laceless canvas pair she'd given Laura. Laura's new job was insole cutter. She'd sit at a table with a thick sheet of pinkish-beige rubber in front of her, and trace various-sized metal dies with a razor knife, flipping the die over as needed to cut either a left or right sole. On her first session she'd slipped with her knife and cut deeply into her left hand as it held the die in place. She'd cried as much from surprise as pain, but of course the nice clean slice healed in no time. Now, already her work was going more smoothly and the soles stacked up beside her according to shoe size.

That time she'd cut herself, despite knowing the wound would heal quickly Lynn still bandaged it with a scrap of cloth. Sucking up her sniffles, Laura was embarrassed about having cried. "I guess I should toughen up. Things get really scary around here, and something like this is nothing."

"You'll harden," Lynn said. "Don't try to force it. It's a natural process."

"Lynn...as the years go by...well, you know what I mean. Even though my body will stay fourteen, will my soul get older? Or my mind? Will I get, like, the mind of an adult? You know, wisdom and knowledge and all like that? Or will I always be immature...just a weak kid? A victim?"

Holding Laura's injured hand in both of hers, Lynn looked up and repeated, "You'll harden, hon—whether that's for good or ill. Whether you stay gentle like you are now, or become strong and assured, you just stay my Lady Blue, okay?"

Laura tried not to let her eyes fill up again. "Okay, Lynn."

Now, today—as they thought of it—Laura saw that they were on their last sheet of pinkish-beige rubber for the soles, and when she told Lynn, her friend said, "Can you go out to the warehouse and drag a couple more sheets in here? They're on a pallet not far from the door; you can't miss it."

"Okay." But Laura hesitated, and Lynn looked up from where she sat sewing together the animal-hide pieces of a shoe, built around the base of a hard, foot-shaped "last."

"You're afraid, hon?" Lynn said. "Are you spooked from that asshole Billy?" Lynn rested the shoe last on her workbench and stood. To her other two workers she announced, "Laura and I are going out into the warehouse to fetch some supplies—we'll be right back." Then she nodded to a door of her wall cavity apartment and said, "Let's go."

Whereas the door in the opposite wall led into a storage room of the Mall, through which they could enter the Mall proper, the door they passed through now took them directly into Warehouse C. The ceiling was high in here, supported by metal joists, and tall metal racks were filled with boxes, crates, and drums. Pallets took up much of the floor space, and Laura did indeed spot the pallet of rubber sheets right away. Immediately upon entering the warehouse, however, Lynn had audibly gasped. Though Laura had only been in here with Lynn a couple of times before, she immediately saw the problem, as well.

"What the hell has *happened?*" Lynn exclaimed, navigating through pallets as she crossed the floor toward the far wall. "Well, geesh, now I guess I know why it felt colder in our flat today."

Laura followed, hugging her arms against the frigid air, crunching through a thin layer of snow that had blown into the warehouse from outside. This was because a portion of the far wall was missing, as if its construction had never been completed. One might first suspect an explosion had occurred here, but Laura saw no rubble inside or out. In fact, it was as though a half dozen good-sized blocks, of which the wall had been built, had been carefully removed, leaving a gap with an irregular but clean-edged outline.

"Did someone do this to get inside?" Laura asked, suddenly looking to left and right, expecting to see some new monstrous brand of Demon come rushing at them from their hiding places in the shadows.

"There are much easier ways to get into these buildings," Lynn said, but she too looked nervous as she stood at the edge of the opening and squinted out into the blowing mists of snow. "We have to tell the others. I guess we'll have to…repair it, right? But we should send a team out to take a look around the complex, to see what they can see."

Laura came up beside Lynn. "Who do we tell? Who's in charge to do anything about this?"

"Volunteers." Lynn wagged her head. "We can only get others to listen, and see who's willing to do what."

An eerie, ululating cry came to them on the wind. At first, Laura assumed it was in fact the wind, but Lynn said, "Oh man." She took a step back from the opening, grasping Laura's arm and pulling her with her.

"What is it?" Laura hissed.

Together they saw it rear up in the distance: a gray-white pillar through the clouds of gusting snow. Laura couldn't judge the animal's size, but she guessed it to be about as big around as a school bus, though much longer. A worm? A serpent? Whatever it was, it was covered in white fur, and a black opening at its end gaped toward the storm clouds as if to suck in their discharge. It was from this hole that the haunting, weirdly forlorn cry came.

"Oh my *gosh*," Laura said. She had already learned not to evoke the Creator's name: it made others, and herself, uncomfortable even if He might not hear it Himself. She said, "Did that thing tear our wall apart?"

"I don't see how it could," Lynn said. She squeezed Laura's arm and whispered, "Get ready to run back to our flat if it comes this way."

Laura couldn't understand how it might spot them, as she noticed no eyes on the thing. In any case, after having towered vertically for only about thirty seconds, the immense infernal creature gave one more howl, which sent a tremor through Laura's nerves, before curling and plunging headfirst back into the snow. A plume shot up where it had burrowed, but when this settled there was no sign—from here at least—that it had ever been out there.

"Good luck getting people to go outside to check on what happened to the wall," Laura said, now better understanding why that man Sam didn't want to lend aid in retrieving the crucible the Yetis had left behind.

-5-

Laura had accompanied Lynn and Brad up to the Mall's expansive roof. Brad had been first up the ladder to reach it, and had struggled pushing the metal access hatch open. When Laura followed the older two Damned up there, she saw what the difficulty was. Snow was piling up on the flat surface, deterred only a little by the warmth the Mall generated.

"Damn it," Brad said. "You see? When the Yetis were here, they had people come up and shovel this off regularly. Do you think anyone wants to do that now, on their own?"

"We might have to just organize a group of shovelers ourselves," Lynn said. "If we don't, and the snow builds up too much, I'm afraid the roof will collapse."

"We can't cover all the bases just on our own, Lynn. Other people are going to have to take some incentive around here."

"I'll talk to Gabe about it."

Laura thought Gabe was the best person to appeal to. After all, it was Gabe who was down there on the ground right now, with Mitch and Emmanuel, making a circuit of the Mall and its satellite structures to see if they could figure out the cause of that curious breach of Warehouse C. Still very curious about that event, Lynn and Laura had come up here to look down at the investigative party to watch from a safe vantage point, with Brad tagging along. Therefore, they trudged through the gathering snow to the edge of the roof, gazing down past the slightly shorter flat roof of Warehouse C.

"I don't see them," Laura said.

"They must already be on the other side of the Mall. Maybe they found a lead."

"Thought I saw you come up here," called a familiar voice behind them.

Laura turned to see another trio of people had just ascended to the roof through the access hatch, and she recognized all three of them. The one who'd spoken was Billy. The other two she remembered from her first day here: Marjorie, who had taken it upon herself to eat what was meant to be Laura's red cake, and Eric, the man who had snatched the remaining chunk of that cake from Emmanuel's hand. Eric held a flat strip of metal with a taped up handle, one length of the metal sharpened into an edge.

"What do you want?" Lynn asked the approaching trio. Her voice sounded harsh, but Laura could hear the nervousness behind the bluster.

"It's my own fault," Billy said through his hiccups, tramping toward them through the accumulating snow. "I was stupid, wasn't I, Lady Blue? I told you a secret I shouldn't have."

"What are you saying?" Brad said. He was trying to sound hard, too, but Laura was sure his eyes were on that improvised machete, as were her own.

Billy and the others stopped a few feet from them. Laura was keenly aware of the drop behind her.

Eric growled, "This girl knows what Billy means." He pointed the machete at her. "Where is it, bitch? Where's the red cake?"

"I don't know where any red cake is!" she said.

"You don't, huh? What a fucking coincidence. Billy tells you about a big block of red cake the warehouse boys stashed, and then suddenly it goes missing."

"Just tell us where it is," Marjorie said, looking miserable. "We don't want to hurt you, honey."

"You aren't hurting anyone!" Brad cried. He stepped in front of Laura. "You'd better get away from us before you get yourself in trouble!"

"Trouble with who?" Eric snapped. "The Yetis? Better go find them, Brad, and tell on us. We'll wait here for you."

"I've never even been into your…your Warehouse B!" Laura said, peeking around Brad. "You didn't say where that stuff was hidden, and how could I move a whole block of it by myself?"

"Who said you moved it by yourself?" Eric said. "You seem pretty close with these two assholes. And it isn't a whole block anymore…it's like forty percent of a block, now."

"You're insane if you eat that crap," Lynn told him. "You see what it does to you?" She pointed at Marjorie. When last Laura had seen the woman, Marjorie had been been haggard and wasted but at least she'd still had lips. Since eating so much of Laura's red cake in one go, on top of what was already in her system, now her lips had entirely rotted away, leaving all her teeth exposed right to the gums, like someone suffering advanced syphilis.

"You worry about your own damn self," Eric told Lynn, waggling the machete at her now.

"Come on, Lady Blue," Billy said, grinning like some lovable oaf and spreading his arms. "Just tell us where it is and all will be forgiven."

Laura stepped out from behind Brad, and said, "I'll tell you something. I'm going to talk to Mitch about this. He told you to stay away from me, didn't he? You mean to say you're not afraid of him?"

"Let me cut her," Eric said. "I want to cut her up a bit." He swiped the machete in a figure eight in front of him, making a swooshing sound. "Yeah, you'll regenerate, you little droopy-eyed slut, but until you do you won't feel very good."

Laura knew he was referring to the fact that one of her eyelids was noticeably sleepier than the other. It had always bothered her, and his remark hurt worse, perhaps, than that machete blade would.

"Mitch is down there right now," Brad snarled at them, pointing behind him. "Why don't I give him a shout? I know he put that spear of his through your head once, Billy, for trying to trick one of the kids in the playground into going off with you somewhere. Sure, if he put his spear through your head again, you'd regenerate, *but until you do you wouldn't feel very good.*"

"That's it." Eric started to lunge forward, or at least to bluff a lunge forward, but Billy put a hand on his chest. His big dumb smile had faded, leaving him looking just doughy and morose. "I think the kid's telling the truth," he said. "How could she carry that red cake off with her?"

"These two fucks helped her!" Eric shouted.

"Why would they, though? They don't use the stuff."

"To trade it for stuff they *do* use!"

"Let's go," Marjorie whined, wringing her bony hands in front of her. "I don't want trouble with Mitch! You didn't tell us Mitch was protecting this girl."

"Come on," Billy said to Eric. "Someone else must've taken it."

"So it's just a coincidence, huh?" Eric said. "You tell this cunt about it, then suddenly, poof, it's gone?"

"Yeah...something like that, I guess."

"*Fuck!*" Eric said, lowering the machete and stomping off toward the open hatch.

"No hard feelings, Lady Blue, okay?" Billy got a vestige of his smile back. "No need to get Mitch riled up, right?"

"Just get out of our face, fucker," Lynn said to him.

"Sorry, honey," Marjorie said to Laura, her words distorted by her lack of lips. "Sorry!"

Then Laura, Lynn, and Brad watched Billy and Marjorie follow Eric to the hatch, and disappear down into it.

When they were gone, Lynn turned to Laura and asked what she knew about this. Laura had told her before about Billy trying to coax her to his apartment, and about Mitch intervening, but not about some big secret stash of red cake. So Laura explained about that, and said, "It just didn't concern me, or whatever, so I didn't bring that part up. I wasn't trying to protect him or anything."

"Oh, I know that, hon. I know you wouldn't."

"Scumbags," Brad hissed, clenching and unclenching his fists impotently. "Worthless scumbags. Things are really going to shit. I'd better start carrying a knife or something."

"Good idea," Lynn said. "Laura, from now on, you keep your razor knife on you at all times, okay?"

"Okay, Lynn."

Brad looked over the side. "Where the hell are those guys? I wonder if they've found anything. I wish Mitch had been down there a minute ago."

Then, the three of them heard a strange sound, like a series of hard raps on a snare drum, carrying from far away. A few ticks of silence, in which they held their breaths, then another series of raps. At the first occurrence Laura had snapped her head up, and now she gasped, "Oh my God!" This time she didn't catch herself from invoking that word. She knew this sound too well, but still she asked, "Was that a *gun?*"

"Sounds like it," Brad said, scanning the horizon. "We'd better get inside. It's in the distance, but still."

"Who has guns in Hades?" Laura asked, incredulous.

"You kidding me?" Brad said. "Demons use them sometimes…but Angels, too."

"You mean, those people from Heaven, who come to Hell to, like, hunt the Damned and stuff?"

Lynn said, "Some of them also help the New Ones fight against the legacy Demons who've sided with the Damned. It's an adventure for them, like fucking military reenactment. It's not like Angels can get killed, right? Not like the Demons."

"I sure hope whoever it is, they're not heading this way," Brad said. "With any luck, whoever it is doesn't even know about the Mall."

"Good luck with that," Lynn said. "What else is there, way out this way?"

"Let's go," Brad said. "Inside."

As they headed back toward the hatch, Laura said, "I hope Mitch and the others are okay."

-6-

They learned that Gabe, Mitch, and Emmanuel were already back inside and on the ground floor of the Mall, at about its center, where there stood a circular fountain pool that with the Yetis gone no longer sprayed water. Lynn had told Laura she believed someone had shut it down on purpose, thinking it to be a foolish waste. People had been scooping the water out with buckets so as to boil it and make better use of it, though the boiling was more for the psychological effect, since the water was as much a clever illusion of the Creator as their human bodies were, which were apparently composed of about 60% illusory water.

Here, Gabe was calling on others to gather around to hear what he had to report after having investigated a strange event. A crowd was slowly gathering, as workers and shoppers left the stores, and other workers trickled in from the factories and warehouses.

Lynn, Brad, and Laura wove through the crowd to get close to

Gabe. Lynn asked, "What did you find?"

"Let's wait until I can tell everyone at once," Gabe said.

"Gabe, thanks for stepping up," Brad said. "We all need someone like you."

"Hey, now, I'm not exactly running for office, here…just doing my part. We all should be."

"Mitch," Lynn said, "we need to talk to you about something that happened with Billy."

"Yeah?" Mitch said. Laura could see his already stern face gear up to get sterner.

"Wait until after I share what we found," Gabe said, "then we'll talk about that."

Laura noticed someone else edging through the crowd to get close to Gabe. She remembered him from his baseball hat and abrasive voice: Sam. "Hey, Mr. President, before you give your state of the union address, maybe you should come see something I just found out about, myself. Then we can talk about all this stuff at once."

"What is it, Sam?"

"I said…*come see.*"

Gabe sighed and looked around at the still-gathering crowd. He raised his voice to be heard over the growing chatter. "Folks, please don't go anywhere, unless it's to get more people to come to the meeting. I have to check something out real quick, then I'll be right back!"

Lynn asked Sam, "Does this have something to do with a weird hole opening up in a wall?"

Sam blinked at her. "How did you know that?"

"Because I found one. I want to see this, too."

So when Gabe and Mitch accompanied Sam up to the second floor, Lynn, Brad, and Laura trailed after them.

❦

Laura had taken a quick look around in this store once before. Its walls were covered in paintings and drawings, framed or unframed, that varied widely in artistic merit. Many a pleasant memory from the artists' mortal existence had been manifested in pigment, charcoal, or ink: childhood homes, favorite vacation spots, favorite pets, the faces of remembered loved ones. Of course, there was abstract art, too, and some pieces that were dark, disturbing, violent. Laura could understand the artists' need to vent these emotions, but who would want to hang such things on the walls of their humble living quarters, already bleak enough?

She overheard Sam explain to the others that the store's proprietor, a woman named Monica, had been the one to tell him what had happened here. Laura had the impression Sam and this Monica were involved with each other.

Today, the shop was much colder than Laura remembered it, and there was a thin film of snow on the floor. It was sifting in through an open doorway at the rear of the store, and Sam led the way into a smallish back room.

This time, Laura was not quite as shocked to see that several large blocks, of which the Mall's outer walls were made, had gone missing just as in Warehouse C, though this opening appeared to be two or three blocks smaller.

"What is even going *on?*" Lynn said.

Mitch went right up to the opening and gazed out into the blizzard, squinting his hard eyes against the moaning wind. Meanwhile, Lynn told Sam what she had discovered, and Gabe gave in and told them of his party's findings, in advance of the meeting with the greater populace.

Gabe said, "We found two other places like this, where building blocks have gone missing, neatly removed. Part of a side wall in Warehouse A, and a whole corner of the sled garage." Laura assumed this to be the building she had been brought into when she'd first come to the Mall.

"Did the Warehouse A folks not see it happen?"

"They were in a pretty excited state when we got there. They'd only just noticed it, but one person *did* say they saw something weird."

"And what was that?"

"They noticed a funny noise—probably the wind coming in— and they came out from behind a rack and saw the opening, and then they said they saw a person walking off into the storm. It was only a silhouette, but they said the person was *big*."

"Big, huh? So was it a Demon? If it was, why walk away from the Mall instead of coming inside to fuck with us?"

"What, are Demons going to just sneak in and dismantle the Mall block by block when we aren't looking?" Brad said. "Well, that's a new kind of punishment."

"I see it," Mitch said.

The others turned to him, saw his broad back framed against the bright white opening, an imposing silhouette himself. "See what?" Sam said.

"The big thing the guy in the warehouse told us about."

Sam, Gabe, and Lynn crowded in fast around Mitch, unintentionally blocking Brad and Laura, who craned their necks trying to steal a peek.

"Oh my God," Lynn whispered. "What's it doing out there? Just standing around like a statue?"

Sam said, "It's hard to tell, but doesn't look like a Demon...I mean, in shape. No horns or weird proportions or anything. Looks like a person."

"You kidding me?" Lynn said. "That thing's too big to be a regular person."

"What I mean is, it's a human kind of Demon. So it's a legacy Demon, not one of the New Ones. There's going to be all types of New Ones, but they're all supposed to a lot less human, right?"

"Even if it *is* a legacy Demon," Brad said, behind them, "that doesn't necessarily mean it's going to show us any more mercy than the New Ones would. It could be some legacy Demons have been ordered in here to get the Mall under control again, until New Ones can replace them later. A lot of the old-type Demons are still going to obey orders right up until they're thrown in the dumpster, so to speak."

Laura crouched down low beside Lynn, and finally got a clear view of the outside around her friend's legs.

She sucked back whatever exclamation she wanted to make, and stared through the particles of snow that stung her face. Below, out there, stood a dark human-shaped figure just as the others had said, and Lynn was right about it remaining as still as a statue. Laura wasn't good at judging such things, so she couldn't tell how far away it was… or truly how tall it might be. Through the shifting veils of snow, which occasionally almost hid the figure entirely before it would be revealed again, she also couldn't tell if it were facing toward or away from the Mall. She looked up at Lynn and said just loud enough to be heard over the wind, "Shouldn't we get back, in case it looks this way and sees us?" But Lynn didn't answer, and she wasn't sure she had spoken loudly enough after all.

Mitch had leaned his upper body out through the opening in the wall, and now he pointed off to the left. "There's another one."

"Careful not to fall," Gabe said, putting a hand on Mitch's back and leaning out, too, to look around his body.

"Same thing?" Sam asked.

"Same thing," Gabe replied. "Identical. Just standing there."

Sam leaned out on the right and peered that way, but apparently there wasn't a third figure. Stepping back from the opening, he said, "The kid's right—let's not call attention to ourselves."

Mitch and Gabe withdrew from the opening, and Brad said, "So do we send another party out there to sneak a closer look?"

"Yeah," Sam said. "Why don't you head that party, Brad?"

"Well, do we just wait to see what happens, then? What do we do?"

"We do our meeting," said Gabe.

Laura couldn't prevent herself from crying out this time. She jolted back so abruptly from the opening in the wall that she fell onto her bottom. The others looked down at her sharply, startled.

"What the hell, kid?" Sam hissed. "You want them to hear us?"

"I had my hand on that block," Laura said, eyes wild. She pointed toward where she had been crouched, bracing herself with her left hand on one of the blocks that framed the irregular opening. "It moved!"

"What do you mean, it moved?" Brad asked.

"I'm sure of it…it felt like it kind of swelled up, and then went flat again. Like, like it sucked in a breath."

The others turned from her to warily study the block she pointed to. They saw no such movements. "You sure?" said Gabe.

"I told you, I'm *sure!*"

"Let's get the fuck out of here," Sam said. "We need to lock this store up...the warehouses, too. Any room where this is happening."

"And if it keeps on happening?" Brad said.

Lynn helped Laura regain her feet, and as Laura stood she said, "I don't think those things out there took away the blocks. I think they *are* the blocks."

-7-

Because there were numerous races of Demons, all quite different whether of the old or the newly produced breeds, the Damned found it best to give them nicknames by which to identify them. They were soon enough calling the figures they'd spied in the snow Golems.

They filled in all those who had gathered thickly around the fountain, and spilled over onto the balconies above, about what had been discovered in Warehouse C, in the back of the art store, and outside during their reconnaissance mission. People gasped aloud, like an audience of movie goers, when they heard a bout the Golems.

"So what are they doing just standing around out there?" someone asked.

"I think they're getting into position," Sam said. "Maybe surrounding the Mall, while they wait for further orders."

"You're probably right," Gabe said.

"But what *are* those things, Gabe?" someone else cried.

"We can't be sure yet, exactly, but Laura here had an idea, and she may be right." Gabe rested a hand on the girl's shoulder. "We know how red cake is made up of microscopic infernal animals...that's why we're all sick like we are. Well, it's possible that all along, the blocks we use to build with...to craft with...that we *eat*...the stuff we call gray cake...it's possible that material is composed of microscopic creatures, too."

"Like nanites," Laura said.

"Like *what?*" someone said.

287

"Nanomachines, nanobots...you know, nanotech?" Laura said. "Except, they're Demons. Tiny, tiny Demons all working together!"

"With a hive mind, maybe," Lynn said.

"All along the gray cake's been like that?" Emmanuel with the M brand on his forehead said. "Then why's it only starting to act this way now?"

"A failsafe mechanism, maybe," Sam said, "in case the Damned ever overpowered the Demons here. With the Yetis gone, it activated."

"I don't think so," Gabe said. "This is New Ones stuff that's happening, but the Mall's been here for a while. Maybe the powers-that-be do know the Yetis have left, and they want to replace them, or maybe they don't know, and they did this thinking to replace the Yetis while they were still here. Either way, I believe they've reached out to the gray cake somehow, and changed its nature. Reprogrammed it, so to speak. Why grow a crop of new Demons and send them all the way out here, when you can just repurpose the material that's *already* here?"

"Anyway, theories aside," Sam said, "we need to get out of here."

Gabe blinked at him a moment before speaking. "Get out of here? And go where? Into the frozen wasteland?"

"The train," Sam said. "That big sled the Yetis left, with the crucible...we drag that to the tracks, then *onto* the tracks, and we wait. A train will come sooner or later, and when it does, the Demons will stop the train to move the sled. Whether they move it themselves, or they have Damned prisoners move it, either way we storm the train and take it over. Then, we take that train wherever it looks promising to go back on foot."

"You overpower a train...manned by Demons."

"There's probably less Demons on a train than can be produced here by all these blocks of gray cake!" Sam snapped, growing louder and gesticulating more fiercely. "How many blocks make up the Mall, Gabe? If this theory about *nanodemons* is true, every single block in here could become one of them! *Thousands* of new Demons!"

"Think of why we're here, Sam...who we are, who they are," Gabe said. "What their *job* is, the Demons. Their job is to punish us, yes, but not send an army to kill us. We can't be *killed*. They won't disassemble the entire Mall to overwhelm us with thousands of Demons. They'll make about as many as there were Yetis, to be our overlords here. Maybe these new overlords will be more harsh than the Yetis were—that's probably part of the whole New Ones deal. Get tougher with the Damned, no more sympathizing with us. But in the end, we'll stay here and go on more or less as we have been. And in the whole of Hades, from what I've experienced and what I've heard from other Damned, that's about the best we can ever hope for. You've heard the stories. A lot of Damned in other regions have it a lot worse."

But Sam was wagging his head. "No...nope, Gabe. I like my idea. I don't want to just willingly put my head on the chopping block, to get chopped off and regrow—wash, rinse, and repeat—into eternity. We have an opportunity here, a window between the Yetis going out and the New Ones coming in. How often would anyone in Hades ever get a shot like that? I want to take it. I want to take my own destiny in hand...not just sit here with a bunch of other chickens in their cages, like I say, waiting for the cleaver."

"You're free to do what you want, Sam," Gabe said. "We're all free to do what we want...at least at this point in time, like you say. We do have a window in which to make a choice." Gabe slowly looked around at the faces that encircled him, then looked up at those on the balconies, too. "My choice is to stay, and see what happens. That's taking my own destiny in my hands, isn't it? Same as you, Sam?"

"Bullshit it's the same," Sam said. "Well, you aren't forcing me, and I'm not forcing you. But whoever wants to go with me –" he looked around at the others, too "– make up your minds fast while this window is open. I say we move quick as we can, before this place gets surrounded by these Golems and they decide to close in."

"The best people to go with us out there," said one of Sam's intimidating-looking friends, whom Laura recognized from the other day when Sam and Gabe had been arguing about the sled with the crucible, "are the hunters. You hunters are the toughest motherfuckers we got, and you know the wasteland, and you've fought those monsters out there before. Fuck, why did the Yetis even allow you to go hunting for game? Because they knew the hell you had to go through out there in the cold, fighting those things."

"Yeah," Sam said, and he turned to look directly at Mitch. Laura realized, then, that Mitch must be one of those hunters. "Mitch, come with my team. I'll make you my righthand guy. Just think of the possibilities. We could stop that train out in the middle of some wilderness where it isn't freezing cold and it isn't fiery hot, and where there aren't any Demons at all in sight. Hades is so huge, man, there *has* to be in-between places like that. What do you say?"

Mitch stared back at Gabe, then shifted his narrow-eyed gaze toward someone else. Laura followed his eyes. He was looking at a middle-aged woman who held two small children at her sides, children who couldn't possibly be her own for reasons Lynn had explained to Laura. Mitch then looked to a boy of about eleven, Laura estimated, who watched the hunter's face anxiously. It was Mitch, perhaps more than any other of them, who had protected the children of the Mall from the worst of the inhabitants of the Mall.

"No," Mitch said.

"No, as in…"

"No, as in no."

"Fuck," hissed Sam's beefy friend.

"I'll go with you," said another of the hunters, however.

"Me, too," someone further back called out.

Sam thus began assembling his team on the spot. People shouted down from the balcony, expressing their desire to join him. Still, when it was all said and done, Laura figured less than a quarter of the Mall's people had signed on to Sam's group.

"Let's start planning this, then," Sam said. "We definitely want to make our move without these Golems seeing us, so we're going to have to check what it's looking like outside. We're going to have to bundle up, because it's a real hike to those tracks and we don't know how long we'll be waiting once we get there. We're going to need whatever we can use as weapons. And, we'll need a few smaller sleds to haul supplies, and carry people who get weak. Though of course, we sure as hell won't be bringing any gray cake." He turned to Gabe. "Unless Gabe objects to us taking any of this stuff."

"And if I did?" Gabe said. "But no, Sam, I don't object. Believe me—I want you people to succeed. I do."

"Good. Okay, then." Sam then shouted, "If any of the rest of you think you might change your minds, don't wait too long for it. You've heard like I have, that all across Hades now groups of the Damned are rising up and fighting back. These little groups are going to start to link up, and become bigger and bigger groups. Let's be a part of that, not a bunch of trembling lambs waiting to be slaughtered!"

Brad leaned in close to Lynn, and Laura heard him ask, "Did Sam use to work on a farm, or something, with all this talk about chickens and lambs?" Then Brad looked to Laura and winked.

Despite the terror that had hold of her, Laura smiled.

And she knew she was staying.

-8-

With the meeting over, Sam's people went about preparing for their escape, with the two hunters who'd volunteered to join him suiting up to sneak outside for an update on the Golems. Meanwhile, Gabe started organizing small teams to seal up access to the various known areas where blocks had gone missing from the outer walls.

Heading back to their apartment with Lynn, Laura said, "It's going to be bad if we have to lock up some of the warehouses and, like, can't get at the things we need in them."

Lynn reminded her of what Gabe predicted. "When the Golems are enough in number, or get their final orders or whatever, hopefully the Mall can be at least *mostly* the way it was before the Yetis left."

"Why even bother locking up these rooms, then?"

"Mostly just for the psychological value at this point, I guess."

They went through the back of the storage area that gave access to Lynn's apartment cum miniature shoe factory. The shoe workers hadn't come back with them, too afraid right now of that compromised room just on the other side of a flimsy door.

Staring at this door now, Laura realized it didn't even have a lock.

"What can we do, then?" she whispered. "We shouldn't stay in our apartment like this!"

"Gabe's people will be here soon; they'll figure some way to bar it, or board it up, or whatever. They're getting tools and such together. You stay here…I'm going to take a peek."

Lynn cracked the door, and Laura felt an icy wisp of air slip past her friend. Lynn peered into Warehouse C beyond, and Laura heard her say, "Oh…oh man…"

"*What?* Let me see!"

Lynn hesitated, then opened wider the door that gave access to the rear of Warehouse C.

Even from here, Laura could see that the opening to the outside was larger by several blocks. More distressing, one of the blocks that remained—outlining the irregular opening—was undergoing a bizarre change. A limb, shaped like a human arm, had emerged and was bracing its palm against the warehouse floor. This appendage was just as gray and rough in texture as the rest of the block of gray cake, and therefore didn't look like it should be flexible, not without splitting and breaking at the joints of its elbow, and wrist, and five fingers, and yet it moved as if it were supple. Then again, hadn't the mall dwellers discovered long ago how adaptable the material was to being crafted and processed in different ways?

Even as they watched, further along the top of the block a pointed hump swelled up. Would this become a leg on that same side of the body? A moment later, with the one hand braced against the floor, the forward end of the rectangular block rose several inches from the block beneath it.

"Back inside!" Lynn whispered.

But Laura had noticed another source of anomalous movement off to her right, and she gestured for her friend to look that way. "Lynn!"

Off to that side, in a gloomy corner formed between the end of a metal rack loaded with cartons and the wall that divided the warehouse from Lynn's apartment, a figure stood immobile. Immobile, that is, except for its head, which was moving so rapidly—back and forth or in circles; it was too frenzied to tell—that it was just a blur. The rest of the body, though, was revealed to be a humanoid form composed of a raspy-looking material like the gray cake, except rusty red in color, like dried blood. Though Laura had only seen that first Golem outside from a distance, this figure appeared to her smaller in height, perhaps only as tall as herself.

"It's what's left of the red cake Billy thought I stole!" Laura said. "It looks glitchy…like it wasn't supposed to come alive with the other ones!"

A thump caused them to snap their attention back toward the opening. The animated block had tried sitting up with only one arm and one leg so far having been extruded from its flat surfaces, and this clumsy effort had caused the block to tumble out of the opening so that it now lay on its back on the floor. Its one arm flopped sluggishly, and the sole of its one foot slid dreamily forward and back along the warehouse floor, as if the shapeshifting Golem were trying to establish the best way to plant its weight firmly so the block might rise vertically.

"Enough!" Lynn said. "Let's go!"

They both ducked back into the apartment, and Lynn closed the door. Laura found this gesture of little comfort. "We *can't* stay here, Lynn."

"You're right," she said. "Let's go find Gabe…tell him what's happening."

They worked their way back out into the Mall's main concourse, and there found groups of people had gathered at the two primary exits to the outside, at either end of the great hall. The main doors had been opened, and Laura assumed these people were gazing out at the Golems. What was happening? Had the New Ones entirely surrounded the complex by now? Would Sam's people already find an insurmountable obstacle to their escape?

Laura noticed something else upon emerging into the concourse. Incongruous sounds, looping in the air outside the building. A motor of some kind, buzzing and revving and putting? No, it was more than one; she heard the buzzing sound recede from one direction, only to grow louder at another point. She turned her head sharply, hearing the buzz pass outside the Mall behind her, as if a gigantic hornet had swooped by. Was this, then, the sound the Golems made when they came out of their dormant state? They were, after all, machine-like. It sounded to her like chainsaws being wielded in the hands of crazed runners…but who could run that quickly through deep snow?

"I know that sound," Lynn said, putting a hand on Laura's arm. "That's snowmobiles."

"Snowmobiles? Who would have those in Hades?"

Then, another sound. The sputter of automatic gunfire. Again, from a different direction. Snowmobiles and guns, circling the Mall together.

Lynn said, "The same people who would have guns. Go, Laura! Get upstairs to the shoe store…go hide in there!"

"You, too, Lynn! Come on!"

The people who had gathered at one of the two doors were suddenly crying out, trying to back off and break up and flee, but getting in their own way. A good number of them were falling, but whether it was from being shot or tripping each other up, from here Laura couldn't tell.

As more Damned fell and piled onto each other, writhing and screaming, Laura saw that a number of figures clad in white, hooded robes were entering the Mall. Now inside, the clatter of their guns was much louder, rebounding off the concourse's high ceiling. On top of the gunfire and the screaming were wild whoops and bursts of laughter.

The concourse became full of fleeing Damned, scattering toward the stores that lined its length. Where else was there to go? And now, the same scene at the other end of the hall, as several more of the white-clad strangers entered there. Fired their weapons there.

The unmoving escalators that gave access to the second floor, and hence the shoe store, were too close to either exit. Laura would be running *toward* shooters, and even if she made it to one of the escalators she'd stand out too much upon it. Second floor was out of the question. In a panic, her only thought was to return to the place she knew best: Lynn's apartment.

As she raced in that direction, she looked around her for her friend, but they had become separated in the chaos. Was Lynn still making a run for the shoe store? Laura hoped not.

She ran briefly beside Emmanuel, and between gulping breaths asked him, "Who are they?"

"Angels," he panted. "Motherfucking Angels on a joyride!"

She and Emmanuel became separated, too, however, but by now she had reached the storage area through which one reached Lynn's flat. Here, she hung back behind the storage room door but kept it cracked enough to listen to the scene of horror in the concourse. "Come on, Lynn," she whimpered, "come *on!*" But her friend didn't come.

She remembered what she had been told about Angels; she remembered it had been Emmanuel, in fact, who'd told her. He'd said that when mortals died in the good graces of the fickle and unforgiving Creator, they went to Paradise. *"They become what they call Angels. And the Angels get bored up there, even with theme parks and mansions, casinos and fountains of wine... they come here to rape and pillage and kill us. They hunt the Damned and they kill us for sport."*

She flinched at one particularly loud voice, an Angel booming in a heavy Southern accent. "Look at this, man, would you? Look at these stores! This is crazy! What do these people think this is? Do they think they're us, or something?"

"I want a new pair of Nikes!" another of them howled. "Where are the Nikes at?"

"Where's the motherfucking Starbucks, bitches?"

She continued to listen. Occasional gunfire, now mostly just individual shots from weapons switched from fully automatic to single fire mode. Laura realized what was going on now in the main hall. This band of Angels was rounding people up there. Getting them herded and under their power in one location; at least, those who hadn't already successfully hidden, or hadn't already returned to their apartments and places of work following Gabe's big meeting.

Laura left the storage area to steal into the little side hallway branching off the concourse, and from here peeked out to get a real view. Her suspicions were confirmed. Mostly men, but two female Angels as well, had lined up in front of a dense mass of Damned not far from the dead fountain. The Damned all had their arms raised, even the children among them. Over padded snowsuits that looked as though they'd be pricey in the mortal realm, the Angels wore white, hooded ponchos that identified them for what they were. She counted seven of them, six of these seven carrying a gold-plated assault rifle, though she didn't know if these weapons corresponded exactly to any terrestrial model. The Angels were too far away for her to see their faces clearly, but Laura knew none of them wore the brand of the Damned on their foreheads.

At their feet, lying between the Angels and the rounded-up prisoners, lay Mitch in a wide pool of blood, growing wider. His spear had been kicked away from his hand. He was motionless; a dead man dead again. Though Laura knew he couldn't really be killed, would heal from his bullet wounds eventually as she had healed from her own, the sight filled her with a sadness and an anger beyond anything she could remember ever having experienced before. Not even on the occasion of her own death.

She spotted Lynn's face among the prisoners. And there was Brad. Gabe...and Sam...

Laura slipped back into the storeroom, turned and bolted for Lynn's apartment.

-9-

Whatever the Angels had planned for the Damned they'd captured thus far, if even they knew, they had been distracted from it by the arrival of the Golems.

Laura saw that four Golems had already entered the concourse: two from one end, two from the other. Towering, perhaps eight feet in height, with snow accumulated on their shoulders and the tops of their heads. Laura saw that they had the indentations of eyes, and the bumps of noses, but they were essentially faceless and reminded her of figures she had seen in a book at school, of molds cast from people buried under the ash at Pompeii.

One of the male Angels, watching as a fifth Golem came ducking through one of the entrance doorways, said, "Man oh man...and I thought these things were just statues out there."

"Not too close, you," said one of the female Angels. She had pushed her hood back from her dyed blond hair, and leveled her gleaming gold assault rifle at this latest approaching Golem. But just as the Angels had assembled in a line in front of the Damned prisoners, so too did the Golems assemble into a line, facing the Angels. As if waiting, Laura thought, for their commands.

As the fifth Golem joined the line, Laura wondered what bullets might do to one of them. Demons like the Yetis, she knew, could be killed and killed for real, having no immortal souls as the Damned did. But, where one Golem was apparently made up of a multitude of infinitesimally small, primitive demonic animals? Maybe only a fraction of them would truly die, and either the Golem would simply reconstitute as she herself would do, or the broken fragments would find each other to slowly fashion a new individual. New improved Demons, indeed. No ears to hear pleas, no voices to bargain or reason with.

Laura was crossing the concourse toward them all: the Golems, the Angels, the Damned. She kept her face composed and her steps bold and unwavering.

"Whoa, whoa, hold up there, missy!" barked one of the Angels, he of the pronounced Southern drawl.

Looking around to see who was coming, another of the Angels, with thinning gray hair and a barrel belly pushing out his white poncho, grinned when he saw Laura and said, "Well, hey, this one looks fun."

"Wait!" Laura called as she closed the distance between them, holding up a palm against the rifle barrels swinging her way. "I'm an Angel too, damn it!" As she came, she pointed to her forehead. "See?"

Peripherally, Laura saw Lynn's face: her dropped jaw, her widened eyes. Laura ignored her. She held back her black hair from her forehead to better demonstrate to the Angels that her skin there was devoid of the brand that would have marked the sin of a Damned soul.

The white poncho she wore was the sheet Lynn had hung up in their apartment to partition off a little private corner for her. Laura had cut a hole from the center of the sheet with the razor knife she used to cut insoles from rubber, then slipped her head through it.

"You're not with us," said the blond, her hard face with its abundance of apparently blizzard-proof makeup looking wary. "How'd you get here?"

Laura stopped right beside the one with the drawl. "I was here with some friends...I don't know how long ago now. We were hunting some Damned who escaped from a train, and I got lost in the storm. These assholes found me and took me prisoner. I don't have to tell you the stuff they've been doing to me."

"These fuckers," the barrel-bellied Angel said, though only a moment earlier he had hinted at performing similar acts upon her himself.

"Thank the Creator you're here!" Laura said. She turned to glare at all the Damned, who stared back at her as an astonished audience. The Damned didn't truly need to breathe, so they looked like they might well hold their breath forever as they listened to Laura's words. She tried not to make direct eye contact with any of those people she knew especially well. She went on, "They took my gun...I don't know where it is. Do any of you have a spare one I can use? I think I'd like a little long-overdue payback."

"Here, sweetie," said the barrel-bellied Angel, no doubt trying to make a good impression on the long-haired teen, stepping closer and reaching under his poncho for the handgun holstered there. He brought it up and showed her. "Think you can handle this?"

"Oh! Well, mine was a revolver," Laura said, "not an automatic like that."

"Semiautomatic," the Angel corrected her. He pulled back on its slide to chamber the first round. "There you go." He handed over the pistol. It was gold-plated like the assault rifles, and heavy. "Careful, the safety is off."

"You go, hon," said the one with the drawl. "Whichever of them hurt you, they're all yours."

"Thanks." Laura grinned, raised the pistol at the end of her outstretched arm, and pointed it toward the faces of her friends.

Then she swiveled fast, lining up the handgun with the gray-haired man who'd given her the weapon, and shot him in the side of the head.

She didn't waste a second to put another bullet in him, just adjusted her arm a couple of inches to shoot the Angel with the drawl. His mouth had flung open in dismay, but before he could yell she blew out one of his eyes, leaving a black skull socket in its place. The gun's recoil was bad, though, and in adjusting her aim to shoot the blond woman, this time she missed and the bullet struck a glass shop window somewhere.

The blond woman fired back at Laura, but by this time Emmanuel had charged forward and tackled her around the middle. Together they went flying backward, and the one shot the woman got off also missed.

Another Angel whirled to fire at Laura, but she shot him first, the bullet tearing away the top of his left ear. The Angel staggered back a few steps, taking aim again, but before he could trigger a shot Sam was on top of him, pummeling him. Brad joined in, and they both knelt over his body, raining blows.

Laura shot a woman of about Lynn's age in the mouth, and the woman's eyes bulged as if to pop, a spray of blood erupting in place of a cry.

One Angel had a gold-plated pump-action shotgun rather than an assault rifle, and he swung this toward Gabe, who had scooped up one of the guns dropped by the Angels Laura had shot. Before either Gabe or the man with the shotgun could fire, however, the tip of a metal spear was slammed into the back of the Angel's skull and emerged between his startled eyes. Looming behind the Angel, his body soaked in blood and punched with holes but his face set with stony determination, Mitch used the spear's long handle to lever the pinned Angel to the ground.

In only moments, all the Angels lay at the feet of the Damned, some temporarily dead, some only moaning from their injuries. All their long guns had been confiscated, and they were stripped of their small arms as well.

"Laura," Lynn cried, "*Laura!*" Now that the fighting was over, she ran to the teen and grabbed her in a crushing embrace.

Laura hugged her back, her composure finally fracturing and tears filling her eyes. She smiled over at Mitch, and for the first time she saw the man smile, through the blood smearing his face like war paint.

"Quick!" Sam said. "These fuckers heal a lot faster than us Damned! We need to tie them all up real good…bundle them up like frigging mummies!"

More Damned, who had been watching from their hiding spots within stores, emerged now carrying cords and sheets and such, to aid in this effort. They emerged despite the presence of the Golems. In all the furor, several more had even joined the row of giants, but the Angels had distracted the Damned from their potential threat. After all, throughout all this bloodshed the Golems had simply stood there observing with their eyeless faces, perhaps confused by the turn of events, perhaps still not fully emerged from their dormant state.

Laura realized one of them was the shorter, rust-colored Golem with the madly-whipping head. As she noticed this, she saw the Red Golem take a few steps toward Sam and Brad, who were still pinning down the Angel whose ear Laura had mangled.

As if spurred to action by the Red Golem's lead, two other Golems took a lumbering step forward.

"*Stop!*" Laura shouted at them, pulling out of Lynn's embrace.

And they did. Every one of the Golems that had assembled here within the Mall turned its head slightly on its pumice-like neck so as to face her facelessly. Even the Red Golem seemed to turn its blurring head toward her.

"Don't any of you put a finger on these Damned!" Laura cried. "I'm an Angel, see?" She moved her hair to point to her forehead again, as she had done to trick the Angels.

"Laura, this won't work!" Lynn winced.

But none of the Golems moved any further to aid the Angels as they were manhandled and bound by the Damned.

"It *is* working!" a Damned man close beside Lynn and Laura whispered.

The Golems waited for Laura to speak to them again.

Lynn whispered back to the Damned man, "It *is!* It's incredible. It can't just be because she never got branded. It's because she never got processed or judged or whatever it is the Brainiacs do when she came to Hades, like the rest of us did. Somehow these things sense that. To them, Laura's not Damned!"

Seeing that her command had been obeyed, and feeling even more emboldened, Laura ordered them further. "All of you Demons, go back outside. Get all the other Demons out there together in one place and you stay there until I tell you what to do!"

"And stop producing new Demons!" Lynn murmured in Laura's ear.

Laura added, "And stop producing more of yourself! Enough! No more of you!"

For a few moments, the Golems just stood there, motionless.

"I said *go!* Go outside!" Laura insisted. "I'm an Angel! I'm blessed by the Creator! You *cannot* defy me!"

Then, as one, the Golems shuffled to face one of the concourse's two exits, and began walking stiffly, like sleepwalkers, in that direction.

The last of them was the Red Golem, lagging a little behind as if befuddled. From out of the crowd Marjorie shot after this Golem, strings of drool swaying from her exposed skeletal teeth. "Wait!" she called mournfully, reaching for it. "No, no, no...wait!"

"Marjorie!" Lynn yelled.

Marjorie got her hands on one of its shoulders and spun the Red Golem around to face her. She clawed at its chest, raked it, splintering her fingernails. She sagged to her knees, sobbing wildly, and leaned in to try to bite directly into the Red Golem's hip area.

Laura saw Billy in the crowd, looking on in horror, but only her friend Eric went to Marjorie to drag her away. "Don't," he told her. "Don't."

Laura had feared the Red Golem would harm Marjorie to defend itself, but it had only watched her impassively. With Marjorie being held back by Eric and several others now, the Red Golem resumed staggering toward the exit, through which all its brothers had already passed to return to the blizzard.

-10-

Gabe told Sam he and his people could take all seven snowmobiles. He didn't want any possible search parties discovering them at the Mall. He kept three of the gold-plated assault rifles for his people, however, and three handguns, and allowed Sam to have the other three assault rifles and three of the handguns.

"How about letting us have the shotgun and extra pistol?" Sam asked.

"I tell you what," Gabe replied. "We keep the pistol, and I'll let you take the shotgun, on one condition. You take these two with you." He swept his arm toward Billy and Eric, who had come out with many of the others to see Sam and his party off.

"Hey...no way!" Eric cried. "You got no right to do that!"

"Shut up," Mitch said, suddenly behind the two men and giving Eric a little jab in the small of his back with the tip of his spear.

"Please, don't do this!" Billy whimpered. "*Why?*"

"Eh, okay," Sam said to Gabe. "We could use some extra backs to pull that crucible sled."

When Eric and Billy finally gave up protesting, Eric turned to Marjorie and asked if she was coming with them. She averted her eyes, turned and walked away down the concourse.

Gabe and the others helped Sam's people pack their sleds and the snowmobiles, though Sam shared spare ammunition and other supplies they found on the latter. The seven Angels, by now fully regenerated but gagged and blindfolded and bound as if cocooned, squirmed and moaned from where they were lashed onto two big sleighs. Sam was taking some shovels with him, not just to dig out the sleds and sleighs if they got stuck, but to bury the Angels before they blocked the train tracks with the crucible sled.

"I promise," Sam told Gabe, "we'll wait until we're good and far from the Mall, and we'll bury them so deep they won't get out until Hell freezes over. Or...thaws out, I mean."

So they left, and the mall dwellers waved and wished them well. Sam and his party passed between the figures of the Golems, which stood like megaliths, so much snow accumulating on them Laura thought they might eventually resemble giant snowmen. After having ordered them all outside, she had counted a total of twenty-four of them including the Red Golem. She had then ordered the twenty-four to spread out, equidistant, and surround the Mall complex, facing out rather than in. The Damned hoped that to any other Demons or Angels that might one day come this way, from a train or otherwise, this display would at least provide some illusion that the outpost was under demonic control.

Before the wind-whipped shrouds of snow obscured his party, Sam called back to Gabe and the others, "We'll be back one of these days, you'll see! Us and a whole army!"

"I hope so!" Gabe shouted in return.

"So you'd better have a bunch of cool new shit made to sell us by then!"

"Count on it!"

"Except, no more food made from gray cake, okay?"

⚭

By their reckoning of time, several days passed, and the mall dwellers strained and struggled through the process of bricking up the gaps in the complex's outer walls with spare blocks of gray cake they had kept in storage.

It was while this project was underway that they abruptly heard a lot of distant gunfire.

"Oh no," Lynn said to Laura, and they stepped outside through a side door of Warehouse C to better listen. The blizzard had stopped for the time being, but the ceiling of storm clouds remained overhead and if anything the air was colder than ever.

The firefight continued for a while…finally died down. After it did, they listened to the rumble of a train as it resumed its forward motion following a period in which it had remained stationary. They saw a black plume unfurl into the air and trail away into the further distance.

"I hope they're on that train," Lynn said, "and not lying shot to pieces in the snow."

"I guess if they are," Laura said, "we'll be seeing them again soon enough."

303

Then back inside the Mall, back to their lives in the afterlife.

Someone came by the shoe factory to give Laura a gift she had made: a proper white poncho, with a hood and everything, to replace that sheet with a simple hole cut in it. So that Laura could play the part of an Angel again, and even more convincingly, if ever the need arose.

For this reason, too, Gabe had suggested Laura keep the pistol she had used on the Angels, and she was given a holster to go with it. She kept the holstered gun hidden in her partitioned area of Lynn's long, narrow living space.

Lynn said to her when they had returned inside, "You asked me, once, if with time your mind and soul would get older, like an adult." She cupped Laura's face. "I said it would. I just didn't expect it to happen so fast, Lady Blue."

✿

If hours could be said to pass in the eternity of Hades, then it was several hours later that a number of badly wounded Demons found their way to the Mall. One of them crashed through one of the main entrances and fell onto its face to die, glazed in ice and frozen blood. Three other Demons came limping or crawling after it. The Damned quickly gathered but kept a safe distance. None of them had ever seen Demons of this style before. They certainly weren't anthropomorphic; if anything, they resembled man-sized tardigrades, though not quite so plump nor as cute, larval white, apparently capable of walking upright on one or two of their three pairs of legs. For faces they had only a lamprey-like circle of razor teeth.

One of these surviving New Ones was dissimilar in that it had a bulging orb behind its lamprey mouth, weighing heavily atop its head, like a huge glossy tumor. This creature was torn up with bullet holes, dragging itself pitifully, leaving a trail of viscous white fluid behind it. When the Damned stood around it, this creature lifted its grotesque face toward them. Laura had joined those who'd gathered, and she looked down at this Demon in particular and her eyes widened in horror as she felt the beginnings of a stirring in her mind, like icy skeletal fingers riffling through the folds of her brain.

"It's trying to read me!" she cried.

"A Brainiac," Mitch stated, and he nudged Laura aside to break their contact, then slammed the head of his spear straight down into the bulging tumor-like growth. More of that white fluid spurted heavily from the ruptured orb.

The Damned then slaughtered the rest of the wounded New Ones, and agreed they must burn the evidence quickly, should any more come.

"They must have been on that train," Lynn said.

"I hope this means the others hijacked it okay."

"I think that's just what it means." Lynn turned to Laura. "It didn't get in your head too much, did it? You don't think it processed you?"

"I don't think it did," Laura said. "At least, I hope it didn't."

So the dead Demons were carted away, to be chopped up and incinerated, and the mall dwellers returned to their places of business, and Laura began her wait to see if she was now truly one of the Damned.

About the Author

JEFFREY THOMAS is the author of the dark science fiction series Punktown, which was introduced with the collection *Punktown* (Ministry of Whimsy Press, 2000) and includes the novels *Monstrocity* (Prime Books, 2003; Bram Stoker Award finalist), *Deadstock* (Solaris Books, 2007; John W. Campbell Award finalist), and *Blue War* (Solaris Books, 2008). His other books include the novels *Boneland* (Bloodletting Press, 2004) and *The American* (JournalStone, 2020), and the short story collections *The Unnamed Country* (Word Horde, 2019) and *Carrion Men* (Plutonian Press, 2020). His stories have been reprinted in *The Year's Best Horror Stories* XXII (editor, Karl Edward Wagner), *The Year's Best Fantasy and Horror* #14 (editors, Ellen Datlow and Terri Windling), and *Year's Best Weird Fiction* #1 (editors, Laird Barron and Michael Kelly). His other books in the Hades trilogy are *Letters From Hades* and *The Fall of Hades*. Thomas lives in Massachusetts.

ABOUT THE AUTHOR

About the Artist

FRANK WALLS is an American artist best known for his dark, surrealistic fine art, fantasy illustration, and similarly ominous heavy metal musicianship.

Walls' interests in heavy metal music, dark art, and horror films paved the way to his emergence as the lead vocalist for bands like Embalmer and HateWorks in the mid to late 90's. His passion for fine art underlined his guttural vocals, and he produced CD and t-shirt art for bands like Incantation and Crypt Kicker, while front lining others. This era of artistic experimentation paved the way for his immersion in The Cleveland Institute of Art, where he focused on illustration and graduated with a BFA.

As a post-graduate Walls designed and illustrated book covers for authors such as Jeffrey Thomas, Shane Mckenzie, and Jeff Strand, while pursuing illustration work in the fantasy realm - what would become the backbone of his career. Walls is celebrated for his contributions to game companies like Fantasy Flight Games, Wizards of the Coast, and Alderac Entertainment. In 2015 Walls co-founded his own company Noctis Games.

Walls now hails from Hawaii where he teaches Art and Design, works as a freelance illustrator, and pursues his passion for painting.

www.ingramcontent.com/pod-product-compliance
Lightning Source LLC
Chambersburg PA
CBHW030245030726
47493CB00023B/605